Garbo Laughs

Garbo Laughs

ELIZABETH HAY

COUNTERPOINT
A MEMBER OF THE PERSEUS BOOKS GROUP
NEW YORK

This is a work of fiction and the characters are fictional.

Counterpoint books are available at special discounts for bulk purchases in the United States by corporations, institutions, and other organizations. For more information, please contact the Special Markets Department at the Perseus Books Group, 11 Cambridge Center, Cambridge, MA 02142, or call (617) 252-5298, (800) 255-1514 or e-mail j.mccrary@perseusbooks.com.

Library of Congress Cataloging-in-Publication Data

Hay, Elizabeth, 1951-
    Garbo laughs / Elizabeth Hay.
      p.   cm.
    ISBN 1-58243-291-0 (hard cover)
      1. Motion pictures—Appreciation—Fiction.   2. Alienation (Social psychology)—Fiction.   3. Fans (Persons)—Fiction.   4. Ottawa (Ont.)—Fiction.   5. Friendship—Fiction.   I. Title.
PR9199.3.H3676G37 2003
813'.54—dc21

2003011989

COUNTERPOINT
387 Park Avenue South
New York, NY 10016

Counterpoint is a member of the Perseus Books Group.
Set in 11-pt Janson Text Roman Oldstyle

03 04 05 / 10 9 8 7 6 5 4 3 2 1

To Bella Pomer, with affection and gratitude

We will never know the extent of the
damage movies are doing to us.

PAULINE KAEL

I

THE FERN

I

Kenny and Frank

Kenny lay awake in the smallest room in the house. It had a narrow bed, a narrow desk, and a cupboard-closet that started partway up the wall. In the dark he could make out his desk covered in books – including his bible, the movie guide of 1996 – and his clothes hanging from a hook on the open cupboard door. With his dad he had gone to a used-clothing store and bought the oversized brown-and-white checked-tweed sports jacket and the red-and-pink tie and the long-sleeved blue shirt, his gangster outfit, and his dad had let him borrow, indefinitely, his black fedora. From Bolivia. His dad was a traveller.

Kenny loved Frank Sinatra. His mom – he couldn't believe this – thought Marlon Brando was better.

"Who's better?" he'd asked her.

"Not again," she said.

"No, wait. Just this time. Who's better? Frank Sinatra or Marlon Brando?"

"Are you ready for this?" she said. "Can you take it? I'd have to say Marlon Brando."

"You're *crazy*, you're *nuts*. I can't believe what I'm hearing."

She laughed, as one nut laughs with another, since she too wore her movie heart on her sleeve. "He's a better actor. He's better-looking. Which isn't to say I don't like Frank Sinatra. I do. At least, I like the young Frank Sinatra when he looked like Glenn Gould. He was an awful thug when he got older."

Kenny turned to Dinah, who lived down the street and never minded his questions and always answered them to his liking. "Who do you like better, Frank Sinatra or Marlon Brando?"

"Frank," she said.

"Me too." He was very excited. "You think he's a good singer?"

"The best."

"My mom says Marlon Brando is better."

"Marlon Brando is good."

"But he's not better than Frank Sinatra?"

"Frankie," said Dinah, "is divine." But Dinah had always gone for skinny, serious, temperamental guys, until recently.

They were in the middle days of November, and all the hesitations of early fall, the tentative snowfalls and bewitching spells of balminess, had given way to sudden cold. From under the covers, in the pale green light that came through the curtains, Kenny heard sounds – soft sounds – that froze the blood in his veins. There was tapping, sawing, tiny running feet on the porch roof outside his window. Rats. He knew it would be hard for a rat to walk up the wall, but in the night anything was possible. Then water, flowing water. Then scratching. Bugs were in the walls. Big-eyed, hairy, losing their grip. He heard one land, very softly, on the windowsill beside his head and was about to call out when some-thing else, something hard, slapped against a window.

It sounded like Jean Simmons slapping Marlon Brando across the face.

It worked. After that it was quiet.

Frankie was good in that movie, and Frankie hated Marlon so Kenny hated him too. Jean Simmons was pretty nice, though, on the whole, he had to say he preferred Vivian Blaine.

He closed his eyes. For a while he pictured the fight, Marlon cracked over the head with a chair, Jean Simmons drunk and funny and throwing punches. He wondered if Havana was really like that. His dad would know. Then Big Julie was rolling dice in the sewer and Nathan Detroit was eating Mindy's cheesecake with a fork.

In the morning he opened his eyes when his mom opened the cur-tains and he said, "Let's watch *Guys and Dolls*."

"Why not *Take Me Out to the Ball Game*? You haven't seen that one yet."

"Is Frankie in it?"

"Of course," she said.

2

Harriet and Lew

Three nights later the slow, searching sound of a taxi came up the wet street and stopped directly below Kenny's window. A door slammed, the taxi pulled away, and then Lew Gold was heading up the steps and Kenny was heading down. His sister was on his heels.

Their house was two storeys high and made of yellow brick. The wood trim in the hallway was American chestnut, a tree wiped out by blight in the 1920s. What remained of the old forests was inside. Everything outside had come inside, even the movies. The banister Kenny never bothered to hold on to was American chestnut too, golden brown in color, but the steps themselves were white pine from the forests of white pine that used to grow where this house was standing. Lew's grandfather had built the house in 1928; after he died it passed out of the family, until last spring, when the grandson had the pleasure of buying it back.

Lew came through the door, and then what a tangle of big and little limbs there was. What a scene of affection. He looked so tanned and lighthearted, so eager and beloved and beaming, that Harriet, standing in the living-room doorway, couldn't resist. She said, "Something unpleasant happened while you were gone."

"*Doña*," he smiled, reaching over the kids to take into his arms his northern-eyed, meatless-on-principle, strangely yearning wife. "I've missed you," he said. And the gift, wrapped in a piece of newspaper in his shirt pocket, got pressed a little flatter.

It was late – a Sunday night – but he could tell by the look in her eye that she was still under the influence of her Friday-night movie. A certain distancing look she directed his way that made him feel he was blocking her view. You're a better door than a window, he heard her thinking, why don't you sit down and remove your hat? Then she would be alone again with Sean Connery or Gene Kelly or Jeff Bridges or Cary Grant. The list was endless. He had been gone for two weeks, to distant parts, and she had spent it with who was it this time? A glance at the video box on top of the TV gave him his answer: Frank Sinatra and Gene Kelly in *Take Me Out to the Ball Game*. How could a man compete?

Maybe this would bring her back.

"I have something for you," he said, drawing the gift out of his pocket.

By now the kids were tucked back into bed, and they were alone in the living room, Harriet in the rose-colored loveseat, Lew in the black wicker rocking chair. Nearby, in this room where everything was well used and old, stood a lamp with a cockeyed shade. Lew unwrapped the newspaper and laid the tip of a fern leaf, underside facing up, in her lap.

It was like the tip of a spear. Or a large arrowhead, its own tip broken off and the surface patterned with a series of black lines, arrowheads again, one laid into the next, a most beautiful design.

"No two spore patterns are the same," he said, now that he had her attention. Her eyes, suddenly bright and appreciative, fastened on him and she waited for the rest of the story.

Outside, it was snowing all over again.

Large flakes, drifting down through the yellowy glow of the street-light, melted away on the dark ground. Very gradually, the street began to go white. The neighborhood was quiet, the city like something from another time – safe, protected, clean, well run. From now until spring, as the snow accumulated, city vehicles would come by in the dead of night to cart the snowbanks away. Windowpanes would rattle and eerie blue lights, ricocheting into their room, would bounce off their bed where they lay side by side, listening to a monster snowplough push banks of snow into the middle of the street, forming a single windrow, like the haircut of a Huron warrior. Then it would rumble away, to be replaced by another safe, growling monster that gobbled up the snow with rolling blades and spit it back out through a high snout into the dump truck alongside. It occurred to her – to Harriet Browning – that Ottawa and Havana were alike in this one fundamental way. Both cities were back-waters, seemingly left behind in the 1950s. In their different ways they were a lot like Brigadoon.

She had the fern in her lap. Lew was telling her where it came from. A fern museum, he said, outside Santiago de Cuba, a small estate once owned by a fern enthusiast who, upon finding himself too old to look after it, had left it to the state. Now two *cuñados* ran the museum, and she had to ask the meaning of the word *cuñado*. One man was married to the other man's sister. One of them, he told her, was also a circus performer. A circus performer? Yes. He divided his time between the fern museum and the Cuban circus, travelling the world; he had even been to Toronto, he knew all about the city. What does he do? she asked, and Lew racked his brain for the word. "Master of ceremonies?"

Lew told her these things, his skin smelling of the taxi, the airplane, and surely Cuba; he told her these things quietly. The kids in bed, all the other presents given out, this one saved for last. Quietly, he dropped into her lap the information and the fern itself, letting her absorb how far away he had been and how different other parts of the world were. They agreed that that would be the perfect life, dividing your time between circuses and ferns, and they smiled at each other happily, easily, even she of the mournful countenance, who thought her husband smiled too much.

"Ringmaster," she said.

"That's the word."

And they felt themselves expand, as if they had made a great discovery.

"Dinah will want to see this," she said, turning her interested eyes back to the fern. "Fiona too. And Bill Bender. I'll show it to them." She nodded at the television on top of which, next to a dog-eared copy of Pauline Kael's *5001 Nights at the Movies*, sat the video box showing the young Gene Kelly and the young Frank Sinatra dressed up in baseball uniforms and grinning like fools. She had nothing to hide. "Dinah was here on Friday. She and Kenny are still on their Frank Sinatra kick."

"And you're still on your Gene Kelly kick," he said with the long, unguarded smile she wished he didn't have. She studied his face – the large mouth, the tolerant, hopeful blue eyes – and thought, He's not bad looking. Not Gene Kelly, but not bad.

He continued to smile, however, and she was on the verge of saying again that something unpleasant had happened, when he began to tell her something else, and again he dropped the information quietly into her lap.

In this neighborhood where giant ferns used to flourish before glaciers came down and then retreated, leaving the puddle that is now Dow's Lake and the rocky lip on which their house sits, there is, in a curving line, Lew and Harriet's house, then the house belonging to the old newspaperman Bill Bender, who gardens naked except for his dressing gown, which is always falling open to reveal his long thing hanging down, then luscious Dinah Bloom, then horrible Ray with his one horrible wife and four horrible children. Just below, on the other side of a grassy alley, his knees wet in what ten thousand years ago would have been a glacial lake, lives the song detective in his defiant forest of Manitoba maples, and, next to him, Fiona Chester, the matriarch of the neighborhood ever since Sybil Rump died. Fiona is learning Russian even though she's deaf. Sybil Rump was one of the secretaries around Prime Minister Mackenzie King, typing up the declaration of war in 1939. Sybil never married but she had a wonderful sense of humor, people say, as they always say about unmarried old ladies. Just as they say about homely women: What beautiful eyes! or, What lovely hair!

I'm married, thinks Harriet, but I have no sense of humor. If I lost my husband would I gain a sense of humor? Or should I just change my name to Sybil Rump?

"I need a sidekick," she has said to Lew more than once.

"You need to get out of the house."

"I need to get out of the house *and* I need a sidekick."

No one says of Harriet Browning, What beautiful hair! They say, Oh, oh, still not sleeping? moved by the sight of eyes so deep-set and weary that were you to cover the rest of her face with a book you would see José Ferrer (not Mel, who married Audrey Hepburn, but José, who played Toulouse-Lautrec in *Moulin Rouge*.) Remove the book and you have Vanessa Redgrave's jaw on Carol Burnett's body. Harriet looks like a colt that grew, not into a horse but into a big colt. All angles, all overlong legs, all gauche embarrassment and mutinous radiance. A nightmare on the dance floor.

"I worry," Lew has confessed, taking into his arms a woman so saturated with old movies, seen repeatedly and swallowed whole, that she no longer fits into this world. Her last office job was during the era of the manual typewriter. Her sense of direction is nil. Kanata is Timmins to her, Nepean the Russian steppes. Highways appall her, computers enrage her, paying the bills is beyond her ken.

"What about?" Unfurling her boniness from his (rather like Audrey Hepburn, came the happy thought, dislodging her limbs from Peter O'Toole.)

"You don't sleep," was all he found it wise to say. "You suffer so."

"*Suffer?*" This was too much. "What do you mean *suffer?* Lepers suffer. Victims of ringworm suffer. I don't suffer."

Then, feeling herself to be unfair, a frequent feeling that was both her salvation and her doom, she relented. She smiled. The effect was like a woman in the movies who finally takes off her glasses.

After fourteen years of marriage, Lew still enjoys her face for the contrasts it offers up, the moments when her thin-faced melancholy gives way to a smile. Somewhere, halfway between the one extreme of lentil-fed sadness and the other extreme of movie-fed rapture, she is nearly pretty. He likes to watch her good looks come and go.

Were he to die, how she or their children would manage he doesn't know. They would watch old movies, but what about the real world?

"You met a *blind* photographer?" she repeated, weighing this new piece of information. "*Blind?*"

Lew was feeling the full extent of his exhaustion, weeks of meetings and almost no sleep. For a moment he lost track of the conversation, overcome by a wave of indescribable weakness. As a boy he fainted so often he had to give up baseball. The feeling was like that, but confined to his heart.

"Tell me," he heard Harriet say, but her face was receding from him.

She observed his gentle smile and resisted snapping her fingers. Lew was not an aggressive man except in this, offering part of a story, then refusing the rest until he was questioned. One day she was going to whack him over the head.

Lew smiled at her, but now he couldn't even remember her name. Then slowly he felt his strength return, and with an effort he explained.

They're pictures of objects he knows well, things he can touch. His cane, for instance. He leans it against a wall beside a bucket. He has people arrange the objects for him, according to his directions. He knows from the feel of the sun on his face how much light there is, and he adjusts the light meter accordingly.

She was taking all this in, the fern-and-circus man, the blind photographer, when he remembered one more thing. He had visited the beach where they went together twelve years before on holiday, "but it was unrecognizable."

"Oh?"

Even twelve years before, he knew Havana well, first from photographs and then from visits as an architect working to preserve old cities. Back then the beach was empty except for a group of muscle-bound men in swimsuits: the national wrestling team, of all things. "It's completely different," he said.

"All the tourists?"

"Not exactly."

He paused, and she thought again what a good if infuriating story-teller he was. *He* should be the writer.

"It's like a brothel," he said.

He said it without emotion and she looked at him, startled. He went on. The beach was full of Canadian and Italian men with young Cuban women hanging off them. "They don't let the women into the hotels," he explained, "not during the day. But you go outside and they're waiting in a throng. I couldn't walk down a street in Havana without getting hit on at least once or twice." This is real life, he was thinking. Forget the movies.

"How can that be?" she demanded. "Why do they allow it?"

He didn't know. A few years ago they said it was poverty. There wasn't enough food on the island and women were desperate. But there was enough food now.

The fern was dry and fragile. Like tissue paper, she thought, turning it over in her hands and drawn forward, for a moment, to Christmas.

Then she put an end to their enchanted mood, already complicated by his description of prostitutes, with a question. She prided herself on her questions, imagined obituaries where she was described as having had an inquiring mind. "She wasn't a prolific writer," the obituaries would say, "but often the best writers are not."

She mentioned the present he had brought for their daughter, wondering if it was appropriate. "Is it appropriate," she asked, eyeing him, "for a father to give a daughter entering puberty such a suggestive gift?"

He looked at her. Then he said, "That's the trouble with Ottawa," and he was vehement and angry.

"You don't mean that's the trouble with Ottawa," she returned. "You mean that's the trouble with me. You aren't talking to Ottawa. You are talking to me."

That's the trouble, and he continued his thought, not shifting his weary, saddened, aging-by-the-minute eyes off his honest needle of a wife. "People here don't know how to enjoy their bodies. They don't know how to relax." And more than ever he was struck by the contradiction in her, the contradiction between her old-fashioned scruples and her licentious ease with movies: she was a puritan addicted to Hollywood, and she was leading their kids down the same brainless path. "In Cuba everybody dresses like that," he said stubbornly. "They don't expect anyone to come on to them just because they do. They all walk down the street like that."

Harriet saw the street. She saw what he was seeing. The dark, humid, *relaxed* air where they themselves had walked twelve years before on the *Malécon*, the wide sidewalk that hugged the harbor with the ocean on the left, Old Havana on the right, the colonial fort a large, dark bulk far ahead, and so many people walking because so few had cars. He was seeing that and seeing her long, pale, bony severity curled up on the old loveseat in the same brown sweater she had been wearing when he left, in front of a fireplace without a fire. She saw thick tropical air and fine smooth female skin, and still she thought the present inappropriate and said if her father had given her such a thing – of course he never would have – it would have confused her mightily. The comparison didn't hold, as she knew perfectly well, since between Lew and their daughter there existed a complete and easy love, while for her father she had felt nothing but fear. But that wasn't true either. She had been aware of her father as a sexual being and a complicated man. Martin Browning the dentist, who forbade candy, movies, and soda pop.

The spear-tip fern was in her hand. Dryness made it rough, though no rougher than her winter fingers.

"You're such a prude," he told her.

She didn't deny it, and still she questioned his gift.

The present was a skimpy crocheted top, more brassiere than top, made with loose looping stitches except for the solid little cups designed to cover little breasts. Jane had put it on, thrilled and giddy, then turned around so that her father could do up the back. Young Kenny said she looked like Sandra Bullock . . .

"You'd better have a sexy gift for me too," she had said, earning a pointed if amused look before he reached into his bag to bring out a jar of Alicia Alonso face cream and a bottle of perfume so stinky she would use it once and not again. Cuban cosmetics, she thought. Only Lew would bring me Cuban cosmetics.

The fern was raspy between her raspy fingers and between husband and wife the atmosphere was also raspy. A sudden coldness that made her heart cold. "I have the right to my opinion," she said. "To state my uneasiness." But she knew her opinion went to the heart of his identity as Lew Gold the loving father, and to the heart of their shared geography, this cold country it had been such a shock to re-enter. He would rather be in Cuba. Come *with* me, he had said.

"So did you go with any of the women who hit on you?"

"No," he answered immediately. "How could I?" And he spread his hands. "There's nothing appealing about it. It's ugly. It's exploitative. How could I?"

"But you don't want to be here with your old wife."

"I do want to be here. I want to be with you." And he left the rocker and sat beside her on the loveseat.

In the morning, at her desk, she touches the spear-tip fern. She asked Lew its name but he hadn't written it down and couldn't remember.

A delicate roughness, not the equal of a whiskery cheek or shaven leg: too delicate for that.

Did you sneak it when no one was looking?

No, the circus man broke it off and gave it to me. I asked if I could keep it and he said I could.

She sits with the lamp on and her notebook open, a great early riser, a tremendous second-guesser, thinking how rapidly something wonderful can turn to shit. *Dear Pauline, For a few minutes I felt as close to Lew as I've ever felt, then I stepped onto an ice floe and pushed myself out to sea. I've seen a thousand movies*, she writes, *but I'm still no good at love.*

Harriet puts down her pen and goes to the window. Her second-floor study juts off the west side of the house and runs its full width – a narrow, winterized porch with windows on three sides offering views south, west, and north of other sunrooms and sleeping porches and cases of chronic insomnia. Fiona Chester is up every night from three until five-thirty, when the voice of the morning man on CBC Radio puts her right back to sleep. Bill Bender rises at four to work on the book he has been trying to finish for twenty-five years. Dinah Bloom doesn't turn off her light until two or three in the morning since, when it comes to reading, she is without self-control.

Several days ago, standing here, Harriet saw at eye level a man in a mauve sweater painting the trim on Bill Bender's window (a warm spell between cold snaps). He was applying blue paint to the white window frame against a backdrop of brown clapboard and blue sky when his ladder dropped. And so did he. A foot, before he caught himself. She opened her window and called out, Do you want me to come down? He was holding onto the ladder for dear life. No, he said, I called my buddy. And a young man came around the corner. It broke, said the man in mauve. What broke? The ladder broke. Something broke.

Afterwards, there was a wild smear of blue paint on the brown wall, a foot below the window.

I am wondering about something else – the endless romance in me that makes it a pleasure to watch the same movie many times, as if movies were animated letters with the white screen as the envelope and the movie as the love letter inside. Breakfast at Tiffany's, of all things. I've watched it several times lately, in the middle of the night when I couldn't sleep, and again on a gray Saturday morning with the kids, and the several times took me through delight to mild interest to greater interest to boredom to a new level of appetite. Appetite grows with eating, as they say in Quebec.

At a certain point, I am satiated and the movie is put back on the shelf. But I still have the memory of the appetite it aroused and satisfied, so that in a year or two my hand reaches for it again, and the same process begins of mild interest, increased interest, boredom, and some new level of appetite.

Perhaps boredom is the stage I'm in now, but it's a boredom like winter, which is a preparation for spring. Premier Bouchard, our dark prince, says that to tell Quebeckers independence will never happen is to say that spring will never come. In the face of this, what can an Ontario girl do but watch George Peppard watching Audrey Hepburn and finally telling her (oh, reactionary thrill) that she belongs to him.

What are movies for, except these looks of love – requited, unrequited, latent, growing? I'm so ashamed, but there it is. They send a shiver up my spine.

At seven o'clock she rouses Kenny and Jane, and goes downstairs to make breakfast. Kenny comes down first, bible under his arm. "Mommy," he says. "Who do you think was the best actor in a Billy

Wilder movie? Would it be Jack Lemmon? Tony Curtis? Marilyn Monroe? Fred MacMillan?"

"MacMurray."

"Fred MacMurray? William Holden?"

"I'd say Jack Lemmon as Daphne."

"I don't know. I like Fred MacMurray a lot in *Double Indemnity.* 'Goodbye, baby.' Bang! And then what about the guy with 'the little man inside him'? What's his name?"

"Edward G. Robinson. He was great. Remember the ending? 'I love you too, Keyes.'"

"Is that your favorite Billy Wilder movie?"

"No. My favorite is *Some Like it Hot.*"

By now Jane is downstairs too, dressed in black and white for the school concert. But the big sister is never a talker first thing in the morning.

By eight they've left for school, and now it's light enough to show Lew the unpleasant thing that happened while he was away. "Lew," she calls from her study when she hears him come out of the bathroom.

He's wearing his father's plaid dressing gown – soft and baggy from age and from never having been washed – just as he wears his father's shirts and ties. A sentimental, practical, nearsighted man.

"Look," she says.

"What?" He comes to her side.

"I opened the blinds the other morning and couldn't see out."

He steps up to the window and "Bull's-eye!" he cries with gusto. Across the glass, covering most of the west-facing window, is a wide smear of snotty yellow goop.

"Did they mean it for me?" she asks in a stricken voice.

"Yes! They found out where you live, and they came here in the middle of the night and lambasted your window with an egg. Why didn't I think of it?"

"Somebody who didn't like my book," she says. "Somebody *in* my book."

Only the other day she had gone to a book club, by invitation, and it was apparent to her, as soon as she walked in the door, who liked her book and who didn't, and who would tell her so at some point during the evening; she recognized the averted stubbornness in one woman's face. Only a fool would have come.

She braced herself, but it was still depressing to be told how angry and unforgiving she was. She tried to make light of it. "You'll be glad to know I'm writing a comedy now," she said, and everyone breathed a sigh of relief and passed the peanuts.

But none of those women would have lobbed an egg at her window. Who did she know with a good right arm? What Mickey Mantle of the literary world had she offended so deeply?

Lew got dressed and went outside. From the shed at the foot of the garden he took their ladder, set it up against the side of the house, and climbed up to the window with a wet rag to scrub off most of the congealed egg, the temperature just above freezing and the sky an even grey. When he was finished, the window looked like a child's dirty face scrubbed with a mother's spit.

"Somebody keeps phoning," she told him when he came into the kitchen. "I pick up the phone and there's nobody at the other end. Do you think it's a burglar?"

"In Ottawa?"

He was used to her exaggerations; he was even tired of them. He poured himself a cup of coffee and Harriet watched him take a sip.

Then she said, "There's a letter from Leah."

This was the point. Now he understood.

"Poor Hattie." And he sat beside her at the kitchen table and took her hand. "How's Leah?"

"I don't know. I haven't had the courage to open it."

He stroked her hand, and she swept her gloomy eyes across the room. "I can hardly wait till I'm dead," she said.

Harriet didn't want to be serious. She wanted to be funny. But she couldn't help being serious. She sat down at her desk and seriousness sat down beside her.

Even Dinah Bloom kept telling her to get out more. Lew kept telling her to relax. Whenever he said *relax*, she told him to dry up. Piss off. Drop dead.

The night before, he'd undressed next to the closet door and she was so drawn to the shape and dusky color of his soft penis hanging down like a softly dark thing, more greys, browns in its coloring, less red than usual, an old-leaf color, she thought, and saw soft old leaves on the sidewalk. And his balls too were darker and hanging down. The room was warm – warmer than usual – she wished she could describe those colors better. All she could really think of was the various shades, the velvety-looking darkness of a horse's penis, but not as dark as that, the dusky greys, the long length (though not as long as that), the soft shape, the way it hung down. In bed they'd found a new position. She wondered if they'd ever find it again. It had to do with the way he cradled her so that he was the rocking chair and she the rocker, though you have to picture the rocking chair on its side, its upper part raised off the bed and her legs up on his shoulders. Well, it was very nice until she yelped. *Ouch!*

Still, there was life in the old wife yet.

And something more curious. Leading up to orgasm, inducing it, were her thoughts about her father. An image of her father in the middle of the night coming naked out of the bathroom as she came out of her bedroom, his hand immediately over his groin like a fig leaf, yet the suggestion of something swinging behind and below his hand, and his proximity and smell as they passed each other in the hall. Would her daughter be the same? Was it usual?

She would have to ask.

3

Dinah

Harriet was an asker, and always had been. An inquisitive, reckless, fundamentally timid woman given to strange blurtings that got her into trouble. There were people who no longer spoke to her. Dinah Bloom was not among them, perhaps because she hadn't known Harriet very long.

"Harriet Browning," Dinah repeated the summer night they met. "That's what Greta Garbo called herself whenever she went incognito."

"Harriet Browning?"

"Harriet Brown. I saw her once. In New York. She was buying persimmons in a fruit store at Fifty-third and Second."

"I hate persimmons. Wait a minute. What are persimmons?"

"You do look a little like her." Surveying her with amused brown eyes.

"I do?"

"Your eyelashes," she said. And Harriet lost her heart to Deadpan Dinah. "They were so long," said Dinah, "that people used to ask if they were real, and she would tell them to pull."

"Pull," ordered Harriet, removing her glasses.

Dinah Bloom, who was a journalist and therefore ruthless, pulled. "I wasn't wrong," she said, examining the long dark eyelash on her fingertip.

Harriet, putting her glasses back on, asked if Garbo was still beautiful then or was she too old.

"She was marvellous," Dinah answered. "She was wearing a helmety sort of cloth hat, an army jacket, ski pants, sneakers. She must have been seventy, but she was the most radiant woman I've ever seen."

"Lipstick?"

"I didn't notice."

"And you call yourself a journalist."

"That was before I'd met you," said Dinah, "and knew what questions to ask."

They have been watching movies together since then, that night in July. Not for Harriet and Dinah the intellectual stress and strain of a book club. They prefer ordering in pizza and eating it with potato chips on the side while splayed out on a sofa long enough for two skinny children and two growing women who indulge in rambling conversations about the glorious shortcomings of Robert Redford and Sean Connery. Or, as Dinah likes to call him, *Seen.*

Except when she calls him *Obseen.*

On this particular day, a Monday, they are drinking tea and eating no-name digestive biscuits beside the kitchen window in Harriet's house when Harriet asks Dinah if she pictures her father's penis when she screws. Dinah chokes on her biscuit. She waves one hand helplessly in the air.

"You need more tea," Harriet says, filling her cup.

"My father's penis?" sputters Dinah.

"Do you picture it?"

"Picture it?"

"Does it –" And now Harriet blushes. Even she takes a while to catch up to her questions. "Does it turn you on?"

"I try to keep my father out of it." Gulping down her tea and holding out her cup for more.

It's four in the afternoon. At any moment Jane and Kenny will barge through the door, and that certainty makes of this moment a well of peacefulness under the low kitchen light, while outside the day is losing ground. From the alley below you can see the two women in the kitchen, long-faced Harriet with her thin, dark hair held back by a crooked barrette, and wide-faced Dinah whose bountiful head of silver hair is the envy of the neighborhood.

Harriet doesn't stop, because nothing stops her once she gets going. "What do you think about then? I mean, what images do you concoct in your head to help you come?"

"Robert Redford?"

"Not Robert Redford." She looks at Dinah in dismay.

"A joke. I never give Robert Redford a thought. Your father," she adds after a moment, "must have had quite a penis."

"He still has it," says Harriet. "Well, I don't just picture his penis. Sometimes I think about a horse. Or a bear."

"In the zoo?" asks Dinah, since she has an eye for detail, "or in the wild?"

"In the woods," says Harriet. "Next to a stump."

At this point children barge through the door, one after the other, although there are only two. Jane and Kenny are not impressed by digestive biscuits and Dinah doesn't blame them, but Harriet says they are her favorites, she even has them for breakfast. That is, when she isn't eating date squares.

"George Washington ate pie for breakfast," says Dinah.

"Maybe he had a mother like mine," says Harriet.

"He weighed 350 pounds," says Dinah severely.

"Maybe," says Harriet, "he had a deprived childhood."

Dinah has heard stories of Harriet's childhood: the endless chores interrupted by elevenses when her mother, seated on the verandah, would apportion six cherries to each of the six children; the mashed turnip so full of strings and fibres she had to sieve it through her teeth; ditto the homemade pumpkin pie; the lack of television; the tragic, tragic absence of movies. Harriet's mother, a Scot with second sight, believed that children should be outside acquiring bright eyes and rosy cheeks no matter how much they loathed the out-of-doors. She used to boot her kids outside and lock the door till mealtime.

Dinah, on her third no-name digestive biscuit, tells the kids they should call 911 unless their mother gets in a supply of chocolate chip cookies. But Harriet claims to be too old for chocolate.

"You're not too old," Dinah says. "You're younger than I am."

"How old are you?"

"Fifty-five."

"I'm forty-seven," says Harriet, "and I never dream about identifiable places. Do you?"

Dinah does. She often finds herself inside the movie theater on Bank Street where she worked every Saturday of her childhood, the only daughter of David and Ida Bloom, who ran the theater for twenty-one years.

"Is it still there?" asks Harriet.

"The Rialto. They tore it down a few years ago. It used to be called the Fern."

"That's odd," Harriet says thoughtfully. "I'm not used to things leading somewhere." And she goes upstairs to get the spear-tip fern for

Dinah. At her desk, struck once again by how beautiful it is, she stands for a moment and studies its pattern of spores so clearly etched they could have been drawn by hand. Downstairs, she lays the fern on Dinah's open palm. "Lew brought it back from Cuba."

"I saw Lew on the ladder this morning. A man who washes windows." Dinah looks up. "Do you know how lucky you are?"

"He smiles too much."

"*Smiles* too much?"

"He's too damn sunny. I feel like Mr. Darcy married to Mr. Bingley."

Dinah leans back and hoots, then leans forward and says, "Can I have him?"

At twelve years old, Dinah Bloom knew she would never marry. Sitting beside the lilac bush in her backyard, basking in the hot May sun, she knew she would never marry, she would never have children, and she would never be what she really wanted to be, a nightclub singer like Peggy Lee; she would be a reporter instead, like Brenda Starr in the comic strip. She saw herself living as she lives now, in a house with a small but beautiful garden, a cigarette between her fingers, and tanned bare legs; frequent love affairs of short duration, as in the movies. What she hadn't pictured was being fired, or falling in love with someone she couldn't have.

Five months ago, on a warm July evening, when the street was full of loud children and patient parents, she came around the side of her house to the flower beds out front and stopped to watch them for a moment: six parents wanting-to-be-admired hovering over ten children demanding-everything-under-the-sun. She remembered when it was the kids who were supposed to be good. A soft orange soccer ball went gently from foot to foot, and a new boy was hunkered on the curb, watching. He had a newspaper stuck in his back pocket and a pencil behind his ear, and he was leaning forward with his face in his hands, elbows on his knees, pale, tall, wiry-haired – and nobody was asking him to play.

Dinah knelt on a slab of foam to protect her knees. Her hands stirred up the smell of mint. This was a friendly neighborhood, but only up to a point, and she had never understood the point. How much did it take to invite a new kid to play? When she was just a few feet away from the boy, she said in a conversational way, "I always hated soccer."

He looked at her and said easily, "I love soccer."

"Want me to introduce you?" She nodded towards the game.

"Oh, I don't like playing," he said. "I like watching. I'm going to be a sportswriter."

"Are you?" She leaned back on her heels. "Then you'll have to learn how to drink booze and play cards."

"I know how to play cards."

"Crazy eights? Hearts?"

"Rummy," said Kenny. "Gin rummy. Want to play?"

They laid out the cards on her front porch and sat on the top step. She said, "Gin rummy's what Fred Astaire used to play. But I don't suppose you've heard of him."

"I've heard of Fred Astaire."

"Have you heard of Gene Kelly?"

"I've heard of Gene Kelly." Then, darting her a look, he asked her who she thought was better. Gene Kelly or Fred Astaire.

"Gene Kelly," she answered promptly. "I know Fred's a great dancer, but Gene was a lovely man to look at."

"What about Frank Sinatra?"

Dinah had to smile. "How old are you?"

He told her.

He was tall for ten. Not that she had a lot of experience in these matters. "And you like Frank?"

"Do *you* like him?"

"I'm crazy about him," she said. "Frank and I are *very* close."

Kenny's eyes shone. He grinned.

Dinah said, "Remind me of the rules for gin rummy."

"When you've got seven points or less you can knock. Or you can wait and gin."

"Well, if Fred Astaire could do it, so can I."

"Did he win?"

"That I don't know."

"What kind of useless fact is that?" Kenny demanded. "Fred Astaire played gin rummy but you don't know if he won?"

"What did Frank Sinatra play?"

"He played crap!"

Dinah leaned back against the porch post. She couldn't believe her luck, meeting a kid like this. "How do you happen to know Frank Sinatra?"

"We watch his movies. We listen to his music."

"I'll have to meet your folks," she said, and later in the week she did. She dropped over to say hello and found all four of them – mother, father, big sister, Kenny – on the back porch, reading. The porch was wide and airy with a high sloped roof against the sun and rain. In the middle of the porch was a square table covered in a floral plastic cloth. Around the table were several folding chairs. A hammock hung suspended between one of the porch posts and a hook buried in the brick wall. A workbench covered in sawdust took up another corner. A wide shelf below a window held dishes and utensils, and next to it, on a narrow wooden table, were a dishpan and dish rack, and above the dishpan was an outdoor faucet.

"You could live out here," she said, turning around in one spot and Lew said, "We do. We're out here from morning till night."

"That's what it looks like." And it was quite evident from her tone and the look on her face how much she admired their world of light housekeeping and easy company.

Harriet and Lew were wearing shirts and shorts faded from countless summers; the books in their laps were library books. They didn't look like Frank Sinatra types, thought Dinah, they looked like professors who would never get tenure. And she liked them immediately and without reservation.

To Lew she said, "You're the man who sings the song from *High Noon*."

About a month ago, when she was peeling a late-night peach on the back steps and it was too dark and leafy to make out the source, she'd heard a voice in the alley on the other side of the big oak, just past Bill Bender's garage, a man speaking to a dog in a tone so natural and easy that she'd known everything about him she needed to know. Then he began to sing softly, "'Do Not Forsake Me,'" and that was it: her heart said uncle.

Now here he was. The man with the tender voice.

Harriet said, "Lew knows the words to a million songs," a compliment so heartfelt it produced a smile, since wifely admiration was hard to come by. Lew reached for his wife's hand, but she batted him away. The kids were used to this: their dad reaching for their mom's hand, and their mom batting him away.

Despite the heat, Kenny was wearing his gangster jacket. In the inner pockets he carried a thick wad of paper money, an old lighter, an expired credit card, a flat silver case that contained one of his dad's business cards – *Lew Gold, Heritage Architect* – and a two-dollar toy pistol.

"Who are you?" Dinah asked him.

He smiled sheepishly but not uncomfortably. "Nathan Detroit," he said.

"So, tell me why you like Frankie." Settling deeper into one of the padded folding chairs at the table.

Lew and Harriet observed their son's conquest, and so did Jane. She listened closely but didn't speak, this twelve-year-old girl with the Bette Davis eyes who put herself to sleep every night planning what she would wear to the Oscars.

"Because he's a great singer. A good dancer, not a great dancer, and a great actor. And he hates Marlon Brando."

"What's the matter with poor Marlon?"

"He's a bum. He can't sing, he can't dance, he can't act, and Frank Sinatra hates him."

Dinah laughed her smoky, raspy laugh, and Harriet, bringing out cold drinks and an ashtray, stopped in her tracks to listen. *Sandpaper calling to its mate*, she thought, having read the description of Louis Armstrong's voice in a Pauline Kael movie review. "You have the best laugh," she said, looking down at Dinah and her son, and she quoted the review and gave credit where credit was due.

Lew said, "Hattie writes to Pauline Kael."

"You know Pauline Kael?"

"No," Harriet admitted sadly.

"But you write to her. Does she write back?"

"Oh, I don't mail the letters."

"Why not?"

"They're stupid. The first letter I wrote to her was about Cary Grant. It was an incredibly stupid letter. Actually, it was a story. It was an incredibly stupid story." And she meant what she said about the story, but if she'd been pressed she would have defended the letters. She was a writer who wasn't really writing *except* for the letters, except for this ongoing, one-sided intimacy that she didn't have to justify to anyone. It relaxed her and kept her company.

"Well," said Dinah, stubbing out her Craven A, "that's one way to save on postage." And she laughed until she nearly choked. One manicured hand slapped the table, the other flew to her face, which for all its

years of hard living was still extremely pretty. "Excuse *me*," she sput-
tered, pushing back her silver hair. It was early evening and still light,
but they were the only ones outside.

"No," shaking her head at the beer, "just a glass of water if you don't
mind." And she lit up again and stifled a cough.

And then they got down to business.

"Now listen." His mother's face took on the ardent, competitive look
that Kenny liked best. "Kenny tells me you don't like Fred Astaire."

Dinah, amused and imperturbable, winked at Kenny and Jane. "Give
me Gene Kelly any time."

Their mother leaned closer. "I'm going to have to educate you."
And Dinah replied, "You don't like Gene Kelly?" and their mother said,
"Nobody loves Gene Kelly more than I do, but Fred was in a league of
his own," and Dinah came back, "Gene was sexy, something you could
never say about Fred," and their mother said, "But Fred was inventive.
He was far more inventive than Gene Kelly could ever be, for all he
tried," and Dinah said, "But Gene had a body and Fred was a dry old
stick," and their mother said, "Cyd Charisse said it was like dancing with
glass dancing with Fred," but raucous, irreverent Dinah wasn't buying it.
"What does that *mean?*"

"The point is," their mother said, "Gene was always trying to be
artistic, that was his big mistake."

At this Dinah turned to Kenny. "Tell your mother that Fred Astaire
doesn't compare to Gene Kelly or Frank Sinatra for excitement. Tell her
the difference between Fred Astaire and Frankie."

Kenny answered thoughtfully. "Fred Astaire is a little bit distant.
Frank comes on and blabs and blabs and blabs and you get close to him.
Fred Astaire is distant. I like him though." Looking at his mom.

Her eyes twinkled back. It was obvious that his mother liked Dinah
as much as he did, and he felt beside himself with pleasure.

Immeasurable, the relief a child feels to see his parents make
friends. Here they were in a huge world, after all. Night was coming on.
The porch, outfitted for outdoor living, was Huckleberry's raft on the
Mississippi. "I took the bucket and gourd; took a dipper and a tin cup,
and my old saw and two blankets, and the skillet and the coffee-pot."
They were floating high above the mosquitoes in the grass and far away
from the mosquitoes in the cedar hedge, but even so, as night fell, a few
found them out. Lew tugged open the little glass door of the Mexican

lantern in the middle of the table, lit the candle inside, then went into the kitchen and from the fridge got his box of Cuban cigars. Soon clouds of smoke filled the air, and that, for the time being, was the end of the enemy.

"Browning," mused Dinah. They were talking about names now, having their conversation about Garbo and eyelashes.

Jane hadn't spoken, but not because she wasn't listening. "Who's Greta Garbo?" she asked.

"You know Frank Sinatra but you don't know Greta Garbo? I'm going to have to educate you," said Dinah, and Harriet smiled. "She was the most beautiful woman in the world," said Dinah.

They continued to sit on outside. Lew opened another beer, Jane played with Dinah's cigarette butts and felt herself turn into Dinah (a feeling that persisted when she went to bed and remained when she woke up, so that she came downstairs for breakfast feeling silvery-haired and husky-voiced and desperate for coffee), and Dinah played cards with Kenny. She asked him what his favorite Frank Sinatra movie was.

He moved the cards around in his hand, sucked in his lower lip, chewed it, raised his eyes and looked at her. "The one he acted in best was that one about Chinese spies."

"*The Manchurian Candidate.*"

"And the army movie where he dies?"

"*From Here to Eternity.*"

"Yeah. He acted best in those two. But I have to say I liked him a lot in *On the Town.*"

"More than *High Society?*"

"*High Society*'s next."

Dinah said, "I have a copy of that one. You can watch it with me any time."

"Okay."

"What about Friday night? I'd be glad to have your company. Jane, will you come too?"

"I'd love to," Jane said eagerly.

"Then it's a date. Shall we invite your folks? We can start a movie club."

Harriet said, "Lew talks through movies. People who talk through movies should be taken out and shot."

"Rule number one: No talking, except by us."

Which is how the Friday-night movie club began.

Lew didn't mind. It was a small price to pay, sharing his Friday nights with movie stars, if it brought in Dinah's good sense and marvellous laugh. Usually, after the movie started, he headed upstairs and played his mandolin. He was learning the song "Tom Dooley."

4

Married Life

Harriet was one of Ottawa's tall women. It was among the first things Lew noticed about the city. The tall women, the huge full moons, the many rainbows.

She would remove her glasses, lay them on the table, and punish her eyes with the flattened ends of her fingertips. Don't, he would say. She would chew the skin around her fingernails until it was red and worked and sometimes bleeding. He would take her hand away from her mouth and hold it. Every tea towel had a scorch hole from having caught fire when she lifted things in and out of the oven. Hence the baking soda at the ready beside the stove.

In the morning he would ask her if she'd been able to sleep.

"I barely slept at all," she would say. "I feel terrible." Or, "I woke early, but I don't feel too bad. No doubt I'll feel terrible later."

To Dinah, Harriet said, "He's too good. Do you know what it's like to be married to a good man? Awful."

They were in Dinah's kitchen this time, Harriet having discovered that Dinah never locked her back door and never seemed to mind a visitor.

"I don't know. Tell me."

"It's all right if you're a grateful person, but I'm not. So I look for faults. I find things wrong with him. I blame him for not arousing enough love in me to make up for all my bad qualities. It would be a relief to be with someone rotten."

"Not for long," said Dinah.

And once again, Harriet felt glad to have Dinah in her life. Usually with people you were in one element and they were in another. You were

27

a fish mouthing words to a fowl. But Dinah was a fish too. They swam along comfortably, side by side. Harriet said, "I just wish he wouldn't smile so much."

"But why does Mr. Bingley smile? Why does Jane Bennet smile? Because they're happy? I don't think so."

Dinah had Harriet's attention. "You don't think so?"

"I don't think so."

"You're as bad as Lew. What do you think, you infuriating woman?"

"They smile to ward off their ridiculous families. Jane Austen was surrounded by hypochondriacs. She knew how people protect themselves."

"I should have thought of that," said Harriet.

That night, when she lay down beside Lew and turned out the light, he said into the darkness, "I love you."

"What prompted that?" she asked.

"I felt you drifting away."

"When?"

He didn't answer.

"Now? Earlier? All the time?"

"Just now. Earlier. Like there's nothing between us."

"And then we drift back," she said.

"That's why I said I loved you. To bring you back."

Sometimes, passing through the living room, he sees her curled up on the sofa, bathed in the flickering blue light that makes her grow, irrevocably, away from him. *Tropism*. He remembers the word from school.

What he can't remember is the moment when she first began to watch videos alone, taking pains to make sure he wasn't in the room, though less overt than she is now with her suggestions that he go elsewhere. "Weren't you going to bed?" she'll say. Or, "You should be in bed!" But he suspects the trouble goes back a long way, to the years they lived in New York City (where he worked for a small architectural firm, but only part-time, since even then architects were going the way of trains and letters), and their ground-floor apartment was so dark and narrow it could have been an art cinema. They set up their first VCR at the midway point of this long, dark passage. On the other side of the

VCR were the pigeons in the air shaft, and beyond the pigeons, five feet away, the peeling wall of an abandoned building. As luck would have it, the best video store in the city was just down the street, and for Harriet, he remembers, this was Shangri-La.

She told people it was like an old-fashioned library, every movie encased in a neat black box and filed on shelves that went from wooden floor to high ceiling. Droopy-eyed Don worked behind the counter. He knew every movie ever made. Once he had actually shaken hands with John Wayne, and another time he'd gone to a party where Hermes Pan was the special guest. "What was he like?" she asked, and not of John Wayne. She was working her way through the Fred Astaire–Ginger Rogers oeuvre and knew that Hermes not only choreographed the dances but practiced with Fred, filling in for Ginger until they perfected the moves, at which point Ginger was allowed in to practice. "A flaming gay," said Don. "And Fred?" "Who knows?" he answered. "He had two kids with his first wife and he was devastated when she died. Have you watched *Picnic* yet?"

It was in New York where she first began to watch the same videos repeatedly, giving herself up to the lengthy seductions made possible by the new steam engine of romance. *A Room With a View*, for instance. She rented it on a Friday and watched it that night, then thought about it all weekend while they visited friends in the country – the scene on the hill-side when George Emerson comes to Lucy through the waist-high barley and takes her in his manly grip; the scene in the hotel when he comes down the corridor as she opens the door, and their faces leap with desire. She thought about the scenes and anticipated the pleasure of watching them again, for such was the beauty of this new invention that multiple viewings were possible, and at will. But how to rent the movie again right away without appearing to be what she was? A lunatic? She would control herself. She would be indirect. She would read the book. "Ah," laughed Lew as he passed her reading in bed, "the movie again."

The trouble was, the book diluted the movie. The movie had covered her with a patina of romance, and now the book lay heavily upon that and made her want to see the movie even more, to shake off the book. No, she would have to wait for Lew to go away and then rent it again. His first trip, and she was out the door like a shot. Liberated – starved even – but ashamed of herself. She was no better than the blue-rinse ladies who used to hang out with the sourpuss librarian in her youth and hog all the Harlequins.

Then one cold day, in the fall of the year, thumbing through bad books about Hollywood in the movie stacks of the library, she came upon the writings of Pauline Kael. *Have I ever told you the story of how I discovered you? How one Saturday morning at the Lincoln Center branch of the New York Public Library, when Jane was hopping about in pre-ballet at the 63rd Street Y, I opened up one of your books and found your essay about Cary Grant: The Man from Dream City. Within seconds, I was beside myself with joy. So this is allowed! I thought. So it isn't altogether stupid! You loved Cary Grant too, and unashamedly. But you loved him in a hardbitten way, condoning our addiction and wondering at it and mocking it, but above all understanding it. A woman with the courage of your romantic, skeptical, humor-filled convictions. That's when I began to write to you, sometimes on paper, often in my head, your company as freeing as the movies, but more bracing, and without the after-taste of guilt.*

For the most part Lew leaves her alone with her movies, but occasionally, late at night, he'll stand for a moment behind her, or sit to one side with the paper, aware of her discomfort as she holds herself still, willing him to go away, and as testy as someone who wants to be alone with a lover. He could write a treatise on the effect of VCRs on romance and marriage: to bring the unattainable into your home, to watch it repeatedly, to fast-forward to the hot spots again and again, to press the zinger of romance until you were well and truly electrocuted – all this he could write about at length.

One morning, on the bus headed downtown, he saw a young man reading a book called *1001 Ways to be Romantic*. He was on Number 66: Flowers. A fellow of average height in a long tweed coat, light brown boots, dark hair, moustache, wire-rimmed glasses. He held a briefcase in his left hand, the book in his right – open to Number 66 – and leaned against the pole for balance. Lew looked over his shoulder as he squeezed by.

"What did they cost?" she asked, arranging the roses in a vase.

"Price is no object," said Lew.

"Now that's a silly thing to say," she said.

A woman without a romantic bone in her body, until she sat down in front of a movie, that is. Context is everything, he thought. Or proximity. Hang Picasso in an art gallery and you have a masterpiece. Hang him in the shed, and it's a scrawl by Percy the neighborhood nose-picker. In the wraparound presence of a movie, his wife yielded every ounce of her common sense. After the movie ended, she was even tarter than before. Tart, peevish, out of sorts.

"If you do this again, I'll skin you alive." She often spoke like that, overdramatic and savage, but what did it amount to? The first time they met she was so fierce he couldn't have imagined her present retreat from the world. They met in Italy the summer she was nineteen. She was working in the kitchen of her Aunt Leah's villa, a film institute with a guest house where he was staying for a week, when one morning Leah's stepson, beefy Jack, insulted Leah (who wasn't even there) and Harriet punched him in the nose. Ice had been necessary. Later that night, while all the other guests were beside the pool, she said to Lew, "I don't even like Leah. She's an awful person."

"But you like Jack?"

"*Jack?* I like him even less." Her bewilderment touched him, and her temper bewildered him.

Ten years later he saw her again. This time she was reading a biography of Sean Connery and blushed crimson at being caught. They were in Montreal, in a café so crowded he asked if he might share her table. She looked up at his oddly familiar face, glad to return to reality since the book was so terrible. (*Thinking about all the movie-star biographies I've read, I have to ask if they're so bad because bad writers write them, or because movie stars are so boring? I wish you'd take over. Please get cracking.*) For his part, Lew was amused by her book and beguiled by the blush, since it vanished as reluctantly as a headstrong sunset. Rather shyly, she explained that although Sean Connery was her first love, she also had room in her heart for Fred Astaire. In other words, she had an open mind.

The third time he saw her, which was the very next day, blood was running down her fetchingly long, slightly knock-kneed legs. She was standing on the porch of her first-floor apartment on Rue Crescent as he came up the sidewalk, and he asked her what happened. She came down the steps, smiling, and held out her hand, which he took.

"Your legs!" he said.

She looked down. "Oh. I shaved them in your honor. Aren't they beautiful!"

Bruegel's *Hunters in the Snow* was above her sofa. He looked at it while the tap ran in the bathroom. Then she was by his side again. She said, "Hemingway said he learned how to write about landscape by looking at Bruegel. What do you suppose he meant?"

Nothing she has done since then has lived up to those fiery beginnings, but he likes to think the potential is there.

Harriet is less sanguine. "You know what we're like?" she said to him once, looking up from the book she was reading to the kids. "Jack Sprat and his wife. You won't be sad, and I won't be cheerful."

But physically, they are similar. Tall, thin, built like greyhounds. He, an affectionate man whose wife commits safe adultery with every movie star under the sun. She, a dreamy soul, deprived of movies as a child and making up for it now.

Outside, he catches sight of Dinah Bloom and they raise their hands in mutual despair about the weather. "I wasn't made for this," she says with her wild, beautiful laugh. "Just look at your heavenly tan."

"Cuba," he smiles.

"And you didn't take me with you."

Dinah is wearing a red winter coat fastened with several black braided loops. "Frogs," he observes, illustrating his point by touching one, and sniffing, as if the loop were all that interested him. He hunches his shoulders against the cold. "Used to be common before zippers," he says. An expert on materials of all kinds.

Sometimes, in the evening, they walk together, Dinah out with her dog, Buddy, and Lew (working off an affection for dogs thwarted by Harriet's allergies) with Fiona Chester's old collie, Buster. They're a slow-moving foursome, poking along, noticing things on the street, exchanging horror stories about work, bits of gossip that Lew passes on later, if Harriet asks, and she usually does. On their walks they redesign the neighborhood, replacing the epidemic of antique shops with a hardware store, a magazine-and-cigar store, a stationer's, a grocery store, a theater, a post office, a good bakery, a dance hall. Often Lew stops to examine the surfaces of things. "I get that from my dad," he says, his dad having been a building inspector for the city of Montreal. "He was always stopping to point out the way bricks were laid, or stones."

Now, with the northeast wind cutting right into him, Lew surprises himself by saying, "Dinah? What should I do about Harriet?"

5

Harriet's Deprived Childhood

Of the few movies she managed to see, she recalls in most vivid detail *From Russia with Love*. One summer's night, when she was twelve and her father was away (repairing the rotten teeth of native children on James Bay or of welfare kids in Vancouver: the charity work he did every August), her mother relaxed the reins and let her go.

It was evening when she went down the hill to the Berford Theatre on Main Street, and dark when she headed back up the hill, and darker still when she lay down on her bed, overwhelmed by the experience of Sean Connery's hard, humorous eyes and hairy chest. There was the cruelty of the movie, the speed, the enormous fun. The flagrant sex, the glitter, the hard-edged tenderness followed by the near indifference. She had never seen anything like it, and yet it was familiar. That is, Sean Connery's body was familiar.

When she sat in the dental chair under her father's shadow and closed her eyes, when she opened her mouth wide for his fine, long fingers to prod, lift up, examine her tongue, teeth, and gums, then there was something similar in his quick, decisive actions and his jesting, man-of-few-words manner. Once, in anger, he had taken a dental knife and whipped it at the wall, where it stuck fast. Her father went through many nurses.

Earlier there had been *The Country Girl*. Grace Kelly, William Holden, Bing Crosby. Which her mother took her to see when she was five. Miracles occur. Her mother, having given birth to her sixth and final child only two months before, was desperate to get out of the house, and on this first outing she elected to take along the last child but one – Harriet Lily – who had been displaced by the baby Owen. This time it was spring and they wore their coats.

Grace Kelly was very severe. She wore glasses. She slapped William Holden's face. Her husband, Bing Crosby, was down on his luck, and a drunk. Or was Grace Kelly the drunk? Empty bottles rolled out from under the kitchen cabinet. All this happened because they had lost their beloved son under the wheels of a car when they weren't paying attention. Grace Kelly could have gone off with William Holden, who was deeply in love with her, but instead she ran after Bing, in the rain? while William Holden watched from an upstairs window.

Already, at five, Harriet considered this a real mistake.

At the age of six came the strange set of circumstances that led to her first disaster as a writer. A Halloween double bill on Saturday afternoon, and her mother allowed her to go for the simple reason that admission was free if you presented six Pepsi-Cola bottle caps at the door. She and two of her older brothers scoured every back alley in town – a small town on the water, where the baker sometimes stood in the back door of the bakery and tossed them balls of dough, as if they were stray dogs, and in a way they were, roaming freely until their mother stood on the porch and blew a whistle either at noon or at six o'clock sharp.

They found enough bottle caps and paid their way in to see, first, giant footprints on a back road where lovers were kissing in cars, and then the giant itself, amid screams, planting his foot on top of those very same cars. At intermission Mr. Pepsi stood in the aisle, while everyone stayed in their seats, and he called out the numbers of several winning tickets. Small Harriet, looking down at the red stub in her hand, saw her number correspond to one of them. She made her way past knobby knees to the aisle, showed him her ticket, and heard him say, "You can go down there and choose anything you want." *Down there* was the front of the theater where a long table was covered with prizes. She walked by herself down the aisle to the table and chose a blonde walking doll in a blue satin dress, and held it in her lap during the second movie, the story of two sisters who wanted the same handsome man. First, he married the good sister, but she drowned while he was away and while the bad sister watched in apparent helplessness because she couldn't swim. Then he married the bad sister, who fell off the dock one night as she tried to rescue her cat in the middle of a storm. Having come home without warning, the handsome husband tore off his jacket to swim to the rescue, only to stop dead: for there she was, the evil one, swimming perfectly well to shore. The look on his face, and then the look on hers as she rose out of the water and saw his horror and repulsion – those looks constituted the final moments of the movie.

Harriet walked home and said, "Look at what I winned."

The next morning she took out a black ballpoint pen and wrote in indelible ink on the doll's neck her own name. Harriet Lily Browning. A long name. A long ink-necklace. She took her handiwork to her mother, still in bed on that Sunday morning, expecting her to be as thrilled as she had been the day before. Her mother took one look and said furiously, "You've ruined it. You've completely ruined it."

Harriet has had trouble writing ever since. Stubbornly, she ruins perfectly good things by writing about them. Her mother wishes she would stop. "Why does she do that?" Gladys will say to Martin. "Is she *so* unhappy?"

But Harriet can't resist. Why did she write about Leah? Because she couldn't resist.

6

The Letter

The letter lay untouched on the blue kitchen counter for several days. Harriet covered it with other mail, so that its brightness wouldn't hit her eyes so hard.

"You open it," she said to Lew when he discovered it among the bills. "I'm afraid it will blow off my hand."

"She's not so bad," said Lew.

"Just tell me she's not coming to visit."

"She's not coming to visit," he said as he read it, "she's coming to stay."

Harriet sank to the floor.

Lew looked down at his wife. "So is Jack."

"*Jack?*"

"Jack's coming first. Any time now." Perusing the letter. "Leah's not coming till January."

"You mean John the Baptist, and *then* the Crucifier?"

He read to the bottom of the page and turned it over. "They're researching and writing a book together."

She found the butcher knife in the kitchen drawer. She pointed the blade at her chest. "I'm going to kill myself," she said.

"They're not so bad," said Lew.

"I'm going to kill you," she said.

She walked over to Dinah's to be reassured. It was November 19, and there were traces of snow in the air. Earlier in the day, at the corner store, the man behind the counter whose hair was very thin on top said this was his wife's first Canadian winter. They were married in India nine months

37

ago, and she thought it was cold, and he told her: You haven't seen anything yet. Ahead of Harriet, as she waited, was a thin, dark-haired man with many unbrushed teeth who said that in Italy thirteen was a lucky number; he had a gold *13* hanging from his wristwatch. Harriet thought, So maybe bad luck isn't bad luck, after all. Maybe, under certain circumstances, it's good luck. But she thought it without conviction.

She knocked on Dinah's door and heard bristly old Buddy start to bark. Buddy was the sort of dog you take a child to see to dissuade him from getting one. Or take yourself to see, if you feel yourself weakening.

To be reassured. Such a miserable business, this one of needing reassurance.

"An egg," she said, "on my window. That's why Lew was washing it."

"Kids," said Dinah. "Boys out larking around."

"How bad was what I did? *How* wrong was it to write about Leah?"

"You changed her name?" asked Dinah.

"Yes."

"You changed her appearance?"

"A little."

"You changed the geography?"

"No."

"Next time," said Dinah, "change more. In the meantime, stop worrying."

Harriet shook her head in despair. "I really think that egg was meant for me."

Dinah took her into the kitchen and passed on the secret of good cappuccino, something she learned not from the Galloping Gourmet, whom she interviewed at home one morning years ago – he came downstairs at nine, lit a cigarette, then made himself a cup of instant coffee – but from her Italian teacher, who paced the classroom in red pumps. "Pina was her name. You bring milk nearly to a boil, then whip it in a blender, let it sit for sixty seconds, then swirl it around as you pour it into the coffee and that way you get creamy coffee and good froth. What they make in this country is so *bitter*."

"Yes."

"Canada," said Dinah. "Where taste buds get buried at birth."

Harriet stared at her cup. She saw her taste buds six feet underground. They were pink. She said, "The phone rings and nobody's there. It happens two or three times a week."

"It happens to me too."

"*But why?*"

"Who knows? Think about Friday. Our Sinatra double bill."

"Yes." Harriet stirred herself. "That's something to look forward to. I think."

"I'll bring the pizza." Dinah pronounced it *pee-zah*, and Harriet had to laugh. But then she said, "I haven't told you the worst thing. Do you want to hear the worst thing?"

Dinah watched the worried blue eyes look away – Harriet always looked away when she was thinking – the angular jaw and cheek-bones, the soft, blowy, nondescript hair, the skittish, shy, serious and determined-to-be-less-so manner of a writer-in-trouble who looked, thought Dinah, like Paula Prentiss on a bad day.

"She's coming in January. She says she wants to move here, though she's probably just trying to scare us."

"Then she's not mad at you."

"She's going to tear me limb from limb."

It wasn't my fault, thought Harriet, that Leah climbed into bed with me.

But it *was* her fault that she had written about it. You betrayed me, Leah said on the phone after the book came out. I trusted you and you betrayed me. You don't understand a thing about being old and lonely.

Oh, drop dead, thought Harriet after she hung up.

But then, on a Friday night a few weeks ago, in an old Frank Sinatra movie called *Robin and the Seven Hoods*, she saw a character, a fleshy man who drank cocoa out of a teacup, who reminded her physically of Leah, the fleshy face and smile, the fleshy wiliness and hurt. And it was his image more than Leah's actual call that upset her. Aunt Leah, her father's sister who ran away to Hollywood and married a famous man.

7

The Hat

A gray-and-black hat sailed past Harriet's head. She stooped to pick it up and recognized it as the second one they had bought for Kenny in as many months. When she turned around she saw him – red-faced and braking at the sight of her – tall and skinny, hair in need of a cut, pants that were too short, and no mittens. He came up to her, took the hat, and said quietly, "Thanks."

"Where are your mittens?"

He reached inside his coat into one of the deep inner pockets that were among the greatest joys of his life and pulled out lined leather mittens, inherited from his dad. Then, "Bye," he said, and ran to join the other boys, some of whom were huge and others quite small in the varied way of adolescence, but none of whom looked at her. She thought, Did they take his hat and throw it, making mean sport of him? It was his first year at this school.

Kenny caught sight of her looking with concern, and turned his back. He wanted her to move on, and she did.

Into her mind as she walked to the fruit store came sad-eyed Buster Keaton, who wore the clothes of an old man "and always felt old," even when he was a boy. And no wonder. By all accounts his dad was a lout and their vaudeville routines were extraordinarily violent, starring Buster the human mop. As a grown man he hated quarrelling of any sort, at the first sign of conflict muttering, "No debates, no debates . . ." She hadn't been able to get his films in Ottawa, apart from *The General*. Yet on the strength of Pauline's capsule reviews, she felt she almost knew him. That morning she had looked up every entry under his name. Then her eye kept going, from movie to movie, and an hour had passed before she'd raised her head. It was like eating chocolates on a treadmill. *You're very tough. I have to hear pleasant and unpleasant things about my favorite actors. In general, though, we like the same ones and some of your phrases I know by heart: Cary Grant's "hooded eyes," Sean Connery's "virile manner."*

In the afternoon, when Kenny got home, she asked him how school went and he gave her his customary high-pitched *great?* Then he brushed aside any further questions. But at least she managed to pin him down on the matter of his haircut.

"You have hair like Harold Ross," she said, getting him to sit on a stool with a raincoat over his shoulders.

"What movie was he in?"

"He wasn't. He was a famous editor at *The New Yorker*. Ina Claire, the actress who married John Gilbert after Garbo ditched him – I'm talking about the 1920s – Ina Claire said she wanted to take off her shoes and walk barefoot through his hair. Everybody thinks Dorothy Parker said that, but it was Ina Claire. His hair stood straight up."

"*Ouch!*"

"Like yours. I want your hair."

"And my brains."

He squirmed and complained so vigorously that out of desperation she began to ask him questions. "What's the funniest movie of all time?"

"*The Life of Brian*," he answered promptly. "Keep going. I like this. Ask me what's the saddest movie." Suddenly he was perfectly intent and still.

"What's the saddest movie?"

"The movie that overall depressed me was *My Life as a Dog*. That's my favorite foreign film. Saddest ending? *Cinema Paradiso*. Poor Alfredo. It isn't the best movie but the ending was so sad I cried."

For once movies and movie talk were serving a practical purpose. She was cutting his hair rapidly now. "What was the ending?"

"You don't remember?" He was incredulous.

Jane sang out from the living room, "*West Side Story*'s a pretty sad movie." By this time she was home too.

Kenny said, "When he put together all the kisses he had to censor from the movies."

"I remember. Well, I always thought Alfredo was just a vehicle for a lousy filmmaker's vanity and sentimentality. What's the most romantic movie?"

"*Breakfast at Tiffany's*," he said. "And *The Russia House*. That's a thinking person's spy movie." Competitive and serious, and not to be derailed by his mother's bad taste.

From the other room Jane said, "Do you mean erotic or true love?" This was the girl who, at the age of three, saw Marilyn Monroe in *Some Like it Hot* and said, "I'm her."

"Romance," yelled Kenny.

Jane came into the kitchen, furrowing her brow and asking herself, "Which movies had a lot of chemistry in them?"

Kenny said, "Katharine Hepburn and Spencer Tracy in *Woman of the Year*."

"You think Katharine Hepburn and Spencer Tracy had chemistry?" Utter disbelief from the big sister.

"Oh yeah. Sparks flew. *Casablanca*'s pretty romantic too."

"Let me think!" said Jane.

"Ask me the best musical," said Kenny.

"Go," said his mom.

"The one with the best songs is *Fiddler on the Roof* but the one with the best dancing is *West Side Story*."

Jane snorted. "You're crazy. The best musical is *Singin' in the Rain*." And she wouldn't hear otherwise. But then she had always known her own mind: sitting self-contained and erect at a friend's dinner table after all the other children had run down to the basement, chewing the steak she didn't get at home. And this at the age of eight.

"Scariest movie?" asked Harriet.

"Most suspenseful movie," he corrected her. "That has to be *Charade*."

"Movie with the worst ending?"

"*The Lady Vanishes*. I hated that ending. Everything was so good, the way Hitchcock set it up, and then he ruined it at the end."

"Movie with the best beginning?"

"*Breakfast at Tiffany's*," he said, giving her a look, since that's what she herself had said only days before. Then, "Or *Get Shorty*. I love that beginning, when he puts on his gloves and knocks on the door and punches Ray Barboni in the nose."

Harriet was sweeping up Kenny's hair and remembering Lew's lament the last time he saw these beautiful, almost coppery locks spread across the floor. But now Kenny wouldn't leave. "Ask me another one. Ask me the best baseball movie."

"Okay."

"*Bull Durham*, of course. Ask me the best line in a movie."

"What's the best line?"

"'Fasten your seatbelts, we're in for a bumpy night.'"

"Put that on the list," she said. "We should watch it with Dinah."

And Kenny added *All About Eve* to the movie list on the fridge.

8

A Green Globe

The fern brought a feeling of peacefulness and possibility into the house, if only briefly. It sat on the corner of her desk, looking more and more like an ancient artifact as it faded from green to parchment brown. *I think of you in your rambling house in Massachusetts, and of a sentence I read in a book about Chekhov: "The doors of the Russian house are wide open." I'm tired of pretending to like things more than I do. Like Ottawa more than I do. Like Lew more than I often do. I'm tired of having to work up an attachment to things. Tired of life being so much less vivid than it could be.*

It was three in the morning. In the sky a half moon shone above the mighty oak in loud Ray's backyard, a tree that used to shade four yards, including her own, but now half of it was dead and the rest was dying, branch by branch. Lew had his own idea why. Last summer he'd said thoughtfully, "I think it's tired of listening to all the traffic on Bronson Avenue." But Lew had a sensitive ear and a fine voice, unlike herself, who took two days to recognize "Auld Lang Syne" when the Ceremonial Guard was practicing it day after day on the open fields at Carleton University nearby. Once she even failed to recognize "Happy Birthday" on the radio. She thought it was "God Save the Queen."

Hanukkah is coming in a few weeks. Then Christmas. Maybe you have what we have, a menorah for eight days followed by turkey . . .

Fiona Chester's light came on; it was half-hidden by spreading lilac bushes in the summer but quite visible now. Fiona, she knew, was waiting for the morning man "whose voice just has that effect," she said one day. "What's the word?"

"Soporific?"

"I beg your pardon? I'm sorry." Shaking her aged head, and smiling. "My hearing is too awful."

Harriet wrote the word on a piece of paper.

"That's it," said Fiona. "Nobody can sleep, haven't you noticed, and?" – with her little lilt – "it doesn't matter."

Age had put its heavy hand on Fiona's head and pushed her half over. She was Groucho Marx as a leaf in the wind, lifted along on her daily trek to Bank Street, a plucky Scot from the Isle of Lewis who arrived in Canada on a Saturday, started work on the Monday, and two months later, on October 29, woke up to the stock market crash of 1929. "The girl at the next desk said, 'Did you know that so-and-so, some big shot, kicked the bucket?' Where? 'On the bridge over there,' she said. And? I looked out the window and pictured a man on the bridge kicking a wooden bucket."

And? was the link that joined each of her utterances to the next, making her unstoppable in conversation no matter how deaf she might be. "I am reading Chekhov, and? I manage several paragraphs at a time."

Now that's pure love, thought Harriet, to go to the trouble of learning Russian in order to read Chekhov in the original, and to do so at such an advanced age and off the back of the public education available in Scotland in the 1920s. That's what oatcakes will do for you. Harriet had gone to Fiona's house for tea (Fiona always invited neighborhood newcomers to tea, taking her job as Sybil Rump's successor very much to heart), and eaten five oatcakes. "To the future Sir Sean," she said, raising her teacup.

Fiona nodded and smiled and nodded again, as deaf as a post, having mislaid both of her hearing aids earlier in the day.

Harriet has since looked up the marvellous name Sybil Rump in a biography of Mackenzie King, but Sybil, who probably kept King and therefore Canada afloat, didn't warrant a mention. Now there was a man who tilted at windmills, at least by night. Harriet looked northeast, in what she thought was the general direction of King's house on Laurier Avenue, where fifty years ago he held the late-night séances that put him in touch with his dead mother and his dead dog Pat. Then she found her thoughts drifting back to the fly in the neighborhood ointment: loud Ray, who planned to cut the mighty oak tree down. Come spring, he said. He was going to put in a pool. If that tree weren't there, he told everyone, he could drop a swimming pool into his backyard and have room left over. As if to accustom his appalled neighbors to the prospect, he spent hours outside with his snow blower, ruining their peace of mind.

She knew she ought to lie down for a while, even if she couldn't sleep, but Bill Bender's kitchen light came on next, and something about the play of light and shadow took her back to the day last summer when she came upon him lying flat on his back, his head and shoulders hidden under a clump of tall ferns, his long legs stretched out across the grass, his feet in red sneakers.

She had knelt down, rested her head at the base of the ferns, and glimpsed what he was looking at: deep, navigable shade. How beautiful it was. And to think she had never looked before. It was like an emerald forest – primeval, peaceful, huge – and only visible from this boyish, unembarrassed angle. Bill Bender was looking up the skirts of the world when it was young.

Some half-remembered words came back to her. "A green globe," she murmured, "in a green shade."

The old man sat up, then. "'A green *thought* in a green shade,' you numbskull. 'Annihilating all that's made / To a green thought in a green shade.'"

"Marvell?"

"Andrew Marvell. Member of Parliament for Hull and secretary to Milton."

"I thought so," she said.

She was impressed with herself, even if he wasn't. Afterwards, she looked up the poem in the library.

The nectarine, and curious peach,
Into my hands themselves do reach;
Stumbling on melons, as I pass,
Insnared with flowers, I fall on grass.

A complicated garden, she thought. Not unlike Leah's with its olive trees and butterflies. And she saw the two of them, Leah and famous Lionel, sitting in the shade, cosseted and embittered by their warm and pleasant exile. Lionel withdrawing into drink, retiring to his study to write his memoirs, and dying without a word of them written down.

Then Leah sitting on alone in the garden, nursing her grievances, cherishing her anger.

The spear-tip fern could have come from such a place. And turning her gaze from the frost ferns on the window to the fern on her desk, she felt for a second time that subtle nudge, as if things might be leading somewhere.

9

The Phone Call

On Saturday morning Harriet made trays of Christmas shortbread, even though her cholesterol was so high it could have been the stairway to paradise. The doctor who broke the news was astonished that a woman so thin would have such high cholesterol. What do you eat? he wanted to know. No-name digestive biscuits, said Harriet. How many a day? he asked. Eight? said Harriet. That's too many, said the doctor.

Dinah said, "I couldn't stand doing what you do. Sitting at your desk all day long, trying to invent stuff out of thin air. I have to get out and sniff around the city every day." Her voice was even huskier than usual from a cold she hadn't been able to shake.

"That's because you're a newshound."

"A newshound," repeated Kenny with relish.

"We could be a scriptwriting team," Harriet said. "Browning and Bloom as the new Comden and Greene. Or a vaudeville act. What were Fred and Judy in *Easter Parade*?"

"Hannah and Hewes," said Kenny, who had a mind like a steel trap.

"Gene Kelly was supposed to have that role," said Harriet. She was clocking the shortbread in the oven. "But he broke his ankle playing volleyball, so Fred Astaire came out of retirement and stayed on for another decade. Lucky for us."

"Your mother's been reading Pauline Kael again."

"I didn't learn that from Pauline."

"Pauline Who?" asked Jane the late riser, wandering into the kitchen in sunglasses and a Guatemalan hat because she felt like summer.

Her mother, deep in her own thoughts, didn't reply, and so Dinah murmured "the movie critic" and Jane sighed "oh," while Harriet rolled on. "Was she ever wrong about *Easter Parade*. Sometimes she was just too harsh, too sweeping, she missed the joy of certain movies. But I love her. I really do."

Kenny had a goofy grin on his face, as he always did when Dinah came over. He strode back and forth with his hands in his pockets. The night before, during *Pal Joey*, he had nodded his head to the music much too vigorously he was so excited, so anxious that everybody like Frankie as much as he and Dinah did. His mother noticed and understood. She herself had never recovered from the shock of hearing, at fifteen, someone malign Rudolf Nureyev. "Nureyev," the brutal someone said, "is so full of himself that Margot Fonteyn can't stand him." Her world, she remembers well, was rocked to its foundations. She had enough sense to know that this addiction to purity, which her son shared, was neither good for her nor good for him. Therefore, she said, "Shouldn't my son have a different role model than Frank Sinatra? I mean, not to do Frank an injustice," as three pairs of frosty-alarmed eyes turned in her direction, "but what's wrong with Nelson Mandela? Or even Sean Connery?"

Dinah snorted. "*Seen* Connery was a truck driver and not too bright, but Frankie had all the right instincts, no matter what you say."

"Sean improved with age," said Harriet. "Frank looks like a sausage in a silver wig."

"I'm leaving," Dinah said.

"Forgive me. I won't say another word. Except that somebody was afraid to go bald and somebody wasn't. And do you know why? Because somebody is a real man."

"I hate to say this," Dinah said to Kenny and Jane, "but somebody in this room is talking too much."

"*Yeah*," said Kenny.

"*Yeah*," said Jane.

Lew spoke to the newspaper: "I don't believe that for a minute." Then he tossed it aside. He didn't understand why Harriet was making shortbread when he was allergic to butter.

The phone began to ring, but Harriet made a policy of never answering the phone if she could help it. "You know the movie I want to see? I've never seen it."

Dinah's eyes followed Lew as he headed to the phone in his study.

"*Ninotchka*," said Harriet.

And Dinah returned to the interesting unreality of Harriet's mind. "When Garbo laughed," she said thoughtfully. "Except no sound came out. Did you know that? They had to dub in her laughter."

"Was Greta Garbo's real name Greta Garbo?" asked Jane, wide awake now.

"Gustafsson, I think. She was Swedish. Gustafsson," Dinah said.

"Greta Garbo has a nicer ring to it than Jane Gold."

"Vanity, vanity," said the mother of the prospective movie star.

"Well, I like my name but they won't let me keep it. They'll make me change it. It doesn't have a ring to it. *Greta Garbo*. What's that called?"

"Alliteration," said her mother.

"Alliteration. I should be Janey Jersinski."

The call was for Harriet. She squared her shoulders and picked up the phone in the study. Her mother said, "First, I want to know how Lew is." And Harriet felt the hair prickle on the back of her neck.

"Lew is fine. Why?"

"Because something happened. And I just wanted to make sure."

It would be better not to ask. But she asked. "Tell me what happened."

And her mother told her. She and Martin were just back from a dental conference in Trieste: they had stayed on for an extra week, renting a room in a house similar to a bed and breakfast and preparing their own meals in a small kitchen. One night, at midnight, she got up to use the bathroom across the hall. Stepping out into the hallway, she saw a strange man at the end of the corridor and stopped, suddenly aware that she was only in her nightgown. The man was tall and skinny with short hair and glasses. The light glinted off his glasses. He stood outside the doorway to his room, she stood in the doorway to hers, and they looked at each other. Then he turned and appeared to go into his room.

Those were her words. *He appeared to go into his room.*

Over the next few days she befriended the woman who owned the house, and her daughter. Their English was limited but she questioned them carefully, and learned that no one else was staying in the house. The daughter was married, yes, here's my husband's picture in the photo album. Yes, she had a brother. His picture is here too. Neither man looked anything like the man in the hallway. The man in the hallway looked exactly like Lew.

Harriet listened to her mother's low, clear voice telling her that she had seen Lew's ghost and she felt herself enter the grip of something inevitable and shapely. Her mother had been twelve when her father died. Jane was twelve. Jane adored Lew as much as Gladys had adored her father.

Harriet sat beside the phone after she hung up. She would keep this to herself, she decided, as she wished her mother had done. But she felt touched. Touched by the future.

Harriet ate a shortbread thoughtfully. "Of course, you're right. I do need to get out more."

"Exactly." Dinah shook her head. "It's no wonder you're nuts."

"You think I'm nuts?"

"Certifiable."

Harriet cracked up and her face was transformed. It's notable, thought Dinah, what laughter does for the woman. A different haircut would also help. To say nothing of an adventure.

"I haven't told you," Harriet said.

"What?"

"You won't believe this. *I* don't believe it. I've been asked to teach a course on comic writing."

"*You?*"

"I know." And she spoke with despair. "It's like asking Hitler to teach a course in the humanities." She pulled out a chair and dropped into it. "Henry said you don't have to be able to *do* something to teach it. Very kind of him," she said, "and crazy."

"Who's Henry?" asked Jane.

"Sometimes," Dinah said, "you are funny."

Harriet looked at her with hope mingled with hopelessness before dropping her head into her arms and mumbling something unintelligible.

"What?"

"I said my letters are funny." Raising her head and looking sideways at Dinah. "I can be funny in letters. I don't know why." Although she guessed. Writing letters pulled her out of herself, gave her an occasion to rise to, made her connect with the rest of the world. "The trouble is I don't write letters, I mean real letters, unless I'm travelling."

"It sounds," said Dinah, "like you'd better take a trip."

"I'm going away," Harriet said. "I'm going in search of my sense of humor and I'm not coming back until I've found it."

She headed to the corner store.

"Bon voyage," said Dinah.

At the corner store Bill Bender was buying his morning papers and horrible Ray his daily allotment of chocolate bars. Three papers so the one could find mistakes "sprinkled like parsley" on every page; six chocolate bars so the other could poison himself to death, though not soon enough for Harriet. The moment she came through the door, he pinned her with his expressionless eyes. "Last night you and Dinah were watching movies again."

She looked at him.

This was Ray's style. He watched you and told you what he saw, not because he was curious but because he wanted you to know that nothing escaped him. He was the neighborhood spy, the sort who would provide the necessary evidence to have you sent to the Gulag as a social parasite.

Harriet said, "Did you happen to see who threw the egg at my window?"

His eyebrows rose a fraction of an inch.

She thought there was a good chance he might know, since he was the one who had warned her about the dirty old man next door. Just days after they moved onto the street, he pointed to the upstairs sunroom at the back of Bill Bender's house. "You know he waters his plants in the nude?" Keeping his eyes fixed on her. "Heather – she used to live in your house? She had two little girls? She had to shield their eyes because he likes to garden in his dressing gown, which has a tendency" – his eyes were flat but glinting – "to fall open."

Now he asked, "Which window?" And then, being a high-school math teacher who couldn't bear to be without the answer, "University students," he said.

Harriet escaped to the back of the store and stayed there until he left, then joined Bill Bender at the counter, a stooped old gent in his eighties, big-shouldered, white-haired, whose pale old eyes looked at her and momentarily drew a blank. She helped him out. "Harriet Browning," she said. "Our sunrooms overlook each other."

"Oh yes. Very good, very good, very good."

They walked home together, taking the alley and avoiding a wide van by stepping over a low snowbank into someone's little backyard. "They shouldn't allow cars," muttered Bill Bender. "Should be just for walkers. No cars." He was one of the neighborhood's oldest eccentrics, draping his living-room wall with the Quebec flag, erecting a weather vane in the shape of a maple leaf. Opinionated, contrary, abrupt. "Be off with you," he'd say when he tired of your company, whether you were six years old or sixty. "Go away."

"Let's ban cars. Let's blow up Bronson Avenue," Harriet said.

"Yes, count me in. Count me in."

"We could establish a car-free republic."

"Dominion!" thundered Bill Bender. "A car-free Dominion."

They reached their street and she invited him in for coffee, enticing him with the prospect of seeing the Cuban fern. "And Dinah is visiting," she added, knowing their fondness for each other. But no, he had to take Fiona the milk for her tea. His long courtship of Fiona Chester was one of the first things Dinah told her about the neighborhood. "He's devoted to her," she said. "He calls her Shortie."

Raising his cap, he continued down the alley to Fiona's house, while Harriet turned right and headed home, walking as usual with her head down, and as a result she didn't see Jack until she started up the walk.

He had put on weight. A meaty man had become meatier.

"I don't like meaty men," she would say to Dinah later, and no opinion could have been firmer. "I never have."

You would be able to hear him barrel up and down the stairs, she thought, and you wouldn't like it. Wouldn't like the thumping weight of him. Or, and she felt the peculiar pull she always felt with Jack Frame, you might like it.

He stood with his back to her, so he must have rung the bell. And since there was nowhere to hide, she groped desperately inside herself and discovered, wonder of wonders, a teasing gaiety. "Good Lord," she called to him, and he turned. "I know I'm irresistible, but what are *you* doing here?"

"Harriet."

From the porch he watched her come up the walk, the only woman who had ever punched him in the nose.

Rod Steiger, she thought, as she came up the steps. The same heft. The same sardonic look he had in *Dr. Zhivago*. She said, "Leah told us you were coming."

They hugged each other as Jane opened the door, and Harriet asked, "Is that a six-hundred-page manuscript in your pocket, or are you just glad to see me?" She was all too prescient. A few days later, after he'd settled into his lodgings, he came by with a seven-hundred-page novel for her to read. The man was without mercy.

She let him into the house – this old friend and terrible stranger – and in pictures taken soon afterwards she looked radiant and keyed up, and she was laughing.

IO

John the Baptist

When Harriet first knew Jack Frame he was wild and woolly, a draft dodger, a jabberer about politics, a full-paunched graduate student with bushy hair and beard – one of Leah's stepchildren acquired when she became Lionel Frame's fifth wife. That was in Italy, that first meeting. She saw him again in Montreal after he'd fallen in love with the French professor who would become his first wife. Years went by and Harriet thought of him as her before-and-after man: bristling with politics, denuded by love. He shaved off his beard, trimmed his hair, lost weight for the sake of Sara Tremblay. Then that Sara disappeared and another Sarah took her place, to be replaced six years later by his third wife, Sally, from Chicago; she didn't last either. (Just as another friend of Harriet's went from David to David looking for the perfect one. He's here right now, if you want to meet him, she told Harriet on the phone. He's in the backyard and he's perfect: handsome, well-hung, fabulous company. Harriet drove over and there he was, in the nude, chipped and on a pedestal, in among the lilies.)

All of Jack's wives labored hard to pay the rent, since he had no real profession beyond that of novelist and part-time film critic and some-time rehab counsellor, but none of his wives was a writer or even much of a reader of fiction, so every few years he wrapped up his latest big, whopping manuscript and mailed it to Harriet, into whose lap it landed like a giant overfed cat. Over the years her response time lagged farther and farther behind, until she hit upon the bright idea of responding immediately: Received your manuscript, looks good, best of luck with it. Then she buried it, unread, in the farthest corner of her study and proceeded to write about him. Calling him Harry Juniper, she included him in the story about Leah, having him say behind Leah's back that he couldn't stand her company, "not even for ten minutes," before making a move to wheedle more money out of her.

Why had she written about him? Because she didn't trust him. But in writing about him so transparently she had made herself untrustworthy. And now they were gathering like Iroquois at the gates, the people she had written about.

Inside, she hung up his winter coat while he pulled off his boots and socks, a man who always made himself at home. He padded into the kitchen in bare feet, baggy pants, soft grey sweater, and Harriet introduced him as Leah's stepson from Chicago.

Dinah said, "You still haven't told me who Leah is."

"A terror," said Lew.

"My father's fifth wife," said Jack, who had never taken to Lew, a man he found irritatingly thin. For his part, Lew thought Jack a grandstander, a peacock, a self-infatuated scribbler. Say no, he told Harriet when another manuscript arrived. Send it back. But he doesn't include postage, she cried. Do you know how much it costs to mail a parcel these days? You could buy a mink coat!

"And who's your father?" Dinah asked him.

"Lionel Frame?" Inviting her to recognize the name. "A friend of the Hollywood Ten. Blacklisted in the fifties, so he went from successful screenwriter to unpublished alcoholic."

Kenny, who was all ears, saw his opportunity. "So, what's your favorite movie?" he asked.

Jack replied as swiftly, "That's an awful question." By now they were at the kitchen table, except for Harriet, who was leaning against the counter, and Lew, who was in his study but within earshot, going through sheaves of music. "Endless movies run through my mind."

"All right. If so many movies are running through your mind, what are your three favorite movies?"

Head back, staring at the ceiling. "Okay. To get you off my back, I'll answer." And he began to list movies.

As far as Harriet could tell, Jack made no allowances for anyone. He sat in his bare feet, seemingly not feeling the cold, and rocked back on his kitchen chair – something she was always telling Kenny not to do – and named one movie after another that curdled her blood.

"*Blue Velvet*," he said. "*Leaving Las Vegas. Apocalypse Now. The Deer Hunter. The Godfather* movies."

"See!" Kenny swung on his mom. And to Jack: "She won't let me watch *The Godfather*! Can you believe that? Is that fair?"

"We watched *Jaws* a few months ago," she said, to show she wasn't a complete stick-in-the-mud. "We held hands," and she twirled her hand to indicate the kids and Dinah and herself.

"Now that's a *terrific* movie," said Jack, rocking forward in his chair and planting his elbows on the table. He said, "Allow me to be boring for a minute."

She looked for traces of Lionel in the son – the bushy eyebrows, charcoal black; the black, flashing eyes; the charismatic smile – but saw the big, crude, dominating person she had written about – Harry Juniper – and went cold at the thought. Had Jack read her book? He had never said so, but he must have. Must have read it. Unless he was completely uninterested in her, except as a reader of his own work, which was altogether possible.

He was describing the "wipe shot" when Roy Scheider is on the beach and the crowd behind him is a blur, when his vision is blocked and so is yours, when the only way to see is to lean forward in your seat – and then Scheider sees something, and it's the fin! which turns out to be a hoax, while the real shark is bearing down on Scheider's son who happens to be swimming in the safe side of the bay. Or the moment when Spielberg – "he's a genius, there's no way around it" – has all your attention focused on the lower left corner of the screen, and the decapitated head bobs into view in the upper screen, giving you the very shock that Richard Dreyfuss gets. Or the parody of being macho when Dreyfuss crumples up the Styrofoam cup.

Or the one-upmanship – now Harriet had joined in – between Robert Shaw and Dreyfuss about who has more scars, which Dreyfuss wins by baring his hairy chest and saying, Here! Mary Jane what's-her-name. She broke my heart!

"Mary Ellen Moffit," supplied Kenny.

Jack said, "They had a lot of trouble with the shark. It actually got loose and headed out to sea. And there they were, chasing their million-dollar shark." He gave himself up to a great, mirthful belly laugh.

Kenny, who looked as if he had found the promised land, leaned forward with both elbows on the table, and said, "What's *The Deer Hunter* about?"

"Blood and guts," said his mom, rolling her eyes.

"Ten to one she hasn't seen it," he said, cocking an eye at Kenny.

"I don't have to." And Lew, listening in the next room, began to worry. He heard her say, "It's one of those big, violent, overripe movies all about men and meaning. No jokes. Nothing simple. Just pumped-up, self-important, very expensive nonsense. And there would be scenes that I wouldn't be able to get out of my mind – ever. Depressing."

Kenny said, "'Expensive and depressing. I hate those words. I like the word *peppy*. And I like the word *cheap*. Peppy and cheap.'" He was quoting from *Soapdish*, and Jack's mouth moved in a half-smile.

Harriet said, "I'm not alone either. Pauline Kael agrees with me about *The Deer Hunter*."

"*Pauline Kael*." He swung his big head in derision. "Wretched woman."

These were fighting words. Lew almost headed to the basement. Kenny sat in shock. Dinah said, "We'd better hold hands again." She took Jane's hand and Kenny's, causing them to giggle. But Harriet wasn't paying attention.

"What you have to appreciate about Pauline Kael," Harriet said, "is that she knows movies from beginning to end, from the silents through the talkies, the Second World War, the Cold War, Vietnam, and since. Not just Hollywood but everywhere else. She's smart, no-nonsense, incredibly well read, with a remarkable visual memory and a great writing style. You could learn a lot from her."

"All right."

"She has no time for bullshit." Harriet paused, then went for the jugular. "Especially poetic bullshit."

"Aye-aye, captain."

He looked amused by her, the sort of man who says, I love it when you get angry. The sort of man who begins life as the sort of brother who takes his sister below the elbow and gets her to hit herself over and over again. Why are you hitting yourself? he laughs, until tears spurt from her eyes. And then he relents.

"I haven't read her in years. You're probably right."

From his study Lew heard Dinah lead the conversation into safer waters – *All About Eve*, a movie everyone could agree on – and he felt grateful. She was saying, "When Anne Baxter makes a pass at Gary Merrill? And he says, 'Don't worry, just write it off as an incomplete forward pass.' What a fabulous script. And what about *Damage* by Louis Malle? That's a movie I've watched four times. Tell me why."

Now Jack gave her his full, smart, easygoing attention. "That last scene," he said, "with her photograph covering the wall?" Dinah nodded, remembering Jeremy Irons in dusty exile with Juliette Binoche's face projected on his wall. "Every so often you meet someone like that," he said. "Something happens to them and they can't swallow it." He put his hand around his throat. "They veer away, they go along the side of their lives from then on."

"Yes." Dinah nodded again, taken by his point, and wondering if he was thinking about his father.

Harriet saw the two of them share a look and a smile, and the very real pleasure of agreeing about a movie. But she couldn't even remember the last scene. "You're such romantics," she said with genuine surprise.

"And you're not?" laughed Dinah.

"Well, I don't take movies *literally*." And she actually thought this was true. She had the knack, she thought, for floating between the two worlds of real life and movie life without losing her perfect grip on sanity.

But Dinah gaped. "That," she said, "is the funniest thing I've ever heard." And she chose that moment to tell Jack that Harriet would be teaching a course about comic writing, and he said, "Are you? Then I'll take it."

"Don't. I'm just filling in for a few weeks."

"I'll learn something."

"Have a shortbread," she said.

"I don't eat butter," said Jack.

"Since when?" She was outraged at having her baking turned down. "Let me guess. Since you watched *Last Tango in Paris*."

"Now that's a powerful film," Jack said. "Brando was extraordinary."

"You like Marlon Brando?" asked Kenny, as keenly interested as anyone who feels himself to be at a turning point.

"Not as a human being, but onscreen. Onscreen there's nobody better."

"And nobody handsomer when he was young," said Dinah.

"He had a fat bottom," said Harriet. "I know someone who met him when he was young, at a party for Harry Belafonte, and he had a fat bottom even then. This woman, the mother of a friend of mine, decided that the real Brando was her husband. Her husband was actually better-looking."

"He didn't have a fat bottom," said Dinah.

"That's right, he didn't have a fat bottom."

"Wives," said Dinah with amusement, "they've got the best imaginations in the world."

In the summer, after so many things were no longer the same, Harriet would write, *Dear Pauline, How do you know whether you've misjudged someone? Misjudged how far someone will go? There's the never-ending doubt when you aren't sure. When you won't allow yourself to dislike someone and have done with it.*

What we persuade ourselves of: That a book is better than it is. That someone attracts us, who didn't attract us at all. That e-mail isn't so bad after all. That the death of letters doesn't break one's heart.

But now, for some reason unknown to herself, after Dinah had gone home to nurse her cold, and Lew had taken the kids to their piano lessons, she went to the trouble of showing Jack Frame the Cuban fern. "Ah," he said, "a cryptogam. Do you know what that means?" His soft eyes held hers. "Hidden marriage," he said.

He turned the fern over and pointed with his thick finger. "It was a big mystery for a long time, the sexual lives of ferns. They don't have flowers, they don't have seeds, so how do they reproduce? Spores. They reproduce by means of these beautiful spores." He held it up to the window and the fine herringbone pattern was backlit by late-November light.

She asked him then how long he was staying and he told her a few months. The National Library had Lionel's papers, he would be there much of the time, and then when Leah came in January they would pool their information and memories about Lionel. The book would be part biography, part family memoir.

"You're really going to write the book with her?" Harriet couldn't picture it.

"She's doing the chapters about their life together, and I'll handle the early life and the politics."

"But I thought you couldn't stand Leah."

"She's paying me," he said.

And this time it was Jack and Harriet who shared a smile. "There's another movie I like," he added. "An old one with Charles Boyer, Danielle Darrieux, Vittorio de Sica. Directed by Max Ophuls."

"*The Earrings of Madame de . . .* ," exclaimed Harriet, and she gave him a long, startled look. "It's one of my favorite movies."

"I thought it might be."

"It's the most romantic movie I've ever seen. And the saddest. Men are so different from women." She ran her hands through her hair and shook her head. "Why did he reject her at the end? Did you understand it? She lied about the earrings, but so what?"

"Honor," said Jack. "Pride. She made him look foolish."

"That's what I mean. A woman would never let pride or honor get in the way of love."

Late in the afternoon, back from his piano lesson, Kenny said to his mom, "I like Jack Frame, don't you?"

"Sure." But in a tone so tentative that he stopped and stared at her. "You don't like him?"

She looked at his face – young, eager, quick, intent on not being fooled, but foolhardy. What a boy he was for sentimental attachments. "I like him," she said, and his face relaxed. "I like him. But not as much as you and Dinah do."

And Kenny was satisfied.

At dinner Lew resurfaced from the basement, where he'd been for the past hour working on his design for an office down there that would include his drafting table, desk, radio, bookshelves, armchair. He asked Harriet where Jack was staying, and she told him in an apartment on First Avenue, an exchange with somebody who was using his place in Chicago.

"And you survived the visit?"

"Oh, I'm fine," she said.

This he would never get used to, the breeziness that followed hard on the heels of her panic.

Harriet took off her glasses and laid them on the table. "He's entertaining," she said, rubbing her eyes and drawn onto the rocks of being fair. "I always forget that. I don't know why."

Then having dispensed with one worry, she had room for another. She put on her glasses and turned to look at Lew. "My mother saw your ghost," she said.

II

In Deeper

She noticed herself looking for him. A sort of quickening when she entered stores, or passed restaurants or barbershops, or when she went for a walk. Down every aisle. In every window. From behind every tree. She expected to see his big, bushy head pop into view.

Even as she reached for a grocery cart, she turned to survey the mounds of fruit and vegetables, expecting to see bent over bananas, sorting through persimmons, bagging potatoes, that big figure in the soft grey sweater.

On a walk through the Arboretum she not only looked for him, she listened for his voice.

"Brook!" she heard.

"*Brooklyn!*"

"Camille! *Camille!*"

"Wayne!"

Having reached the topmost level of parkland, she had an unbroken view of dogs and dog owners on the treed and snowy slopes. From here Ottawa rose up on the opposite side of the canal like a small city on the far side of a plain to which the traveller is destined to go. She liked, at night especially, to stand in her boots, or on her skis, and stare across at the ribbon of city lights, the visible rooftops, the lighter evening sky beneath the darker night sky. It was lovely. "Except for Bronson Avenue," she told Jack in her head, detecting its roar in the distance. "One of these nights, under cover of darkness, I'm going to hijack one of those contraptions – what are they called, those bulldozers? Six lanes! *Six*. I'm going to plough a trench from Dow's Lake to Fulton Avenue. I'm going to flood that sucker."

"Flood what?" Horrible Ray was at her side. She had been talking out loud.

She gave him a furious look. "Bronson Avenue." She waved her hand in that direction. "It's time to reclaim the landscape. Your dog." She jerked her head towards the little white dog barking incessantly at a German Shepherd. "German Shepherds don't like little dogs."

Ray went to the rescue of defiant Fluffy and Harriet made her escape, striding across the top of the steep sliding hill that children hurtled down all winter long, courting concussion and death. A big black poodle crossed her path. The poodle's owner looked to be retired, a gent in a tweed cap and velvety brown corduroy pants.

"Felicity," he called anxiously.

"*Felicity!*" he implored.

It happened when she was thinking about something else. She had gone to the post office on Fourth Avenue and proceeded to the supermarket on Bank Street. It was the last Friday in November, and she was thinking about *Ninotchka*, the movie they were going to watch that night. She came down the potato chip aisle, her eyes fixed on the rows of chips, only dimly aware of a large man staring intently at the shelves of canned tomatoes and beans. She looked around his dark-green back at the various brands, and beyond, hoping something better lay ahead, but it didn't. She glanced back up the row of chips then down the row again, and recognized the man in the dark-green jacket.

"Jack," she said.

Then he looked at her. He said her name without surprise. She guessed he had seen her from the first. He said her name in full. *Harriet Browning.*

How can someone disquieting, who looks unprepossessing, who openly farts, become attractive to you? Time. Repeated viewing. Familiarity, but at a distance. And something more. You push against him and he doesn't give. That's what she liked. His massiveness was the massiveness of a solid steamed pudding: the very thing for winter.

She told him what she was looking for, and he replied that a certain brand was unquestionably the best. She chose the biggest bag of that brand, even though she didn't trust its bright garish looks. Then he leaned over and brushed something off her face, just near her left eye.

"What have I got on me?" she asked.

"I don't know. But you look ridiculous," he said, making her laugh. His tone was neither caressing nor rough, but somewhere in between. In between familiar and intimate. In that place where things can go one way, or another.

Harriet looked up from Pauline Kael. "Have you seen *Rio Grande*?" she asked Dinah, who was stirring honey into her tea. It was almost four o'clock on the same afternoon. In a few minutes the hour would strike on Parliament Hill, much too far away from this part of old Ottawa South to be heard. It was the time of day when tones of red emerge from the dead flowers and wet grasses.

"John Wayne and Maureen O'Hara? They're separated, but still in love. There's a son who brings them back together."

"Pauline says they're very effective together," said Harriet, "'so that the viewer deeply wants the final reconciliation.'"

"I was at the *Winnipeg Tribune* when he died. They splashed it all over the front page. That never would have happened if women had been running the paper."

"That's a good storyline. 'So effective together that the viewer deeply wants the final reconciliation.' What are we going to do about your cough? You sound like a swamp."

"*Nothing*. I have this every winter."

Harriet looked at her with concern, but thought better of making some remark about her smoking. She said, "I keep wondering if Sarah Brown and Sky Masterson are happy together."

"No." Dinah was very firm. "If he reforms enough to satisfy her, he won't be happy, and if she corrupts herself enough to satisfy him, *she* won't be happy."

"No miracles," Harriet said sadly.

But she was romantic and given to fond hopes. She continued to believe that Sky and Sarah were making each other deliriously happy in some fashion. In some fashion? In bed. She pictured them running a Salvation Army Thrift Store on the main street of a small town, and, above the store, a poolroom: corruption and goodness coexisting like a two-layer cake. She thought about *A Streetcar Named Desire* too, especially when she heard the song detective calling into the night, "Stella! Stell-aaaa."

Stella was his five-year-old malamute.

About a year ago she had watched *Streetcar* with Lew (for once they watched a movie together), then afterwards she reread Pauline's review in which she called Stanley part infant, part brute – a man without compassion. And surely this was true. But the image of Brando crying and on his knees, while Stella came down the stairs, drawn to him, drew her too. And against reason, she hoped for a happy ending. "Do you think she'll go back to him?" she had asked Lew.

"Why do you care?" he had wanted to know.

"I've been thinking about it all day. Don't you wonder what happens to people after the movie ends?"

"No."

"I want them to be happy." She had been wanting it all day.

"What are you saying?"

"Nothing. No agenda. I just wish they could be happy."

But she knew he didn't quite believe her. She thought he must wonder, as she wondered herself, if a woman who was really happy with him would be so addicted to romantic movies. Perhaps he thought it was a phase she would get over. And it might be. *I go at movies the way I go at food. Only Cary Grant interests me, then only Gene Kelly. The same thing over and over again until I'm sick of it. A serial enthusiast.*

"I'm funnier with you than I am with Lew," she said to Dinah. "Why do you suppose that is?" She looked moodily out of the window. "I know why it is."

They were talking about her comedy class now.

"I'm sad because he's cheerful. If he weren't so *sprightly* I'd have to lighten up."

They can't help it, thought Dinah, these married couples. But it broke her heart to see Harriet wasting Lew's capacity for tenderness.

"Have you ever asked him what's going through his mind? When he seems cheerful, have you asked him if he really is?"

Harriet felt suddenly foolish. But she defended herself. "When I do he's evasive. That's what gets me. He doesn't *react*. Now Pauline Kael, there's someone who's not afraid of her own reactions. I can't imagine her not knowing what she wants to eat for dinner."

"I could say you're lucky, but I'd be repeating myself, wouldn't I?"

"You like him?"

"He's a sweetie. And handsome too."

Harriet cheered up immediately, and Dinah tried not to be too critical of a woman who couldn't see what she had until someone else admired it.

"Well, at least I'm not as badly off as my Auntie Lottie," said Harriet. "On her wedding night Uncle George put his head under the covers and sucked his thumb."

"I think that's endearing."

"*Endearing*?" Harriet looked at Dinah with wonder. "What a generous woman you are!"

"You don't agree?"

"Are you telling me you wouldn't mind a husband who sucked his thumb?"

"I'm just saying that's love, isn't it?"

"What's love?"

"Feeling tender towards another's weaknesses."

"These tests of love," said Harriet. "I flunk them every time."

It being a Friday, when Kenny arrived home from school he called out to his mom, "Did you get a movie?"

She said yes. "It's called *Nails*. It was made by the National Film Board, and it's fascinating."

"No, really," said Kenny.

"*Ninotchka*. Greta Garbo and Melvyn Douglas. It's a classic," she said, seeing his doubtful face.

"Is Dinah coming?"

"She's not feeling very well, but I persuaded her to come anyway."

"Good," said Kenny, heading upstairs and leaving Harriet to remember the Christmas when her mother, as a treat, borrowed a film projector and brought home some educational films to watch, among them, *Nails*, a documentary about the manufacture and production of miles upon miles of nails. *And you wonder what drove me into the arms of Cary Grant?*

Garbo came on and they stared. No one said a word. Harriet thought, Her hair is flat. Her tummy sticks out. Her shoulders slump.

And that *hat*.

Ina Claire is better, thought Harriet. To Jane she said in a neutral voice, "Do you think she's beautiful?"

"Yes."

Surprised. "Why?"

"Her skin. Her eyes. Her mouth. Of course, it could be makeup. It's hard to tell if somebody's beautiful when they've got makeup on."

Dinah agreed with Jane. "She's marvellous. Look at her stride across a room. Nobody else was like her. Nobody came close. Even the smart ones didn't have what she has behind her eyes."

Harriet thought, She has herself behind her eyes. She makes love to herself.

The laugh was worth waiting for. To be accurate, the attempt to make her laugh was worth waiting for. How attractive of Melvyn Douglas to be attracted to a serious Russian and to want to make her laugh. "It sounds natural to me," said Dinah. "It doesn't sound dubbed. Does it sound dubbed to you?"

"She's good at being in love," Harriet said. "But she's not in love with Melvyn Douglas. That's easy to tell."

"They wanted Cary Grant for the part," Dinah said.

"Ah! That would have been a different story." And Harriet imagined Cary in the part, and in other parts he had turned down. How different *Love in the Afternoon* would have been had Cary said yes, and *Sabrina* too. "You read that somewhere?"

"Jack told me."

"Jack?"

"I saw him when I went for the pizza. He asked about you, by the way." She looked at Harriet. "I think he likes you. But I guess you know that."

Kenny said, "He's good." His eyes hadn't left the screen.

"Melvyn Douglas?" said Harriet, feeling more pleased than she knew was sensible.

"What else is he in?" asked Kenny.

"He was in *Hud*. But he was no fun at all."

"He *is* good," agreed Dinah. "They're good together."

Harriet thought, No, they're good apart. Later, she said, "Too bad Garbo didn't choose to keep on laughing. She could have been a comedian, but she chose to be sad and lonely instead."

Dinah said, "What makes you think comedians are happy?"

But Harriet just laughed, still mildly aglow from what Dinah had said about Jack.

After the kids were in bed and Dinah had gone home, she watched *Ninotchka* again. "'The whites of your eyes are clear. Your cornea is excellent.'

"'What kind of girl are you?'"

Then once more, a day later, by which time she had convinced herself not only that Garbo was beautiful but that she was in love with Melvyn Douglas. The falsity and strangeness of her acting fell away, and Harriet became accustomed to her mannerisms, which now seemed like truth.

12

Family Life

Jane said to her brother, "You're wasting water, Kenny."

They were standing side by side at the sink, and Kenny had emptied a glass, half full, down the drain, then filled it anew.

"Just an ounce," he said.

"Ken, do you know that farmers don't have enough water for agriculture because it's being *taken*? By city folk? For bottled water? That's wasting water, Ken. Just because I touched the glass, you don't have to throw it out."

"It's just an ounce," he said again.

"But it adds up. If we had a social scale, you'd be lower on it than I am."

This occurred after school. Before supper Harriet said, "I just looked in the mirror. That was a mistake. I'm looking less and less like Julie Christie every day."

"So is she," said Lew.

They were all in the kitchen, the table covered with homework spread far and wide, and the air full of bickering about who would clean it up.

"Who's Julie Christie?" asked Kenny.

"A famous movie star."

"Then why haven't I heard of her?"

"Because you're dumb," said Jane.

During supper, eaten around piles of homework, Kenny said to his mom, "Remember how you said after you watch a movie you feel emptier than before?"

"Not always." Remembering, and qualifying what she'd said.

"It's true. Except for two movies. *My Life as a Dog* and *The Black Stallion*. After they were over, I felt great."

"But you said *My Life as a Dog* depressed you."

"The thing is, it had some very depressing moments, but it had a very happy ending." She nodded, and then he said, "Name a movie star who was good at dancing, singing, and acting, all three."

Lew reached for *Canadian Architect*. Harriet said, "Gene Kelly and Judy Garland."

"I agree," said Jane.

"And not Frank Sinatra?"

"He was good at singing and acting," said Harriet, "but not so great at dancing."

"Have you heard the new scandal?" Kenny had a twinkle in his eye. "They finally discovered that Gene Kelly never really sang. And his feet were computer-animated."

"And Frank Sinatra was dubbed," snarled Jane.

"Now that joke isn't funny," Kenny protested. "Now it's not funny any more! You ruined the joke!"

He pushed aside his plate and stomped upstairs. In his room he put on his gangster jacket and his fedora, sat down at his small desk, and began to type, two-fingered, on the old typewriter he'd lugged up from the basement. *I parked my Rolls-Royce and walked into the bar wearing my light-brown tweed jacket and my black fedora, smoking –* "What's the name of a cigar?" he yelled to his mom, who was coming up the stairs. "White Owl," she yelled back – *a White Owl cigar. That's a typical outfit for me because I'm so underpaid I can't afford new clothes. The Rolls Royce is my late sister's. She left it to me in her will. At the bar I saw the Sinatra sisters. They were each having a drink. For Dinah Sinatra it was Scotch. Same for Harriet. I went over to the counter and got myself a Bourbon. Then I got another Bourbon. I went up to the Sinatra sisters and said,* "I think your father's better in the movies than he is singing. I especially like* High Society, On the Town, *and* Guys and Dolls. *How about you?" But when I looked up they were gone.*

In the basement Lew heard his son typing away. Lew was wearing one of his father's shirts since he, too, was looking for inspiration. Any design problem, and he put on his father's old plaid shirt; mixing drinks, and he wore his father's polka-dot shirt purchased in Miami Beach in 1947. How to create a small office as efficient and exact as a small boat? That was the problem he had to crack, this son of a melancholy building inspector whose nervous breakdown at fifty-four had delivered young

Lew and his brother into the tender hands of their grandparents for several summers, in this very house.

Late one night, when Lew and Harriet were folding the tablecloth after a dinner party, Lew said, "A beautiful color. My father's favorite color."

"Coral," she said.

"Salmon. My father would have said salmon. One time at dinner we were eating lobster and he kept picking up different pieces and saying: This is the color. No. *This* is the color. He was trying to find the shade to paint our house. That was the same night he cut his hand on the broken jar and said afterwards *That was the color*. The color of blood dripping down his hand."

A pebbled-glass orange juice jar, used for storing water in the fridge: it slipped out of his grasp on a hot, humid night and he caught it as it smashed on the floor. A shard of glass severed the tendon between finger and thumb, and a hand surgeon with the memorable name of Dr. Nailbuff repaired the deep wound.

Harriet was agog as she listened to the details. From the first, she had reminded him of his father. Intent, serious, easily hurt. Tempestuous, susceptible, blunt. Kenny had some of the same qualities, perhaps too many, while Jane was more like his own mother: capable, determined, energetic, yet subject to various physical afflictions, as was he. He didn't always understand it: this marriage of his. He loved a crowded house. Harriet hated company. He loved plump, full-bodied women. Harriet was tall, bony, rangy; given to insomnia and sadness, which she doctored with old movies; often embarrassingly direct, and furious for no good reason. And what held him? Oddly enough, the way she left him alone.

His dad used to kiss him on the mouth. Ancient fatherly affection. Unembarrassed. Without guile. He loved his sons. No one was good enough for them, not their wives, not the sons themselves. For Lew he had had the highest hopes, imagining a fine career with a large firm, and it hurt him – Lew knew that – to see his sons refuse to climb the ladder from which he himself had fallen. He spent his final years typing bitter letters to the editor with two long fingers, his lips moving in silent battle with the old enemies in his head. But Lew's ambitions had never been material. Teaching, offering his services to international heritage committees, an occasional high-paying private job for extra money. And his designs were invariably simple. As a boy his favorite word was *room*. After that, *boardwalk*, from playing Monopoly. What is it? he had asked his dad. A wooden walkway by the sea, came the answer. And Lew thought, No wonder it's the most valuable property on the board.

"I fell in love with his room," Harriet answered, when Dinah asked her how it happened that she fell in love with Lew. "He'd made every-thing himself – desk, bed, shelves – and everything was placed – arranged – with an eye for proportion and balance." Dinah nodded. Yes, she thought, there was an atmosphere around Lew of nothing being too much trouble.

He rarely watched a movie. Harriet liked to joke that the last one he'd seen was Bertolucci's *1900* made in 1977. Once, she'd asked him what movie star he drooled over as a boy. He thought for a time, then said, "I liked Marilyn Monroe." How old were you when you first saw her? "Thirty?" he said.

He was the sort of man who mended the tears in a map. Who spent hours pressing cloves into an orange to hang from the rearview mirror and dispel the car-stink that made his daughter want to puke. The only one who had the patience and dexterity to put her tiny pierced earrings into her ears.

"If it hurts, you let me know, okay?"

"Okay."

He turned the light to its brightest setting. "Come on, get through. If it hurts, you tell me. Is it hurting?"

"No."

"It's not going through. Let's try the front. Turn your head. Now it's through. The hole is still there. There it is. Right through."

So tender-hearted that when he picked apples in an orchard he picked them all, scabby, small, lopsided, unable to leave any behind. He came home with boxes of apples and Harriet went through them and said, "Did you wear your glasses?"

A man so kind and calm that when he was less than that, it took your breath away.

A year ago she was in New York doing some research for her magnum opus, *Mapping Canadian Self-Doubt* (a title that Dinah told her had to go: "I would never, and I mean never, buy a book called *Mapping Canadian Self-Doubt*"), and one afternoon she called home collect. Lew answered. She heard the operator ask him if he would accept her call, and through the domestic chaos in the background she heard him say, "I guess so."

A day later she called again and heard the same tepid answer.

I guess so? I guess so?

And she felt everything that had ever been between them fall instantly away.

"You want advice about Harriet?" Dinah asked gently the morning she stood outside in her red coat and learned the correct name for her braided black fasteners.

"She's up all night," he sighed, "and awful all day."

"Is she up now?"

"Now she's in bed. She might be sleeping. I hope she's sleeping."

"You'd better get a new mattress. A good mattress makes all the difference."

Dinah, observing his tired face, remembered her first impressions of him: the tender voice, the sexiness of his domesticity, his easiness in any situation, his courtesy. She pictured him making the lunches and getting the kids out the door, and she felt sympathy but not pity. Her mother would have felt pity, but Dinah belonged to another generation. Her father, too, had been a devoted dad. She used to think all Jewish men were the same, but then she went to New York and discovered that there were poor Jews and bad Jews. Lew's Jewishness lay easily upon him, like an invisible cloak. He worked hard, but never talked about how hard he worked, "It used to be," he said, "before everybody was in such a rush, that the first question people would ask was *Who are you?* Meaning are you Jewish, French, Italian, Puerto Rican? Then, *What do you do?* Meaning are you a doctor or lawyer or Indian chief? Now they ask *Are you done yet?*"

His own not-so-secret wish was to run a slow-paced neighborhood coffee shop. Harriet would make the pastries. She had actually offered. She would bake, she said, every night from six until ten, so long as she didn't have to speak to anyone. Of course, what appealed to Lew, a sociable man caught in the coils of an unsociable wife, was the chance to visit with people all day long. There were times when Dinah thought the two of them oddly suited to each other: one fulfilled by little, the other unfulfilled by a lot.

"She can't stand visitors," he said, "except for you." Giving her an appreciative look.

"We have fun with our movies."

"*Movies*," groaned Lew. "That's all she cares about."

"Don't be a jealous fool," she teased, but to her surprise he didn't smile.

Ah, she thought sadly, so that's the trouble. He's suffering from Rhett Butler syndrome: he wants his wife to fall in love with him.

13

The Crucifier

They were downstairs when the phone rang. It was the last Saturday in November. Lew answered, and said, "Leah!" To be exact, he said, "Leah! *Where are you?*"

That was the clue. They knew more than one Leah, but only one Leah could have drawn from him such a resounding note of cheery panic.

Harriet, reaching for the coffee, froze in her tracks. Then, without a coat, she headed out the back door into the snow. She was wearing slippers. In her slippers she went around the side of the house, squeezed through the narrow passageway between verandah and wooden fence, got herself past the car parked in the driveway and around to the front. She came in the front door, removed her slippers, tiptoed upstairs and pulled the blankets over her head.

Lew sat on the edge of the bed. "I saved you," he said.

"Where is she?"

"With Jack's sister in Chicago. It's all right."

"She's not coming?"

"She's coming, but not till January, like she said. She just wanted to complain about not hearing from us."

"What did she say she's doing? What is her life like?" Harriet could ask now that the immediate danger had passed. She was very curious to know.

"She said she spends all her time writing angry letters she doesn't send. She said it's a good thing she doesn't send them. Then she read me one."

"Right."

Even a calm letter from Leah was like a missive from Liza Minnelli. Hectic, overemphatic, crammed with capitalized words and exclamation marks. It made you long to be a Quaker.

"I said we'd be happy to have her stay, but we always put a limit on guests of three days. Otherwise you can't work."

Harriet looked at him gratefully. "Except Jeff Bridges. If Jeff calls, he can stay for a week." She reached for Lew's hand, and he said to her, "You know, she's a fund of information. Get her to talk about Hollywood."

"I don't believe a word she says. She trashes everybody. She hates them all. You remember what she said about Cary Grant?" Fixing him with livid eyes. "You don't remember. Well, I'm not going to repeat it."

"She's lonely," he said.

"She's a bully and a lush. She leaves Attila the Hun in the dust."

"You're afraid of her."

"*Afraid?*" squawked Harriet. "Try terrified. Oh, for heaven's sake," she said, sitting up. "This is ridiculous. *I'm* ridiculous. When in January?"

"The first week."

"Why would anybody come to Ottawa in January?"

Lew shook his head, equally confounded.

"She's demented, that's why."

"I know," he said.

14

Sunday

You give in so easily, Ratty said to Mole. Harriet had been reading to Kenny and the words come back to her at three in the morning. Timid Mole and Imperious Ratty. She thinks of Frank Sinatra and Marlon Brando in *Guys and Dolls*. She thinks of commanding figures and weak ones. She thinks of getting up, but she doesn't. Her shoulders are cold. She lies in bed and worries some more.

Her class. She must prepare for tomorrow's class. And Leah. She must build herself some armor.

In the morning, while the kids and Lew sleep in, she makes coffee and takes it to her desk upstairs, and there she sits remembering the previous week – the last week of November, when for a day or two it was unexpectedly warm and she became aware of the birds singing and the highway going on and the wind picking up. *Life isn't so bad, though it would be better, it would be much better, without wind chimes. Listen to them. Listen to them ruining my life. They sound like Auntie Muriel clicking and sucking her false teeth. To be twenty-one, to be at Covent Garden, to be listening for the first time in my life to* Carmen *and to have it ruined by my opera-singing auntie with the blue eyeshadow and the great crooked nose that turned black in the cold and the long fingernails painted red except where the paint had chipped away – to have it ruined by my dear old auntie clicking her teeth and humming over the arias. Is it any wonder? Is it any wonder that I get depressed?*

Ottawa has done this to me. Ottawa has sucked the juices from my brain and the marrow from my bones. But I can't say so or Lew's eyes will light up and he'll exclaim: Montreal. Cuba. Brazil.

One night earlier in the week, when they were lying in bed together, she said, "I am one-third my mother and two-thirds my father. One day out of three I work hard, everything interests me, I am glad to be alive. Two days out of three I rot. I sulk. I'm incapable of anything but self-pity. My mother should have married someone else. She should have married an Asian."

Lew, only half listening, said, "You think you'd do better if your dad was an agent?"

"Okay. My mother should have married an Asian agent. Then my book would be a howling success *and*" – returning to her own point – "I wouldn't have so much body hair."

The hair on her legs was thickening as was the hair on bucktoothed beavers in their lodges and glutted raccoons in their holes. It would continue to grow and flourish until the end of April, when the summer harvest would begin. Then she would take a razor to her legs and the yield would be enough for a little fur coat. She could sell these coats, she thought. If *that* failed, if worst came to worst, and no doubt it would, she might develop a line of gum makeup. She had acres of gums. Voltaire on Canada? Nothing but a few acres of snow? Well. Check out these few acres of gums.

She tried out her idea on Dinah. "You're a career woman," she said, "what do you think?"

"A career woman? I was fired ten days ago."

"Dinah."

"Not to worry. I've already lined things up. Dinah Bloom, speech writer."

"So you're all right?"

"And as a career woman with a new career, I think gum makeup has a great future, so long as you do a little modelling on the side."

They had watched *Bells Are Ringing* not long ago, and as soon as Judy Holliday began to sing about the Bonjour Tristesse Brassiere Factory, where she did a little modelling on the side, Harriet took a page from her daughter's book and said, "I'm her."

"You can't be Judy Holliday," said Dinah. "You're Greta Garbo."

"I can be Judy. I have room for *many* enthusiasms."

"Okay. Have it your way. But I'm Audrey Hepburn."

"We're *both* Audrey."

Dinah looked at Jane and Kenny. "Your mother," she said, "is out of control."

Dear Pauline, wrote Harriet the morning after *Bells Are Ringing. Now I'm in love with Dean Martin. Tell me. What is it, exactly, that makes him so sexy? Dinah says he has the look and manner of someone from her father's generation, the sort who only has to say, Hi, dollface, and you feel like you've died and gone to heaven. But Dinah is cruder than I am. To say nothing of older. I would say it's his relaxed but ardent humor, his easy good looks, his perfect timing, and unabashed appreciation of quirky, good-hearted, funny women who loosen up and relax in his company. I don't suppose you've watched many Dean Martin movies in your day; you don't even include* Bells Are Ringing *in your* 5001 Nights at the Movies, *a clear sign of disfavor. I hope I'm broadening your mind.*
    H.

Eeyore is more interesting than Mole, Harriet tells herself at her desk: self-pity beats timid charm any day. Her mother introduced her to Eeyore. *My mother exactly*, her mother had said, laughing and shaking her head at Eeyore's prickly gloom as she read aloud to Owen, the youngest of the six and the one for whom she had time. The only one she read to. Harriet discovered Eeyore that way. She was a witness to the cozy hilarity on the sofa.

Her mother had a sense of humor. She used to laugh over Mark Twain until tears streamed down her cheeks. Her mother insisted that Harriet's father, Martin the Martinet, also had a sense of humor. "A great sense of fun. Don't you see it?" Harriet didn't see it, so busy was she avoiding the back of his hand. Her mother never accused her morose daughter of having a sense of humor. She accused her of being just like her own mother, the one who was just like Eeyore.

Now here she is, proving her mother right. Sunk in gloom at her desk because who was she? She was Harriet Browning, who taught writing sporadically, and for peanuts. How she hated the donkey work of preparation and the unspeakable slave labor of reading her students' weekly efforts. How she hated being reminded that what she knew would fill a thimble. How she hated pretending that what she knew would fill more than a thimble. The truth was, she was fooling her students and her students were fooling themselves – what was it Elizabeth Bishop had said about students of creative writing? "I wish they wouldn't." She hated her diplomatic lies. What else did she hate?

Oh yes. Wind chimes.

Escaping her desk in the middle of the week, she went outside to stand under the trees, and Fiona Chester came down the sidewalk, a look almost of sorrow on her face, as if about to tell a tragedy. "Oh, Harriet, it's so beautiful," she said with a catch in her voice.

She meant the day. It was so beautiful it was breaking her heart.

A mere wisp of a thing, this tiny woman with the grand appetite for knowledge. Bill Bender joined them, closing his front door on the four radios all tuned to the CBC from morning till night, since he hated to miss a thing as he moved from room to room between stacks of books so heavy there was genuine concern for his buckling floors.

"I've never asked you: have you got any books about Garbo?" Harriet said.

"I saw her once," he said, jiggling some coins in the pocket of trousers worn white at the knee. He did his own laundry, hanging out a few shirts at a time and a pair of pants, from which sight Harriet concluded that he wore no underwear, ever. "In Central Park," he said, staring down the street. "She was walking in the rain."

In the rain, thought Harriet, imagining it.

"Under an umbrella?" she asked.

"No umbrella."

And they stood there picturing Garbo getting wet.

"What about a hat?"

"Yes," he nodded. "A wide brim. Dark green."

"Sunglasses?"

He nodded again.

"Lipstick?" she asked.

"Pink," he said. "Soft pink."

That's my man, thought Harriet. She knew more about him by this time – the photographic memory, the mild alcohol problem, the fine way of getting mad. According to Dinah, his wastebasket at the *Journal* was dented in a dozen places and there was talk of a telephone he had kicked to pieces. Also, absences of several days when he stalked out in a rage over some managing editor's stupidity. Mainly, though, he was known for his brilliance and his rubbery posture, a physically eccentric and talkative man. Dinah loved him. She had moved onto the street because he was here, and still checked her facts with him. The name of the Catholic hospital in Winnipeg? Misericordia. The name of the beautiful old library across the street? The Cornish. The spelling of Freiman's department

store, long gone, on Rideau Street? The *e* comes before the *i*. The reason
Mary Pickford visited Ottawa in 1948? To make an appeal on behalf of
UNESCO. The reason she got along so well with Prime Minister Mackenzie King? She loved her mother too. Like most newspapermen he
knew far more than he had ever put into print, and that was what he was in
the process of correcting. His book, the newspaperman's encyclopedia he
had been working on for so many years, would be a compilation of every
story he had ever written plus its shadow story, all the embarrassing facts,
deep background, and multiple connections he had never been allowed to
make. Journalists write less than they know and novelists write more, he
told Harriet when he learned she was a writer. A journalist will know the
premier has a mistress kept in a hotel at government expense while his
battered wife regularly visits the emergency ward, and not write about it.
A novelist will not only write about it but come to sweeping conclusions
about the nature of man. What fun they must have, he said.

Oh, I don't know, said Harriet.

Nicotine oozed from Bill Bender's walls. His bathroom ceiling, said
Dinah, was speckled with brown bubbles the color of old urine. A two-
pack-a-day man from the age of twelve, and a meticulous documenter –
he wrote the date beside every cigarette burn on his kitchen floor.

Harriet itched to ask Fiona Chester why she wouldn't marry him,
wondering which of his eccentricities might be the stumbling block,
since there were more. There were, for instance, his long-running feuds
with the sparrows who moved in on the swallows every spring; with
Mort the squirrel, who led a guerrilla army against his tulip bulbs; with
the song detective, whose ribald, rebellious backyard bordered his and
produced the thousands of Manitoba maple seedlings that clogged his
experimental patches of ferns and goldenrod. Against sparrows and
squirrels he aimed his grandson's pumped-up Super Soaker, and against
the Manitoba maples he wielded a pair of clippers in the dead of night.
They're not maples, he told the song detective more than once, they're
box elders. WEED TREES, he said, *in anyone's language*. Brittle, shapeless
trees that multiplied like starlings. But the song detective was no less
stubborn, having lived in the treeless Arctic for twenty-two years,
where, again according to Dinah, who seemed to know everything about
everyone, he passed the long dark nights learning how to knit. (In retal-
iation, Bill Bender planted ragweed along their shared property line,
since he knew the song detective was prone to bouts of hay fever.)

"Why won't you marry him?" she asked outright one day.

"Too many mirrors," was the answer. And Harriet thought Fiona's hearing aids had stopped altogether.

"How many?" she asked.

"I don't know in total, but?" with that little swing in her voice, "in his bathroom there are three large ones."

"He doesn't look like a vain man," said Harriet in some perplexity. "He doesn't dress like a vain man."

"That's the trouble. He can't get undressed fast enough."

On Sunday mornings, Harriet always heads downstairs to catch the song detective, who comes on the air at twenty minutes to eight and provides, in the next twenty minutes, three stories, each with a beginning, a middle, and an end. It's rather like hearing three little three-act plays. There's the letter requesting a song that has meaning in the listener's past, the search for the song, and then the song itself – a most satisfying progression.

The song detective doesn't look a bit like his educated voice. Always knocking about in jeans and army jacket, no gloves, no hat. A smooth baritone with a mischievous laugh, but socially a misfit: a solitary, burly man who walks down the middle of the street never greeting anyone. Never, according to Dinah, stepping on a crack.

You seem to keep a close eye on him, observed Harriet one day.

He's not my type, came the surprisingly curt answer.

Harriet heats milk for her second cup of coffee as she listens, the volume turned low so as not to disturb the others. *"The memory that has prompted this request goes back about twenty years when I played an old record for my son who was then about ten years old . . . "* It was the *William Tell Overture*, a Columbia recording the listener was given as a boy. Two large discs with blue labels. Harriet listens to the music and her thoughts wander to Bill Bender and his endless book. *Everyone is writing a book, have you noticed? And why? Because books are about to expire, that's why. Any plant under stress puts out many blooms.*

No doubt writers will be the silent-screen stars of the 21ˢᵗ century – left behind – unable to make the leap to the next stage: books without paper.

When I was little I used to visit the post office and go through the tall wire-mesh waste baskets to find beautiful used envelopes and discarded business

forms. What treasure. Once, coming home with my hands full, a little dog came
out of nowhere and bit me. Papers everywhere. Tears, of course. And home.
Books without paper, and, I should probably add, without readers.

Later, under a sky that couldn't make up its mind whether to snow or
rain – such nervous, indecisive, Jack Lemmony weather – Harriet walks
to the fruit store and looks up from the bananas straight into the eyes of
Dinah Bloom, who is stocking up on oranges because she feels so run
down. "It was in a store like this," says Dinah, "a little smaller, that I saw
Greta Garbo." They push their carts to the front, where it just so
happens that the most beautiful woman in Ottawa is working the cash.
While they wait in line Dinah asks if Kenny is still writing his
Humphrey Bogart stories, and Harriet tells her he's too busy listing
reasons why he should see *The Godfather*.

"What a great kid."

"Not everybody thinks so," says the mother.

"Who doesn't think so?"

"His teacher."

"What's her name? I'll slap her silly."

"Well, he can be hard to take. Sometimes he comes at you like
something shaken up."

"You mean somebody put some Benzedrine in his Ovaltine?"

"Exactly."

"No," Dinah says, "your kids are great. You're adequate, but your
kids are great." Her face takes on a wistful look. "The first time I met
Kenny and he said he loved Frank Sinatra, I thought, This is bliss.
Where does he come from? And I wanted to see him grow up. I wanted
to stick around long enough to see him grow up."

She puts her two bags of oranges on the counter and the beautiful
woman, working quickly, smiles and says, "Hello, my dear," in her strong,
Middle Eastern accent. She is slender, dark-haired, olive-skinned, oval-
faced. She works the cash only when the store gets suddenly busy, otherwise she sorts fruits and vegetables in the back, or sets them out on shelves.
Always she wears a long blue apron over a straight black skirt, dark stockings, ankle socks, small leather boots. Yet she looks elegant. Harriet doesn't
know how she does this, except that it seems to require no effort, but it
must require some. Some lipstick, some rouge, some eye makeup. She has

a beautiful smile and good white teeth. Her hands are work hands, rough from sorting through dry, wet, earthy vegetables at cool temperatures. "Do your hands ever crack?" Harriet asked her once when her purchases were being sped through, and she smiled and ignored the question the way beautiful women always ignore questions about beauty.

"Are you ready for tomorrow?" asks Dinah.

"You mean my class?"

"Jack said he's going."

"You saw him?"

"I told you I did."

His name drops like a sexual pebble into the stream of their conversation, and for a moment they both look down. Beyond them, on the other side of plate-glass windows painted with enormous red cherries and yellow bananas, falls the first snow of the day. November 30. It gathers on the roof of the unfinished-furniture store across the street, and on the trees beyond.

Dinah says, "Just remember what George Cukor said. 'Don't panic and don't wilt.'"

"What's left?" asks Harriet.

They take the long way home, heading over to the Rideau River and passing the Strand on the way, the old movie house abandoned to bingo, and then abandoned by bingo. Located just beyond the fruit store, it sits empty and faded in the falling snow.

15

The Comedy Class

"**I**t's not that I'm funny," said Professor Harriet, standing at the front of her Monday-night class. She was wearing the long black sweater, shapeless and already streaked with chalk, that was passed on by a late cousin once removed. Her hair was pulled back into a ponytail and her brain had tightened in alarm because Rod Steiger was in the front row.

"But I'd like to be," she said. "I've decided," she went on, "to take a serious approach to comedy. I call it the Buster Keaton approach. This way we get to have our cake and eat it too. We get to be serious *and* funny. We don't have to be funny all at once, or all the time. We'll read Calvin Trillin, James Thurber, Beryl Bainbridge. We'll figure out what makes them funny and then we'll steal from them. We'll steal like raccoons. We'll watch movies too, or at least scenes from movies, since life isn't worth living without them. Why is Cary Grant funny here and not here? You could spend your life figuring that one out."

She saw Jack Frame looking at her the way a vegetarian looks at meat. Desire? Distaste? Who could tell?

"Three weeks," she reminded them. "I'm just filling in for three weeks."

"You see," she went on, "I think it's the need to relax and the impossibility of ever doing so that makes for comedy." Now she was reading from her notes. "The struggle to keep going in the face of humiliation, the mounting dismay until you either laugh or go nuts. In other words, seriousness heading off the rails is funny. A deadpan attitude towards the outrageous. Laurel beside Hardy. George Burns beside Gracie Allen. Lily Tomlin beside Lily Tomlin.

"This is my approach," she said.

"What is?" asked someone she pretended not to hear.

"Now," she said with great firmness, "open your notebooks and, for ten minutes, write about the last time you laughed out loud."

They looked at her. Eight people seated as far away from each other as chocolate chips in a no-name cookie. I could bicycle between you, she thought. You could be my paper route. In her nervousness, she could not absorb, let alone remember, any of their names.

There was 1.) A short, squat young man who looked like Toad of Toad Hall. 2.) A middle-aged roué who arrived late, his face soft and dark from lack of sleep. 3.) A woman in her sixties who looked like Vanessa Redgrave without the neck. 4.) A young Asian woman who wrote with pencil, since by now they were all writing; this was the miracle. They were all, without exception, writing.

There was 5.) A woman in her thirties whose skin was the color of Cheerios. Her sweater was the color of Cheerios. Drop a Cheerio and you would never find it again. 6.) A man in his seventies with a North of England jaw and a North of England nose.

"I'm saying," North of England announced to the room, "that I can't remember the last time I laughed aloud."

"Perfect," said Harriet.

They were united by the delicate knowledge that none of them knew what he or she was doing, including Professor Harriet. Thank God, she thought, for courteous obedience, even if it did lead to Scott's death at the Pole. How would a Norwegian teach this class, she wondered. What would Amundsen have done? He would have started with the first comic writer the world produced – Euripides? Did any of the Greeks have a sense of humor? – and worked forward, training himself in every step of comical progress mankind had ever made. She knew this because Kenny was doing a project on the race to the Pole. Kenny had very decided views on the matter. Amundsen, he said, was a hothead. He liked Scott.

Just wait, Harriet cautioned. Read some more before you make up your mind.

But Kenny had to be on someone's side all the time. He had to commit himself, and he had to know whether you were on the same side.

Then there was 7.) A woman in a shawl who looked strangely familiar. Beware of shawls, thought Harriet, after the woman gave her a deadly look.

And 8.) Rod Steiger.

Her glance went back to the Shawl, who chose that moment to look up. Their eyes locked briefly, because that's all Harriet could stand. She looked away. Then, hunched over her notebook, she wrote, *Dear Pauline, What would you do?*

When Harriet discovered Pauline Kael years ago, that cold fall in New York, she was in the middle of another crazy time, trapped as she was with two kids in a tiny apartment. That fall, Pauline's old movie reviews were the only things she could read. Reviews of movies she had never seen, most of which she never would see, but what did it matter, so captivated was she by her sharp tongue and uncanny grasp of the shape of a movie and the pitfalls into which actors and directors consistently fell. The greatest trap, she gathered, was wanting your audience to like you. A mediocre actor in an unlikable part would always find a way to figuratively wink at the audience: this lousy person isn't me, I'm really quite lovable. A great actor, on the other hand, threw himself into the part, no holds barred. Brando never winked.

You would square your tiny shoulders and glitter with dark wit. You wouldn't droop. You wouldn't need to be liked. You would brass it out.

Professor Harriet girded her loins and looked once more at the Shawl. Something about her was so familiar. Had they met?

"It's time to stop," she said, and everyone stopped. "Now I'll ask you to read your pieces aloud." And she turned to North of England directly on her right.

North of England, as he had warned, couldn't remember the last time he laughed aloud, but he remembered the last time his wife did not. They were at the weekly meeting of the Society of Friends. Quakers, he explained, whose meetings of worship were held in silence so that every sound your poor body made was audible to all but the stone deaf. It was summertime and the meeting was in someone's home in the country. They walked up to the front door, and, before knocking, he turned to his wife and said to her, "This is your last chance to fart," not realizing that the windows were open and his voice carried like a bell. Or so said his furious wife.

Everyone laughed – no-neck Vanessa laughed the loudest – and Harriet led the clapping. A round of applause after every reader. That was her strategy. Plus homemade cookies (the shortbreads), which she would produce during the break.

The roué was next. The last time he laughed aloud was at a Bill Murray movie, and his girlfriend didn't laugh at all. They broke up after that and his personal reasons for being in Canada evaporated. For some reason he stayed. He had always wanted to be a comic writer and most of the comic writers come from Canada. "Why is that?" he wanted to know. "And the three authors you mentioned, are any of them Canadian?"

"Good point," said Harriet. "Nothing is written in stone," she said. "Let me think about that." Like Scott, she would improvise her way to her doom.

Cheerio-woman spoke up: "Who did you say we were supposed to read? Somebody Bumbridge?"

Harriet wrote the name on the board with such vigor that the chalk snapped in half and bounced off Jack Frame's desk. He picked it up and handed it to her, producing, she could feel it, a violent blush.

"Beryl Bainbridge," said Toad, looking at the board. "I think my mother reads her."

"How would you like a kick in the pants?" muttered Harriet.

"What?"

"Next." Nodding to Cheerio-woman, who said the last time she laughed aloud she choked. She was drinking a glass of water and the man she was with had to thump her on the back. Why was she laughing? Because he'd told her a dirty joke.

"Yes?" said Harriet, her insides expanding with hope. "Go on."

"I've written the first part down."

"Yes?"

"But I can't remember the ending."

The Shawl snorted. "I knew this would be a waste of time."

"That's the trouble with jokes," commiserated Harriet.

The Asian woman who wrote in pencil read so softly that no one could hear her. Pencil Voice, thought Harriet. "May I read it for you?" she asked. But the writing was too faint to decipher. "I wrote in pencil until I was twenty," Harriet said, and she gave Pencil Voice a pen.

No-neck Vanessa said she laughed aloud that very morning. Over *Cathy*, the comic strip.

"Not *Cathy*," protested the Shawl.

"I love *Cathy*," said Vanessa.

Harriet intervened, perhaps too quickly. "Remember," she said in her shapeless chalk-streaked sweater, "that humor is subjective."

"Do *you* laugh at *Cathy*?" demanded the Shawl.

"Sometimes."

"Then I must be in the wrong class."

"Give it time," said Harriet.

"Not that I'm expecting a lot," said the Shawl. "I read your book."

Like Robert Falcon Scott, Harriet did not flinch. She turned to face Rod Steiger, who said that the last time he laughed aloud was over a book by Nick Hornby. That's who we should be reading. Not Thurber. You read Thurber in high school. Thurber was outdated in 1950, for Christ's sake. Why Thurber?

"Nick Hornby," said Harriet. "Good idea." She turned around and wrote in her notebook: *Who the fuck is Nick Hornby?*

Then it was the Shawl's turn.

The last time the Shawl laughed aloud was with her friend Leah. They were reading a review of a book called *Moonglow* and laughed to see it dismissed as "narcissistic twaddle." Her friend felt vindicated because the author had written about her in an unflattering, untruthful, nasty way. She – the Shawl, that is – was taking this course out of curiosity. She was curious to know how writers justified their various betrayals.

The classroom was quiet. Harriet's arms were folded. She rubbed her nose with her finger and left a white streak across the tip.

"'Drivel,'" she said with a weak smile. "'Narcissistic drivel.' To be exact."

She was remembering now where she had seen the Shawl. At Leah's house, years ago. "Do you know each other?" she asked, looking from the Shawl to Jack.

"Since forever," said Jack. "Emily used to stay every winter. She taught me how to swim."

And so the chickens were coming home to roost. Under a shawl you could hide several chickens and many eggs. "But your name wasn't Emily, was it?" No, her name had been Janice Bird, a name that brought nothing but bad luck. So now she was Emily Carr-Bird, after the painter.

The newly minted Emily said, "How do you writers live with yourselves? I'd really like to know. Using people you know in your stories."

One person – Toad – spoke up. "But it's not really the real person. You change them in the story. The story takes over."

The roué said, "I wish my stories took over. I never get beyond page three."

"Some stories," Jack asserted, "are from life, every last detail."

Silence again, save for the humming overhead of the fluorescent lights.

Toad made another good-hearted effort. "Any story that's good *seems* as if it's from real life, whether it is or not. That's the paradox, right? We don't want it to seem invented, we want it to seem real."

"You're talking about real fiction," Emily said. "I'm not talking about real fiction. I'm talking about pretend fiction that isn't made up."

Harriet leaned back against the hard edge of her desk. What if it were summer, she thought. Or midnight? What if everything were the same, except for one crucial thing? What if she had never written about Emily what's-her-name – for she had written about her too, as Leah's friend, the latent lesbian, who moved like a large lake inside her clothes. So much soft flesh. So much fugitive typing in that complicated garden with the olive trees and the rosemary hedge and the games of Scrabble played on the lawn. But she looked different now. Illness? Could it be terminal?

It would seem that no one had escaped her pen, despite the fact that she had written so little. And now she would escape no one.

Her butt had gone numb but she didn't move: her legs were too weak. She didn't have Scott's valiant desperation, or Hemingway's grace under pressure. She didn't have Atwood's don't-fuck-with-me wit. She didn't have Richler's raunchy intelligence. She didn't have Carver's lumbering goodness. She didn't have Woolf's teeming brilliance. She didn't have Austen's measured wisdom.

What *have* I got? *I've gotta get out of here.*

She unfolded her arms. She looked past Pencil Voice to Vanessa, and cleared her throat. She said, "Pauline Kael says that Warren Beatty *is* Warren Beatty, but Cary Grant *wants* to be Cary Grant. Who is more interesting to watch?"

"Warren Beatty," said Vanessa.

"Look," said Harriet. "Every time you write something you do the best you can. You make mistakes. You wish you'd done some things better, other things differently. You learn, or you don't learn. And you go on. You *want* to get better at it."

"I don't know what in blazes you're on about," North of England said. "What's she on about?" he asked Vanessa.

"Mordecai Richler is a funny Canadian writer," said Harriet. "Let's read him."

"*Who?*" asked North of England.

"Richler, Mordecai Richler. He's Canadian and he's funny."

"No, he's not," said the Shawl. "He's offensive."

"What *I* don't understand," said Cheerio-woman, "is this stuff about Cary Grant. I don't like Cary Grant."

"Didn't you read the fine print?" said Harriet. "You're not allowed in this class unless you like Cary Grant."

"This is stupid," said the Shawl.

Two classes left, thought Harriet. Three minus one equals two. She was walking home beside the canal and stopped to look up at the dark, city-softened sky, the muffled stars, and then around her at the curving canal with its dreamy, generous lights – a whole string of them, like white baubles, and tonight only one of them was out. It was inexcusable, that story about Leah and Janice and Jack, inexcusable and true, the things she had said in the story. A runner jogged by on the other side of the canal. She heard footsteps behind her, and turned to see Janice coming towards her.

Harriet was much taller than Janice, and her Rollerblades were in her backpack. She could always club her over the head with them, the way Newfies club seals.

Janice stood in front of her.

"I'm sorry, Janice." She had said this before, during the class, but if Bill Clinton was anything to go by, you can't say it too often.

"Emily," barked Janice. But her eyes were red.

Harriet heard the snuffle, as of a seal. She reached into her pocket for a tissue for Emily.

"Your story was so unfair," Emily sniffed furiously. "You said I looked like a marshmallow."

"I said your dog looked like a marshmallow. You look like Gertrude Stein."

"I do?"

Ah. This was the way out. Why hadn't she thought of it before?

"I liked what you wrote tonight. It was energetic and tough."

Emily raised her tear-stained face to Harriet's. "Really?"

"You should keep writing. I mean it."

And Emily smiled, despite herself.

Dinah, stirring a pot on the stove, heard a mighty banging on the door. "Buddy," she coughed. "Have we got a gentleman caller?" Buddy hoisted himself upright, and the two of them headed for the hallway.

And here was Harriet.

Harriet saying, "I insist on having a heart-to-heart with Sara Lee."

In the kitchen her eye alighted on Frank Sinatra, old and dying, in the upper right-hand corner of *People*. "Have you noticed," she asked, flipping through the magazine, "that the young Frank Sinatra looked exactly like the young Glenn Gould?"

Dinah had her head in the refrigerator.

"Only when they were young," continued Harriet. "Once they got old they didn't look like each other. Or like themselves, for that matter."

What transformations await, she thought. Her upper lip had begun to develop the accordion furrow that, of all signs, is the most telling. The robin of old age had dropped directly onto her face.

"I'm so glad I'm younger than you are," she said, accepting the last piece of cheesecake. "And skinnier. I'm only eating this to save you from yourself."

"Somebody's class went well," Dinah said to Buddy, who had thrown himself on the floor at Harriet's feet.

"It was a disaster."

"I don't believe that."

"After I finish this I'm going to strangle myself. By the neck."

"I wish I had your nice long neck."

"Lew's the one with the Audrey Hepburn neck."

"You're the one with the long waist. When they were giving out waists, I must have had my nose in the cutlery drawer."

"Well, you've got great legs. Nobody asks me to take off my pants and put on shorts."

"You've got a great husband. Where the hell was I when they were handing out husbands?"

"We'll share him," said Harriet.

"Oh, yeah?" Dinah's laugh was cracked and rollicking and almost pained. "Sure we will."

Harriet finished the cheesecake, wishing she hadn't said something so witless. "You're cooking," she said, looking intently at the stove. "It smells like – what *does* it smell like?"

"Beeswax."

"Flowers?"

Dinah picked up the paint stick and stirred. "Face cream. I even have a name for it."

Harriet peered into the pan. "If that's gum makeup, I want a cut."

"*Bloomsbury*," said Dinah. "'Face creams for smart women.'"

It was nearly midnight. Harriet stood on the sidewalk. There was nothing to see in the sky, and underfoot it was more wet than snowy. She walked with bent head towards her house, springing back when her foot came down on a dirty tissue, but it was a small clump of leaves. Once, in October, she had mistaken a few wild white roses next to a path for tissues balled up and tossed out by some jerk with a bad cold. It was one of those early-winter nights so damp it reminded her of England, the month she spent on British Rail with a mother so thirsty she fell upon every drinking fountain as if it were her last, and generally it was. They didn't like water in England, not to bathe in and not to drink.

She had checked the clock on Dinah's stove before saying, "I don't have the self-respect to emerge from this sort of thing with any dignity."

"You didn't see her name on the class list?"

"She's changed her name, and she looks different too, much thinner." *Self-respect is everything, isn't it? All the rest is shifting sand.* "She used to be Janice Bird, now she's Emily Carr-Bird. I should call myself Greta Garbo and be done with it."

"Somebody's been sending me roses," Dinah said. She dropped a pouch of crystals on the table and sat down. "Sticking them in my door at peculiar times. It's spooking me." She was wearing a thick blue turtle-neck which she kept rolling up to her chin so that she spoke from behind battlements of blue – swooping, rapid talk punctuated with hacking coughs and flourishes of her beautiful, manicured hands. "I drop these all over town to get rid of the bad luck and I burn the paper the flowers come in." Her silver hair kept falling out of the large clip she continually took out and put back in, pausing to take sips from her can of Diet Pepsi. Only cans, she said; bottles don't taste right. *The Pepsi purist with the beautiful nails*, Harriet will call her in a letter to Pauline. *It isn't anger that throws Dinah, it's roses appearing out of nowhere.*

"I used to review books," Dinah said. "I still do. I used to write about TV. People would cut out my column, take a razor blade to my face, and mail it back to me. I took it as a sign of success."

"But you were writing about strangers."

"Not always," Dinah said darkly, wearily. "Some of those authors I'd met. One was a friend. The TV people? I knew some of them too. Anyway, what you're doing is teaching a class. They've come to you to learn about writing."

"But I don't know how to teach. Even if I knew how to teach, I wouldn't know how to teach comedy."

"Ask them questions. Ask them to write about the funniest person they've ever met. That will take their minds off you."

Harriet loved a joke, especially at her own expense, so laughing – holding on to the table – she felt for a moment the sweet relief that comes from what the ancient Greeks called the last and greatest gift of the gods: a sense of proportion. "I love you," she said to Dinah.

"If you love me, you can do something for me. I need a control for my face cream."

"Okay."

"You'll have to use my cream on the right side of your face, and your regular cream on the left side. What's your regular cream?"

"This stuff from Cuba that Lew gave me. Something Hydrating Cream. It's supposed to protect your skin from external aggressions like wind, sun, and the U.S.A."

"Will you do it?"

"Of course," said Harriet.

Kenny called to his mom as she climbed the stairs. She went into his room, and he spoke from his pillow. "Where have you been?"

She sat on his bed and reached out to stroke his hair, but he took her hand and held it against his cheek. Where had he learned to do such a thing?

"Talking to Dinah," she said.

"What about?"

"My stupid class."

"It wasn't good?"

Hearing his alarm, "It went fine," she said hastily. "Dinah says I should get them to write about the funniest person they've ever met. I can't think of the funniest person I've met."

"You don't have to."

"You're right. They have to."

This was the room Lew had slept in as a boy. Sometimes, coming in the front door, he said he still caught a whiff of his grandmother: talcum powder and Dove soap. A house holds smells for a long time. He'd told them that on one of those childhood visits he got locked inside the cupboard in this room. Hide-and-seek, and his brother locked him in the cupboard and forgot about him. Where's Lew? his grandma asked Artie, who by then was watching television. They found him where Artie had left him, curled up between the floor of the cupboard and the first shelf, patiently waiting.

"Can't you sleep?" she asked Kenny.

He shook his head.

"Something's worrying you."

And then it came out that his teacher wouldn't let him do his project on Scott and Amundsen because somebody else was already doing it. Rachel was doing it.

"You should have a race," she said. "See who finishes first. Do you want me to suggest that to her?" No, he didn't. "Well," she sighed, "now you know how Scott felt." She stroked his hair. "In the morning we'll come up with another idea. Here." And she held out her arm. "Fill up my arm with your worries. Then you'll be able to sleep."

He took hold of her arm with both hands, and squeezed.

"Whoa," she said. He loosened his grip but continued to hold on, and she felt her arm get heavy, and then it started to ache. She smiled gamely, but it was like being electrocuted. Next time, she thought, I'll offer him a block of wood.

16

Man of La Mancha

Friday nights, upstairs with his mandolin, Lew would hear them laughing down below and remember a time when Harriet was more like Dinah. When she edited books on economic theory for a small left-wing press. When she was so fearless in her job that she got herself sacked. When she even read Proust.

"Remember when you read Proust?"

"I never read Proust."

"But there were volumes beside the bed . . . "

"I borrowed them from the library and returned them unread. I was just pretending."

Since then – those intellectual glory days – movies had engrained her with Peter O'Toole's every wrinkle and Sean Connery's every hairline. Sometimes she joked that she was another Miss Havisham. The clock had stopped when Cary Grant died.

In the first week of December, when Dinah wasn't answering the phone or returning calls, something she did periodically, Kenny had the idea to invite Jack Frame to the Friday-night movie club. They had dubbed their club the *Fern*, in honor of Dinah's old movie house. "He knows movies," Kenny said. "He really knows them."

Lew said, "And he never lets you forget it."

"But you like him?" asked Kenny, with the anxious tone he brought to such matters.

"I like him fine."

"He talks too much," said Harriet. "Talks too much? He writes too much, that's his problem. Actually, it's my problem." And her voice was savage. "No," she said. "He'd want to see movies I couldn't bear to watch and I'd end up wringing his neck. We're not having him." And she stomped upstairs.

Lew said to Kenny, "She's worried about her class."

"Yeah."

"Kenny, did Dinah say she was going to be away?"

"Is she away?"

Upstairs at her desk, thinking about Jack's simple eloquence in person and his gassy grandiloquence on the page, brooding about his treacherous presence in her class, Harriet wrote, *Something happens. He can't be direct when he writes. He can't even be grammatical. But it's not the first time I've noticed this paradox. Someone sad in person will be funny in print, or gallant in person, brutal in print. As if the act of writing puts him in touch with his other self. But wouldn't it be nice if it put him in touch with both selves? This new novel is like the others. Incest, amputation, and suicide play a queasy role, and every character is a fat cartoon that triggers his disgust. Writing brings out the worst in him, yet he's dedicated to it, indefatigable. The sort who papers his room with rejection slips while becoming deeply, deeply bitter.*

Who is he going to take out his anger on?

After a moment she added, *You see, he sends his books to me. I am his reader. It's like being his mistress.*

And then the phone rang, and it was for her.

She picked up the extension in the hallway and heard his soft voice. "Harriet, this is Jack." An unnerving voice, the tonelessness of which she only noticed on the telephone. In person he sounded full of life, a smart, massive, opinionated, inordinately talkative man-between-wives. As they conversed, however, she realized that he was waiting for her. The more she warmed up the more did he. She became talkative, then, almost flirtatious, teasing him, and he responded in kind, until he said suddenly, "I've been angry at you."

"Angry?"

"I thought we were very close, and you didn't stay in touch."

This bear of a man, who only drank tea. No coffee. No alcohol. He knew all about tea. He could be boring about tea.

I've been angry at you, and the pieces fell into place. There had always been something sexual between them. The time he lay on her bed in that small room in Italy, asking her to wake him in half an hour, and when she did he reached for her hand. On some level she's been running away from him ever since. All their subsequent encounters seemed to flow from that moment on the bed, when she realized that he had interpreted her punch in the nose as her way of making a play for him.

"I've been reading *Don Quixote*," she said. "Have you read it?"

"You're changing the subject," he said softly.

"We've been out of touch for a few years. That's not so unusual. It happens."

"I saw the show and it broke my heart."

"The show?"

"*Man of La Mancha*."

"Why?" she asked. "Why did it break your heart?"

"Watching him go mad. Watching him pursue a love that was completely unattainable – that broke my heart."

She was struck by the sad force of his answer, the grave sentimentality, and suddenly she felt grateful to him for quickening her interest, even though she still wanted desperately to get off the phone.

He said, "I dreamt about you last night."

"Did you?"

"We were making love. Sally was furious."

There was a pause. Then Harriet asked, "Was it nice?"

"It was fabulous."

———◆———

There was talk of a windmill on Dow's Lake, a gift from the grateful Dutch that nobody wanted. Harriet wanted it. She wanted to hear through the hot summer nights the thud of heavy wooden sails turning in the wind just as they did in that old Hitchcock movie with Joel McCrea, the one where he realizes something is wrong because the sails are turning *against* the wind.

One morning she found herself in a coffee shop on Bank Street, having ordered the wrong thing: something small and expensive instead of the larger special that came with free coffee. So busy was she trying to figure out what a Turkey Temptation might be, and how it might differ from the Herby Turkey Bagel, she hadn't seen the simple word *special* on the counter. Too many words, she thought, too many highways, and not enough dreams of recognizable places. The loss of a free coffee hurt.

Months ago Lew asked her to take five minutes and draw a map of Ottawa. Okay. She sat down with a sheet of scrap paper and drew a line for their street with a circled X for their house; then the connecting alley to Bronson Avenue; then Bronson Avenue itself as multiple lanes peppered with crosses inscribed RIP. Beyond Bronson she drew the trees of the Arboretum with a big square for the chip wagon on Prince of Wales Drive. On the right she brought the curving line of the canal into Dow's Lake, beyond which she drew the wavy lines of the Gatineau Hills. On the left she made the Rideau River curve unrealistically but protectively towards the Arboretum, and below it all, under a straight line, she wrote *U.S.A.*

This was his wife's world. A world defined by water, trees, roads, french fries, and death. He scratched his head. "How do you manage?" he asked, truly wondering.

"By being with you," she said simply.

At his request Kenny and Jane drew maps too, and so did Dinah. Research, he said, as part of the course he was teaching about urban design.

"Ask them," Dinah suggested, "to draw a map of something important. Their first kiss, for instance."

"Their first kiss?" said Lew.

"Draw a map of where it happened. That will get them thinking about the concept of place."

It got Lew thinking. Dinah's map was still in his wallet, folded up and not forgotten. She had drawn Bank Street, accurately locating and naming every single bar.

Harriet, in her coffee shop, was a block and a half north of Irene's Pub. *Grabbajabba*, she thought, looking around her: it should be the name of a boxing ring. *Sing Sing*, as Audrey so perceptively said to George Peppard: it should be an opera house.

She had ventured out to purchase an undershirt, but she would never find one. Undershirts weren't made any more. Central heating had taken care of undershirts just as electricity had taken care of peace and quiet. It was as noisy as a truck in here. Perched on a tippy stool, trying to read her book, thinking about streets devoid of bookstores, of movie houses, of decent five-and-dimes, she recalled reading something that Salinger had said: Write about what you love. But what about what you hate? Why couldn't that get a little press? Because then writers wouldn't have an out. I wrote out of love, they say, while their victims writhe in agony on the floor.

As if on cue, she heard her name: *Harriet Browning*.

Startled, she closed her book.

Jack perched one heavy buttock on the stool beside her, and took the book out of her hands. Then, with a frown, he put it down.

"I like Chekhov," she said.

"You would." Jack gazed at her. "He's a very measured writer."

His eyes were cool, inscrutable, and she smiled. Was this a compliment or a measured insult from the least measured writer she had ever met?

"You don't like him."

"I prefer others," he said.

What she did next was not a big mistake, but it was a mistake. She pedalled forward instead of backward. "Maybe it's time to give Dostoevsky another try," she said. Guessing correctly that Jack was a *Crime and Punishment* man.

She was at home when Jane got back from school. Jane told her that her French teacher hadn't bothered to teach today. She showed a video instead. *Gandhi*.

"In French?"

"In English."

"Why?" asked Harriet. "Why was she showing you a movie in English?"

"I don't know," Jane said. "And I'm not going to ask. She doesn't like me anyway."

"She doesn't?"

"I don't think so. I'm not really myself when I talk to her. I'm not really myself when I talk to lots of people. Does that happen to you?"

"It does. It happened today."

———◯———

Kenny would remember that his mom ate her grapefruit standing up. That she used a nail to test a cake for doneness, "since what do you think they used before toothpicks?" That she said no when he tried to buy an Oh Henry! bar. "Do you know what Nestlé is up to?"

Until one day, when they were driving south on Bank Street, they saw a great yellow truck sail by with *Oh Hunger?* painted on its side, and remembered, in unison, the moment in *Desire* when Gary Cooper comes up with the right slogan for the new American car that Marlene Dietrich is going to steal from under his nose.

The boy with the movie brain knew the scene by heart. "His boss says, I can't decide between these two: I'm *delighted* to drive a Bronson 8 or I'm *glad* to drive a Bronson 8. And Gary Cooper says *Delighted.* That sounds snobbish. It's too snooty. Then the boss says, So *glad* is better? And Gary Cooper says, If I bumped into you in the street, I'd say, I'm glad to see you. No, I tell you, glad's the wrong word." Then Kenny made a grand sweep of his hand to indicate the sign on the back of Gary Cooper's car, and said, " 'I'm *happy* to drive a Bronson 8.' "

"Is that what it was? A Bronson 8? You have an amazing memory," said his mom, and Kenny, taking advantage of this propitious moment, inquired if she wouldn't like to see *Toy Story 2*, and she said, "Does it have Cary Grant in it?"

Together they would walk to the library to pick up *My Favorite Year* and *Man of La Mancha*, since some secret philanthropist had recently left his sizable collection of old movies to the public library. At the checkout counter, Harriet talked to the librarian with the bum knee and friendly manner who read the English papers and kept her up to date on Peter O'Toole. "He's back on stage, acting in a play in the West End," the librarian said. And how are the reviews? "Not bad, I think." Thank God for that, said Harriet.

On the way home, Kenny said aloud to himself, " 'If you can't sleep, it's not the coffee it's the bunk.' "

"What brought that to mind?"

"I don't know. It's from a movie."

"*Christmas in July*. Preston Sturges."

"Did you like it?" he asked her.

"I loved it."

Tall mother and tall son walked along, the personality of one extending into the personality of the other. Coming towards them they saw Dinah, who said she wasn't the least surprised when she spied *Man of La Mancha* under Harriet's arm.

"He's a smart man," said Harriet of Peter O'Toole.

"So it's brains you're after now," said Dinah.

"He was handsome too, in his day, really exceptionally handsome. I admit his body leaves something to be desired."

"His chest is a size twenty-eight."

"Like mine," said Harriet, "and with the same hair count. Jack Frame recommended it. He said it broke his heart."

"Then Jack Frame has a silly heart."

Kenny, ever alert, asked, "Don't you like Jack Frame?"

"Do *you* like him?"

"Don't you?"

Harriet, too, was most curious.

Dinah said, "I've never been able to resist a man with dry, freckled lips."

17

All of This Would Seem to Have Significance Later

Harriet would remember that the fall of 1997 was drier than usual, and the weather prevailingly cool. The first snow fell on October 22, a layer of soft wet stuff that clung to everything and was very beautiful. Kenny and Jane were up early, as if aware of the transformation, and when they came downstairs Jane said it looked purply outside, like her teacher's hennaed hair. The same day Harriet was in a fish store in the market, fascinated by the beautiful blues of the blue crabs and of the lobsters too, whose armpits were a powder blue. A young woman with blood on her fingers and scales on her hands took her money. Harriet asked what lotion she used, and she said lots of Lubriderm. Is it the best? No. Neutrogena is the best. When she worked as a cleaner in Halifax and Maine, she said, Neutrogena was the only thing that helped her hands, so sore and dry were they from all the cleaning fluids. And it was only then that Harriet realized she was talking about cleaning houses, not fish.

The end of October was sunny and the painters came back to finish the trim on Bill Bender's house. Indian summer returned on November 8 and left for good on Remembrance Day, November 11. While the warmth continued, the song detective ate outside, and in the morning Harriet would see an empty wine bottle or two on his picnic table. On Remembrance Day, the temperature dropped and she pinned Kenny's poppy to a warmer jacket. A week later Lew came home, and a few days after that she cut Kenny's hair, kneeling on the floor afterwards and sweeping it into the dustpan, reminded of a previous time when Lew was the barber and said afterwards in a soft moaning voice, "Such beautiful hair, such beautiful hair. I'm so glad it grows back."

That fall she slept very little, usually waking at three, worried that she couldn't remember words. It took her hours one night to remember the word *waffle*; only *tortilla* would come to mind. When the teachers went on strike for two weeks, it wore out her nerves having the kids underfoot; then her comedy class began and one of the students, she discovered, had an exceptional memory. Every morning, as she dressed, Cheerio-woman would think about that same day a year ago, remembering the weather, her wardrobe, everyone she had met and everything they said. A year ago, she said, there was none of this: snow falling and muck on the roads. It was a beautiful day. She drove to Eganville to see her father, who had lost the use of his right arm after a stroke, and he said to her, *I feel that I've wasted my life in idleness.*

By early December, frost ferns provided her study windows with a permanent curtain, and she no longer felt so eerily visible to Bill Bender, but Dinah had disappeared. She wouldn't return for a week, and when she did, her mother, Ida, came with her. On December 25, Harriet raised the blinds and snow was falling outside. In a sign of things to come, she saw a woman walk by under a large umbrella.

At first, Dinah thought she had the flu that everyone else had. But the symptoms persisted. She was tired, and coughing all the time. She went to her doctor. They did blood tests and took X-rays at the end of November, and she went to her mother's for a week without telling anyone where she was. Then, missing her own place, she persuaded Ida to move in with her. My illness is serious, she told Harriet on the phone, but my mother is a saint.

Harriet found her in bed, with an old and scented lawyer at her side. He wore a silver tie and leaned back in his chair as if he were at the beach, fixing his gaze on Harriet and asking her what she did for a living. Very nice, he responded, very nice. He confessed that he too wanted to be a writer. He wanted to write an epic, he had it all planned out, though he hadn't begun to write it yet. It will be like Tolstoy, he said, laughing with great, fleshy-faced gusto. Very nice, he said, turning back to Dinah. Very nice.

"You should take Harriet's writing class," Dinah told him. And he laughed and laughed.

Dinah's bed was big and white with many pillows. Her silver head lay against three pillows, piled up; her face was the color of pewter. "I should have had a physical every year, the way they tell you to." The lawyer had left. She and Harriet were alone. "So should you."

"I'm only forty-seven."

"Don't boast. I hate boasting."

"I've got an appointment with the sleep clinic. But not till February, unless there's a cancellation."

Ida appeared in the doorway and Dinah said, "Mother, tell Harriet to get a new mattress."

"Have you thought of a new mattress?" asked Ida. Her hands were stained from dying a pink sweater a shade of plum. And she had a good system, she said. She did it in the washing machine. First, she dissolved the dye in hot water, then she put in the clothes and ran the wash cycle twice, and *then* she let it go to rinse.

Ida was one of those less-than-beautiful women who turn into old beauties. On the bedroom wall there was a picture of her holding Dinah in her lap and she was nothing to write home about. But now! Her face had finally forgiven her big nose and taken it to its soft wrinkled self. Framing the truce was hair as thick and silvery as Dinah's, whom she had named after Dinah Shore. "I wanted to call her Gilda but I knew Rita Hayworth would come to a bad end."

"I loved Dinah Shore," said Harriet. "At least, I loved her closet."

"She was Jewish," said Ida proudly.

"They had a picture of her closet in the weekend magazine when I was a kid. A walk-in closet with so many clothes and so many shoes. That was out of this world."

"She was a game girl."

Ida headed downstairs and Harriet said, "Your mother is wonderful."

"She is," said Dinah.

On the bedside table was Esther Williams's autobiography. "Abysmally bad," Dinah said, "but there's a part where Esther, who I loved as a girl, all those swimming scenes, describes working in a clothing store patronized by movie stars." A loud bang came from below. "Close the door," she said, and Harriet closed the door.

"Garbo used to come to the store," continued Dinah, "and they had to pretend they didn't recognize her. Usually, she left empty-handed, since all she was interested in was getting a deal. Marlene Dietrich came too, and Esther had to model outfits for her. She would go into Dietrich's dressing room and find her stretched out on the sofa, stark naked."

Dinah was in the mood for spilling any secrets but medical ones: about her health she didn't want to talk. And so Harriet adjusted her worried ways and entered into the fragile spirit of things. In grade thirteen, Dinah said, she took a Garbo biography to school and read it in English class, tucked inside her textbook. She was supposed to be reading Keats. They also did *Macbeth* that year and *Antony and Cleopatra*, and because her hair was so long and fell forward over her face, she was asked to read Cleopatra's lines aloud and was horribly nervous. "What did I do in high school?" she said to Harriet. "I grew my hair." Inspired, she said, by a movie that came out in 1958. She was sixteen, and her aunt had invited her to Toronto for a visit. She went by train, it was Easter, and her aunt took her to see *South Pacific*. Dinah thought the Hawaiian girl with the long dark hair, the one who played the secondary love interest, was the most beautiful girl she had ever seen, and on the way home, on the train, she thought of nothing else but how she was going to grow her hair long and look like her. By grade thirteen her hair was down to her waist. "I loved Mitzi Gaynor too. Loved all those Mitzis, Angies, and Debbies. I was furious with my mother for naming me Dinah."

"I loved Rossano Brazzi," said Harriet.

"He was awful," said Dinah. "But I thought John Kerr was thrilling, a Montgomery Clift kind of actor, and the story was tragic."

"You like eggheads," diagnosed Harriet with a certain pity. "I never saw *South Pacific* as a girl, but there was a movie I caught one night on TV. *A Certain Smile*. Joan Fontaine and somebody young, some girl, who fell for Rossano Brazzi. Well, he was completely irresistible. That olive skin, those melting eyes, that chest hair. Then she fell apart when she realized that he wouldn't leave his wife, ever."

The clock ticked beside the bed.

"Why wouldn't he leave his wife?" asked Dinah.

"Oh, they'd had a son who died. The usual nonsense."

Dinah nodded. "Yes," she said. "So how's my Kenny?"

"He can't sleep. His stomach aches as soon as he goes to bed."

"Take him to the doctor."

"I have. He's fine. There's nothing the matter with him."

"Change teachers. Change schools."

Harriet took off her glasses and rubbed her eyes, then put them back on and smiled at her friend. "When did you cut your waist-length hair?"

"When I went to the *Journal*. I cut it shoulder-length. It was shoulder-length in the picture people sliced up with razor blades, especially after I panned that rotten singer Our Pet Juliette."

"Well," said Harriet, "you deserved it." She reached for Dinah's hand and held it. Then she got up to go. "More roses," she said, spotting them on the desk in the corner of the room.

"From silly Jack."

"Jack?" And the expression on Harriet's face slid around like a too-large watch on a wrist. "Jack Frame? He's the one?"

Dinah nodded, amused.

"Do you like him?" Still amazed. "I mean, I understand why he would like you, but do you like him?"

"Why not?" Dinah said. "You do."

18

Cary Grant

They were supposed to be discussing plot. "I've never understood the word 'plot,'" Professor Harriet admitted. "One thing leads to the next thing. But does it?"

Her students looked at her.

"It seems to me that one thing often leads to the same thing. Or back to an earlier thing. Or, more likely, to nothing at all."

The Shawl wasn't there. "Death is a good plot device, though. Even I can see that."

"Only in a tragedy," said North of England. "Tragedies always end in death, and comedies always end with a wedding."

"Not Buster Keaton's comedies," said Harriet. "They end with a tombstone."

And into her mind, as she picked up a broken chalk off the blackboard ledge, came the old burial ground in Halifax – gravestones weathered black on a grassy, shaded slope – a black as black as charred toast inside a halo of green, and English toast, not North American. Almost wafer-thin. The stones abloom on the back from years of having lain on damp soil.

Pencil Voice interrupted her thoughts with a question she had to strain to hear. "I wanted to ask you about having children? Is it good or bad? If you're a writer?"

"Oh, I never recommend having children," Harriet answered. "I never recommend it." Scanning the class list, stopping at Miin-ling. "I could tell you homework stories that would make your blood run cold. On the other hand, I've written more since having children. You convince yourself that raising children is a job, and then you get some child care, and you have a few spare hours every day . . . "

Only six of the eight, and so unsteady was the pole of humiliation, jokiness, ruefulness, shame on which she wobbled that it hurt her to see there were students who couldn't be bothered to come, even when their absence was a godsend. She assigned an exercise. I'll give you the first line, you go on from there. And she wrote on the blackboard: *She remembers waking up in the middle of the night to the sound of an egg smashing against her window.*

"No," said Rod Steiger. "That's not a good first sentence."

"All right. Give me a better one."

"It's not funny. You won't get a funny story if you begin that way."

She held out the chalk to the man who wooed with roses. He stood up and walked slowly towards her, saying, "My brother wouldn't come downstairs if we had eggs for breakfast. He couldn't stand the smell." He took the chalk, but stood there thinking.

Harriet said, "I wonder why pie throwing is funny and egg throwing isn't. If you want revenge you throw eggs, if you want laughs you hit somebody in the face with a custard pie. It's still eggs, but in a different form."

"They're both cruel," Cheerio-woman said, and Harriet agreed. Then she turned to Jack. "Okay, Einstein. What's your idea?" As usual she felt aggressively unsettled in his presence.

He wrote on the board, *My brother the egghead hated the smell of eggs so much he stayed at the top of the stairs and held his nose during breakfast.* Harriet rubbed out everything after *the smell of eggs*, thinking as she did so that if Jack Frame turned out, in the end, to be a good writer she was going to slit her throat.

While her students wrote about their brother the egghead, she remembered a peculiar experience that occurred many years ago. She was sitting in a pew on Sunday morning, finding refuge from the loneliness of university life, when she felt a visitation of physical warmth. It came into her left side and for several minutes beat about her heart, filling her chest cavity and radiating through her limbs. Had she been someone else, someone less skeptical, she would have taken the sensation of warmth as an incident of spiritual moment. A benediction. She might have gone in that direction – towards the spirit – instead of falling into the wispy arms of cinematic flesh. *Did you know,* opening her notebook and writing to Pauline, *that Cary Grant ate sandwiches of thinly sliced turkey breast on thinly sliced bread? A most sparing lunch.*

Strange – she went on – *how puffy his face became in old age, reverting to the youthful roundness we see in his early movies. Fred Astaire stayed bony, but Gene Kelly and Cary Grant widened, and not with fat. More like girdles giving way. I learned the business about Cary's favorite lunch from one of the trashy biographies I read secretly, shamefacedly, when I was old enough to know better. At the time I was writing a letter to you, since your affection for Cary Grant gave my own free rein. I said to myself, if smart, pixie-faced Pauline Kael can call him "The Man from Dream City," then so can I. I wanted to put my mind at rest about his sexuality – a silly quest, a small-town girl's quest. As if I were going to marry the man. In my letter, which was really a story, I asked you why you didn't spell things out. Was he gay or not? Then I reread your essay and saw that for a careful reader all the implications were there. You let the two halves of his personality fall on the table like a pair of gloves, to use someone else's excellent phrase.*

North of England read aloud his piece about his older brother, a great reader who used to sneak outside during the wartime blackouts in London – only later did they move to Manchester – because he loved the dark, he would do anything to be in the darkness. He even begged his mother to let him bring the clothes in off the line at night. After the war he found the darkness inadequate. But he fixed that. He took his life at thirty-five.

No-neck Vanessa filled the sudden silence. She was sitting beside North of England – an easy intimacy had developed between them – and she said she knew lots of suicides, having grown up in Niagara Falls. The year they stopped the American falls to make repairs, they found all sorts of bodies in among the rocks. It draws people, she said. Well, said North of England, you know it will work, for one thing; why die alone in a motel room when you can step into a river and be swept over the side? And, of course, Harriet added, they want to make a point of their unhappiness. *You* think you're happy now, you newlyweds, but just you wait.

Jack Frame read his piece next, sticking to his own first sentence. "'My brother the egghead hated the smell of eggs so much he stayed at the top of the stairs and held his nose during breakfast. Then he married Debbie, whose breasts looked like fried eggs. "No," he'd say every morning, "Not sunny side up. I can't face the look of them twice in one day." His kids called him Egg-beater. After she was institutionalized, they called their mother Scrambled.'"

"That's not funny," said Cheerio-woman.

One summer, Jack Frame and his first wife had a small trailer in the woods north of Montreal, rounded and old, fitted out so neatly that when Harriet entered it she thought, This is what I've been looking for. And she didn't want to leave. But the next time she went, in place of the neatness were buckets to catch the drips, and an all-pervasive mess. Jack always spread himself sloppily wide, even as he went to almost magnificent lengths to be attentive.

In Dinah's room he sprawled in the chair beside her bed and peeled a grapefruit, one of a box of twenty-four huge, beautiful grapefruits he had brought to her. With thick-fingered dexterity, he divided one of the grapefruits into sections and shared it with Dinah, then Harriet. Dinah asked in her croaky voice if either of them knew who got the grapefruit in the kisser in that movie with James Cagney.

"*The Public Enemy*," said Jack. "Not Joan Blondell, the other one." He used his upper lip to work some grapefruit from between his teeth. "Mae Clarke," he said.

Harriet tried to think of some light remark, to lift Dinah's spirits, but her mind was blank. "What happened to Rod Steiger in *Dr. Zhivago*?" she asked finally.

"Murdered," said Dinah.

"He was good in that role," said Jack.

Harriet said, "He was the *only* good thing in the whole movie. I mean, apart from Julie Christie."

She had been trying to figure out what to tell Jack about his manuscript. In the past she had softened her damning words with some skill, or so she liked to think, focusing on the questions his novels addressed and feeling like a low-level diplomat keeping her nose clean. But this time was different. As they left Dinah's house he said to her, and his voice was brusque, "If you're not going to read my manuscript, just say so. I'll show it to Dinah."

And in her mind the small, perfectly outlined trailer receded into the distance like a child's toy. This was the real world, this vast canyon that opened wide between people, no matter what you did.

That night the phone rang. She went into the hallway to answer it, but no one was at the other end.

19

Kenny's Laughter

When Harriet told Kenny and Jane about the tumor in Dinah's lung, she explained that Dinah's mother was living with her now, and Jack Frame visited all the time, with flowers. It was dinnertime. They were at the table and Kenny and Jane stopped eating.

"How is she feeling?" asked Jane.

"Tired. Very tired. But they'll treat her. They'll do more tests and she'll probably have an operation and then radiation and chemotherapy."

"That's terrible," Jane said.

Harriet began to say more about her fatigue, the size of the tumor, her doctors, but Kenny interrupted. "Can't we talk about something else?" And he stood up abruptly and left the table.

But they couldn't talk about anything else. Next it was Fiona, who felt an uncomfortable pain in her chest, and later in the evening fainted. It turned out to be pneumonia. Harriet went to see her in the hospital and Fiona put her wonderful, tiny hands around her face.

Their beautiful snowy backyard didn't have a single child's footprint. Children weren't drawn outside to that beautiful surface, and parents didn't force them. It was 1997, and all the children were inside all winter long. Other changes: no one shook a mop outside, winter clothes came in riotous colors, cars started with ease.

Christmas was coming. Old Martin would leave Sarnia at midnight and pull in to Harriet and Lew's at six in the morning, a man who loved to go from A to B and to wake you up. Gladys would go to their youngest, Owen, who was no longer speaking to Harriet. It touched her to see how hard her parents were trying. They would not disown their children, neither would they favor one over the other, and that included Owen. The little shit.

Lew was talking to himself more and more. She heard him two rooms away castigating himself for forgetting the antibiotics he was supposed to take prior to a dental appointment to protect his heart. It unnerved her, the agitated way he spoke to himself. It was so different from the unfailingly calm way he spoke to everyone else.

Then one night, early in the second week of December, she woke up to the sound of Kenny's bare feet on the floor – toilet seat raised – lowered – his return to bed. And then his laughter. He was laughing hysterically, laughing with enormous uncontained glee. She lay still for a moment, having only just managed to fall asleep, or so it felt. Then, when the laughter continued, she got up and went to his room.

He was under the covers, curled up on his side. She bent over him and kissed his head, which smelled like it needed a good wash. Boy smell. Everything's all right, she murmured, and he rolled on his back and laughed in her face, although she knew he was sound asleep. Too much excitement, she thought. Too many worries. He was eleven years old now, and overtired, overexcited, worried by what had happened at school – the sudden good luck turning to sudden misfortune. He kept laughing and he laughed so hard that once or twice she thought he was sobbing. But no, it was more laughter. She pulled up his covers, discovered the sheet twisted around his knees, straightened it, and tugged everything up. Left him in stitches.

In bed Lew asked, "Is he laughing or crying?"

"Laughing."

"Is he in bed?"

"He's in bed. Sound asleep."

But carrying on like Grace Poole, she thought. And she imagined him going off his head in the trenches.

He had come home from school and immediately she'd known that something was wrong. He let his knapsack fall to the floor and his *hi* in answer to hers was flat and dejected. He said, "Do you want to hear the tragic thing that happened to me?"

"You went to the Aviation Museum. I'm sorry. I forgot to send money along."

But he borrowed from a friend. Three dollars. The chips in the vending machine cost $1.10. He put in a toonie and got two loonies. Put in a loonie and got not nickels and dimes but four loonies.

"Congratulations."

"Wait," he said.

Everybody gathered around him and tried to do the same thing, but they lost their money in the machine. In the meantime, with his new-found wealth, he gave James one dollar, bought a Coke for two dollars, bought chips for one dollar, and lost a dollar. Then the boys who had lost their money in the machine returned with the teacher, who told him he had to pay the boys for their missing money.

And so Harriet had sat down beside him and figured out the transactions on a piece of paper, saying, first, "The thing to never forget is that vending machines fuck you up. First parents, then teachers, then vending machines." She discovered when it was all written down that if he paid Robert the one dollar he lost, and another boy the two dollars he lost, he would come out even. It was all right.

He cheered up. They'd gone over to see Dinah and he told her the whole story. He sat at the foot of her bed and rattled on, full of gestures, his hands as long and beautiful as Gary Cooper's when he held the reins in *High Noon*, his thin, young back curved, the muscles in his neck strained. Then, as suddenly, he ran out of steam.

Ida came to the rescue. She took him downstairs and served him apple pie. A Mrs. Smith's, a tad burnt, and curdled milk in the small pitcher, but Kenny drank Pepsi so it didn't matter. He ate three pieces of pie he was so eager to please, and almost passed out. Then he demolished most of a bowl of green grapes, except for the few he fed to Buddy. Then lost himself in *People* magazine.

Upstairs, Dinah said sadly, "He's changing."

"Changing?"

"Haven't you noticed? He doesn't talk like he used to."

"He talks a lot."

"Not like he used to."

Harriet thought he had done so well, and felt hurt on his behalf. Dinah expected too much. Too much from a boy who was shocked by the change in her: her color, fatigue, decline. "He's growing up," she said, and shrugged and let it go. But she thought he was the same boy, of limited but intense interests, who could read the same book repeatedly, watch the same movie repeatedly, stay close to home indefinitely – clear in his attachments, and open about them: as demonstrative as ever.

Dinah felt her take it the wrong way and was too tired to set her straight. But she could see it, even if his mother couldn't: the beginning of Kenny's drift into shy adolescence.

On the sidewalk Kenny said to his mom, "Do you believe there's life after death? I don't mean angels. I don't believe in that. But being able to read?"

That night his stomach ached, but it was different from nervousness; it was a real ache. His mom told him to go to the bathroom. Then, when he came back still clutching his stomach, to lie on his back, to rub his tummy with his hand, this way; to think about Christmas. Too much pie, she said. Then added, "Remember, we put all your worries in the hallway. Everything is going to be all right."

Even though it was dark, she saw him relax. His body eased a little as he lay there. That much she could make out. But what does it mean, she wondered, *everything is going to be all right*? And why does it have so soothing an effect? It must mean that deep within us we have reservoirs of calmness we can draw upon, since everything, as we know, is never all right.

"Put your worries into my hands," she said.

But this was less satisfactory. First, her joined hands couldn't hold much. The worries were bound to spill through her fingers, or over her wrists. Second, it was coy: stupidly literal, yet not literal enough. If she managed to hold all of his worries without spilling them, and took them into the hallway, they would still be in the hallway. Lurking outside his door. Pressing to get back in.

No, she would have to take them into herself. So this time she'd given him her left arm to electrocute.

20

A Poem

Fiona was recovering at home. Bill Bender looked after her, and a nurse came every day, a very fine nurse, she said, who made her a laxative of fruit and senna. She recognized the bitter childhood taste of the senna through the nurse's mixture of apricot and prunes. In childhood the mixture had been prunes, figs, raisins, and senna. A spoonful each morning.

She looked older and even more pushed over, in a sweater and pleated grey skirt, her hair more windblown and white, her old translucent skin unpowdered. She used a mixture of Vaseline and baby oil on her skin, rubbing it on and wiping it off with a cloth; something she learned on a visit to France, she said. I'll tell Dinah, said Harriet.

On the table beside Fiona, in a stack, were a Russian grammar and dictionary, and copies of Chekhov and Akhmatova in Russian and English. Old Buster lay asleep at her feet. Harriet always found it restful here, away from her own study, which was so chaotic with papers and the wrong light. It revived her, seeing the arrangements Fiona made of her person, her furniture, her walls and plants and windows. The house was warm, the air biscuity-smelling; every armchair had a footstool and every side table had a lamp. Bill Bender served tea on a tray, then read aloud one of Akhmatova's poems. It was the one about letting "the terrible stranger" into your house. When he finished, Harriet said, "A terrible visitor is coming to us in January."

Fiona said, "In this case, the terrible stranger was death."

"Yes," said Harriet.

Bill poured more tea and Fiona returned to the subject of her dedicated nurse. "Dedication not romance," she said, "is what drives the nurse in *The English Patient*."

Harriet smiled. "It might be the nurse's dedication, but what about the author's sense of romance? The wounded man tended by the beautiful nurse is a most romantic situation."

"Dedication," repeated Fiona. "Not romance."

But it seemed to Harriet that nothing was more romantic than Bill Bender tending to Fiona in his gentle, lumbering way.

When she stood up to leave, Fiona put out her hand and asked about Lew. How is he? she wanted to know, and watched with some concern as Harriet answered. But Harriet's reply was casual, easy. He was well, no doubt he'd be over tonight to walk Buster.

So she didn't suspect, thought Fiona. But then I'm the one who sees them together. All fall Lew and Dinah Bloom had dropped over most nights, Buddy in tow, to pick up Buster and take him along for an evening walk, and one night they were already out the door when she remembered that she was out of bread. She called after them and Dinah, turning too quickly, lost her balance and Lew reached out to steady her. He held her elbow longer than necessary, and Fiona nodded to herself: It's as I thought. That poor man is in love with Dinah, but he doesn't know it yet.

21

More Intimations

It was Friday, December 12. Movie night for the Fern foursome, since Dinah had insisted upon bundling up and coming over to escape Ida, who was beginning to drive her crazy, although what she really wanted, she said, was a smoke with her old pal Bill Bender. "The least, the last, and the lost," they were fond of saying whenever the two of them stood hacking and coughing on the sidewalk. "To quote the Salvation Army."

"Give me some news," Dinah commanded.

"I've rented *Two for the Road* from Tony," said Harriet. (Tony was the owner of the only video store in town that had copies of *Trapeze* and *The Pajama Game*; a tiny man with an English accent who filed everything alphabetically, "excluding definites and indefinites.") "We had a most interesting conversation. He told me the women men go for. Greta Scaachi. They see her once and never forget her. Charlotte Rampling. Kathleen Turner, for a while, and now this new one, Catherine Zeta-Jones. Ellen Barkin, even though she isn't pretty, because she has something men respond to, a magnetism."

"And women? Who do they go for? I know the answer."

"Harrison Ford."

"I knew it."

"Brad Pitt. Gene Hackman. Paul Newman. Robert Redford. And last but not least, Sean Connery. How are you feeling?"

"So much better. I can't tell you."

"There's more. I've got an idea that will make your fortune: a sure-fire beauty product." Harriet ran her hands down the sides of her face. "Facial Brylcreem. I've got cowlicks in my peach fuzz."

"You need varnish," said Dinah.

"I have to keep smoothing my cheeks down. It's driving me nuts."

"What about my face cream?"

"It's greasy. I feel like greasy Joan keeling her pot."

"I was afraid of that."

"Lew coined a word: *greasome*. He calls me Greta Greasome."

This was the night they beheld Audrey Hepburn in a swimsuit ("Quelle sight!" said Dinah) standing beside an equally sunburned Albert Finney. Dinah, stretched out on the sofa and wrapped in an afghan – since watching movies made her cold (a phenomenon that affected them all, this drop in body temperature, as if they were frogs at a January matinée) – Dinah said, "She gets the Fred Astaire Body Building Trophy, hands down. Peter O'Toole, Audrey Hepburn, Fred Astaire. Body Builders Unite."

Harriet said, "All she ate for lunch was half a tomato."

"Shhhh," said Jane.

Outside, there was snow on the ground and a sharp wind, but they weren't aware of it, for on the screen it was thirty years ago and Audrey and Albert were meeting and falling in love, then growing older and falling out of love, and with every shift in time and place Audrey had a new wardrobe, and what could be more wonderful than that. What a pleasure it was to see their beautiful, interesting, expressive faces, to watch them move and talk and joke around, to have them young again, and in Audrey's case, alive again.

When the movie ended, Dinah drew the afghan close and said into the air, "What is the meaning of life, anyway?"

Harriet got her another pillow and tucked a blanket around her feet. "The meaning of life is good potato salad," she said. "You should know that."

"I forgot."

"And I have the recipe. A boiled egg for every large potato, plus black olives, chives, paprika, salt and pepper, and plenty of Hellman's. Hellman's and nothing but Hellman's."

"That's what I want in my final minutes," said Dinah.

Kenny and Jane gave the same question serious thought. Kenny said if he had a choice between a milkshake and a Dr. Pepper, he would probably have a Dr. Pepper. Jane said she would have a tall glass of cold lemonade. Harriet said lemonade would be good, but she would rather have a cup of scalding tea and a date square.

"You and your square dates," said Dinah. "What movie would you watch in your final minutes? Personally, I'd choose *Annie Hall*."

Kenny, who loved this kind of question, said he'd want to watch a comedy. "I'd want to be laughing. Probably *The Life of Brian*. Or maybe *Palm Beach Story*. Rudy Vallee was great. J.D. Huckensucker. Or maybe *The Crimson Pirate*."

"*Top Hat*," said Harriet.

"I don't know," said Jane. "Maybe I'd watch parts from a whole bunch of musicals. The night club scene in *Singin' in the Rain*, and Fred Astaire and Cyd Charisse dancing the detective mystery in *The Band Wagon*. She was such a good dancer! I'd watch Judy Garland sing 'Get Happy' in *Summer Stock*, and the dance in the garage in *West Side Story*. I'd watch auditions too. They're my favorite parts. The audition in *The Full Monty* and the one in *The Fabulous Baker Boys*. And *All That Jazz*."

"I'm so glad I raised you right," smiled her mom.

Later, after Dinah went home and the kids and Lew were asleep, Harriet lay in bed thinking of *The Killers*. Burt Lancaster waiting for his fate. A black-and-white movie she had seen on TV at a friend's house when she was a girl, and the suspense was terrific. Burt lying on his bed in that seedy room above the bar, knowing they were coming to get him and there was nothing he could do about it.

Leah would be here in a month. The last time she'd seen her, five years ago, her aunt was badgering an old friend, a woman of seventy, who was flying to Italy for a holiday, badgering her to take two of her own suitcases back to Italy for her. The old friend agreed to take one. Leah insisted she take both. "Have pity!" cried the friend. "Pity?" said Leah with scorn. "You should have pity on *me*."

Harriet couldn't sleep. And so she turned on the bedside lamp without disturbing Lew, put another pillow under her head, and began to read a magazine, coming to an article about cancer and thinking, as she began to read it, about Ingrid Bergman finding a lump in her breast as she lay reading a story about someone finding a lump: and she found a lump. The princess felt the pea under all those mattresses.

22

The Magic Table

Kenny came downstairs in his gangster jacket and white shirt and messy hair. "Is it all right if I watch the rest of *Guys and Dolls*?"

"It's all right," said Harriet.

"I don't know who I am. Nathan Detroit or Sky Masterson."

"Who do you like more? Vivian Blaine or Jean Simmons?"

"In this movie? Vivian Blaine."

"Then you must be Nathan Detroit."

That settled that.

In the afternoon they got the Christmas tree. Harriet sat in the car reading a book by someone much funnier and nuttier than she was – she liked the book enormously and she was jealous; so it goes, she thought, sue me – while snow fell softly on Lew and the kids and the young man sawing the bottom off the tree they'd picked out. He wore a Santa hat and a blue jacket and grey pants. Lew's shoulders were hunched up. He was reaching into his pocket for his wallet and Harriet had to look away. She wouldn't ask.

"Roll down your window," said Kenny through the glass.

She rolled it down.

"This guy's really popular. People keep coming by and saying hello to him. I wouldn't mind having a job like that. In high school. Selling trees. Talking to people when they come by. Giving 25 percent to the Humane Society."

"Habitat for Humanity."

"Whatever."

Lew tied the tree that cost a fortune to the roof of the car with a jump rope and jumper cables. The alpha male of the seal pack, trussed up in a net and crunching on the roof. The snow kept falling, swirling around like the torn-up pages of a letter borne away by gusts of air. *Wouldn't you agree that part of Danielle Darrieux's generosity of spirit was her ability to tear up the baron's love letter and let the pieces fly out the carriage window and drift away with the falling snow? All that love, which culminated in his inexplicable rejection – his punishment of her for her frivolous falsehood about her earrings, earrings which travelled from person to person, unifying the story and directing it.* The Earrings of Madame de. . . . *A movie you call perfection. I never would have heard of it if it hadn't been for you.*

Cold poured off the tree when they brought it inside. They trimmed it, then watched the Marx Brothers in *Horse Feathers*, and then *Christmas in July*, the early Preston Sturges movie they had seen once before; the first not nearly as funny as they expected, and the second a delight. But when Harriet stood up to rewind it, and turned around, there was Kenny, water spilled on the floor, a nest of crumbs where he'd been sitting, his denial that they had anything to do with him, and her shouted commands. Sponge! Vacuum! His repeated denials. Lew's admonitions to her, nipping at her heels like a pesky, good-hearted dog.

Who has the heart to write these things down? The way a parent ruins Christmas for a child. She flicked Kenny's head hard with her finger, threw the sponge at his back. So furious, so suddenly furious, that she could have throttled him.

"Are you all right?" Lew asked her carefully. She had come upstairs and shut herself in their room, and now he was checking on her.

She had to look away. At the bedside table. Away from his careful self-control and everything he kept himself from saying.

"We'll get through it together," he said.

Later, she would try to make up for her sins by reading *A Christmas Carol* to the kids at bedtime. She read: "He had frisked into the sitting-room, and was now standing there: perfectly winded." Lew, on his way to the kitchen, said, "How can you *stand* in a sitting room?"

Harriet said, "I know someone who died in a living room."

"You mean he was rubbed out in his drawing room?"

Then all her tension relaxed into laughter, and for the first time she thought he was like Chekhov in certain ways. Slender and mild and funny.

Lew had taken to calling Dinah *muchacha*. When she came over for their Friday-night movie, he said, "*Muchacha*, how are you feeling?" And he hovered around more than usual, and even stayed to watch the beginning of the movie. Tonight it was *Grand Hotel*: John Barrymore murdered by the blunt end of a telephone, and Garbo left out in the cold and never knowing why – never knowing why he didn't join her on the train, in the kind of misunderstanding so awful it ennobles all the silliness that came before. Dinah slept through most of it. She woke up when it ended and said stubbornly, "I want to skate on the canal. I've been thinking about it for days. As soon as the ice is thick enough."

Kenny said, "I think the canal is highly overrated. The ice is usually terrible, it's overcrowded, and you have to wait twenty minutes to get a Beaver Tail."

He was referring to the Ottawa delicacy of fried dough sprinkled with cinnamon, sugar, and lemon juice, or spread with jam. A Beaver Tail was about the same size, and as flat, thought Harriet, as a large breast squished by a mammogram machine.

Earlier in the week, at the hospital, she had asked the technician about Clint Eastwood's breasts. The technician was wearing three gold earrings, two in her left ear, one in her right. She said the machine was fussy today. She was just going to turn it off for a moment to make it smarten up. A short, stocky, red-faced blonde who lifted Harriet's left breast onto a plate and spread it flat like pastry, then lowered the plate above, removing her ringed hand as the plate came down. *Paddle* and *bucky* were the proper terms: the paddle pressing down until, to Harriet's eye, her breast looked like a giant white strawberry that's been stepped on. "What do you think of Clint Eastwood's breasts?" she asked her, after she was able to breathe again.

The technician had been smiling all along and she kept smiling, but more vacantly.

"You haven't seen his most recent movie?"

"No."

"Nor have I. But they say he was unwise enough to take off his shirt."

"I've done men's breasts," she said. "That's hard because they're so muscular."

"Not Clint Eastwood's."

"Well, you get all kinds. You get every kind under the sun. I've seen every kind of breast there is."

A day later Harriet would be sitting in another hospital, in a small waiting room on the second floor. She was waiting for Dinah, who was having a CAT scan. Beside her sat a plump little white-haired woman who looked to be the picture of health, but had had one mastectomy seventeen years ago, and was having another now. She had rolling veins, she said, which makes it hard to draw blood. They put a needle into the vein and the vein rolls away. She made a large, easy motion with her hand like a dog rolling over.

The little woman went off to her appointment, and Harriet pulled out her notebook and began to write. *I don't know why, but I've been thinking about Katharine Hepburn, asking myself why I find her so embarrassing that I have to look away. She's all over her own face, somehow. So aware of herself and how smart and shiny she is. Always being seen. And I agree with you that she's good, she's often very good. But I can't watch her. Ida told me that she much preferred Barbara Stanwyck. We got talking this morning when I went to pick up Dinah. Ida confessed that when she was a girl all she wanted was to walk around – swagger about – as the older girls did, in open, unbuckled galoshes.*

Harriet laid down her pen and leaned back in her chair. She thought about Dinah. A beautiful, mouthy woman in terrible health, who only the other day admitted to having had cancer once before. But you smoke, said Harriet. Yes, said Dinah, but I don't drink.

Dinah was too blithe, she thought, too hardened by journalism, a craft of short attention spans and rapid turnover, a profession for young women and coarse old men. She suspected that she herself felt things more deeply. She was more sincere than writers who were more successful, *that* was why her book had failed to sell more than a few dozen copies. Yet if she felt things so deeply, how could she have been so casually cruel? And down came Leah–Jack–Janice like an iron collar of guilt around her neck. On the other hand, she couldn't be all bad or she wouldn't be here, keeping Dinah company.

She leaned forward and added, *I do like her, however, in* The African Queen.

Dinah, undergoing the CAT scan, was thinking about her will, and then about Harriet and Lew. She had been fending for herself for so long that a woman like Harriet, largely dependent on a husband for support, struck her as near-exotic and worth scolding; but she didn't have the energy to scold. She liked them both, and Lew she loved. She liked the way Harriet's long, too-slender body advanced at a tilt, as if it were folding up or unfolding and who could tell which? She loved Lew for being funny, smart, sexy, and humane.

On the way home, riding in the passenger seat, she said to Harriet over the music on the radio, "I want to get married."

"Have you got somebody in mind?"

"Yes."

"You don't mean Jack Frame?"

Dinah looked out the passenger window at the suburban houses going by, the front yards, driveways, plate glass windows. Today they looked lovely.

"Dinah?"

"What's wrong with Jack Frame?"

"He's a lousy writer and he's never done anything with his life."

"The trouble with you," Dinah said, "is that you don't appreciate the wonderfulness of modest lives."

"Are you nuts? Jack Frame isn't modest!"

On Tuesday of the following week, in an appointment squeezed in before Christmas, a woman in slacks and a striped shirt took Harriet to the room that had the magic table. It was pink, and sunken in the middle. In the most sunken part there was a hole the size of a one-holer in the woods. She climbed a stool to get onto the table. She lay down, naked from the waist up, on her stomach, and dropped her breast through the hole. She turned her head to the left, as instructed, away from the action. Then they raised the table higher so they could work underneath her, locating the lesion and calcifications. They were going to take tissue samples. *Strange how frightened I am. All around me people are in trouble. Dinah's tumor might be inoperable; the Kosovars are burned out and burning up; and here am I, on my little hilltop, waving a flag in the air: over here! over here! over here! don't forget me! I have a one in a thousand chance of having cancer.*

"You must feel like you're working on an old Chevy," she said aloud.

"We prefer to think Mercedes-Benz," said the technician.

"Silver," said Harriet.

"With the top down."

"Red," Harriet said. And then she was quiet for a while.

By the time she got home there was a dark patch of blood on her tan-colored shirt. She took a dry face cloth, folded it in half, and pressed it on her breast for five minutes. The bleeding stopped. She got up and put on the kettle. The bleeding started.

She lay on the sofa, staunching the blood with her face cloth, and watched *The Empire Strikes Back*. Pauline Kael said it was the best of the three, so it was okay to watch it. When she met St. Peter at the gate, she would say, "Pauline said it was okay." And then she would meet Pauline. The conversations they would have! Was Cary Grant gay or not? What other movies was Dan Dailey in besides *It's Always Fair Weather*? Was Judy Garland in love with Gene Kelly? And how, *how* could you like Katharine Hepburn?

And then, together, they would meet Cary Grant.

She got up and found a king-sized bandage and slapped it over the Band-Aid provided by the hospital, then dug out her copies of *North by Northwest* and *Notorious*.

In the wakeful, painful hours that followed she wrote a long, rambling letter in her head to Pauline, inspired by the sight of Cary Grant's sagging chest. *Remember? The scene when he's in the hospital after pretending to have been shot dead by Eva Marie Saint, and he's wearing only a towel around his waist because the* FBI *won't let him have his clothes? Hitchcock tracks him from the side, in close-up, as he paces back and forth, and his chest looks aged and sagging. Then the camera pulls back, and it's like someone sliding in their false teeth: once again he looks youthful and fit. Cruel Hitchcock with his sudden cameo-jolts of Hitchcock-reality.*

You aren't crazy about Hitchcock and neither am I. These early movies, of course, but not the later ones when his seamy sadism ran riot. In Notorious *Cary Grant was perfect because he held so exquisitely to the edge of his own and Hitchcock's ambivalence. "I was a fatheaded guy full of pain," he says. And then how did he put it when he finally admitted that he'd always been in love with Ingrid? "Long ago, all the time, since the beginning." One of my favorite lines, though you have to hear him say it. You have to hear his voice and see his face as he finally admits how torn up he was about not having her.*

She was thinking about the disease of video love. How it had changed her life, perhaps more than anything else ever had. The ability to see Cary Grant's face, a certain look on his face, over and over again.

To see Fred Astaire, the "beautiful mover," walking alone on a train plat-form and singing "All by Myself." To hear the intonation Kevin Kline gives "I want you." Or George Peppard gives "Will you marry me?" Or Humphrey Bogart gives "The Germans wore grey, you wore blue."

More recently, the latest *Pride and Prejudice* had been her undoing. She had borrowed it from a neighbor, then ended up deserting her desk in the middle of the morning to watch long stretches of it, fast-forwarding through Wickham to get to Darcy. Why toil away on some story that was boring her to death when Colin Firth was waiting in the next room? She had confessed as much to Dinah, who said, "What is it about women that fills us with this terrible need for a contained beauti-ful world, where no ugliness intrudes? We need to tramp over great chunks of parkland and arrive at a welcoming cup of tea. We never have the chance. We all need our own five acres."

Harriet told her that five acres wouldn't do it. And she hadn't been thinking about the landscape so much as the emotional line of the story – a man in utter control falls uncontrollably in love with a woman who very gradually discovers that she loves him. She also had a sudden understanding of the dreaded Leah and herself as she watched Charlotte Lucas hopping about to please Lady Catherine de Bourgh. There she was, scurrying to get a chair for Leah, dancing attendance, being servile, solicitous, ignoble.

Finally, she'd had to take herself in hand and return it. This required going out the back door, down to the foot of the garden, left along the alley, right along another alley, through to Sunnyside Avenue by means of a gravel driveway, and then right again, one, two, three houses to the neighbor who had lent it to her a week earlier. But yesterday she had gone to her and borrowed it again.

Harriet leaves the sofa – by now it's one in the morning – drawn irre-sistibly to the VCR. In a moment Darcy's eyes are spilling their bountiful love for Lizzy's bountiful breasts. She watches him walk with his two greyhounds through the halls of Pemberley, his curt mouth moving in a barely perceptible smile – what a transformation! – back into the room where earlier in the evening their voluptuous eye contact occurred, and where now, hand on the mantelpiece, he resolves in his mind to hie himself off to Lizzy first thing in the morning.

She presses rewind once again.

The next morning in the shower she cups her little breast with one hand. It looks like someone's first attempt at making a dairy queen.

But she feels better.

Dinah, too, feels better, great quantities of fluid having been drained from her lungs. Her oldest mannerism is back in full swing: repeatedly she fools with her hair, using both hands to sweep it back, coil it around, then hold it in place with a long-toothed clip. Harriet notices the fresh roses in the corner of her bedroom.

"Jack?"

"The same."

"He called me." Harriet rubs her eyes behind her glasses, then settles the glasses back on her nose. Once again she'd been struck by the soft flatness of his voice – like an untoned thigh – asking her to do something. "He wants me to help him and Leah with their book about Lionel."

"Are you going to?"

"I said no."

At her *no* his tone had changed. It softened another notch. He said he had seen a movie she would like. *Bridges of Madison County*, he said. She reminded me of you. Meryl Streep? Yes, he said. You have certain things in common. *Like what?* You're both very direct. You fold your arms the same way. Your mouth and eyes are the same.

You need new glasses, she snorted.

He laughed a little. He said they would like her to be the editor. She was their first choice.

No, she said again, I don't think so.

His voice was gentle. "Harriet Browning, you owe it to us, don't you think?"

And she felt the inky letters of her name encircle her neck like a noose.

23

Dinah's Boots

On the last day of December, Dinah sat on a wooden bench at the side of the frozen canal. She lit a cigarette out of sight of Ida – just to smell it – and watched a couple dote on their baby in a stroller. The father could have been the grandfather, except that the mother, once she raised her head from crooning over the baby, wasn't much younger. In fur hat and twill trousers he arranged the blanket in the stroller, smoothing it like an artisan, while the mother put the smiling baby – such skin! – into a second snowsuit, then laid her on the blanket, folded the blanket, spread a down-filled bag over her feet and lowered the clear plastic windbreak over the stroller. They were a couple who couldn't seem to believe their good fortune at having such a beautiful, patient, good-willed baby. Turning to her, asking her if she would kindly put out her cigarette, they moved to sit beside her on the bench and put on their skates. They would skate together, this pair, pushing the baby ahead of them in an outdoor display of pluck and luck and skill.

Dinah was husbanding her resources. In a while she would stand up and push off. She said to the couple, "I wonder what would happen if you came back and someone had taken your boots."

"Oh, that *never* happens," the woman said, horrified. "I've been skating for fifteen years and that *never* happens. Almost never."

"I guess you'd walk home in your skates," the man said.

Two miles away, at the other end of the canal, seated on a bench near the Laurier Bridge, Lew watched perfect stars, six-pointed and filigreed, land on his black corduroy pants. For several minutes he was completely absorbed by the tiny, weightless complexity of one snowflake, then another, then another. A dozen pairs of boots were beside the bench, all innocence and trust, and he felt a burst of affection for a city where you could leave your boots for several hours and return to find them untouched. It was almost Islamic, as if people had gone off to say their prayers in stocking feet, just as it was almost Japanese, the custom of shedding your shoes whenever you entered someone else's home. It was four o'clock. He stuffed his boots into a gym bag (he was skating home) and slung it over his shoulder. Directly ahead, the canal was straight and narrow. It curved after it passed the University of Ottawa, then widened – opening itself to every gusty headwind from the west – then narrowed again under the Pretoria Bridge, and widened again as it passed the many tiny lights of the Canal Ritz. It narrowed to skirt Lansdowne Park, narrowed more under the Bank Street Bridge, narrowed even more as it continued its curving way towards the end of a subdued sunset over Dow's Lake. The ice was rough and uneven, but it would get better; the season was only beginning. By the time Lew reached the Bronson Street Bridge, half an hour later, the sun was down and light emanated from the surrounding city and from the snow and ice itself. Somebody was searching among the boots around the bench to which he was headed. He swerved over and came to a halt.

It was Dinah, and her boots were gone.

"I can't believe it," she said. "They've stolen my boots."

"No."

"They aren't here." And she laughed in uproarious amazement.

"Sit down," he said, taking her by the arm. "What do they look like?"

"Last year they stole my snow shovel off the front porch. I thought that was as low as you could get." Her voice was its usual raucous, sexy self. "Navy Sorels, size six."

He searched around the bench, holding on to the back with one hand to keep his balance, then farther afield among the snowbanks. "I'll help you get home," he said, sitting down to unlace his skates.

She looked with gratitude at his reliable face. "You're a darling. I've always said so." And when he offered her his arm, she took it. They made their way across the few yards of trodden snow to the wooden staircase, and up the steps to the sidewalk. Cars whizzed by, the wind picked up. Lew felt waves of fatigue roll off Dinah as she leant into him. There was another bench next to the iron railing, he helped her over to it and she sank down, and then he knelt at her feet. "Enough already," she said. "I'll marry you."

He unlaced her skates, pulled them off, shoved them into his gym bag. Then he got her to stand on the bench and climb onto his back. "I'm too heavy," she said into his ear. She had her arms around his neck as he set off with a lurch, adjusting his walk to her weight, which was heavier than he expected. "I'm too heavy," she said again. He grunted. Soon he was sweating. They had to wait for the traffic to thin before crossing Colonel By. And then two more blocks. He had his arms around her legs and the gym bag in his locked hands, a lean, wiry, surprisingly strong man who managed to carry her 131 pounds on his back like a voyageur, she thought, on a portage between canal and home.

"I feel like a polio victim," she rasped into his ear.

"Your legs feel fine to me."

At her house he sank backwards onto the steps and she slid off. He disentangled his arms, then helped her stand up and that was when they stumbled. His knees gave way, and they caught each other. "Oh, Lew," she said. And that was it. That's what did it.

II

THE ICE STORM

24

Leah

It began raining six days later on Monday, January 5. The holidays were over, Kenny and Jane were back in school finally, but what a ruination. The rain meant the death of skiing, skating, going for walks. After supper, when Harriet remembered that they needed milk, she went out into the wet, slippery night and made her cautious way, under an umbrella, to the corner store. An umbrella in January!

The next morning they woke to a wet glass world. Rain was falling on frozen rain and freezing too, coating everything it touched and being coated in turn.

Fiona Chester, looking out her window, thought of the banished poet in the frozen town. And what was Akhmatova's apt and moving phrase? "The ice like a paperweight." Her spiked cane was in the closet, as were spiked overshoes made in Germany with studs from racing-car wheels embedded in rubber sole and heel. She tugged on trenchcoat, footgear, plastic bonnet, took her cane, and stepped outside.

Every stem, twig, branch, pole, car was swollen by the frozen rain. It came from the southwest and the west-facing sides of houses were slick with ice. At the end of her street she turned right (to avoid the sloping alley) and on the next block heard a commotion at the Golds. A door slammed and Lew Gold, the most patient of men, burst impatiently, dangerously, down his front steps, losing his balance then regaining it, while Harriet followed in her dressing gown, saying what? "I meant it all / in fun. Don't leave me, or I'll die of pain"? So went another of the great Russian's poems.

Lew turned around and spoke to his wife. Perhaps he, too, like the husband in the poem, smiled calmly, terribly, and said, "Why don't you get out of the rain?"

An old woman's premonitions. Several days ago, on her way past this same stretch of houses, she saw Dinah Bloom stumble into Lew's arms. Saw his face afterwards as he turned out of Dinah's walk right into her path, quite unaware of himself or of her. And thought, Now he knows, and felt such a pang of sadness.

Harriet caught sight of Fiona Chester and waved, and hoped her hearing aids weren't in. Lew was in the car, backing out of the driveway.

Later it dawned on Harriet that she should have offered to do Fiona's errands for her. But she was in a state of despair. The school buses were cancelled and she had lost, after only a day, the solitude she had finally regained. The kids would be underfoot again, the radio said the freezing rain would continue, and Lew was on his way to the airport to pick up Leah.

The day before the rain began, Harriet and Lew saw, without knowing what it was, a signal from the sky. They were in the woods, cross-country skiing near Mackenzie King's country estate, where the prime minister, half crazy for love of his mother and all dead things, had brought and reassembled pieces of demolished old buildings, fashioning them into something Italianate and temple-like. What a kook, thought Harriet, standing on her skis inside the phony ruins and thinking of the man his friends called Rex. She pictured him with Mary Pickford on his arm, and Shirley Temple, since the latter had also made his day by visiting Ottawa. A man who loved movies, but called them "plays." A man who loved power and held on to it for all he was worth. Not unlike Leah, she thought. Not unlike her short, square, obstreperous aunt who ran a restaurant, and ran it well, until she became the last wife of a famous man, the controller of his papers, booster of his reputation, presenter, defender, champion, to say nothing of critic.

Harriet looked up at the winter sky, then out through an empty Gothic window at a handsome day of white-toothed snow and whiskery trees. Rabbits were about. She saw their tracks on either side of the path as she skied down to join Lew: sizable indentations that put her in mind of Richard Burton's pockmarked face. Then dainty traces made by a chipmunk: Elizabeth Taylor before she put on weight.

A tree had fallen across the path, making lines in the snow and leaving a second imprint, hovering above the first, of twiggy shadows. The tree was too heavy to move. They went around it on their skis.

After a while they stopped to eat oranges. Harriet was for burying the peels under the snow, but Lew wouldn't have it. He took them from her and stuffed them into his pocket. The day before he had learned that a colleague of his had a tumor at the back of his tongue. For two months Duncan had had a sore throat and now they knew why.

Look at this orange, she said, holding the peels nearly reassembled in her hands before he took them from her. The color was brilliant, cupped in her hands above the pure snow and below the astonishing sky.

Lew said, "They paint them, you know."

She smiled. But here was a change: Lew did not.

With sudden feeling, he said, "We should do what we most want to do, right now."

"While we have the money," she agreed, "and the health." Running her hand lightly over her chest. Her lump had turned out to be benign, just as she thought it would. And Dinah had some of her old energy back, at least for now. She said, "Dinah's looking so much better, have you noticed?"

She didn't ask him what he wanted to do, thinking she knew already and not wanting to encourage him: a move to Latin America (she was far too set in her ways) or Montreal (she'd end up humming "O Canada" under her breath).

He said, "When Duncan told us he had cancer, his breath was so bad it was hard to be in the same room. You never know your breath smells bad."

"I do."

"It's impossible. Physically impossible. A person with bad breath never knows it."

"Of course you do. You exhale into your palm." She demonstrated. "And the smell of your breath comes back in through your nostrils."

"A medical miracle," he said, testy and unconvinced, since he had heard the opposite stated as fact on the radio.

Neither of them remarked upon the color of the horizon, or the color of the snow.

Today our skis slid over fallen beech leaves bleached to near-ivory by winter, and fallen maple keys, she wrote when she got back to her desk. *We skied alone, the two of us, over a pattern of delicate shadows thrown by twigs that made the fresh snow look like a Japanese screen. We stopped to peel an orange and it was then I noticed how strange the light was on the horizon. Greenish, almost emerald, in color. The snow too had a greenish tint by then, and there weren't any birds in the sky.*

You become aware of the surfaces of things because every surface provides an opportunity for ice. The weight builds and builds.

On his way to the airport Lew drove slowly and saw several cars slipping, skidding, going slowly into the ditch, and birch trees starting to bend like women in the first stages of washing their hair. By week's end their heads would be pinned to the ground.

A most beautiful catastrophe. Photographs wouldn't do it justice, any more than they do justice to many faces, failing to capture the expressiveness, the tone, the quality of the stillness.

Waiting for Lew to return, throwing salt on the icy steps, thinking of the bad luck of being chosen not for dislike but for love, for a certain kind of hostile love, Harriet's nervousness was fuelled, stoked, whipped up by thoughts of Leah and her difficult ways. The way she settled on you, for instance, as her favorite. The way she adopted you and referred to you as one of her "kids," the way she wanted to have a following of young people who would admire and amuse her, the way she played one favorite off another out of some bedrock conviction – where on earth did it come from? – that nothing less was owed to her.

And what Harriet wanted for herself, she thought, was the very opposite. What she really wanted was to be left alone.

She stood on the porch and looked out at the awful world. *How do you deal with bullies? How did Garbo deal with Louis B. Mayer? She went home to Sweden; she let him wait.*

But Harriet had nowhere to go. She was about to be trapped inside with one of Chekhov's nasty women who take over your life and abuse everything, even the spoons.

The car pulled slowly into the icy driveway, and because Leah was the last person on earth she wanted to see, Harriet couldn't have been more welcoming. She embraced her aunt, took her coat, helped her with her boots, led her by the arm into the kitchen. She hid her true feelings under an excess of cordiality, managing to convince even herself that she liked Leah far more than she did.

"Here she is," she said to Kenny and Jane, who were reading the sports pages and the comics at the kitchen table. "Do you remember your Great-Aunt Leah? It's been a long time."

They looked up and saw nearly at eye level a very short, brisk-looking old lady with beautiful deep-set eyes, an extraordinary blue. A thick neck, soft veined cheeks, and gray hair that was shorter than Kenny's. They didn't remember her at all.

Well, she would fix that. She began to sing "Kennies from Heaven," causing both children to light up and laugh, and their mother to laugh too. Harriet hadn't seen her aunt in this new manifestation: as the widow of Lionel, who had died two years ago, a very old man. Leah, at seventy-six, was on her own; she would have to be nicer to people, and so far she was succeeding.

"How tall are you?" Leah asked Lew when he joined them. "Six-foot-four?"

"Six-three."

And she got up on a stool to see what the room looked like for somebody nearly a foot and a half taller than her. She even got them to snap a picture of her in that pose, admitting quite freely that she had always wanted to go on stage. Then she established herself at the kitchen table and began to give out gifts.

Like Jack she wore pants, and a loose shirt that she didn't tuck in, but her shirt was made of silk and her pants of the finest wool. Harriet had known her to stand in tears in the middle of a busy room – a party – and weep in memory of a long day of shopping when nothing but nothing would fit. *I want to look rich! I want to walk into a store and have people look at me and think:* RICH. A peasant-duchess, thought Harriet, vain about her good taste even as she sucked air through her teeth, making a sound that was somewhere between a thin whistle and a squeak. Harriet pictured a mouse sliding to a halt on a polished floor.

"In Italy today it's *Il Giorno della Befana*," announced Leah, "and I'm *la Befana*, the old woman who gives out gifts on the Feast of the Epiphany. You Anglo-Saxons," she said, "you don't know what you're missing."

Harriet looked at the others. "My anti-English aunt," she said wryly. But Leah seemed to enjoy the crack.

Was it going to be easy then? Harriet wondered. Was all her alarm mere stage fright? So often it was exactly that. So often her wild trepidations gave way as soon as people arrived, and she rose to the occasion and outdid herself, urging everyone not to leave as it got late, but to stay longer. From having been dangerously overwrought, she became oddly, dangerously disarmed.

You're always like this, Lew would remind her, his old-school hospitality completely at odds with her various fears. But he was like the Irish king she'd read about, who was so constantly giving that his right hand grew longer than his left.

The gifts were from Florence: a box of fine writing paper for Harriet, leather gloves for Jane, leather wallet for Kenny, silk scarf for Lew. Without a doubt, they were being wooed.

And Harriet thought, Where has her sharpness gone?

Harriet had lasted only the one summer working for Leah, that summer she was nineteen and chopped onions and made beds under her aunt's flattering, tyrannical eye. Leah went through as many servants as Harriet's father went through dental nurses. A panther in the kitchen. Moody, unpredictable, muscular in her watchfulness. In later years, on return trips as the favored visiting niece, Harriet had had a chance to study further her aunt's effect on people. *Dear Pauline, This is how you have to be in Leah's company: subservient without being servile, attentive without being spineless, opinionated without being disagreeable. You have to be interesting and insecure, and in need of love. She chooses her prey well: plucky, nervous women who want to be liked. There are plenty of them around. For instance, the Sarah she chose as her Sarah was Jack's second wife: tall, thin, eager, kind – a funny generous woman upon whom she lavished many gifts. She had nothing but praise for her, and indeed she was a lovely woman with just the right amount of insecurity (large), deference (medium), and loyalty (total).*

After the gift giving, after Lew and the kids drifted away, Leah began to talk expansively and at length about one thing: the way people treated her, and how she reacted. And she wove Harriet into the picture. "You would never do this, you are not that kind of person," she said. "They are, but you aren't."

First came the story of the stepdaughter with whom she had always been at odds, Lionel's last-born and favorite, Enid, who had written to her to say, *For thirty years you have burrowed into my life in order to undermine it.* And Leah was all innocence, all amazement. She admitted that, yes, she had taken Enid's son to one side to tell him how terrified he was of his mother when he was little, but it was Enid who was unstable and always had been; it was sad. Then she told Harriet about the nephew who avoided her, and the cousin who refused to let her stay in his house, relating these stories to show how well she coped with rejection, and how she got even.

This is how she got even: she set traps. She pretended not to have taken offense, inviting her lulled victims to meet someone they wanted to meet – Enid to meet an important movie producer whom Leah happened to know – or to have some memento of Lionel's they couldn't resist owning – a first edition of *The Leopard* to the nephew who avoided her. Then at the last minute, and innocently, she pulled the olive leaf out from under their feet.

This is where her sharpness has gone, Harriet realized. Into covert operations. Into an elaborate centerpiece, and the centerpiece is loyalty.

It was hard work. Hard work to have to be so buoyant and apparently well balanced in her widowhood. And hard work to be her niece.

The day before, in preparation for the visit, Harriet had hidden most of their movies in the basement: all of Cary Grant, *West Side Story* (bad old Jerome Robbins), *On the Waterfront* (down with Elia Kazan) – leaving out John Sayles, *Some Like it Hot*, Charlie Chaplin, and a documentary about the father of the documentary, John Grierson. She advised Kenny not to mention Frank Sinatra when Leah was around. "I don't think she's a fan." She reminded him and Jane about Lionel's history of being blacklisted. "Lew?" she said. "You explain."

But Kenny said he knew what being blacklisted meant. Your name was put on a list and you couldn't get work. Yes, said Lew, and the list was circulated to all employers by the FBI in the States or by the RCMP in Canada, telling people not to hire them. Not just for being communist, or friendly with communists, or being anti-fascist before the war, but for being union organizers, "which they saw as being communists," piped up Jane. "I know about the Cold War," she said, "but why did they call it *cold*?"

Lew, who was standing at the sink wiping tomato sauce off his shirt – "Your father's a Red," teased Harriet – said the Cold War was the battle between the U.S. and the Soviet Union for world supremacy, and they called it *cold* because most of the time they weren't killing each other, they were killing people in the countries they were trying to dominate. "One of Lionel's books has a lot about it."

"One of his books that went nowhere," Harriet said. "Poor Lionel. A sad old gentleman."

"Nobody was able to defend themselves," said Lew, still scrubbing away at his shirt, and calmly explaining the immoderate past as he was in the habit of explaining urban travesties to his architecture students. "Right-wing politicians linked the enemy outside to the enemy inside. They claimed that union organizers were communists and communists were foreign agents. The only ones who didn't get blacklisted were the ones who turned in their friends."

"And if you didn't turn in your friends," Harriet said, "they were indebted to you for the rest of your life."

Leah picked up a spoon and rolled the handle between her small, capable fingers. Harriet saw her eyeing it to see if it was clean, saw her taking in the kitchen, the whole house, and judging them on their taste and income. But what Leah said was, "You've done a good job with your kids. I mean it, darling. You've got nice kids. I always know what the parents think of me by how their children treat me." She made that squeaking, sucking sound with her teeth. "I can always tell if the parents have said nasty things about me."

"Lew's the wonderful parent," said Harriet, getting up and going over to the sink.

Leah followed her with her dirty cup. She saw the baking soda beside the stove. "That's smart," she said. "Everybody should do that." Then she looked around for the dishwasher, but Harriet didn't have a dishwasher. "But everybody's got a dishwasher," Leah said.

"We don't want one. We don't need one."

"You mean Lew doesn't want one. It's Lew, isn't it? He won't spend the money."

Harriet's face tightened. She returned to the table and Leah followed her and sat down too. "What I don't understand," Leah said, "is why the children of all my friends make less money than their parents."

"Stop it," Harriet said softly, but Leah wasn't deaf.

"Stop what?"

Harriet didn't answer.

"*Stop what?*"

She sighed. "Stop putting Lew down."

"Don't be ridiculous, darling. I like Lew more than you do."

Harriet glanced at the clock on the wall. It was only ten-thirty in the morning, on the first day of a visit whose duration she was too cowardly to ascertain. As a child, *you were loud*, her mother had told her. Then some line to her tongue snapped, and for years she had almost nothing to say. Leah, she knew, still saw her as the tall, shy kitchen help in that villa full of intimidated guests. Unknown to Leah, however, was Harriet's violent temper, which erupted only once in a while. As a girl she had smashed a plate over awful Owen's head. At school she electrified her classmates by banging her fist on her desk in an argument about the word *oblivion*. Once, she threw a telephone across the room. Also a quart of partly skimmed milk. The milk she'd aimed at Lew.

Kenny came into the kitchen and asked if they'd heard of whist. Was it like bridge? He'd been reading Jules Verne's *Around the World in Eighty Days*. Leah said it was. Before there was bridge, there was whist. Then he asked if she knew how to play, and she said no, neither game. Then Harriet said she thought bridge was a waste of time, that in her experience people who played bridge – people like Lew's Uncle Milt and Dinah's mother, Ida – were not too bright.

Kenny couldn't believe his ears. He couldn't believe his mother would say such a thing of someone who was a friend. To Harriet's astonishment, tears filled his eyes. He went to the drawer in the kitchen counter and got out a paper napkin to wipe them. He said, "How would you like it if I called Ida up and told her she wasn't very bright?"

"I won't tell her. I don't tell people they're not very bright. I don't even like the word. Actually, I hate the word. But some people aren't as bright as others. Ida isn't as bright as Dinah."

"I can't believe it," he said, wiping the tears off his face. "I can't believe this."

"What? That I'd say someone isn't as bright as someone else?"

"That you'd say someone isn't very bright who thinks she's your friend."

"I could say I'm not bright enough to play bridge. That's true too."

She watched his thin, reproachful back as he headed upstairs again, then turned to her aunt, embarrassed by her bumbling, stupid self, embarrassed and worried about her infinitely sentimental son. "He gets so worked up," she said.

"He's perfect," said Leah. "I want him."

———◯———

Dinah Bloom dropped by in the early afternoon when Leah was upstairs with the kids. "So is she moving to Ottawa?" asked Dinah.

"I haven't asked."

Dinah gave her a look of amused pity. "Then I'll ask."

Outside, the weather was turning every house into an icy ship on an icy sea. Branches were coming down, more and more people were without power. Dinah said that she'd gone out to use her car and found it completely encased in ice with the ice scraper inside. She'd had to borrow loud Ray's, and he was wearing an eyepatch because a splinter of ice had flown into his eye when he scraped off his van. Her mood was jaunty, even excited, while Harriet could only think that if she took Leah anywhere at all, her aunt would fall and break a hip, and then they would never be rid of her.

Dinah had been on the phone to Fiona Chester, and Fiona had told her about a bad ice storm during the war when soldiers had to break up the ice on Bank Street with picks. She had called an editor at the *Citizen* too, offering to write some articles for them. "I love a disaster, I can't help it. It's in my blood."

Leah came downstairs with the kids, and ever afterwards she would refer to Dinah as "that reporter" and Dinah would refer to her as "the formidable aunt." The only two women Harriet knew who called people "darling" and they had no time for each other. From the first moment – when the kids lit up at the sight of Dinah, who took them into her wide embrace, the three of them on the sofa and Leah displaced, Leah side-lined to the black rocker where she pointedly ignored Dinah's greeting – from that moment they had no time for each other.

"How long are you planning to stay in Ottawa?" asked Dinah.

Leah's reply was stiff, cool. "I can't tell you. I haven't made up my mind yet."

"The weather might make up your mind for you," said Dinah.

There was an awkward silence. Harriet, in her discomfort, felt the tug of loyalty and the pall of disappointment. She had hoped, somehow, that Dinah and Leah would hit it off. It was the Kenny in her, the wishful matchmaker.

Dinah asked, "Where's Lew?"

"I'm here," he said, and Dinah turned around. He was in the living-room doorway, gazing at her. Their eyes met and it was like fingers in a socket.

Leah's narrowed eyes went back and forth between them. But Harriet was distracted by a descending spider. She held out her hand to it. A little one, colorless. It landed and raced across her palm and over the side. She turned her hand to keep it in play. "Look." To Kenny, whose fear of bugs she wanted to allay. "It means no harm."

It travelled the length of her hand, pausing on one knuckle while everybody watched, and she began to tell the story of how she murdered a spider in cold blood. She was visiting an Irish friend one Christmas, and when she put on her coat to leave, she saw a spider race across the hallway floor and instinctively reached out with her foot and stomped on it. Her friend was horrified. *Don't you know they're good luck? And now it's going to rain.* "I've never stepped on a spider since, but somebody must have."

The spider, so tiny and alert, sat quite still, and she saw that it wasn't really colorless at all: its body greeny white and its legs like the pale eye-lashes on a redhead. What interesting, silent, creaturely company it was.

Then it bolted, and though she rolled her arm around she lost it to the floor. The conversation resumed, but more musingly. She said, "Last night when I couldn't sleep I watched part of *Nashville* again."

Dinah drew in her breath approvingly, and Harriet said to her, "So. Did Keith Carradine really care about Lily Tomlin or not?"

"Well," Dinah said with a knowing smile, "not very much."

"But remember after they make love?" persisted Harriet. "When she says she has to go home and she's moving around getting dressed? He phones another girlfriend? But as soon as the door closes behind her, he hangs up. Remember the look on his face?"

"I think he cares about her more than he knows." Amused by the interrogation.

"Exactly," said Harriet, glad to have pried loose an answer closer to the one she wanted to hear. "More than he knows, and more than *she* knows."

What a marvellous scene that was, she thought, the way the movie led up to it, then concentrated upon it so fully: in the bar when he sang to her and we get the change, the surrender in her face, the sexual letting-down, as of milk in a woman's breasts. And then the scene in bed when, for the first time, he actually shows interest in a woman. Asking her a question. Pleading with her to stay. *I like the way you put it. You say we see him "with one bed partner after another – with Geraldine Chaplin, whom he'll barely remember the next day, and with Lily Tomlin, whom he'll remember forever." Not diminishing what you call his moody narcissism, yet not leaving it at that.*

Dinah spoke again, a little flushed. "I dropped in on a friend of my mother's. Dottie Greenburg. She's been without power since last night and she looks ten years older."

"You look ten years younger," Harriet said. "Really. You look remarkably well."

Lew said he'd been downstairs listening to the radio list school closures and cancellations of plays and evening classes. "I phoned Duncan," he said, "and he's sitting in candlelight in the hospital. It's going to keep raining."

"Yes, it's getting worse," said Dinah.

Now Leah joined in. "You could get a book out of this," she said to Harriet. "I'm serious. You should be taking notes for a novel. You might win a prize and get somewhere."

"Delacroix never won a prize." Harriet meant it as a little joke.

"Delacroix?" Kenny's ears perked up. "Robert Mitchum was Charles Delacroix in *The Grass Is Greener*."

"I didn't like him at all," Jane said. "I liked Cary Grant."

"Actually," Harriet said, "he was very good. Cary Grant shouldn't have agreed to do a movie with a man's man like Robert Mitchum. Mitchum was sexier."

Leah said to the room, "I give up."

"Leah, *you* write a novel if you think it's so easy."

"I'm too old. So are you. Lionel used to say if you haven't written a novel by the time you're forty, you never will."

"But he's not read any more, is he?" observed Dinah in that amused and husky voice of hers that allowed her to get away with saying anything. "Don't write Harriet off. It's unkind."

"*Unkind? Unkind?* I'm the kindest person I know."

———————◆———————

Harriet picked up the binoculars off the kitchen windowsill and trained them on the world outside. She saw air bubbles inside an icicle, the wood grain on the bird feeder, individual seeds under layers of ice, and not a single bird. Leah was in the study on the phone. Dinah had left. It was only three o'clock of the same Tuesday, according to the slow-moving clock on the wall.

"That was Janice," Leah said, coming back into the kitchen. "Janice Bird."

"You mean Emily." Turning around. "She changed her name to Emily."

"Whatever. You'll have to drive me to see her. Not today." Looking out the window. "But when this is over. Today I want to talk to you about the book I'm writing with Jack."

"Why talk to me?"

"Because you know how to write. I want you to read what I've written so far. It won't take long. It's only fifty pages."

Harriet raised the binoculars again and focused on the wire fence lacquered with ice, the two cars marooned next door, the maple tree transformed into glass, and – sweet Jesus, would she have no peace? Jack Frame lumbering up the side lane, hands in his pockets, eyes on his sliding feet. Harriet watched him until the house next door hid him from view.

"Get Jack to read it," she said, putting the binoculars on the windowsill and sitting down across from her aunt.

"We need an editor. I've got the experience. Jack is doing the research. You can be the one who polishes the prose. And don't tell me you're doing other things. I know what your life is like."

Harriet unfolded her long body and stood up. Why was Al Pacino more ruthless than Marlon Brando? Because he was shorter. She stood over – towered over – her short torturer with the beautiful eyes. Then she went to the cupboard and rummaged for sustenance. "Here," she said, putting Oreos on a plate. "This is what we're reduced to."

But Leah was reaching into her bag, taking out a copy of Harriet's book, putting on her reading glasses. "As for you," she said, "when are you going to stop writing these *little* pieces? I read your book and I wouldn't know what to call it. It's just bits and pieces strung together." Opening the book, she began to read aloud the scene describing an elderly woman with veined cheeks and grizzled hair who climbed drunkenly into bed with the narrator and nuzzled her neck and wept. Her aunt was going to punish her by reading aloud a story that a kinder person never would have written – but do people write to be kind? – and Harriet was going to suffer through it. She had written the story to free herself of Leah, but, instead, she had given her aunt an extra indelible life, a sort of amplified existence, from which she could not escape.

Leah lowered her reading glasses, and Harriet stood there, her arms suddenly too long, and said, "I read a horrible story last night. I can't get it out of my mind."

And then came a big knock on the front door.

She went to open the door and saw Jack in front of her, and the mail off to the right. "Jack," she said, avoiding his eyes and reaching across to the mailbox on the side of the porch.

He grabbed her hand. He held it and fished out the letters for her. His face was inches from hers.

"You've come to see Leah."

"I've come to rescue you," he said.

For the next hour Jack took Leah off her hands. Kenny was especially glad to see him, since Kenny liked a man who liked to talk. Harriet was free to lean against the counter and watch. Jack, no less than Leah, she thought, liked to have an effect on people. His effect on her, at the moment, was not unpleasant. *Dear Pauline*, she would write in her notebook, thinking about the insidious nature of attraction, *Who are the most memorable lovers, and why? The ones we're ashamed of, that's who and that's why. The ones we're angry at ourselves for liking. The ones who excite our resistance, which breaks down over time. The stronger the resistance, the more complete the breakdown and the more memorable the affair. Think of screen lovers. I do. Cary Grant and Ingrid Bergman in* Notorious. *Burt Lancaster and Gina Lollobrigida in* Trapeze. *Humphrey Bogart and Ingrid in* Casablanca. *Colin Firth and Jennifer Ehle in* Pride and Prejudice. *Now why are they memorable? Because the woman gets under the man's skin. She puts him off balance and makes him angry: angry to find himself attracted to someone he'd dismissed.*

Jack Frame puts me off balance.

———————◉———————

That night Leah discovered the martinis in the freezer (five parts gin to one part vermouth, mixed ahead by Lew and kept in an old whisky bottle). She replenished her glass, then set it down hard on the living-room floor beside her chair.

"That's what I can't forgive Lionel for," she said to Harriet. "What was he doing all that time?"

She meant those final years when she cooked his meals and wiped his bottom, secure in the knowledge that he was writing his memoirs and praising her to the skies. But after his death there was nothing in his study except blank paper, cans of tobacco, piles of cheap paperbacks.

So she would write the memoir. She would write something important, something lasting. Unlike Lionel, whose books were out of print, every single one of them. With sudden fury, she said to her niece, "Don't let anybody tell you what to write about."

Harriet looked at her in bewilderment.

"I mean it. I really don't care if you write about me. Oh, I might for a bit. But so what? The important thing is to write. Do you know what it's like, finding nothing but blank paper when you're expecting a book?"

"Well," said Harriet with a deep and sympathetic sigh, "I don't always see the point of writing either."

"THEN DON'T!" The panther pushed herself out of her chair and stalked into the kitchen. Yanked open the freezer-compartment door. Refilled her glass once again. Then went to the window and stared out at the ghastly night.

Nothing was visible through the dark kitchen window, but you could hear the rain, like spittle, falling and sticking to itself, becoming more and more engorged, until by morning mosquito-sized raindrops would have bloated up into glass balls.

Harriet went upstairs to listen to Lew read Frank McCourt aloud to the kids. First, his "On the Town" piece about his landlady named Klein, who wasn't Jewish, and then another chapter of *Angela's Ashes*. She sat on the hallway floor, her back against the linen cupboard door, while Lew sat in the doorway of Jane's bedroom, doing the accents, and the kids chortled and guffawed in their beds about "sore arses" and "speakeasies." Then Harriet took herself back down to Leah and found her weeping in her dressing gown, a kimono-like affair of patterned blue silk – weeping about her long, sad years without sex. After his first minor heart attack, when he was still in his sixties and she in her forties, and they had been married less than ten years, Lionel gave it up. "You

know what Anglo-Saxon men are like," she said. But couldn't you have
had an affair? asked Harriet. And Leah cried out that she couldn't have
done that to him. "It would have killed him." But did he have to know? I
mean, it's not as if *he* didn't have plenty of women.

But she wasn't meant to question these confessions, or let on that
she'd heard them already, years ago, in another kitchen, martinis in the
glass, alas.

Harriet led her aunt to bed. Then upstairs, reading the fifty pages
that her aunt had entitled *The Way We Were* (while Lew slept peacefully
beside her), she thought of the hold Hollywood has on all of our minds,
even on tough Leah's, so that everything, finally, is a cliché. Her pages,
peppered with name-dropping, laced with bitterness, larded with
wishful thinking, were a cliché: good woman rescues hounded genius,
and theirs is a true romance. But it was nothing like that, not really. She
remembered the villa, the garden, the way her aunt used to shower
Lionel with savage compliments. *Listen to him*, she would say whenever
he played the piano. *Is there anything he can't do? It's disgusting!* More
furious than proud, because he did so little. It was Leah who kept them
afloat; Leah who'd had the idea to go to Italy after Lionel was deported
from the U.S., a Canadian citizen, as was she; Leah who'd had the idea
to trade on his friendship with Roberto Rossellini and buy a rundown
villa behind a high stone wall and turn it into the Frame Institute for
Politics and Film, an institute that paid handsomely for many years by
drawing on the bottomless guilt of the North American Left, a pitcher
that never emptied.

Now her aunt was using the phrase *our romance*. "Our romance," she
wrote, "was like something out of Hollywood, right up to the end."

But Harriet had known her to stop in the middle of a crowded sidewalk and cry out, *There have been people who loved me unconditionally. Who
adored me.* And she certainly didn't mean Lionel. Raising her face in wet
appeal, spreading the tears across her cheeks with the side of her hand,
she had wailed over the traffic, *But they're all dead!*

Leah Margaret Frame. Who hadn't spoken a word to Harriet's father
in twenty-seven years, not since they quarrelled about how much money
the family cottage was worth. Who prided herself on being a radical but
wanted to be rich. Who nursed Lionel into his nineties, having seen his
influence wane and his friends fall away even before he died, but especially afterwards. And that was the end of *The Way We Were*.

Harriet reached for her notebook on the floor and wrote, *Dear Pauline, The ability to watch movie stars whenever we want to and for as long as we like – what has this done to our minds? Pickled them. We are pickled in the juicy brine of movie love.*

Sounds came from below. Coughing, muttering, tossing, turning. Leah stewing like sauerkraut. Fermenting. In her crock.

Yes, everyone is writing a book. Leah too. But at the same time I've spent years watching people who want to write avoid writing: Leah too. She's stuck, and now she's come to me. We spring away from the page as if it's a trampoline. Fear, self-pity, laziness – that's the trampoline we bounce upon, while down below, fading from view in a sickening fashion, is the grassy, private paradise of writing.

25

Jealousy

That night Harriet dreamt she was walking with Chevy Chase down a wide sidewalk in Paris. She kissed him and left black lint on his lips. They were going to the Oscars. But when she looked more closely he wasn't wearing a tuxedo, but rather a black and silver vest. She had been wrong about their destination. Lew stirred beside her and she told him her dream, and he responded by telling her his. "I was in Paris too, working on some newsletter or magazine. I was in my twenties. We all were. In the office I had my eye on a woman and hoped we would find ourselves alone. And suddenly we did. I was in bed and she got into bed with me."

"What did she look like?"

"Short. With curly hair and a wide face."

"That sounds like Dinah," she said. "But I'm not worried." Then she wondered why she had bothered to say that, even jokingly.

It was early Wednesday morning, barely light. She turned on the radio beside their bed, thrilled to discover that they still had power, and kept the volume low since no one else seemed to be up. The announcer said another wave of freezing rain was on its way, and went on to report about broken hydro lines and thousands of people without electricity. Lew was lying beside her, eyes closed, but awake. She said, "How old do I look?"

"Your age," he said, without opening his eyes.

When he regained consciousness, she was saying, "Seriously, I want to know. What do you like about the way I look?"

"Let me see." He sat up and turned her face towards him and studied it for a while. "Your eyebrows," he said, and she dissolved in laughter.

Afterwards, stretched out beside each other with a towel covering the wet spot, she said, "I do like a laugh." But then she heard Leah moving about downstairs and moaned aloud.

Lew said, "I like what Groucho said."

"What did Groucho say?"

"Time wounds all heels."

Kenny poured Cheerios recklessly into a bowl and Harriet, standing at the stove, heard them spill from counter to floor like a broken string of pearls. "Kenny," she groaned.

He picked some of them up and said, "In this magazine's top-100 list, *Casablanca* beats out *The Godfather*. Do you approve of that?"

Leah came into the kitchen in her dressing gown and Harriet poured her a cup of coffee. "It depends," she said. "One has a claim on the heart . . . "

Leah took her coffee over to the kitchen table. "Tell me about that friend of yours," she said. "That reporter. Who does she work for?"

"Dinah? She freelances and writes speeches. She used to work for a magazine."

"Magazine writing. That's like being a cigar roller eighty years ago." Leah settled herself into a kitchen chair. "Something written on paper and delivered through the mail? What future has it got?"

Kenny tapped his mom on the shoulder. "You should have an opinion," he said. "You have to have a preference. You can't like them the same. *Casablanca*'s number two. *The Godfather*'s number three."

"What's number one? Not *Citizen Kane*."

"Yeah."

"God."

By now Lew was in the kitchen too. "But *Citizen Kane* stinks," he said, which gave Kenny his Jack Frame foothold.

Standing in the middle of the floor, waving his long hands in the air, he declared, "It was something new. It paved the way for everything else with camera angles and direction. Even if it isn't the best movie ever made, it deserves something. Personally, I would have given it one-hundredth place."

Leah said, "They're wrong about *Casablanca*. *The Godfather* is the better movie."

"You see? Thank you. Now, do you think it's fair that my mother won't let me watch it?"

"I'll rent it." Leah stood up from the table, a dumpy figure wrapped in silk. "We'll watch it together."

Harriet yelped in protest, and Leah said, "Darling, do you mind? I'm out of cigarettes."

The errand runners, dressed in coats and boots, stepped outside at ten in the morning and opened their black umbrellas. Harriet took a scoop of salt from the bag on the porch and scattered it as she and Jane headed down the steps. They were Hansel and Gretel in reverse, since going forward was the challenge, not finding their way home. "Why is frozen rain slipperier than ice?" Harriet asked into the air. "I suppose it's wetter." They could barely stand up. "Listen to it. It doesn't sound like rain. It sounds like church." She meant heavy, meaningful, dank, on their umbrellas.

They stood in the street and looked around at something being made in slow motion – a slow-motion disaster. Nothing could have been simpler.

Or, indeed, more complicated. Twigs were undergoing warm-wax therapy, except it wasn't warm and it wasn't wax. Dipped repeatedly, they were thickly gloved, fatly swollen, mittened with ice. At the same time drops of frozen water hung suspended off their tips – "An old game I liked to play when I was little," Harriet said to Jane, reaching for a twig and pulling it low, "to lift my hand out of the bathwater and watch the water form long glamorous nails on my fingertips." She was struck by the twig's beauty, just as she'd been struck by the beauty of the spear-tip fern. Inside the casing of ice, inside the glass coffin, you could see the dark slender lines of the twig, and almost forget about the ominous weight.

They inched forward, not lifting their feet off the ground, past street signs fringed with foot-long icicles and a stop sign that wore a buckskin jacket of ice. Fine rain was coming down. They stepped over a tree limb and heard road crews in the distance, but here it was quiet, not a car, not another soul in sight. Harriet stopped again and looked around, so relieved to be outside, so glad for the respite from her aunt, that in sudden high spirits she began to hum, and then to sing "Waltzing Matilda." At Seneca Street they saw a woman out with her dog. The woman was standing beside her dog and then she was flat on her back, without having taken a step, and looking around fast to see if anyone had seen her. Harriet inched over to help her up: She was pretty and dark-haired, with a space between her front teeth, red-faced and laughing about having been caught out in her embarrassment.

Then they continued across the street to Mike's Barber Shop with its ice-bloated swirly pole, and Harriet thought of Garbo at fourteen, lathering men's faces and writing in a letter, *I feel as though I've been alive for an eternity*. That thought led to another, less welcome: the horrible story she had read only a couple of nights ago. It was about Garbo, and by some strange coincidence it involved a shawl. Harriet had set the book to one side, thinking, *later*. *A Spanish Shawl for Miss Garbo* the story was called, and it was written in 1938 by one of *The New Yorker's* footloose correspondents, and reprinted in a biography of the actress.

Garbo was in Italy, staying in a villa with Leopold Stokowski, and every day, the story said, fifty or more letters arrived for her. She ordered all of them to be tossed into the furnace without being opened. Sometimes packages arrived. One contained a new brassiere, with the request that she wear it, sign it, and return it to the sender. Then "a package too large to be burned unopened came and was unwrapped for destruction. It contained two Spanish shawls: one in colors – this was rather fine – and a handsome white one." Garbo kept the colorful shawl, the story said, and gave the white one to the housekeeper in lieu of a tip when her visit ended. After she drove away, the housekeeper unfolded the shawl to try it on, and a letter fell out. It was from a Sicilian baronessa who had fallen on hard times, who wrote that her family dated from the fourteenth century, "that they were impoverished but had been able to go see Miss Garbo in a film in which she had exhibited much pity for those in trouble, that she was *una grande artista* and so must also be as compassionate as she was talented," and they asked Miss Garbo to be the purchaser, at such price as her generous soul saw fit, of these two valuable shawls, the last of their worldly possessions. The housekeeper, "thin-lipped, put the white shawl in a new package and in the folds put a note, saying she was returning the white shawl but that Miss Garbo had taken the colored shawl and gone off with it, no one knew where on earth to."

The story stopped me in my tracks when I read it. The baronessa's desperation, the housekeeper's hostility, the whole terrible misunderstanding, if true. If the story was true.

I was reminded of the movie Shoeshine, *in which life conspired to turn two friends against each other, to corrupt them and destroy their friendship, and each other. It was a movie I watched by myself one morning years ago in New York. I started to watch it and could see the external circumstances being set in place – two boys who were best friends unwittingly entered a trap: they were set up, caught, and thrown into a reform school where they eventually betrayed each other. I finished watching it at midday – noon, but dark in the living room, and cool. I was wearing a jacket and felt colder at the end. The ruined friendship and the ruined punishment, and the knowledge that there would be no leniency. Pasquale held the dead Giuseppe, where he had fallen on the rocks, and the future held only more grief, more fruitless punishment.*

I remember that I stopped watching it when I first put it on. Stopped, because I knew that it was only going to get worse, and because I thought the whole thing too predictably sad. It was predictably sad, but the events were far from predictable.

And now this real-life story about Garbo, which was also far from predictable.

When they achieved the corner store, they discovered Dinah, buying all the papers. At their cry of *Dinah, what luck!*, she looked up, and they embraced each other. "So how is the formidable aunt?" she asked them.

"Out of cigarettes," said the errand runners, and Dinah's face relaxed into knowing amusement.

Then they stood to one side and talked for a while. Dinah wanted to know if Leah had always been like that, and Harriet said she used to be worse. People would come to see Lionel and if she didn't want to see them she'd say, *Not you!*, and slam the door in their face.

"And they put up with that?"

"For Lionel. Everybody loved him. I never knew a man so loved – by men and women both. I think Leah couldn't believe how lucky she was to have landed him. But then he got sick and she ended up being a full-time nurse, which is what happens if you marry a guy more than twenty years older than you are. Don't ever do that," she said to Jane.

More customers came in, all of them wanting bags of salt, but none was left, as Dinah could have told them. She had parked in her driveway last night only to discover when she got out of her car that she couldn't stand up, it was so slippery underfoot, and so she drove over here to buy a bag of salt, but all the salt was gone. She ended up scattering cat litter ahead of her as she inched her way up the front walk.

Harriet asked Dinah, "How do *you* deal with difficult people?"

"Directly."

"Directly," replied Harriet, thinking about it.

"I say no a lot."

"You're so much better with people than I am. You're better at love too. You're the one who should be married."

Dinah winced, and Harriet saw how wrong-footed her so-called compliment was. "I'm sorry." She touched Dinah's arm. "I have a big mouth."

"It's all right," said Dinah, summoning up a raspy laugh. "I like your mouth."

She paid for her newspapers, and Harriet for two packs of Craven A Light. "Jack's coming for dinner tonight," Harriet said. "Please come. Bring Ida. Saying no is not allowed."

"Then yes," said Dinah. "I can't speak for mother. She's afraid to go outside. But I'll come."

And it was yes to the next question, too. She felt surprisingly well. Better than she had in months. I know it hasn't gone into remission, she said, but I feel so much better.

Before they parted company, Dinah asked Jane if she and Kenny would come with her to see *Titanic* in the afternoon, a movie of the moment so apt that she was writing about it for the paper. Then, having made Jane's day, Dinah offered them a ride home (she was on her way downtown). But they declined, embarking instead on the treacherous adventure of going home by foot. They were merry, inching forward down the ice-palace laneway, Harriet falling, then Jane, but neither one getting hurt. But at the halfway mark Harriet went silent and morose, and Jane asked, "Why are you afraid of Leah?"

Harriet stopped and looked her daughter in the face.

"You get to this line," Jane gestured with her hand, "and suddenly you're serious."

"You think I'm afraid?"

"I understand you *can* be frightened of her, I just don't understand why you are."

Harriet would have liked to ask Lionel about the story of Garbo and the shawls. He had written his own article about Garbo, one so appreciative and thoughtful that she let him on the set of *Queen Christina*, a particular favor since normally everyone – journalists, screenwriters, producers – all of them were banned. She let him stay for an hour, and when he had a chance to thank her he apologized for the pestering ways of reporters. Laughing, referring to them, she said, "I don't like little birds." He loved to imitate her accent and tone of disdain. *Leetle* birts. Reminiscing late at night in the large, spotless, Italian kitchen, to Harriet and anyone else who was around. With Harriet he talked about writing, candid about his sense of failure. He knew his best screenplays and books were written as a young man, and nothing he'd written later was nearly as good. He knew more about writing, he said, so they should have been better, but they weren't. He also talked politics. The FBI began their file on him in 1943, "when Russia was our ally, don't forget. Strange," he would say, "how hysterical even the most sensible people can get about communism. In its basics it's no different from Christianity."

"Then why not simplify things," Harriet asked him the last time she saw him, "and just be a Christian?"

She didn't expect an answer. She was just trying to point out that communism and Christianity were different kettles of fish and it was silly to pretend otherwise. Lionel took her point. He was always at his most affable with young women who kept Leah company. In his small study, the smallest room in the house, he had a long desk that ran the length of the room. A chair-spin away was an extensive set of shelves full of cubbyholes that Harriet coveted – they came from a post office dismantled long ago. He worked at his desk every morning, joining Leah and the students of all ages for dinner at two, then lecturing about politics and film from four to five, then taking his late-afternoon swim in the pool, where son Jack learned to swim, and others (like Janice Bird, at work on a screenplay about garment workers) sunbathed. After that he settled down to one glass of wine after another. Harriet remembers his amused and gratified smile when Ronald Reagan was elected to the White House. "Who would have guessed that our first fascist president would come out of Hollywood?" In those days he was writing a book about the diaspora of exiles created by all the dictatorships in the Americas: Argentina, Uruguay, Chile, Brazil, Guatemala, the United States. He was tracing the pattern of migration to Cuba and Mexico, Canada, Spain, and Italy. That book and his memoirs were what Leah expected to find after his death, but there wasn't a scrap of paper, not a pencil mark, not even a leetle note.

Leah, looking out the living-room window after lunch, said, "Most disasters are ugly. I'll give it that much."

"Nuclear explosions are beautiful," Harriet said. "At a distance."

"This isn't at a distance."

"Thank God we're not in a tent." Coming to her side. "Thank God we're not birds."

In the quiet house, Leah eyed the plaid armchair in one corner of the room, and said, "Wrong fabric."

"It's the same plaid as Lew's father's dressing gown. He says he sits in that chair and it's like sitting in his daddy's lap."

"You need a solid color."

"I need a good haircut."

"One thing I have, everybody tells me, is good taste." Leah studied her niece. "Get bangs. They'd soften your face."

She had been thinking of getting bangs. Like Meryl Streep. "You think so?"

"It's a shame your hair is so thin."

"It's not thin. It's fine. But there's a lot of it. Every hairdresser says so."

"It's thin."

Harriet kept herself from saying *It's not thin! You want thin? Look in the mirror!* But from now on she would find herself running her hand through her hair and saying that hairdressers said there was a lot of it. They were surprised, but they *all* said the same thing.

"That friend of yours has wonderful hair," Leah said. "You want to be beautiful, you have to have thick hair."

"She is beautiful, isn't she?" Always an eager champion of Dinah's good looks.

Leah shrugged. "Lew thinks so."

"Lew?"

"I've seen the way he looks at her."

And there it was – what had been waiting in the wings all this time.

"How does he look at her?"

"Open your eyes."

Jealousy. She felt it sit down heavily in her lap.

26

Nobody's Perfect

Leah went to her room for a nap and Harriet stayed where she was, on the rose-colored loveseat, thinking about Lew and Dinah, the way Lew looked at Dinah. She tried to picture it, and it wasn't hard. Dinah was the kind of sumptuous, full-bodied woman that he found attractive, she had always known that. It's indisputable, she said to herself. And she recognized what was happening to her: the kind of calmness that occurs after the first shock of bad news. But it wasn't to be trusted, this calmness.

She stood up and went into the kitchen, and turned on the radio. The power was still on, but parts of the city were without, and in the countryside the blackout extended for miles, from farm to farm and town to town, east and west, north and south. It's also indisputable, she thought, that my needy aunt is a born troublemaker. As blind as she is perceptive. But then so am I.

Looking out the window, seeing things getting worse and worse, she thought: Buster Keaton would be happy. The out-of-doors was one big accident holding in its arms many small, old-fashioned accidents: chimney fires, falling trees, kitchen fires, electrocutions. Cattle, in particular, were dying in droves. *Dear Pauline, I was watching him the other night, and he was breaking my heart. I had to turn it off.* Speak Easily, *a talkie I borrowed from the library. He is Professor Post, too frightened of life to live. He saves his money, reads Aristotle, never goes anywhere because he's never invited. Then he receives a huge inheritance and goes out into the world, where Jimmy Durante steals all of his thunder. 1932. He was no longer in control of his pictures, already drinking too much. A talkie, as I say, and you hear his voice. A low, pleasant-lugubrious voice, an old-man voice, as he falls in with Jimmy Durante and doesn't get the jokes. Durante grinning like a maniac and Keaton on the sidelines. And you can see what the studio is up to. They're going to make a star of Durante – he's their new favorite – and they're going to ditch Buster Keaton.*

She started to run water for the dishes, remembering how Keaton was made to look stupid, slow, masochistic, out of it. *You would see what Leah is up to. You would know not to trust her. And yet what she says makes sense. If I were Lew, I'd prefer Dinah too.*

Then Harriet heard the study door open and Leah's footsteps coming towards her, and her heart sank. She turned and said to her aunt, "That was a short nap."

"I only ever need twenty minutes," chirped Leah with the appalling conceit of the energetic.

They were listening to the radio in the kitchen and waiting for the return of the moviegoers. It was nearly four o'clock and it was still Wednesday. "Did Lionel ever meet Buster Keaton?" asked Harriet.

"Buster Keaton was a nobody," she answered.

And Harriet felt her world narrow even more. She felt so pained that she had to look away. "So that's all there is to say about Buster Keaton?"

"Chaplin's the one Lionel knew," said Leah. "Chaplin was the genius."

"I hate Charlie Chaplin." Harriet's voice was hot and emphatic. "Did you see *Limelight*? Keaton was a hundred times better than Chaplin and Chaplin knew it, which is why he left most of Keaton's footage on the floor. Unforgivable. The applause-hogging little jerk."

"Harriet Browning," observed Leah. "The one person in the world who thinks Charlie Chaplin was a jerk. Pardon me. The second person. The other being Joe McCarthy."

"I'm not saying he didn't make some great silent films, or that Keaton didn't make some terrible talkies." She knew she was red in the face, and felt sick with growing dismay. These transitions, she thought, these terrible transitions: from silent to sound, radio to television, typewriter to computer, friendship to love.

Jack Frame, for instance. He couldn't make the transition from talking to writing, no matter how many novels he wrote.

And soon he'd be here too.

But it was lovely Bill Bender who showed up first, and, inspired by the strange weather, he reminisced about the yellowy, balmy, very still atmosphere that stretched past Christmas in 1918 as thousands died from the Spanish flu. He was in Winnipeg then. Four years old. There was a field hospital down the street, and when the horse-drawn ambulances went by, he and his friends covered their noses and mouths with their hands to keep from breathing in the germs.

They had moved into the living room when Bill came over, and now Leah yawned, visibly bored, in her rocking chair.

I don't want to kill the woman, thought Harriet, I just want to dislike her to death. Make that the first line of your story, she instructed her class in her head.

"Bill's writing a book too," Harriet said to her aunt. But Leah was especially uninterested in him if he was writing a book.

"I began to write poetry last night," he said. "By candlelight. Like Pasternak." He shook his head in amusement. "I was inspired by the ice storm."

"Leah?"

Leah rocked back and forth and ignored them both.

Awful, thought Harriet. Her aunt's lack of curiosity was awful.

In bed last night, when she was lying awake and Lew sneezed and then lay awake too, she had murmured to him that Leah talked about people, either to let you know they were treating her the way she wanted *you* to treat her or they weren't; it was so manipulative. And Lew had replied that it wasn't just manipulative, it was the only thing she was interested in. His quiet remark soothed her: he not only agreed with her, he was even more stringent in his estimation of her aunt. He wasn't incapable of being hard, she thought. She couldn't count on that.

"Leah?" Harriet's voice was tired. "Bill knew John Grierson when he was here setting up the National Film Board."

"I knew Grierson," she said. "Norman McLaren was more interesting. He came to us a few times to talk about his thing – making films without a camera, drawing directly onto film." She shrugged. "I never could see it. What's the point?"

"I think I'll write a book without words," Harriet muttered to herself.

"Well, it was cheap," Leah said. "He was one of those Scots. Stingy."

"Frugal," said Harriet, stung. "Ingenious."

"Mean."

"I knew Grierson more in the last years of his life," said Bill Bender. "But he was still sharp, sharp, sharp. Opinionated, opinionated, opinionated. More a talker than a listener. A splendid writer too. Like all those Scots. Well, he got cut down in the Red scare."

"He wasn't a Red," said Leah.

"I'm not saying he was. I'm saying he got cut down in the Red scare."

"What would you say he was?" asked Harriet.

But before he could speak, "A *liberal*," said Leah with contempt. It would always be the ultimate insult. *You liberals.*

Harriet raised her spear and attacked. "They weren't the best screenwriters in the world, you know, the ones who were blacklisted. I've seen some of their movies and they were pretty bad. *Woman of the Year*, for instance. It was awful."

"Ring Lardner, Jr.," said Bill Bender.

"*Thirty Seconds Over Toyko* was even worse."

"Dalton Trumbo," said Bill Bender.

Leah drew air sharply through her teeth, rubbed the fingers of her right hand against her thumb, and said levelly, "Faulkner could write any old shit for the screen, nobody held him accountable. But a radical writes a bad screenplay and he's no good, never was, never will be. Liberals use any excuse to dismiss the Left."

Liberals. And she meant them. Everybody in sight. And she had a point, thought Harriet.

But Bill Bender said, "I've always thought Walt Disney was worse than Joe McCarthy. McCarthy ruined a few lives, but Disney destroyed good taste."

He got up. He'd come over hoping to find Dinah, directed by her mother, who had thought she and the kids might be back from the movies by now. He had an old newspaper clipping about the ice storm of 1942, when streetcars were frozen fast for sixteen days, and he handed it to Harriet to pass on to her.

He missed Dinah by an hour. The moviegoers returned at six o'clock, just as Jack Frame came through the door and Harriet burned the soup. Leah told her to empty it into another pot and add a potato, it absorbs the burnt taste. "Don't stir up the bottom," Leah told her.

Then everyone else descended upon her. Jane starry-eyed and peevish, as she tended to be after seeing a movie; Kenny impressed and eager to talk about the enormous queue (they'd had to step over fallen electrical wires to get to it) and the size of the sinking ship; smart Dinah quick to point out the missed opportunity. *Titanic* should have taken a leaf from *High Noon*, she said, and been made in real time. How long did it take the ship to sink? Two hours? The perfect movie length. They could have focused on a Gary Cooper hero, some courageous man on a ship of fools. Then the suspense would have been real.

"You're talking documentary," said Harriet, looking up from the soup and thinking about Grierson.

Jack Frame, clean-shaven, but still padding about in bare feet, said, "*High Noon* wasn't documentary. The crop-dusting scene in *North by Northwest* wasn't documentary. They were real time."

I know that, thought Harriet.

Leah's fifty pages of memories, single-spaced, stapled together, were on the kitchen table. Jack picked them up and asked Harriet if she'd read them yet, and she said yes, last night, and she liked it best when Leah wrote about food. This comment was more or less truthful, but far from satisfying, she knew. "She's lucky to have you to help her," she said to him. Then, "Would you do something for me? Lew isn't home yet, and we need a fire in the fireplace."

Jack took in her hot, flustered face, and she saw in his glance a flicker of amused condescension. "No problem," he said with a relaxed smile.

Her eyes followed his powerful, pudgy back as he headed into the living room, Leah trailing after him. Then she was alone with Dinah, who pointed at Leah's pages and raised her eyebrows, and Harriet replied in a hard whisper, "It's like fudge filled with gravel."

"Fudge?"

"Filled with gravel. Icky-sweet and hard as nails. Gushing and venomous."

Dinah chuckled. But Harriet's shoulders were tense and she was getting a stiff neck. I'm not going to sleep tonight, she thought. I'm not going to sleep ever again.

Then Dinah said, "Lew is here."

And Harriet told herself to *look*. To watch and see how Lew and Dinah greeted each other. But when he came through the back door she couldn't raise her eyes to his face. Only when he came over to kiss her, having hung his coat on a hook on the wall, having left his boots by the door, having put the bags of food on the counter – only then did she lift her face. He saw her distress and she saw his mildness. "The soup's burnt," she wailed. And he said, "Don't worry. It doesn't matter." And he put his arms around her, and this time she didn't bat him away. They stood there, a tall and bony pair framed by the blue kitchen cupboards at the end of a long and difficult day. Harriet was holding a wooden spoon. Whatever awkwardness she felt, since Dinah was only a few feet away, she made no move to step out of Lew's arms.

Then Kenny came into the kitchen. He tapped his mom on the shoulder. "Mommy, what do you think of Sylvia Plath?"

She turned to him. "She's good. She wrote some very good poetry." Taking a moment from her sorrows to give a serious answer.

And Lew burst out laughing at mother and son. What a pair they were.

Dinah was laughing too, watching them. She caught Lew's eye. Then held his gaze and saw what Harriet didn't see: she saw his face go yearningly sad.

Dinah had trained herself not to look away from anything, not tears, stumbles, acts of love, spasms of hate. A self-described old hack, after all. If this were a map, she thought, the X in the middle would have been that marital embrace. In that moment she'd felt the force of marriage set against her: the neediness of marriage, and its roominess. And she'd caught herself thinking rather bitterly that Harriet would always be looked after. Then Kenny had broken up the twosome with his question, and she'd had a chance to see in Lew's face an overabundance of strong but divided feeling.

The night before (after she had sprinkled the walk with cat litter), she'd taken Buddy outside as far as the curb, her old dog no more inclined than any other sane, living creature to venture any farther. Dogs had their own way of dealing with the ice storm: they would stop eating for a few days, since they couldn't get a grip on the ice in order to relieve themselves. It was eight o'clock. The street was empty of people and strewn with branches and twigs, and it occurred to her that it was dangerous to be standing under a tree, but she remained where she was, for here came Lew. He was on his way back from taking Buster outside so that Fiona wouldn't have to.

Under their umbrellas, under the streetlight, they weren't exactly fugitives, she thought, just two people who didn't know what to do, how to proceed. Then, because Buddy was miserable, she turned to go in and Lew came with her. He took her arm and helped her get to the steps, then up to the relative safety of the porch. They stood there, even after he said he should be getting back, the kids were waiting for him to read to them. What book? she asked. And when he told her, she said, "*Angela's Ashes*! But it's heart-wrenching." They love it, he said. "Do you skip the sad parts?" No. He shook his head. He read them every page.

"I'm in love with your kids," she said. "In fact, I'm in love with all four of you." And her raspy, throaty laugh travelled up and down the street, for all the world like a piece of sandpaper that's found its mate. She said, "There aren't enough Lew Golds to go around, that's the trouble. Don't you have a brother you could lend me?"

Lew looked down at her, his eyes too serious, and she was about to say so, when a tree limb came down. It landed fifteen feet away, on the hydro wire, which gave under it but didn't break. They stepped to the edge of her porch and watched: nobody's lights went out.

Only recently she'd heard the most appalling story about a dying woman's selfishness. It had been on her mind ever since, this case of a relatively young woman with terminal cancer who decided to get pregnant because she wanted to experience childbirth before she died: the woman found a sperm donor, got pregnant, gave birth, and two months later she was dead; now her sister was looking after the baby, and would be picking up pieces for the next twenty years.

She touched Lew's shoulder and said she was going in, and so should he. He nodded. Then brought her towards him and gave her forehead a kiss.

She remained where she was after he left, watching his progress down the icy street, until she saw that he was safely home. Then she went inside herself, only to learn from Ida that Jack Frame had called.

That night Kenny was reading his bible as they waited for dinner. "What's *Fantasia* about?" he asked Jane, who answered, "It's a bore. It's incredibly boring. And it's made for children, right? But all children I know think it's a bore." She was having cocoa, hold the milk: chocolate paste eaten out of a bowl, despite what her mother said about spoiling her dinner.

Lew was filling a tray with dishes, Harriet was getting out the utensils.

"And *Bambi* is disgusting," said Jane. "All that cuteness makes me want to hurl."

Then they moved into the living room, joining the others who were around the smoking fireplace. From the loveseat Dinah offered Campfire Jack bantering advice.

Leah said, "When I was a girl we played a game we called movie stars. I was always Norma Shearer, I don't know why, and my friend Effie was Jean Harlow."

"Effie Wineburg?" asked Jack.

"Effie Stone. I haven't heard from either of them in years. But I know why." And she reached for the reason as automatically as you reach for sunglasses on a bright day. "I was held up as a model, and they were jealous."

"A model for what?" asked Dinah.

They balanced bowls and plates in their laps, an awkward business, but the fire was coming to life now that Lew had taken over, and it would be soothing if not especially warm in the old-fashioned hearth that Lew wouldn't change: his dad had watched *his* dad set the stones in place. In a room little different, then, from the way it had always been, Leah was in the rocker, Jack settled himself on the loveseat beside Dinah, Kenny was on the floor and Jane on the sofa, and Harriet sat apart in the plaid armchair. Jack Frame had a way of claiming a woman, thought Harriet, watching him put his arm around the back of the loveseat, grazing Dinah's shoulder with his hand.

"A model for what?" Dinah repeated.

"Loyalty," Leah said from the rocker. "That's what I have to offer, all my friends tell me. Since I was five years old I've judged people by their capacity for loyalty. Well, people who share the same moral attitudes. With them you should be loyal."

Everyone chewed on this in silence. Later, in her study, Harriet would write, *What she really has to offer you is* your *loyalty. Your reward for putting up with her is a sense of your own loyalty.* And she remembered a night of Scrabble in that complicated garden – detesting a game that made her feel stupid, and listening to Leah illustrate her everlasting point by telling the story of Reva, whose brother in England offered to send money to Germany in 1939, enough so their mother could escape, but not their stepfather, whom he hated. The mother wouldn't leave her husband behind, and so they both perished in Auschwitz. "Now that's loyalty," Leah had said.

Dinah was saying, "People with a taste for power are always singing the praises of loyalty. Politicians. School principals. They're crazy about loyalty."

"Are you saying I'm power-hungry?"

"Of course you're power-hungry."

"Harriet, did you hear that? Did you hear what she said?" The formidable aunt was outraged and amused, released, somehow, from her ill humor by Dinah's bluntness. She lit a cigarette and went to stand by the fireplace. In the silence they heard the crack of a tree limb, and more rain, and Harriet was able to concentrate on looking at Dinah and Lew. She saw Dinah taken up with Jack, and Lew still attending to the fire. Nothing of note. But then Jack looked at *her*. That is, he caught her staring at him. And confused, she looked away.

The other day, when he dropped by, saying he'd come to rescue her, she listened as he and Leah talked at the kitchen table, tussling over the book, each of them explaining what they had done so far, what they would do next. And something she'd read about Marlon Brando and Anna Magnani came back to her, something that Sophia Loren had said. "It will be a battle," said Sophia. "And Marlon will win. Because he'll stay relaxed."

Unquestionably, Jack was successful with women. Wooing with roses and grapefruits and a kind of protective presence that seemed to defy the world and to thrive on a certain kind of woman. She thought of Lew's Uncle Milt, the bridge player, who said, "Show me a woman in need, and I'm lost."

Her eyes moved to Dinah now, and, as she looked, Dinah's glance shifted to Lew, who was wrestling two logs into a better position and unaware that he was being watched, unaware that Dinah's face softened when she looked at him, visibly softened. *And Pauline, do you know how I felt? This came as a great surprise. Less jealous than proud. Wifely. Possessive. Not a feeling I've had very often, not a feeling I approve of. But I've noticed before how suggestible I am in real life. Only with movie stars do I go my own way, adamant and loyal to the end.*

She turned to Leah, "The potato worked."

"Onion."

"You said potato."

"I said onion."

"*I* say onion," said Lew. Grimacing, he held up his burned fingers. A slice of onion was the best thing to put on a burn, he'd learned that in Peru. And he went into the kitchen to tend to his hand.

Not Harriet, not Dinah, but Jane followed him, offering to help. Jane, who had once joined a conversation Dinah and Harriet were having about handsome men by saying that her father was the handsomest man she knew. Dinah had touched her arm. "Good for you." Then Jane had added, "I knew before I was born that my father was handsome." Her mother had looked at her earnestly, overwhelmed by her daughter's intuitive ease about matters of the heart, and said, "You're way ahead of me. In every respect."

It was Kenny who suggested they watch a movie, and Jack Frame who said it would have to be something that everybody would want to see, and Leah who interjected, "Not Charlie Chaplin then. Harriet hates Charlie Chaplin."

Kenny swung on his mom. "But you said *Modern Times* was great. You said *The Gold Rush* was one of the best movies ever made."

"I like Buster Keaton more, that's all," came the dogged answer.

"But Mommy, you can't say Charlie Chaplin was no good. You can't say that."

She reached out and took his hand. Kenny was standing beside her armchair, and she took his hand and held it. "All right. I won't say it."

"How about *Some Like it Hot*?" suggested Dinah, and a thrilled Kenny was halfway across the room when the formidable aunt said she couldn't understand why everybody thought that film was so funny.

"Don't you like Jack Lemmon?" Kenny asked her, standing in the middle of the room and trying to hold back the waves of criticism. But Leah made a face and rolled her eyes.

Dinah came to Kenny's rescue. "Jack Lemmon was brilliant," she said, and Kenny revived.

"He was a much better woman than a man," he stated confidently. And Dinah agreed. "So let's watch it," he said, springing towards the VCR.

Leah sucked air through her teeth, making that window-cleaning squeak of dismissive contempt. "It's all right with me. I'm just saying it's supposed to be roll-in-the-aisles funny, and it's not."

"My negative stepmother," said Jack, with a half-smile for the room in general and Dinah in particular.

"I'm honest. There's a difference. I mean Marilyn Monroe isn't exactly Meryl Streep."

And that's when Jack said with quiet passion, "I hate Meryl Streep."

A patient man, thought Harriet. He had set up this punchline three weeks ago. She stared at him. She wouldn't ask why. But Kenny was there. Kenny asked why.

"Because she never looks you in the eye," he said, gazing steadily at Harriet. "She always looks off to the side or down at the ground. She never looks you in the eye."

What jolly arrows, these little zings of hostility that go through the air. She felt a small, foolish smile form on her face. Too stricken by the sudden attack, too skewered to respond. She turned away, but was aware of Jack reaching for a magazine on the coffee table and thumbing through it.

"Is Jack Lemmon still alive?" Jane wanted to know. She had come back into the living room.

"Just barely," said Harriet.

"He's more alive than Tony Curtis," said Kenny. "What happened to him, anyway? He got a huge belly, he lost all his hair, and he marries twenty-year-olds. It's disgusting."

Jane said, "He got older and he didn't want to."

Then they were quiet for a while. Kenny started the movie. Harriet turned off lights, and for the first time in days she felt herself relax. At least, she felt that relaxing might be possible, if all the mouths in the room would only stay shut.

But at the first close-up of Tony Curtis, Leah grouched, "See? Mr. Pretty Face."

Then Dinah – *Dinah!* – said, "You're right. He doesn't have his heart in it, does he?"

And that's when Harriet snapped.

She would have plenty of opportunity to think about why later. At the time it simply struck her as unendurable that one of her favorite movies was being ruined by her dearest friend, who wasn't perhaps her dearest friend, after all.

"Be quiet!" she told Dinah. "I can't hear a thing. *I can't hear.*"

In the kitchen, Lew slowly dried his hands. Then came to see what the trouble was about.

"I'm not allowed an opinion?" Dinah was saying with plaintive good humor. "I'm not allowed to say he's just going through the motions?"

"You're spoiling the movie!"

The big vein was throbbing in the middle of Harriet's forehead. Lew recognized the sign. Just as small Harriet used to recognize in her father's trembling lower lip a sure sign of danger, and would go quiet.

Jack was also gripped by Harriet's face. There it was again: that fierce, pugilistic look.

"Whoa," he said gently. "Take it easy."

Harriet stood up and looked him in the eye: the man who hated Meryl Streep. "*I can't hear. I can't hear a fucking thing.*"

"*Pardon us,*" said Leah. "But you're the one who's talking."

By then, however, Harriet had swept out into the hallway and around the newel post and was going *thump thump thump* up the stairs.

Leah said loudly enough for it to carry: "*Menopause.*"

And Lew protested in a tired voice. "Leah, have a heart."

"*Have a heart? Have a heart?* I'm *all* heart."

Upstairs, in the light of the bedside lamp, Harriet lay on her back, hands folded across her chest, ankles touching, soul aghast. To fall out with Dinah, not over Lew but over a movie. To lose Lew to Dinah and Dinah to a movie.

Menopause.

There should be a fifth season, she thought, a name for the freezing rain that breaks up winter and destroys it. The *leah*. Spring, summer, winter, fall, leah. What's it doing outside? someone would ask. And the answer would come: leah came last night, you can smell it in the air.

Then the tide in her mind went out and stayed out. The rain came down. It fell on a marooned house in a marooned city, and there wasn't any end in sight. After a while, Lew came up to check on her.

"Hattie?" And he sat beside her and took her woeful hand.

With this gesture of affection her memory came back, and she thought gratefully of other times when her feelings had hit a dead end, only to find an exit through some gentle thing he did or said.

"I feel so bad for Buster Keaton," she said, and she meant every word. "He ended up in those beach-blanket movies. With Annette Funicello and Frankie Avalon. *How to Stuff a Wild Bikini. Pajama Party.* He was Chief Rotten Eagle." In the back of her mind she was also thinking about Garbo and the shawls, and the contradictions in the story.

Why did the housekeeper write to the baronessa saying that Garbo had gone who-knows-where, when she would have known exactly where she had gone, and could have conveyed the baronessa's letter to her? It was a story written to make Garbo look as bad as possible. A set-up, she thought. Another set-up.

She squeezed Lew's hand, then let it go. "Why is she here?" she asked him. "Why did she come?"

He shrugged. "She wants to be loved," he said.

Harriet gave him a deadly look. "For one second – just one – will you stop being so understanding?"

"We're probably the last people on earth she's still talking to."

She groaned and closed her eyes, and remembered Leah's wail: *I have been loved unconditionally. My aunt loved me more than anyone else in the world!* And it was only now, as the memory flooded back, that Harriet knew what response might have placated her: *Lionel loves you very much. I know that. Everybody knows it.* But what was the matter with conditional love, anyway?

"She won't be here much longer," said Lew.

His voice sounded weary and distant, and it struck her now that he *was* different. Not in the way he'd looked at Dinah, but in the way he *hadn't* looked. He'd avoided her – avoided them all – the whole night, fussing with the fire, retiring to the kitchen to do the dishes.

"How do you know?" she said. "Anyway, it's not just that."

"What else?"

She couldn't find the words to say what else. Couldn't bring herself to utter the question. Couldn't imagine what she'd do if he said, yes, Leah's right. So she shook her head and looked away.

He said. "I'll take her to work tomorrow and give her something to do. You'll feel better as soon as you have some time to yourself."

"It's too dangerous outside. She'll fall and break her hip. She's killing me," Harriet said. "She's come here to kill me."

"Come on, Hattie. We're her family."

"We're fresh blood," said Harriet.

Downstairs, Leah was implacable. "See what I mean?" Referring to Society Sue and Beanstalk. "Tinny acting." And when Joe E. Brown came on the scene, "Too bad he's not half as amusing as he thinks he is."

She was like Mussolini watching a train arrive late. And then she was asleep. She slept through the last half of the movie and the others were able to watch it in peace.

Dinah said, "That's the best ending in movies."

"'Nobody's perfect,'" Kenny repeated with gusto.

Jack stretched and stood up. He said, "Diamond and Wilder threw in that line at the last minute. They didn't even think it was funny. But that's how brilliance works. You're only brilliant when you're not trying to be brilliant."

"It's so funny because it's so simple," said Dinah. "The movie is one complication after another, one disguise after another, and then the final line says, I'll take you any way you come."

"Timing is everything," said Jack.

"Not timing." Dinah was irritated. Men always said timing was everything. "Surprise. The last line is a complete surprise. It's simple and it's surprising."

Upstairs, Lew had made the mistake of smiling a peaceable, almost begging smile, and the gap between them widened. That smile. She was married to a kind man, but did she want to be? No. She wanted a thug who would go downstairs, grab everybody by the scruff of the neck, and throw them out into the night. Where was Humphrey Bogart when she needed him? Where was Sir Sean?

"What can I do?" asked Lew.

"You can leave me *alone*."

"All right."

He stood up. He'd had enough.

Dear Pauline, Here is my favorite fantasy. Guests have come for dinner. We are talking in the kitchen, or on the verandah, or in the living room, depending upon the weather, and one of the guests insults me. Then evenly, without rudeness, I say, "There's a very nice restaurant down the street. Why don't you try it out?"

The insulter laughs. Coarsely. Like a horse.

"I mean it." And I am very calm. "I don't make food for people who insult me."

Sometimes, if it's winter, I hand him his coat. Then he realizes that he is going to have to leave. He is going to have to go to bed without his supper.

He leaves.

And because my little performance, necessary but unfortunate, has ruined everybody's appetite, they leave too. And I get an old movie, Charade, *say, and watch it.*

She heard Lew in the hallway downstairs, getting their coats, saying goodbye. And she stayed put. Ankles crossed, hands folded across her chest, lighthouse eyes searching for more disaster. She heard Dinah's husky laugh heading out the front door, and felt sick to think that the friendship might be over.

Then the footsteps of a meaty man ascended the stairs. There was a tentative knock on the door, and Rod Steiger poked his head into her room.

He looked at her with a certain, all-too-familiar smile. It was her older brother's smile when he wanted to make up for having driven her in tears from the dining-room table. Almost chagrined, surprisingly tender. And she resisted her old susceptibility to these smart, hard, sardonic boy-men who, in the movies, are capable of all-out love, but in real life are infuriating, hurtful, not to be trusted.

He said, "I just wanted to say that nobody's perfect."

And in spite of herself, she had to laugh.

27

Under the Tree

The second big wave of freezing rain came that night. Wednesday night. Kenny lay listening to it. He liked the cracking, sighing, bumping sounds, since they were clearly going on outside. He liked having visitors too. Leah disagreed with him about movies, but that didn't matter; she had opinions. He could ask a question and she didn't say, Ask me another question. Or, That's a terrible question. Or, Kenny, when will you learn to ask questions that people want to answer? Or, Kenny, if you don't stop asking me that question I'm going to kill myself.

He slept with his blue plastic flashlight under his pillow, in case the power went out.

Harriet and Lew were lying side by side. "Is self-righteousness one of the seven deadlies?" she asked into the darkness.

"The seven deadlies?"

"It's come to this," she muttered. "A Puritan in bed with a Jew. Gluttony, lust, envy, anger, avarice, pride. Maybe that's what they call self-righteousness. Pride. What is the other one?"

Lew fell asleep.

Sloth, she thought. Then she was teaching in her head, a much better teacher there than in front of a class. "I can only write in the first person," she confessed to her students. "It's like putting on a pair of old slippers. They're comfortable, but you can't *go* anywhere in them."

A big hurt was pushing against her, and had been for hours. She gave herself up to it now. She allowed the hurt to fill her to the brim, then felt herself sink heavily until she hit bottom, and stayed there. Then after a time – and it was like a miracle – something moved off her heart and she felt herself rise, not into the arms of Jesus but into a joke. In her mind she was phoning Dinah. "Hi, this is Tony Curtis's mother. This is the president of the Tony Curtis Fan Club." A new tide came in and lifted the barnacled weight off her chest; a tide of humor – of splashy comediennes – washed over her.

She didn't want to be left alone at all, she wanted to be funny. To tear open her chest with both hands and let her funniness pour out. She would do anything, she realized, to make things all right again with Dinah, and Lew, and herself.

So much of the time, she thought, we're either at our best or at our worst, either concerned or vicious, funny or humorless. Unjoined somehow. *Then come moments when the parts of one's personality connect, when you hold them all in your mind at the same time. When instead of going from room to room in your personality, you're a summer house full of screen doors. You remember the range and array of your feelings and don't censor them, either from self-interest or shame.*

She lay there, saying these thoughts to Pauline, awash with the fullness of life, and she expected that she would slide easily into sleep. But she didn't.

At one in the morning she was shaking the formidable aunt awake. She had figured out something else, and Leah – who had tried to destroy her peace of mind – was going to have to listen. "You're wrong," she said. It was cold in the house – they always turned down the heat for sleeping – and she was in her dressing gown. Leah, sitting up, was in a thin nightie. "It's snobbery and I hate it," said Harriet. "Snobbery that keeps people from appreciating a genius just because he isn't ingratiating."

"Can't you save this till morning?" Leah's reaction was surprisingly mild, all things considered, but she wasn't used to Harriet on the attack.

"I can't." And Harriet, having turned on the light, was fully visible as possessed.

She handed Leah her kimono, led her into the living room, put *Limelight* into the VCR, and made her aunt watch. "Chaplin cut out Keaton," she said. "Jerry Lewis did the same thing to Dean Martin. He couldn't forgive him for being funnier than he was."

Leah said, "These old movies are like Latin. Dead."

Harriet pressed fast-forward. "Chaplin played the Tramp, that's why he was the darling of the left. Keaton played rich saps. But Keaton died poor and Chaplin died rich."

"So?"

"Chaplin knew how to suck up to an audience, he was always trying to ingratiate himself, always begging for admiration."

"You said that."

"It can't be said enough. Look." She had found the brilliant few seconds when Keaton as the nearsighted professor spills sheets of music onto the floor. Then the camera cuts to Chaplin and stays for an eternity on his outrageous, egotistical mugging. "See?" She stopped the tape and pressed rewind, returning to the spot where the two of them are in the dressing room, then played the scene again. "It's a tragedy – the waste of Keaton's talent. They wouldn't let him make his own movies full of all those ingenious mishaps and escapes because crummy movies made more money. So he became an alcoholic, and Chaplin could have rescued him, he could have helped him stage a comeback, but he hogged the camera instead. It breaks my heart."

"Don't take it so hard, for Pete's sake."

"Why not? Why shouldn't I take it so hard?"

"Go to bed, Hattie."

She went to bed. And there, thinking about the master of switches and turns who couldn't make the switch to talkies, she recalled reading something in the paper years ago, something that held her, something she'd never forgotten: an actress who couldn't make the transition from silent screen to talkies fell into a depression that coincided with the country's, and died of a drug overdose. Jeanne Eagels. Somebody was writing a play about her, the paper said. But a play had never materialized, so far as she knew.

She turned on the bedside lamp, and Lew opened his eyes. "I'm just going to read for a bit," she said. He stroked her arm and turned over, and was asleep again.

She read about a white lilac so heavy with blossom it snapped under the weight of a sudden snowfall, and a child who ate an orange and drank a glass of milk before going to bed, and died in the night. Innocence and experience, she thought sleepily. Innocence and the terrible shock of experience.

At that moment there was a great CRACK, followed by the sound of a drawer being opened. That would be how she would describe it in the morning. *It sounded like a big drawer being opened in the next room.* Then a thud and more cracking. She went to the window but couldn't see past the darkness.

Lew was sound asleep, but Leah was moving about downstairs, so she must have heard it too. Then it was quiet again, outside and inside.

Leah's bed was the pull-out sofa in Lew's study, even though she had made it plain to Harriet that she should have been given their room upstairs. "Strangers are kinder than relatives," she had said as Harriet made up the bed the first night. "My seatmate on the plane offered me a room in her house any time I needed it, and I'd never met her before!"

That's why, thought Harriet.

"When your parents visit," Leah demanded to know, "where do they sleep?"

"Here."

"You should give them your bed."

"At Christmas I gave dad our bed because he had the flu." An observation she knew would rankle – the despised brother, sick abed and being catered to by his daughter, since Gladys had gone to Owen's for the week. She didn't say it was a blessing to have her father out of the way, especially when she pulled the turkey out of the oven: her father was a master carver, but to carve well you need a turkey that offers some resistance, and this one had been so overcooked she could have reached in and pulled out the rib cage, slick as a whistle. She'd let the bird rest on the counter and had taken her father a bowl of broth. While he spooned it down she studied the fringe of dead skin on his dry upper lip. Davy Crockett lips, she thought.

"Dad," she said, "you've got to drink water."

"No damn water," he said.

Downstairs, they were eight around the Christmas table: the four of them plus Dinah and her mother, Ida, and Fiona Chester and Bill Bender. A reasonable number. Plenty of turkey for everyone, and no competition for the pope's nose. Harriet put it on her plate and said to her cholesterol, This is for you.

She could remember the shade of Dinah's red lipstick and its rapid shift to her wineglass as she had regaled them with stories about elopements and early deaths. In 1938, Dinah said, Stan Laurel eloped with a Russian dancer named Ivanova Shuvalovna, but his wife discovered where they were hiding and stood in the corridor and pounded on the hotel-room door.

"Ivanova Shuvalovna," crowed Kenny. "Ivanova Shuvalovna!" And his head nearly hit the table he laughed so hard.

Dinah said she had also read – "And this is serious, don't laugh" – that Jeanette MacDonald sang "The Indian Love Call" at Jean Harlow's funeral. "She was only twenty-six."

"Jeanette MacDonald?"

"Jean Harlow when she died. She was the daughter of a dentist."

"I'm the daughter of a dentist!"

All eyes turned to Harriet. She looked up at the ceiling. "Up there," she said. "In bed. A dentist."

It was during the headiness of Christmas dinner (the kind of overexcited atmosphere that would have prompted her father to say, There are going to be tears) that Bill Bender had confessed to his boyhood crush on Joan Crawford. He had been crazy about her, he said. "Her mouth was so sexy."

"She was good in *Grand Hotel*," piped up Kenny. "She was better than Garbo. Garbo was terrible."

"Garbo was splendid. I told your mother I saw her once in New York, walking in the rain."

"Yes. But tell me again."

And so he'd told her again. It happened on a day in October, when the rain was light but steady, and didn't let up till evening. This was in 1965, a month before the great blackout. She was in Central Park, he said, and you could tell she was a walker, the way she strode along in flat shoes. "I followed her out of the park at 59th Street and over to Second Avenue and 53rd, where she went into a greengrocer's on the corner, and I went in too."

Dinah said, "But that was where *I* saw her. At 53rd and Second."

"Did you speak to her?"

"I wish I had."

"I didn't either. But somebody else did and she put her finger to her lips."

"There's an awful story about her mouth," Harriet said. "Ingmar Bergman was very mean about her mouth."

"Ingrid Bergman?" Fiona Chester was fiddling with her hearing aids.

"Ingmar."

"Ingrid Bergman had a beautiful mouth," said Fiona.

"Did you follow her home?" Harriet asked Bill Bender.

"To 450 East 52nd Street. The very end of a dead-end street, so there was nothing to block her view of the East River. Her building wasn't like any of the others on the block. It was tall, narrow, secluded-looking. Like a stone-and-brick chateau, but simpler. The perfect spot for her, I thought. She lived on the fifth floor."

"Is that all?" asked Jane.

"That's all. Except that before she went into her building, she took off her hat and gave it a good shake." His voice turned wistful. "She was such a loner. I've always had a special feeling for her."

Harriet had intended to tell the story about Garbo's mouth, but got sidetracked by the pudding, which had to be flamed. This involved three simple steps. She poured brandy into a saucepan and heated it up, added a spoonful of sugar and let it dissolve in the hot liquor, then poured the liquor over the pudding while Lew struck a match and set it alight. The same lovely running blue as a pilot light. "I read a memoir," she said as she served the pudding, "in which the author recalled asking his mother on his tenth birthday to make his cake out of nothing but frosting. And you know something?" She was spooning hard sauce minus pudding onto Kenny's plate. "She did."

"Now that's something I wish," said Bill Bender. "I wish I'd been less rigid with my sons."

"I didn't know you had sons."

"I'm the father of two boys. Men." He spread his hands beside his plate.

"What else do you wish?" Harriet had addressed the table at large, and these were the answers that came back. Jane said she wished she was living in New York City, though any big city would be better than Ottawa. Kenny said he wished he could see *The Godfather* and *The Godfather, Part II*, one after the other. Lew said he wished he was living in the tropics and eating papaya every morning for breakfast. Fiona Chester said she had no wish, none whatsoever, to be alive for the millennium. Ida asked if these wishes had to be about the future or if they could be forsaken dreams from the past, and when she was told forsaken dreams were also allowed, she said she wished she had gone to medical school, but there wasn't the money. Dinah said she wished she had never moved back to Ottawa, and having moved back she wished she had never bought a house, and having bought a house she wished she had sold it before the market went down. Her cigarette-roughened laugh filled the room, and then the fit of coughing that drove her to the sofa. Harriet had joined her, lying on the carpet, her breast still tender from the biopsy, her thoughts clouded with worry. She said to Dinah, "If I've made a mistake in my life, it's holding back. Not flinging myself head-long into things. I wish I'd been less timid."

Dinah had said, a foot or two above Harriet's head, "If you ask me, recklessness isn't all it's cracked up to be."

Upstairs, old Martin had lain with his eyes closed. Harriet went up to him with a cup of tea. "What's it doing outside?" he'd wanted to know.

"Snowing again, I'm afraid."

He turned to the window for a second, like Scott of the Antarctic opening the tent flaps on a blizzard: utter disgust and self-pity. "How in blazes am I going to get home?"

"Weather changes fast," she said. "More to the point," helping him sit up and handing him his tea, "what am I going to do about Leah when she comes?"

His face had softened then, and, uncharacteristically, he had taken her hand, her fingertips really, with his fingertips, which were very warm. "You'll survive," he'd said with a sigh. "I survived her and so will you."

"At least give me another pillow," Leah had commanded the Tuesday night she arrived. Harriet located another pillow, and the next morning she found it on the floor, where she would find it every morning.

Before dawn, Harriet stole downstairs like a Huron avoiding the Iroquois and turned on the gas under the espresso pot made ready the night before. *Did you know that as she neared fifty, and for some years after-wards, Garbo would hide the lower part of her face from photographers, using a newspaper or purse to cover her wrinkled upper lip? The upper lip, more than any other place, she considered to be the site of aging. In this she was perfectly right, as the following incident bears out. On one of her visits to Sweden she met Ingmar Bergman. She sat down in his half-lit office, removed her sunglasses, and said, "This is what I look like, Mr. Bergman." He was astonished to see how beautiful she still was, going so far as to write later that her beauty was "imperishable." For a while they walked together around his studio, talking, meeting people. She was relaxed and happy, encouraged to think that she might work again in film. But when they returned to his office and she leaned forward into the light thrown by his desk lamp, he saw her mouth. In his autobiography he would describe it as "ugly, a pale slit surrounded by transverse wrinkles" that no plastic surgeon or makeup man could ever conjure away. He wrote that she read his thoughts at once, and "grew silent, bored." Moments later she left. She would have been fifty-seven.*

I have no patience with him. Disguising his cruelty as honesty, using the word "bored" instead of "hurt," stripping everyone bare, except himself.

Like a Huron, she carried her coffee through the sleeping house and up to her room on the second floor, where she stood looking out at the southeastern sky as it began to lighten. It was Thursday and she hadn't slept, not really, not well, since Sunday. It felt – going without sleep for so long – like standing on a dark highway and being side-swiped by cars. She and time were being reconstructed. Night and day no longer governed her, because new pockets of time were being hollowed out of her, as if she were a Henry Moore sculpture – beautiful and horrible.

Two great branches torn off the maple lay below, one on either side of the fence on the left. She waited for signs of life. But not a bird, a cat, a squirrel – not a thing moved.

Then she went to the northwest window and the world dropped away, and so did her heart. She was staring out at black, gaping space. The old oak, the dead and dying oak, lay on the flattened garage and in the broken arms of smaller cedars and spruce, and on the lawn.

Then she saw something else. Sticking out from beneath the mattress of crazy branches was something sizable and red. She went downstairs to get the binoculars, and returned.

Ammil was the word she found for freezing rain in a book about the atmosphere, from the old English for *enamel*. Fine rain that turns to ice as it falls and collects so gradually that an ordinary tree might carry five tons of the stuff before it snaps. A twig might bear a weight 130 times itself. How much weight must have accumulated, then, for the branches to come down on Bill Bender's head. He was standing and then he wasn't. And now his lower legs were visible but the upper part of him was not.

She went downstairs and outside, and not quickly either. Moved by horror and a kind of tickling curiosity as she put on her coat and found her hands were clumsy, then her boots, and went out the front door and up his walk – scattering salt ahead of her – and around to the back, drawn by the sight of those red sneakers.

How pitiful his legs were. How thoughtful of the tree to hide his face. Not a sound issued from the rack of branches that sprouted from his torso. Or trunk, she thought.

The oldest oak tree in Ottawa.

He must have come outside in the middle of the night to check on the trees.

Back inside, she picked up the phone and dialled 911. Her hands were trembling. A man, she said. A man has been killed by a tree. Then she had to remember his address. She closed her eyes. After two tries, she was able to give her street and the nearest cross street, and finally the number of his house.

Then she went upstairs and shook Lew awake.

"Who was he, anyway?" asked Leah.

"You met him," said Harriet.

"I know that. But who *was* he?"

"An old newspaperman," answered Harriet. "There was nothing he didn't know. He saw Greta Garbo walking in the rain. He loved baths."

Leah huffed. "Everybody saw Garbo. She dressed up to be recognized. Here comes Garbo pretending not to be Garbo."

That night it was utterly still. She went outside at nine-thirty while Lew read a few more pages of *Angela's Ashes* to the kids, and in the new-fallen snow the streets were beautiful in a way that was different from their previous beauty. All the ice, all the glass trees and bushes and vines, now under a little new snow, seemed less dangerous, though owing to the extra weight they were more so. It was so quiet that she thought, *Benediction*. Once again it was like winter (rather than this strange new season of freezing rain). Once again it was possible to walk. A group of kids were out sliding on the small hummock of a hill between Downing Street and Colonel By. She heard cries of delight, and every so often the sound of ice in the trees, like unearthly wind chimes, different from any she had ever heard before.

At Christmas she had asked Bill Bender what history of the world she should read, and he replied, "I'm reading Parkman again. The history of the forest." She remembered this on her way back from her walk, as she passed his darkened house.

At her own house she stood under the street lamp and looked in. From here she couldn't see much of the living room except the tops of lamps and books and paintings. Fiona Chester was there, being comforted by Dinah and Ida. Leah, of course. And Lew. The kids were in bed. She would join them all in a minute. But it was lovely to be outside for a while, and alone.

And then the power went out.

28

Blackout

There were candles in each room and everyone spoke quietly; even the formidable aunt was subdued. Thursday night, still. But they were back in an earlier time, when houses burned down, kerosene lamps tipped over, nightgowns went up in flames, trees fell on unsuspecting heads. Only half the block was dark. Dinah's house still had power. She had checked immediately and returned with an extra flashlight and more candles. Fiona had power too. She knew just by looking out the window: her upstairs light was on. Dinah offered to walk her mother and Fiona home to their warm houses, "and Leah, why don't you take my bedroom tonight and I'll stay here? You'll be warm and comfortable." Looking to Harriet for confirmation, and getting it, and back to Leah, who said, rather formally, "That's a kind offer." Then she unbent a little more. "I accept."

Dinah said to Ida, who had decided not to go back to her home west of Ottawa until the ice storm abated, "Mother? You won't mind if Leah stays in the house with you tonight? You'll be able to turn up the heat as high as you like, I won't be there to complain."

Leah gathered together her nightgown and toothbrush, her reading glasses and book, and set out with the others. They slid their feet along, save Fiona who was confident in her super-duper ice grippers. Lew took Fiona's arm, Harriet took Leah's, Dinah took her mother's arm. As they passed Bill Bender's house, Fiona stopped for a moment and gazed at the dark exterior. "I'll give you the key," she said to Lew at her side, "and? would you go in later and check on the furnace?" Of course he would.

Then he looked around too, from one end of the street to the other, and remarked that it was like a frozen Havana. No traffic, almost as dark, and the sidewalks just as impassable.

Dinah would spend the night in Lew's study in a house so quiet – no hum from refrigerator or furnace or clock – that she would hear every sound.

They were on the same side of the house: Dinah on the pull-out sofa in Lew's study directly below Harriet and Lew's bedroom. She was lying in the light of two candles and thinking of Fiona as a widow, her mother as a widow, of herself as a widow of sorts, having buried, not a husband, but the possibility of an affair with one. There must be a phrase for that, for putting yourself out to pasture. Grass widow? The envied couple moved around above her head. *The envied couple?* Yes, she envied them, even though she knew it wasn't all roses for them and wouldn't be for anyone. But certainly she was tired of doing everything by herself. I would seriously get married now, came the recurring thought, just for the relief of not doing it all on my own. There was the faint clatter of glass beads as more ice fell. Then quiet. Fiona would be reading in bed, no doubt, or staring at the ceiling. In the afternoon she had gone with her over to Bill's house to locate the phone numbers for his sons – Andrew in Kingston, Jeffrey in Hull – and walking through the book-crammed rooms, Fiona had said, "What will they do with everything? I hate to think. I hate to think what they'll do and? there's nothing I can say. They wouldn't listen to me anyway."

Upstairs, it was dark except for the barest suggestion of light that came up the stairwell from Dinah's candles. Lew got out of bed and closed the door. Then back in bed he and Harriet turned towards each other, aware of Dinah below and awake, and aroused by her presence. They made love.

They were quiet but not silent. The sense of Dinah in the house, of someone left out but within hearing, inspired a looseness, an eroticism. "Turn over," said Lew.

Their bed took up almost the whole of their small room. There were two windows and the shades weren't drawn. The only light came from the windows, the white sheets, the glass that covered the prints on the wall. Everything floated around, in the room and in their minds, and everything aroused them. It made her wonder about the aphrodisiac effect of death, and of sorrowful third parties.

Dinah, on her pillows, picked up her book and tried to read, but the same few paragraphs over and over again wouldn't sink in. She heard a door open upstairs, she heard someone go into the bathroom.

They were a ragged band next morning.

Gathered in the freezing kitchen around the gas stove, and Lew so proud of himself for having insisted upon it. That was what they talked about, the virtues of a gas stove, the foresight, the good luck. Dinah admired his long hands – Kenny's hands – and thought of other fathers and sons she had fallen in love with. Some women fell for movie stars, some for twin brothers (her cousin Ruby), some for bankers or hairdressers, but her weakness had always been for attentive fathers with weedy, young sons. She noticed a long scar on Lew's right forefinger, and drew his attention to it. Cheap glass, he explained, long arms; he'd been careful around windows ever since, not to be so flamboyant in his gestures.

His smile said all. He was happy in the memory of last night and in the presence of people he loved.

It was peaceful with Leah out of the house, and not unpeaceful – eerie, but not unpeaceful – to be in the presence of sudden death. Everything slowed down. The ice storm had suspended life in so many ways, and now Bill Bender's death had shocked them into a different sort of stillness.

They wore hats and coats as if they were winter camping, and Harriet – regarding their wintry selves – thought of Keaton's and Chaplin's ability to see in any disaster the rudiments of a bed and table, the makings of a home. An awning became a roof, a drainpipe a coat rack, a table a bed. And some great longing in her was satisfied by this – the sight of shelves built into a tree, pots hanging in an old jalopy, makeshift rooms folding into the out-of-doors.

The espresso pot had worked its miracle. She held a hot cup between her cold hands, and into her mind came the image of Audrey stepping out of the cab onto Fifth Avenue, her back to the camera – the Pablo Casals of backbones – in her long black dress and ropes of pearls, so alone and so content, looking in the window of Tiffany's with her roll in a bag and her coffee to go. She was elegance-out-camping. Self-sufficient and in such a mood of her own.

Do you remember the brass mailbox equipped with mirror, lipstick, and perfume? She opens it like Buster Keaton opening a suitcase and pulling out

*kettle, teapot, cup and saucer. Light grooming in the middle of anywhere, so
that anywhere contains the basics of beauty and romance.*

*Audrey really had something. I could watch her forever, and stolid, hand-
some George Peppard had something too. In fact, he had what Lew has – that
great wish to look after someone. The sexiness of the nurturing male.*

Harriet turned to look at Lew. He was bending down, scooping flour
into a bowl from the big bag in the lower cupboard, and she saw the top
of his head. He set down the bowl for a moment and knelt on one knee –
his shoelace had come untied – and then she could really see what she
hadn't been aware of. He was losing his hair. He was going bald. The
sight filled her with such tenderness that she had to wonder why. He
stood up, set the bowl on the counter, and went to the fridge for eggs.

Mortality made her tender. Mortality touched her heart, this woman
who didn't care for the weaknesses of men; the cinematic sufferings, yes,
but not the real weaknesses. Life couldn't compete with the movies, but
death could.

Using his hip he held the door open, fished two eggs out of the egg
carton, then shut the door firmly, and it was at this point that Kenny,
who had just come downstairs, grabbed his father's arm to ask him a
question and one of the eggs slipped from Lew's grasp. Then Dinah
sprang forward to catch the egg, and what followed was a slapstick dance
of hands arms chests to keep the egg from hitting the floor (well,
thought Harriet later, it was straight out of *Charade*: Dinah and Lew
were Audrey Hepburn and Cary Grant using their bodies to keep the
orange in play). They succeeded. They saved the egg.

29

A Paperweight

It occurred to Harriet, who was seriously underslept, that the world was especially wakeful too. There was the tissue of freezing rain outside, the membrane of queer sounds in the walls as all warmth leaked away, the rustle of dryness in their sleepless skulls, their bone houses. They were held by it all. By their sleeplessness, by the tracings of rain and ice on the windows, by the intricacies of light and shadow at play in the world.

In her winter coat she went upstairs to tell Jane that breakfast was ready, and found her lying awake and remembering a dream. A nightmare, she said, where she was told that she would be dead in two hours, and she was terrified.

Harriet sat down on the edge of her bed, but Jane didn't move her legs to make room for her mother. Harriet had to give them a nudge.

"My past is gone forever," said Jane. "I'll never go back."

"What do you mean?"

"I miss the way I was," she said, in the same broken-hearted tones.

Harriet looked at her daughter, who was still twelve. An emotional, economical, romantic child, who alternated between dreams of being a movie star and being a pioneer settling the West, travelling by ox-drawn cart to a land where she wouldn't have to go to school. A child who walked on the soft earth next to the sidewalk to avoid wearing out her favorite shoes. Who turned down invitations to go shopping. Who ate after school the cold porridge she hadn't finished at breakfast.

"What way was that?" Harriet asked gently, more intrigued than worried.

"The way I looked, for one thing. My face is longer." Jane squeezed her face and twisted it with both hands. "My hair is straighter and darker. I used to be fatter. I'm so skinny now."

"You're more beautiful than ever."

But tears were oozing out of her eyes.

"You're inside a physical storm," her mother said. "That's what puberty is. You don't have any control over it, but everyone goes through it. You're not alone."

"I know I'm not *alone*," said Jane.

Harriet helped her daughter get dressed in a freezing house that did nothing to raise Jane's spirits. Only Dinah, downstairs in the kitchen, was able to bring a smile to her face. "You and Kenny can go over to my house," she said, "and watch movies. I'll tell Ida to get out the popcorn maker."

It was only one day since Bill Bender's death, but it seemed much longer. Dinah would take the kids over to her mother and Leah, who were getting along surprisingly well. Then she would join Harriet at Fiona Chester's; they were helping to arrange the funeral.

They found Fiona searching for a passage to read at the service. She had Chekhov open on the table to his story "About Love," and she'd located Akhmatova's poem about the town "locked in ice: a paperweight of trees, walls, snow" to which Mandelstam had been banished in 1934. It was a poem about a silenced poet. "The word *paperweight*," said Fiona. "You see its terrible meaning."

Fiona was having one white night after another, she confessed, but so it goes. There was nothing she could do about it. "All night long things fly into my head, things I don't want to remember, especially about myself. And? I ask myself how I could have been so stupid, or naive, or blind, and they all have to do with hurting people."

"Yes," said Dinah, who met Fiona's eyes. Fiona took her hand and gave it a gentle pat.

Harriet nodded too as her mind filled up with hurtful things she had written and said, and in this mood of shared, expansive, almost pleasant regret they sat for a while. Then Dinah pinned down details of the funeral: it would be on Sunday, the regular silent meeting for worship at the Society of Friends – Bill Bender was a Quaker, as she'd known. Out of curiosity, Dinah had gone with him once or twice, she said, and discovered that silent worship brought her close to her *least* spiritual aspects: every physical twitch, every stomach grumble and urge to pass gas mushroomed in magnitude, until she was locked in an agony of self-consciousness. "Bill told me I needed more patience, which was rich, coming from him."

Fiona's hearing aid let out a shriek and she cupped her ear. "I'm sorry. I should get it replaced, but? I don't want to hear *everything*."

She went in search of fresh batteries and was gone for quite a while, leaving Dinah and Harriet alone in the living room. They heard her moving about upstairs. It was noon by this time, on Friday of that unforgettable week. In the summer to come – in the endless heat – they would spread their snapshots of the ice storm on the picnic table, and Kenny would say, "It was worse than that." What it really looked like, he remembered, was a hockey rink after the vicious game was over: trees snapped in half like hockey sticks and the weight of violence in the air.

Dinah reassured Harriet that it was perfectly fine, having Leah at her house. She said, "My mother talks and Leah interrupts, then she talks and my mother interrupts."

"What do they talk about?"

"People they can't stand."

"She talks to me about love. I wish she wouldn't."

Outside, it was incredibly beautiful and birds were dying. Dinah had spoken the day before to a man who had spent the previous day trying to bury his dog: he had to call vet after vet before finding one who was open, then go on an endless drive in search of his street, where, for twenty dollars, the vet had agreed to dispose of the dog.

"What does your formidable aunt say about love?"

"She says Lew is in love with you."

To anyone who knew her, this was perhaps the most alarming aspect of Harriet's personality, her ability to take the wind out of your sails as if she were passing the time of day. It was never planned. When it happened, it surprised her too.

"I don't blame him," said Harriet, impressed with herself for feeling so generous and being so truthful, and forgetting that such feelings are mere will-o'-the-wisps brought on by a death, a time of year, by the tone of light in a room. "I'm not exactly a picnic to live with."

"No," Dinah Bloom said firmly. "He's waiting for you."

Fiona came back, gingerly touching her hearing aids, and there was a need to change the subject. Harriet said, "Last week Bill lent me Kurosawa's autobiography. The Japanese director?" Fiona nodded. Yes, she knew that Bill had been a big fan. "There's a fascinating part," said Harriet, "about the Tokyo earthquake in 1923, which happened when Kurosawa was only thirteen. The devastation was unbelievable. Corpses everywhere. But his older brother made him walk through the city afterwards and look at it. If you *look*, he said, you're less frightened than if you don't look. Mind you, that brother ended up committing suicide."

There had been times in their friendship when Dinah had seen Harriet as typical of so many married women, landing on their feet only to complain about their shoes. But not now. "What happened?"

"The talkies came in."

Dinah's eyebrows shot up.

"Yes," said Harriet. "He worked in silent films as a narrator and sound-effects man, and when the talkies arrived he knew that was the end – they were all going to lose their jobs. He led a strike, even though he knew it was a lost cause. And after it failed, he killed himself."

They sat in the warm living room, thinking about death. Then Harriet said, "What do you mean, Lew is waiting for me?"

"I mean he's waiting, for you," said Dinah.

But Lew wasn't waiting, he was coming around the corner. He called out to them as they made their way back from Fiona's, treading gingerly on the icy street.

"I learned a new word a few days ago," Harriet said, stooping to pick up a fat twig-cigar, enwrapped in a dozen leaves of ice, a very cold Havana. "*Japanned*. It means varnished or lacquered. All the trees are japanned with ice."

Around them the street was full of reflections, like a lake, or a finely polished cabinet, or silver, or a painting of any of those things.

"For you," Harriet said, and gave the twig-cigar to Lew.

They were the only ones in the street, a threesome with the sky falling around them. Off to the left another branch came down with a whoosh and a thud. Lew had news to relay, and as he did so Fiona Chester's cautionary face – *and they all have to do with hurting people* – came back to Dinah. The Château Laurier was renting rooms, he said, for forty dollars a night to anybody without power. He had booked a room for Leah and another for themselves, and why don't we all have dinner there tonight? You too, Dinah. It would give us all a break.

Harriet watched Dinah's face as she hesitated for a moment. Then she looked at Lew to see how he was looking at Dinah. But she didn't have Kurosawa's gaze. She had her own easily embarrassed eyes that looked down: away from losers at the Oscars, from violence in movies, from anyone she had offended, from any moment of private emotion. "My treat," she heard Lew say. And this is what she wished: she wished that Lew hadn't invited Dinah, that Dinah hadn't said yes, and that she hadn't fallen prey to jealousy, once again.

Ida was sound asleep on the sofa when Dinah let herself into her house. Buddy the protector lay on the floor beside her. Quietly, she pulled off her boots, and as she did so she heard voices in the kitchen.

Jack and Leah were at the kitchen table, which was spread with papers and a tape recorder. "Authors at work," Dinah said, with a husky chuckle. She went to the sink for a glass of water (usually she just lowered her mouth to the faucet), and drank it while she looked at them. Jack had told her that he was going to record Leah's memories and work from the tapes rather than from her sentimental notes. It would seem that he had convinced his stepmother to go along. Dinah was impressed. He had taken over and was doing things his own way.

Leah looked up at her and told her what she already knew.

"I saw Lew outside," Dinah said. "I'm coming along for dinner."

"That's nice," said Leah, her tone so unenthusiastic that Dinah shared a look of amusement with Jack.

There were fresh roses on the table. Dinah bent to smell them. "These are beautiful. Where on earth did you get them?"

"It wasn't easy," he said. "But a store in the west end had some."

He had brought strawberries too. They were washed and in a bowl beside the roses. Dinah, pulling out a chair, murmuring her appreciation, sat down and ate several. "Strawberries in January. What a luxury."

"That depends where you live," said Leah.

"True," smiled Dinah. "Harriet told me she met Lew when she was living in your house in Italy."

Leah cocked her head a little, and eyed Dinah. "Lew was just a kid. A skinny twenty-year-old. He wasn't interested in Harriet then. That came later." She took a strawberry and ate it slowly, not taking her eyes off Dinah. "He had to be convinced, you know."

"I don't know. Tell me."

"She's the one who went after him."

"Harriet?"

"Don't be fooled. She seems featherbrained but she's hard as flint. A sore loser too. Oh, yes. We'd be playing Scrabble and she'd get *angry*. Remember, Jack? She'd make up words and insist they were real."

"Good for her," laughed Dinah.

"She hates to lose," said Jack. "She's too competitive."

Dinah said, "I wouldn't have said so. I don't find her so."

"She's more competitive than Lew," Jack said. "But then Lew's not good enough for her."

Dinah stared at him, a strawberry halfway to her mouth. What sort of talk was this? What sort of mean, muddled thinking? For a moment she felt like her mother when she'd been given by her future mother-in-law a badly tangled hairnet to untangle, as a test. Once she'd untangled it, and it took her an hour, her mother-in-law decided that she would do. Ida was suitable to marry her David. But how to untangle all of these personal threads? Apparently, Jack was jealous of Lew. But on Harriet's account? Or on my account? she wondered. Had Leah told him Lew was in love with her? As she'd told Harriet?

She said, "I can't believe you would say that Lew isn't good enough for her."

"Why are you so interested in Lew?" asked Jack.

"I'm interested in both of them. They're my friends."

"Be interested in me instead," said Jack.

"Okay." And she took one of the strawberries and said, "Open wide."

Her mother wandered into the kitchen a few minutes later. Dinah told her about her plans for dinner and about Leah's room at the hotel. They would go over to Harriet and Lew's first, then go on from there. Jack, who had other plans, would get a ride with them to his apartment, and they would continue on to the Château. "I'm sure you would be welcome too." But Ida wasn't interested. The food at the Château gave her heartburn, she said. No, she would stay here and keep Buddy company.

Lew was at the piano when they trooped into the house half an hour later. He was playing Gershwin songs, and immediately Jack grabbed Harriet by the hand and began to dance her around the living room. He was surprisingly light on his feet, propelling her so firmly that when she sank into the sofa afterwards she was laughing with delight. "Louise Brooks said Fatty Arbuckle was a wonderful dancer," she said. "It was like floating in the arms of a huge donut."

"Thanks," said Jack.

"You're not a donut," she laughed. "Unless you're Fatty Arbuckle."

"What's this? You're calling me Fatty Arbuckle? Yes or no?"

"If you're Fatty Arbuckle, then I'm Ginger Rogers."

Lew, seated at the piano, said, "I think Ginger is safe," and Harriet felt the remark enter her like a needle.

"What are *yes* and *no*, anyway?" asked Jane, who had been reading on the loveseat. "They're not adjectives. They're not nouns. They're not verbs. What are they?"

"Adverbs," said Harriet. "Believe it or not, they're adverbs." And she stood up and headed for the kitchen.

Lew said, "No, they're not. They can't be adverbs."

Harriet stopped and stared at him. Then she went into his study, got the dictionary, returned and opened it. "*Yes* is a contraction of *yea, be it so*, and the dictionary says it's an adverb. *No* is a contraction of *not ever*. Also an adverb." She slammed the book shut.

Dear Pauline, she said to herself, *Love only goes so far, even among people who are supposedly fond of you. Remember that. H.*

In her mind she accused Lew of intentional mild malice. He would deny it, of course. He always denied being a shit when she accused him of being a shit. She just wanted him to admit that, yes, every so often he was a shit. But he wouldn't.

And so, when it came time to go to the Château Laurier, she was in no hurry to leave the house. Everyone else was in the car – Lew, Aunt Leah, the kids. Dinah would take her own car and drop Jack at his apartment, then join them in the restaurant. But Harriet was still fishing for her keys. As she was about to step out the door, she turned around for a last look and found herself held by the dark, still interior. The quietness drew her back inside and back in time to the blessed, creative, early-morning hours in university when she wrote poetry before her lectures began. The lovely surprised excitement of writing, and of reading afterwards what she had written, amazed that something was there.

Lew came to the door to get her. "We're ready to go," he said.

"I think I'll stay."

"Don't be like that. Come on. We'll have fun."

"No, we won't." Her pale, exhausted face hovered in the dim hallway.

"We'll have a nice warm room and you'll sleep."

"No," she said, "I won't."

"Hattie," he pleaded.

"I'm sick to death of the lot of you," she said.

The freezing darkness stole around her. She curled up on the sofa, under a blanket. A childish mistake. Lying here on her ice floe, not even knowing what day it was. It was Friday, and outside it began to snow.

An hour or two passed. She was thinking about Garbo stepping onto the private raft she called Harriet Brown. Better, perhaps, to be Garbo-in-reverse: Harriet Browning for the first half of her life, someone vividly different for the second half. I've reached the outer limits of my personality, she thought with sudden clarity. It's time to leap onto another ice floe and push out to sea. To find some new territory – an archipelago, or an island – to explore. The thought came with a strange pain in her heart, and an image of Lew fading into the distance, receding into an icy expanse.

When the phone rang, she was almost too stiff to get up and answer it.

The sleep clinic had a cancellation. Come in tonight, they said. Be here by eight o'clock. What time is it now? she asked, since it was too dark to see her watch. A quarter to eight, they said. Before leaving she lit a candle, found the phone number for the hotel, left a message for Lew about her whereabouts, blew the candle out.

30

The Sleep Clinic

Harriet sat in her long gray nightie with thick socks on her feet, while a young man named Danilo attached fifteen electrodes to her forehead, around her chin, under her eyes, behind her ears, on the back of her head, on her shoulders, and on the muscles just below her knees. She said she was surprised they were operating the clinic this week, and he told her they'd had to close on Wednesday. Nobody could get here.

Most of their clientele, he said, were obese men. Even being twenty pounds overweight was enough to cause snoring or sleep apnea. It's the extra weight carried on the neck that does it, he said, and the way it restricts the breathing cavities. Their wives send them, he told her knowingly, and for her benefit, she thought, since she was interested and amused. They'd never come on their own, he said, because it's considered sissy. "Not too many women come," he added. When she asked him why he said he wasn't sure, but he suspected that women learn how to get by without much sleep. He said, "They don't complain or whine as much as men."

Small and slender, this Danilo, with glasses and a soft beard. Brown skin. Gentle hands. He didn't do this all the time – he was getting his Ph.D. – but this was a way to earn money. She felt the need to explain why she was one of the few women who complained – or whined – and to apologize somewhat, since she had no great physical affliction. She said, "I've been thinking about coming to a sleep clinic for years. I've had trouble sleeping since I was twelve."

Look at me, Danny, she wanted to say, look at these tired eyes. Instead, she asked him what his Ph.D. was about. Neuroscience, he replied. He worked with rats. Just their brains, and so the rats, unfortunately, had to be killed. Their brains are kept alive in a solution, he said, then triggered with certain stimuli to measure their responses. It's to further the work on human deafness.

"Do you kill the rats yourself?"

"I do."

"How?" she asked.

"You decapitate them."

"With a knife?"

"With scissors," he said. "They're made for the job. They're big and very sharp. You just cut through the neck – it's quick and painless. If you have an old rat with a tough neck then you anaesthetize it so it doesn't feel any pain. It's done very carefully. We're not allowed to cause pain. And it's for science," he added.

They were in a small equipment-filled room on the first floor of the west wing of the hospital. She was positioned so that she faced a small black-and-white TV and various charts of the human body. As Danilo hooked up her legs, giving the spot below the knee a close shave, she pointed at the big sleep chart on the wall behind him. "The six stages of sleep?" she asked, because the chart was divided into six sections with a different pattern, of what she assumed were brain waves, drawn in each one.

"Five stages," he said.

"What's the sixth? Death?"

And he laughed and looked over at the chart, and explained that the six stages included a pre-sleep stage, characterized by fast-frequency alpha waves in the brain.

On her left was the open door to the cubicle where she would sleep, a nun-like room with a narrow bed and two chairs. Behind her was a second sleeping cubicle. In that one the other client was being hooked up: she heard the voice of Danilo's colleague explaining as he went along, and she imagined the obese chest and belly of the man at his mercy. She didn't imagine that she knew him, but she did. When he came out, in briefs and a T-shirt, it was the song detective.

He had his knitting in a cloth bag, the needles stuck out the top.

"I'm your neighbor," she told him as he blinked at her. "In the house beside Bill Bender. The one with the big verandah."

He was thickset, but not obese by any means. Lived-in face, unruly hair, craggy brow, dry lips. A bit like Badger, she thought. A Rosanno Brazzi of field and den.

"Is it the neighborhood?" he asked. "As far as I can make out, nobody sleeps."

Gingerly, so as not to dislodge any of the electrodes, he took a chair near Harriet, who said, "Dinah told me you were a knitter."

"Did she?" Sudden interest in his face. "What else did she say?"

"Oh, she's very discreet, which is unusual for a reporter."

"She is unusual." His radio voice – she recognized it – was as deeply appreciative as when he talked about Deanna Durbin: "A better voice than Judy Garland, and she's still with us, she's living in France."

"You've known her for a while?"

"We knew somebody in common," he said. "I heard a lot about her before I met her."

"And when was that?"

"The first time? About fifteen years ago, when she came up north to write some articles. Then two years ago, when she moved into the neighborhood. Two years ago last November," he said.

He fished his glasses out of the cloth bag, and then his knitting, set the glasses on the end of his nose, and began to sort out needles and wool.

"My mother knits in the car," she told him. "When she isn't filing her nails."

"It's for Dinah," he said simply. And the crackle of romance filled the air.

It was warm, almost cozy, in this small room filled to the brim with functioning electronics, while outside trees and wires and pylons crumpled in the fields. Danilo and his colleague fiddled with knobs. Harriet, in her flannel nightie, kept up her questions. "So when did *your* sleeping troubles begin?" she asked him.

"You want the history? Ten years ago when I gave up drinking to please a woman who left me anyway."

"Was her name by any chance Stella?"

A rumpled grin. He looked over his glasses – just like Sean Connery, she thought, in *The Russia House* – at this inquisitive woman with the dramatically tired eyes.

His lips, she noticed, were not only dry but freckled.

He was counting stitches. "Fifty-nine," he said aloud.

Then he put down his knitting, and asked her what she knew about Dinah's cancer. She told him what she knew: since they'd drained the fluid off her lungs she was feeling remarkably well, surprising herself and her doctors, but there would be an operation. Probably at the end of January.

A young doctor came in. Friendly. Mop of brown hair. "Are they taping you up?" he asked as they sat there, taped up.

"She doesn't take care of herself," he said after the doctor left. "Reporters never do."

"Well, she's got an idea for a new career. I'm her test plot." Harriet rubbed the left side of her face. "I had to stop using her lotion because this side of my face was starting to look like W.H. Auden."

Then Danilo told them it was time for bed. They said good night to each other, and wished each other luck.

The sleeping cubicles were soundproofed, the beds rather high. Harriet removed the two pillows and used the one she had brought from home. The young doctor came in again and with many smiles talked about her sleeping trouble as outlined in the questionnaire she had filled out months ago. "I know what I should do," she said. "I shouldn't eat rich dinners or get stimulated by company. I should have a sign on my door that says, No Guests."

"A lot of shoulds," he said. "Are you a controlling personality? Everything has to be just so?"

"Well, I'm not interested in controlling anybody else."

"Obsessive," he said, and wrote it down on his chart.

He left her and went to the other cubicle, where he questioned the song detective. Harriet heard their voices, but the words were indistinct.

Danilo came in and made some further adjustments to the electrode on the back of her head, then asked her how sleepy she felt on a scale of one to eight. She said, "Seven, I think. Or maybe five." She felt somewhere between pleasantly sleepy and wakefully sleepy. Once again she had been up since four, and she was very tired.

It was safe in here, the door closed tight, the TV in the control room turned low, earplugs in her ears, video camera chronicling in shadowy black-and-white her movements in bed, as well as any comings and goings into her room so that no one could sneak in and throttle her, and no interruptions. Not alone, but not interrupted. Safe. Like Virginia Woolf. Or like Mrs. Dalloway as Virginia Woolf described her, in her cell of a bedroom at the top of the house, sleeping in a narrow single bed so that her husband wouldn't disturb her. It was his idea, fretted Mrs. Dalloway. But not a bad one, it seemed to Harriet.

Across the city, in the Château Laurier, an ecstatic Kenny and Jane were stretched out on the bed with Leah, watching *The Godfather*, while the man who didn't watch movies sat in an armchair and read *Jewish Currents* to keep his mind off what had happened earlier. They'd had dinner in the piano restaurant downstairs, Dinah, the kids, Leah, himself, and it was not a success. Leah sent back her soup, saying it was inedible. Then she said to Lew, "Lionel and I never quarrelled. Maybe we should have. They say it's healthy to quarrel."

"We didn't quarrel," said Lew. "Harriet wanted to have some time to herself."

"*In a freezing house?*"

Dinah said, "She's probably opening up a bottle of champagne right now," and her laughter effectively sidelined Leah, and not for the first time.

Lew, smiling across at Dinah, saw her as having the sort of relaxed down-to-earth gracefulness that comes from having survived many difficult things without bitterness. The absence of self-pity made her very beautiful.

It was when they were almost finished the meal that he suddenly felt weak.

"Are you all right?" asked Dinah in alarm. "Is it the food?"

"I will be," he said, leaning back in his chair but keeping his hands spread out on the table for support.

"You're green," said Leah.

Quickly, Dinah stepped over to the bar and asked the waiter to bring a glass of water right away. Then she grabbed a mint from a large bowl, unwrapped the cellophane, and gave it to Lew.

"What does it feel like?" she asked him after he took a deep breath and thanked her, and had a few sips of water, and put the mint in his mouth. The kids and Leah were watching him with considerable interest, and he gave them a reassuring wink.

"It feels," he said, with an amused and weary smile, "as if my life is very far away." He spread his arms wide to show how far. Several feet. "It's as if everything drains out of me, and all that's left is weakness."

Leah spoke up. "That's not exactly specific."

He smiled again. "That's what the doctor said."

"*What* did he say?" pressed Dinah.

"That it wasn't a lot to go on."

"I should have been there," said Dinah, her voice suddenly hoarse. "I would have hung on like a bulldog until I got more out of him."

"Her," said Lew, looking spent but not unhappy.

"I'm serious. I ask every question I can think of and I write everything down."

Ten minutes later Lew felt well enough to get up and leave the restaurant. On their way to the elevators he stopped to look at the Karsh photographs on the walls of the inner lobby. Go ahead, he told the others. The others went ahead, except for Dinah, who stayed with him and looked too – at Georgia O'Keeffe in profile, Pablo Casals from the back, Stephen Leacock with a big smile and eyes so crinkled up they were closed. Surely that was a mistake, she said. She would have liked to have seen the humorist's eyes.

They stood in front of Einstein, and Lew said, "He looks calm." He leaned against her. He said, "I guess that's what a good photographer does. He makes his victims relax."

He was thinking of Harriet. Hoping she was all right. He would call her when he got upstairs. He looked at his watch: it was eight o'clock.

Dinah asked if he was feeling better, and he smiled at her and said it always took a little while to recover. He said it was like fainting away around the heart. He saw himself and everything around him at a distance, with clarity, while he went still and small and hung on for dear life. If he were to make any effort at all, to carry on talking or eating or moving, he would die. And then it passed.

"It's nothing to worry about," he said. "They've done tests. There's nothing the matter except a heart murmur, which is common."

"Unless it happens at the wrong moment," she said. Turning to confront him. "Suppose you're driving, Lew. What then?"

"Then I pull over."

He looked into her worried, questioning, unconvinced eyes and then he put his arms around her, and they stood that way, holding each other. They looked as if they'd been on a long journey and were taking strength from each other for the next stage.

A voice said, "There you are, you lovebirds."

Lew let one of his arms drop, but brought Dinah closer with the other, and turned to face the formidable aunt.

"The kids want to watch *The Godfather*. I thought I'd better check, knowing Harriet's dead against it."

The next morning, at six, Harriet was wrenched out of a deep sleep by Danilo opening the door and saying it was time to get up. She woke up in earnest when he began to tear the tape off her face – neck – shoulders. Ow, ow, ow. Ouch!

When did you wake up? the questionnaire asked.

When they ripped the tape off my face, she answered.

She and the song detective left the hospital together. He had come by taxi since he didn't know how to drive. "Are you a poet?" she asked him. She had never met a poet who knew how to drive.

"As a matter of fact, I am." He looked exhausted, and said he'd had one of the worst nights of his life.

"I've never felt more rested," she said. "I feel reborn."

It was still dark when they pulled out onto Carling Avenue into non-existent traffic, but the weather had changed, and so had she. Her head felt deep instead of shallow. No longer was she skittering across the surface of a world that offered no purchase, her life all foreground and no background. Rather, she had come out of something – out of the most remarkable, dream-filled depths – and the back of her skull retained the feeling of territory occupied, filled, discovered by sleep.

She turned the car into his street, and he said, "I make excellent coffee."

"Good."

She had slept so well that she could actually feel the pouches under her eyes. Her eyes felt moist and more open, and even the pouches were relaxed.

She parked. It was ten to seven by her watch, which was five minutes fast. For the first time in a week the sky was clearing in the west.

He opened the door to an ecstatic Stella, the glamorous white mala-mute in his life. Then he showed Harriet into the living room, let the dog out the back door, and got busy in the kitchen. Harriet, seated in an old velvet armchair low to the ground and next to a row of windows, saw Pauline Kael's *Deeper Into Movies* on the bookshelf; she reached for it and began to read a book that she'd had to borrow from the library because it was out of print.

He said, "I used to visit her," and Harriet looked up in awe as he handed her a mug of his excellent coffee and set down a plate of toasted bagels.

In Berkeley, he explained, when his older brother was a graduate student and he went to visit him from time to time, he heard her movie reviews on the radio and went to the repertory movie house she ran with her husband before they separated. He said the two times he met her she was living in a bungalow. Her daughter was there: Gina, who was thirteen, and so lovely that he was prepared to fall in love with her. Well, he was only nineteen himself. His brother, who loved Hitchcock, was the one who'd had the idea to call up Pauline, and when he did she invited them to come over. "She *hated* Hitchcock."

"That's my Pauline," said Harriet. "What did she look like?"

"I was too busy trying to think of what to say to notice."

"Small, intense, opinionated, fearless." Harriet supplied the adjectives.

"She wrote on a drafting table. I saw it in her living room. And she drank bourbon."

Hunters in the Snow was over his mantelpiece, the same reproduction she had in her own living room. On the near wall was a photograph of a woman seated and nude from the waist up. Harriet said, "She liked early Hitchcock. It was late Hitchcock she couldn't stand." Then she stood up and inspected the photograph more closely. The woman wasn't as immediately beautiful as Dinah, but she had Dinah's wide face, thick hair, full un-Garbo-like lips and breasts. Yes, men liked women with flesh on their bones. It was a well-known truth.

"But she isn't knitting."

"She couldn't."

"Why not?"

"Look at her hands."

Her hands were folded in her lap but you could see that the right forefinger was cut off at the knuckle.

"But you're on the right track," he said.

"And was her name Stella?"

"It still is."

"I like her face," she said.

Even as a girl she had been susceptible to an interesting face: Nureyev; Trudeau; Lyndon Johnson more than Kennedy; Jackie more than Marilyn Monroe. The first time she saw Dinah's wide, lush looks, she thought to herself, I could stare at you for a long time.

Then she turned her attention to *Hunters in the Snow* and, from this angle, following upon her deeply restful night, she understood perfectly what Hemingway meant. Into her mind came the opening paragraph of *A Farewell to Arms* – the dusty road and dusty trees, the river, the hills in the distance – and here was the same detail and depth bringing your eye close to everything, no matter how near it was or how far away. He'd been thinking of this painting when he wrote that paragraph, she was sure of it.

"Would you like to borrow it?" asked the song detective, picking up *Deeper Into Movies* and offering it to her. She took it and flipped to the beginning. His name was written in the front and she said, "I thought it was *Creek* with a double *e*. But this is better." *Jim Creak*. "On Sundays I get up early just to listen to you." Then she closed the book and held it to her chest. "What about you and Dinah?" she asked him.

"I've been waiting for her to show some interest."

These waiting men. Get cracking! "Somebody's giving her roses. All the time. I think you should break his legs."

Then at the door, her coat on, she said, "Why don't you ask her to the movies? The Mayfair's right around the corner."

"When I go to the Mayfair," he said, "I take a pillow."

"I take two Tylenols."

And it was at that moment – as they were thinking about the killer seats in the Mayfair movie theatre – that Harriet Browning had her idea, and she told him what it was. She would take over the empty Strand. She would run a movie house, like Pauline Kael. The movies would be old movies and they would be cheap. "You and Dinah can write the movie notes," she told him. "Jane can sell tickets, Kenny can be the usher, Lew can design the renovation."

"And you?" he asked.

"I'll be the businesswoman."

"Do you know about business?"

"I think I do," she said. And in her bones she felt she did.

31

Shock

When she got home, the power was still off. It was early; she was the first one back. But within minutes, as if giving their blessing, a lamp sprang to life and the refrigerator began to hum. Hallelujah! She took off her coat, put on a pot of coffee and a small saucepan of milk. Then feeling cold as she waited, she reached for Leah's silk kimono, which was hanging on the back of a kitchen chair, and put it on. She had always admired it, and with good reason – the colors traced delicate maps of the Far East; and it was warm. The espresso maker began to bubble and whoosh and at the same moment the milk foamed up, so she reached for the milk with her right hand and the coffee with her left, and the long left sleeve of the kimono brushed against the gas burner and went up in flames.

Dinah would find her an hour later at the kitchen table, drinking the coffee she had made at great cost to herself. Invisible, inside a big-armed sweater, was her loosely bandaged arm, cut free from the ki-mono. She'd slapped out the flames with a square potholder, then held her arm under the tap, then lowered her arm into the cold water, the soft flesh of her left forearm. Reaching for the baking soda, she'd poured it in, and the new area in the back of her skull darkened with pain. Then from the kitchen drawer, a pair of scissors to cut away the kimono.

"There's coffee on the stove," she said to Dinah, not getting up. And that's all she said. Almost against her will – she could feel it happening – her brain embraced the histrionic underside of pain. She would perform a bitter little experiment. Who loved her enough to notice? Or would anyone notice at all?

"You must have frozen last night." Dinah was pouring herself coffee. "I called to get you to come over, but you didn't answer the phone. I was worried about you."

"The sleep clinic had a cancellation. I was over there."

"What did they give you? What's the cure? Your eyes look so different." Dinah had taken her coffee to the table and she was scrutinizing Harriet's face.

"Sleeping alone. I felt like a nun."

Then Dinah sat down across from her and told her that Lew was fine, but he'd had a strange attack of weakness at the end of dinner. Does that happen very often? And Harriet thought, She's come over to talk about Lew, not to check on me.

"Every few months," she answered. "And if he drops dead on me, I'm going to be extremely pissed off."

Despite herself, she laughed. Despite herself, she was glad to see Dinah. But she still didn't tell her friend about her burned arm, hewing to the dark logic dictated by unreasonable pain.

Dinah stared at her coffee. "Last night Lew and I were looking at Karsh's photographs. It reminded me that I interviewed Celeste Holm years ago when she was at the Château for some reason. I'd forgotten all about it. But she was beautiful."

Harriet shifted in her chair. "I always thought so."

"I never did. But she was *beautiful*. Her skin. Her eyes. And she was elegant too. I thought she was just a second-string player, but she had quite a sense of herself."

"*High Society*." Harriet rose from her bed of nails to the movie occasion. "She was more beautiful than Grace Kelly. Frank Sinatra was nuts not to appreciate her more. She had the same sort of braininess as Betty what's-her-name in *On the Town*. The taxi driver. Who wanted Sinatra to sit in her lap."

"Betty Hutton."

"Not Betty Hutton."

"Betty Grable."

"Not Betty Grable." Betty used to be a sexy name, now there was just Apple Brown Betty. "The one who was blacklisted because her husband was a leftie. Betty Garrett. She was beautiful too." She took a sip of coffee. "This isn't hot," she muttered.

Dinah took it out of her hands and put it in the microwave, then returned it to her saying, "Harriet, what is it? What's wrong?"

And Harriet would have told her, since one word of sympathy was enough to break the spell, but just then Kenny burst through the door, and they were lifted up on a wave of noise that didn't deposit them for some time.

"Doña," cried Lew as he came into the kitchen, and his heartiness was like an Indian rub on her singed flesh. "I got your message last night. Are you cured?"

She turned her head and trained her white Buster Keaton face on the peasant-duchess, who was looking for her kimono. But she didn't explain that either, since one explanation would require another.

There was a big bowl of purple grapes on the table, draped with a thick towel (no longer necessary) to keep them from freezing. Harriet stood up and removed the towel. Then, with her left arm held gingerly at her side, she got the grape scissors from the kitchen drawer. What a hope. Leah swept down on the handsome grapes and yanked them off their stems one at a time.

"Leah?" Harriet was standing with her left hand raised and cradled in her right – much as Garbo might have cradled a bag of ripe persimmons. "You've never told us how long you were planning to stay." She heard the edge in her own voice.

"My ticket is open."

"I was afraid of that," said Harriet, a comment for which she would pay later, no doubt, but she didn't care.

Leah's small, blunt, grape-sticky fingers stopped their gluttonous pursuit, and Lew's eyes travelled to the pale strain on Harriet's face. Well, it was a miracle it had taken so long. "I have a colleague who's going out of town for a few weeks," he said. "I'll see if she'd mind a guest while she's gone."

"Or Jack," said Dinah, also coming to the rescue. "Would he have room for you for a bit?"

"Why not Janice?" Harriet challenged her aunt. "You said you wanted to see her."

"I suppose you want to get back to your writing." Leah's voice was mild, but Harriet wasn't fooled, and she wasn't deterred.

"No. I've given up writing. I'm going to open a movie house."

"A what?" said Lew.

"I'm going to take over the Strand, and I want you to do the renovation."

He laughed. "I can see it!" he said. "You'll have movie nights. Harriet's choice one night, Kenny's the next, Jane's the next."

"Second-run movies for two dollars," said Harriet.

"Depression prices," observed Leah dryly. "Harriet Browning: Purveyor of cheap movies."

"I like that," said Harriet. "I'll put that on my business card."

"Where will you get the money?" asked Dinah.

Leah yanked off another grape. "I'll put up the money," she said.

And the cat was among the pigeons.

Harriet went to the window, and what she saw on that familiar slope littered with tree limbs and twigs made her turn around and gaze at Dinah. She said to her, "I'm hoping you and Jim Creak will write the program notes."

The song detective was making his way up the slope with the help of a stout walking stick. He came in the back door without knocking, and Harriet went forward to take his coat.

He said, "You forgot to take the book." Handing her *Deeper Into Movies*. Then he said, "What's the matter with your arm?"

You can't do better than an observant man with dry, freckled lips who makes excellent coffee, even if he doesn't know how to drive.

"I had an accident," she said. "Stupidly."

Then she had to sit down and show her arm to a bunch of onlookers who failed to understand why she hadn't told them immediately, and she couldn't explain. "I'm sorry, Leah. I ruined your kimono."

"You're in shock," said the song detective.

Lew shook his head and moaned, "Hattie."

They were afraid of the wind, since it was strong, from the southwest, and it would take so little to bring down even more branches on the low, sagging wires. But the sky had cleared, and for much of that day it was bright, melting. Dinah Bloom and Lew Gold, walking through the Arboretum and checking on the damage, saw many Mr. Rochester trees: split down the middle like the tree in *Jane Eyre*, the ice having acted like a meat cleaver. Dinah tried to lift up a small, horizontal cedar, but its lower boughs were pinned under ice and snow. A weeping mulberry, on the other hand, umbrella-shaped, compact, low to the ground, was unharmed. The big spruces had fared well. But three of the lovely false cypresses were split in half.

They had driven Harriet to the hospital and she insisted – ordered them – not to stay with her, but to go home. She would phone them when she was ready to be picked up.

They walked over the treacherous, littered ground and once again they found themselves talking about her. "She's a tortured soul," said Lew, and Dinah had to smile. "There's always something," he said to her, "and it's almost nothing."

Dinah could see it. The tiniest speck of egg yolk and the meringue fell. "Not this time," she said.

"Not this time," he agreed. "The trouble is she gets overambitious. Overaggressive. It happened the first time I met her. She got so mad at Jack Frame she punched him in the nose."

"*Did she?*" It was the first Dinah had heard of this, and she laughed out loud. "You've got to love her," she said. Then asked, "But what did Jack do to deserve it?"

"I don't think she was ever sure herself."

Dinah nodded, her eyes on a large bird feeder, recently filled with seed, and drawing birds like a magnet. "I understand," she said. "He gets under your skin." In good ways and bad, she thought.

They came upon two huge hackberries split down the middle. Then a dotted hawthorn. More than half of it lay like Gulliver upon the ground. Lew pulled paper and pencil from his pocket and jotted down the names of the fallen trees. "Harriet will want to know," he said.

That night Harriet said to Lew as they lay side by side in bed, "We have to find a man for Dinah. And I don't mean you."

He turned towards her calm, tough face soothed by painkillers and lit by the bedside lamp. Her arm was bandaged and aware of itself, lying gently beside her. He reached over and stroked her hair.

She took his hand and brought it to her cheek, and held it there.

Kenny lay awake, listening to the movements in the house. Eventually all was quiet, except for the snap of a tree limb or the clatter of ice. Without knowing it, he was listening to the loss of shade. In the spring, gardeners would puzzle over how to turn their shade gardens into sun gardens, and his science class, on an excursion to the woods, would be stymied by the mess of branches on the ground and have to turn back. Dinah would lose her hair, and when it grew in again it would go in ten different directions, much as new branches, shooting out from the tops of snapped-off trees, would grow in wild and thick. But Dinah would still look better at the wedding than his mom.

SPRING

32

The Funeral

On the morning of Bill Bender's funeral, Harriet was up early, swallowing codeine and turning on the radio to catch the song detective, who said he was going to do something out of the ordinary: he was going to play his own request. "Lament for the Children," composed in the eighteenth century by McCrimmon. A pibroch, and he thought on this morning, in particular, it was the right song for Fiona Chester.

An hour later, Harriet was helping Fiona get ready, not that she was of much use with one arm in a sling. "Did you hear the song on the radio?" she asked. "A bit lugubrious, maybe?"

But Fiona said, "I think that man has the loveliest voice I've ever heard and? I don't care what Bill said about him. Now. Where are my black gloves?"

Harriet joined her on the floor as she searched, noticing at this level a dark smudge on Fiona's ankle – shoe polish? – but at least her stockings were free of runs. Down here they continued their conversation about what Fiona might say at the funeral. Chekhov's stories, for all their splendor, Fiona said, didn't lend themselves to such an occasion. Not really. She sat back on her heels and bobbed her head. "I thought of using one of my own translations of a paragraph, but Constance Garnett is so much better. No matter what some say about their inaccuracies, her translations were the best. The most – what's the word?"

"Alive. Intimate. Natural."

"That's the word."

"Open."

"That's the word."

"I'm not sure that's the word." Harriet was thinking on her knees. What she most admired about Chekhov, she thought, was the way he didn't make too much or too little of the changes his characters undergo, because he fit them into the ebb and flow of life. A man died, and on the day of his funeral his mourners were on the floor searching for a pair of gloves.

Fiona discovered them – "you rascals" – gathering dust behind the umbrella stand.

In the end, Fiona elected not to speak at all. It required more poise and bravado than she could muster, to stand up during the Friends' silent meeting and bear testimony to Bill's life. Several colleagues from his newspaper days offered words of tribute and affection, saying that Bill Bender was in a class by himself, there wasn't a thing he wasn't interested in, not a person he wouldn't talk to, not a fact he couldn't locate. Then halfway through the meeting, a familiar voice electrified the room. It was the song detective, dressed in a sky-blue hand-knit sweater. Resting his hands on the chair in front of him, he uttered these words. TELL THE ONES YOU LOVE, YOU LOVE THEM; TELL THEM NOW. FOR THE DAY IS COMING, AND ALSO THE NIGHT WILL COME, WHEN YOU WILL NEITHER SAY IT, NOR HEAR IT, NOR CARE. I WILL SAY IT AGAIN: TELL THE ONES YOU LOVE, YOU LOVE THEM. TELL THEM TODAY.

That got everybody's attention. He had a fine, urgent voice – it was no accident he was in radio; and all the while he looked straight at Dinah, right into her riveted, brown eyes, until she turned beet-red and looked away.

Harriet found it thrilling. It reminded her of the opening scene in *Rules of the Game* when the young pilot blurts out his love on the radio for all to hear. In the afternoon she would leave a note to that effect in Jim Creak's mailbox, congratulating him on his eloquence and inviting him for dinner, since he had disappeared so quickly after the service that she hadn't had a chance to speak to him. Disappeared, thereby escaping the obligatory round of smiles and handshakes and smiles, which brought Harriet face-to-face with North of England and his mute and humorless wife. Later, over lemon loaf and date bread, her former student grabbed her good arm and asked if she ever saw Ruth. Harriet knew who he was talking about. No-neck Vanessa. She had to say no, and watch the disappointment settle on his face.

"Chekhov never went to a movie," Harriet said thoughtfully later the same day. She liked the codeine very much.

Dinah said, "I saw *The Cherry Orchard* once." Her voice was flat, noncommittal.

"And?"

"I fell asleep."

"Yes."

"It was boring."

"It was badly produced," Harriet said. But she too had fallen asleep during a production of *The Cherry Orchard*, a different one. "You have to see *Vanya on 42nd Street*," she said. "Jim Creak is like what's-his-name, the doctor who was crazy about trees."

They were all gathered in the living room: Fiona napping in an armchair; the kids and Lew attending to the fire; Dinah and Ida still dressed in black; Leah in a bad mood. And Jack, who had shown up out of the blue.

"Where were you last night?" Leah demanded when he came through the door. "I called you twice."

But he didn't satisfy her curiosity, and Leah said, "Never mind. I got through to Janice. That's where you'll find me as of tomorrow night."

Jack's arrival interrupted Dinah's reminiscences about Bill Bender, but only for a moment. Harriet suspected he had dropped by with nothing in mind except getting fed; he was content to nod hello to everyone and sit next to Dinah on the sofa. But then he put his arm around the back of the sofa, and leaned closer to Dinah, quite noticeably, and Harriet thought, Something has moved forward when I wasn't looking.

Her eyes went to Lew, who was standing by the fire. He saw her glance and asked if she was feeling all right, then came over and knelt beside her. "Do you want to lie down for a bit?"

Only then did Jack notice her arm.

But Harriet said she was fine, and asked Lew if he would bring them all something to drink, and she steered the conversation back to Bill Bender, his collection of books and maps and radios. His love of language, his love of trees. We're killed by what we love, mused Dinah. I had a cat named Jenny who ran out of the woods when she heard the sound of my car, and straight under my front wheels. It was late at night, and I'd been away for two days; she was overeager, and my headlights probably blinded her.

Jack said, "She might have been chasing something. It might have had nothing to do with you. So much is out of our control," he added, saying that on his way here he had watched a big tree slowly turn as it tore apart down the center. It didn't fall, he said, so much as lie down. And Harriet pictured Emma Thompson sinking to her knees in *Howards End*.

She said, "I heard on the radio that softwood trees are suffering the most. Willows, birches, silver maples, Manitoba maples."

"Manitoba maples," coughed Dinah. "The bane of Bill's existence. His radio was on, did I tell you? When Fiona and I went into his house on Thursday morning. The radio in his bedroom."

Fiona, hearing her name, opened her eyes, and Dinah reached over and touched her arm. "Bill was such a man for facts and connections and history, wasn't he?" And Fiona, nodding her head, fiddling with her hearing aid, wondered aloud what would happen to all of his filing cabinets and to the book he'd been working on for so long.

"Should we go into his house and get it?" Dinah asked her. "Rescue it, before it gets lost?"

"If it's even there," Leah said acidly. "Don't get your hopes up."

"It's there." Dinah stared down Leah. "He showed me the filing cabinet crammed with everything he'd written so far. Should we rescue it?" she said again to Fiona.

Fiona shook her head. "His son Jeffrey came to see me. He needed a key to get into the house, and? I gave him mine. I don't have a way of getting in any more." Then, like the dormouse in *Alice*, she went back to sleep. Since Bill's death she looked tinier than ever, and she was exhausted.

Ida was in the loveseat, the picture of health, her face supple and full, her eyes bright and amused. This is how Dinah will look in her seventies, thought Harriet, if she lives until then. Ida said, "That Bill Bender had a heart of gold. He used to make bread and bring it to Dinah when she was so sick. Can you believe that?"

"Ida," Harriet said later on, after they had plates of food in their laps and glasses of wine within reach, and she and Ida were side by side on the loveseat, "tell me how to run a movie house." Her request made them an island of movie talk amid the other conversations in the large living room.

"Movies used to be wonderful," Ida said expansively. "People would go into a movie at any time, in the middle or partway through. You know when that changed? In 1960, with *Psycho*. Hitchcock wouldn't let anybody in after it started." In the early days, she told Harriet, movies changed twice a week, "and there were all these shorts and double features and animated cartoons and half-hour featurettes like *Blondie and Dagwood*. That dog was wonderful. Daisy." She chuckled with affection, and even remembered the names of the actors who played Blondie and Dagwood. "Penny Singleton and Arthur Lake," she said. "And there was *The Real Benchley*: Robert Benchley, doing his comic-essay films." You could go in whenever you wanted to, she said, starting at noon on Saturday. It cost a quarter or a dime, depending on the theater, and you stayed right through. Children's pictures in the afternoon, adult pictures in the evening. "But lots of kids hid in the bathroom for half an hour and stayed on for the evening shows." She leaned back into the corner of the loveseat. "Going to the movies was a ritual. Larger than life. But now! You watch at home with the lights on and answer the phone when it rings."

"What kind of movie house would make a go of it now?" Harriet had shifted her position, sitting sideways so that she could look at Ida without straining her neck. Her arm in its sling had started to throb.

"You can't make a go of it now."

"One that showed old classics?"

"I don't know," Ida said thoughtfully. "You'd have to find your audience."

"How did *you* find your audience?"

"They found us," said Ida, explaining that she and her David got into the movie business through the back door, after her uncle died and the family needed somebody to run the Rialto. "We ran it on the side. We still had the hat store on Sparks Street," she said. "But the money we made off Gene Autry and John Wayne!"

"What about Joel McCrea?"

"Yes. Joel McCrea too. Good for you."

The other conversations in the room had died away and everyone was listening to Ida now; even Kenny had put down his book. In its day, said Ida, the Rialto was known for the ten cent matinee, and you would get a newsreel, a cartoon, a first feature, a serial like *The Perils of Pauline*, and then the second feature. Cowboy movies, that's what the Rialto was known for. Up the street was the Somerset, with a higher class of movie, and farther up was the Capitol. "It was grand. A crime that they demolished it. It was like a palace," she said. "You had to see it. The chandeliers!" But business began to go slack, she said, and they gave up the Rialto in 1960. The next owners dropped the price from thirty cents to twenty-five cents and showed triple bills instead of double bills, and they did better. "But you see what I'm saying? They offered something you couldn't get anywhere else, a triple bill, and that brought in the audience."

"Schoolkids," said Dinah from the sofa, taking the glass of water that Jane had brought from the kitchen to quiet her cough. "Thanks, sweetheart." And she made room for her on the sofa. "They were always skipping classes and sneaking off to the Rialto. I'd find algebra books under the seats. Geometry sets."

"Single gloves," said Ida. "Cigarette lighters. Student cards. Transistor radios. Hats and scarves and mitts. Once a year we'd bundle everything up for the Salvation Army."

Harriet, the burgeoning businesswoman, wanted to know about the Strand.

"Ah, the Strand," said Ida. "It had a very sad life. It never got going because it was too close to the Mayfair. You have to get out of the reach of other theaters, or you won't get the films. The Mayfair got the pictures first, then the Rialto, then the drive-ins. By the time the Strand got them there was nothing left."

"So the only way it would work," said Harriet, musing aloud, "would be to do something so different it wouldn't compete with the Mayfair."

Leah broke in. "You could do a retrospective of all the later films Lionel didn't get credit for."

"A retrospective of blacklisted screenwriters," said Jack with sudden interest. "That's not a bad idea. I'd go to that."

"Make it the Canadian campus of the Frame Institute," said Leah. "We could have exchanges between Italy and Canada and get the government to pay for it. You'll need start-up money, but I've got that. You'll need a business plan, but I can do that too."

"I thought I'd go to the bank," Harriet said weakly.

"Why go to the bank when you can turn to family?"

"Because banks are simpler."

"See what I mean? You need a business partner."

"That's one thing Leah knows about," said Jack dryly and to no one in particular. But he rubbed his fingers together and tapped his forehead.

Harriet looked around for Lew, and found him in the plaid arm-chair, legs stretched out, arms crossed. He smiled at her and said, "Get Pauline Kael to come to the opening."

"I know her," said Leah. "A real frump." She sent out a particularly long, thin, knowing whistle of air, and Harriet stared at her in disbelief. But it could be true, she realized. Her aunt knew all sorts of people through Lionel, though not as many as she claimed, of that she was sure.

"Stockings in loops around her calves," said Leah. "A hole in her sleeve. She had her daughter with her when she came to us. That was after Twentieth Century-Fox took her and *McCall's* magazine to task for panning *West Side Story*, and she was fired by *McCall's* and didn't write about movies for a year."

"She didn't like *West Side Story*?" Kenny was incredulous. He'd been stretched out on the floor, one leg twisted through a stool, and now he sat up.

"It wasn't *West Side Story*," said Harriet. "It was *The Sound of Music*."

"She hated *West Side Story* too," said Leah.

"Then she's an idiot!" said Kenny.

"She's not an idiot," said his mother. "She didn't like it. She's not an idiot for not liking it, and you're not an idiot for liking it."

"Her nephew lives here," said Leah. "I'll call him."

"Her nephew?"

"I'll call him," said Leah.

After that the formidable aunt was in such a grand, gloating mood that she told Harriet how to write a novel. "This is what you do," she instructed, saying she was passing on advice given to Lionel by a black-listed editor at Knopf. Harriet listened, thinking there were no lengths of triumphant gall to which her aunt wouldn't go. "You write a long letter to yourself," said Leah, "in which you set down in a figuring-out sort of way what you want to write about. Then you go through it and underline what stands out. Those become chapter headings. Then you bring in the things that most concern you, that you want to find out more about. And you don't put anything off, you don't save anything for some later book. You don't kid yourself that you're going to live so long."

"Did Lionel follow his advice?"

"Lionel unwrote in the afternoon what he wrote in the morning," Leah said with disgust. "You know what Anglo-Saxon men are like."

Jim Creak knocked on the door during dessert, and Fiona woke up again. She looked around at the plates of cake and said, "I can't make a cake any more. My hands are stupid, and? there's nothing I can do about it."

Jim came into the room in his woolly garb, rumpled and bashful, saying he was sorry, he just got home, or he would have come earlier. As he sat down, taking the only available chair, his eyes rested on Dinah, whose glance slid away to the younger, beefy man on the sofa beside her: that must be the one whose legs he was supposed to break.

Lew had been observing, from his armchair in the corner, Dinah's apparent coziness with Jack, which he understood, or thought he understood. She needed someone to lean on, and Jack had broad shoulders. But Jack also had the kind of cruel, sarcastic mouth that women seemed to fall for, and he didn't know why. Dinah looked over at him every so often, her glance never less than tender and never more than philosophical. A realist about love, he thought. Unlike Harriet.

The arrival of Jim Creak sparked Lew's interest. Here was the man who wasn't afraid to champion love in public.

But Dinah, he noticed, was looking the other way.

It was Fiona Chester who put her hand out to Jim and thanked him for the song he had played on the radio, "And? I couldn't agree more with what you said about love."

"Nor could I," said Harriet.

Leah's sniff was so audible that Harriet said, "All right. What would you have said?"

"I don't know, but I wouldn't have made such a fuss."

And Jack Frame started to laugh. "You made a fuss at Lionel's funeral. I'll never forget the way you gave him hell for not doing enough. Not writing the books he should have written, or pursuing the contacts he should have pursued. Then afterwards you shut yourself in your room and wouldn't come out."

"That's not a crime. I wanted to be alone."

"Garbo," said Dinah into the silence. "The woman who had everything and threw it away with both hands. But that's why she was so interesting."

Harriet said, "That's not why."

Leah said, "She's not even interesting."

"She was so public," Harriet said slowly, dissatisfied with her answer even as she formulated it, "and then so antisocial. That's what made her so interesting. The contradiction in her personality. And her beauty, of course."

"She wasted her life," said the aunt. "She could have spoken out. She could have made a difference. But there was nothing to her. No politics."

Jack began to yawn.

Lew buried his nose in *Jewish Currents*.

Dinah exchanged going-home glances with her mother, and Jim Creak noticed and stood up when they did and offered to walk them home. " 'I'm with you now,' " he said, an amused, self-mocking smile playing around his lips as he ignored Jack's glare.

Kenny's ears perked up. "Al Pacino!" he cried. "When he was in the hospital with Marlon Brando. Give me another one," he begged.

"He's good," Jim said to Harriet. They had moved into the hallway. He was helping Ida with her coat, and he said, " 'I need him like an axe needs a turkey.' "

"Humphrey Bogart!"

"Nope."

"It's a woman," said the helpful mother. "Barbara Stanwyck, to be precise."

"*Lady Eve*," yelled Kenny, and Ida said, "She's my favorite," and Jim said, "Mine too." They were ready to leave, but Kenny hung on. "Give me another one."

" 'All I know about you is you stole my car and I'm insane about you.' "

"I know!" cried Jane, who had pushed her way into the hallway and was standing beside Dinah. "I know! Gary Cooper!"

"And what's-her-name!" Kenny pounded his fist on his leg. "Marlene –"

"Marlene Dietrich," yelled Jane.

"Shut up!"

"Don't say 'shut up,' " said Harriet. "Say 'be quiet.' "

"But which movie?"

"I know," yelled Jane.

"Shut up!"

"Kenny!"

"*Desire!*" he yelled triumphantly. "Give me another one!"

"No." His mom took him by the shoulders and moved him back a few feet, but he still wouldn't give up. "Have you seen *The Usual Suspects*?" he asked Jim.

"Good movie. I liked it a lot."

"*She* won't let me see it. Can you believe that? She's always so mean."

"No, she's not. She's really nice to you."

At these words, Lew lifted his head from the Israeli–Palestinian impasse and stared thoughtfully through the doorway at the jumble of bodies in the front hall. He knew how easily Harriet was drawn in. Putting down his magazine, he went over to say goodnight, kissing Dinah on the cheek, and then her mother. Shaking Jim Creak's hand and assessing him anew. Behind him, in the living room, Jack took down Leah's new address and Fiona let out a low snore.

Dinah Bloom had known other men like Jim Creak, overfond, overattentive, and wanting too much in return. She was a practiced dodger, prepared, when he accompanied her and Ida back to her house, for him to put his hand on her arm and say, "Come home with me and I'll make you a cup of tea."

"No, Jim. Not tonight."

Having known Stella, she knew too much about him. *He wants to do everything together. He even wants to shower together.* Stella of the many men, and boozy Jim Creak.

"It doesn't have to be right now," he said. "Any time. I'll make you the best cup of tea you've ever had in your whole mouth."

Had it been summer, Dinah's laughter would have rippled into every house on the block. "Don't tell me," she said. "Jack Lemmon?"

"*It Should Happen to You*," said Jim.

33

In Which the Formidable
Aunt Takes Revenge

The next day the kids were back at school, though with a difference. At recess Kenny's teacher fell on the ice and staggered back inside with blood running down her cheek. A concussion and a broken wrist, and that was the end of her for the rest of the year.

The good news sent Kenny to his typewriter, where he banged out the following: *The name is Brackenwood. Brackett Brackenwood. On my estate in the North of England I have vineyards and a putting green. I also have a villa in the south of France. They modelled Cary Grant's villa in* To Catch a Thief *on mine. Also an apartment in Paris and an apartment in New York. Also three dark-blue Porsches.*

Aunt Leah heard the typing and went into his room. "You sound like Lionel," she said. "What are you writing? Read it to me."

Kenny read it to her.

"Put *me* into your story. Can you do that?" She was looking over his shoulder and reading for herself now. "You could have an apartment in Rome too: an apartment in Paris, an apartment in New York, and an apartment in Rome."

"Okay." He scratched his ear.

"Wouldn't that be *great*?" Sounding almost desperate for him to agree. Then, "Wait," she said. She went downstairs and returned with a key ring that had a picture of the Frame Institute on its tab. "I want you to have this. I gave one to your mother but she never uses it. You'll appreciate it more than she will."

"Thanks," said Kenny.

"I don't want you to forget me," she said.

That night she was gone, to Janice's, and Harriet's shoulders kicked off their high heels and dropped four inches. The next day she went to the hairdresser's and found herself in the hands of Julie, a small woman in her twenties who said she was born to have a pair of scissors in her hand. "No matter what tragedy I'm going through, I feel better when I'm cutting hair. I pick up a pair of scissors," Julie said, "and it helps me get through my grief." She was brushing Harriet's hair as she talked, so hard that tears came to Harriet's eyes.

Afterwards, Harriet wasn't sure. She had done what so many women do to make themselves feel better. Now she felt the way so many women feel afterwards. Uncertain, and poorer.

That week, following the ice storm, the snow military were out in their trucks and ploughs removing the snow-and-ice banks, and once they were finished, the street was as broad as a boulevard in Paris. A lesson in narrow and wide. Narrowed by snowbanks until cars couldn't pass, then widened by the plough until street, curb, sidewalk were spread evenly with snow – a mother generous with butter. One night, Harriet came upon the liberation army idling on Glen Avenue. Six dump trucks and several ploughs occupied the block. High up in their glassed-in cabs, the drivers were drinking coffee in summer shirts.

She went in to say goodnight to Kenny, bending over his palisade of books to give him a kiss. "Do you like Aunt Leah?" he asked her.

"Not much."

"Do you like Dinah?"

"Very much. What are you thinking about?"

He was wishing that she liked Leah more, even though he knew perfectly well that Leah was a lot harder to like than Dinah.

"Kenny?"

He looked up at her. "Is *Jane Eyre* your favorite novel of all time?"

"It's among them."

"All right. Give me your top three."

"No."

"Your top five."

"No."

"Why not?"

His mother turned on her heel and left, and he stretched out farther in his bed. Sometimes it worked, and sometimes it didn't.

By the end of the week the formidable aunt had taken her revenge, and it happened this way. Thursday morning, while Harriet was reading about old movie houses, the phone rang. Leah was calling her from Janice's house. She said, "I've talked to Pauline Kael's nephew, and you're in luck."

"How do you mean?"

"She's in Ottawa."

"I don't believe you."

"Fine. I'm a liar."

"But she's old and ill. I can't imagine she travels anywhere, let alone to Ottawa."

"Wait a minute, darling. Someone's at the door."

Harriet waited. Minutes went by. Her arm rested inside its sling.

Leah came back on the phone. "He's her only nephew. They must be close. Anyway, this is the point. We're having lunch tomorrow. Would you like to join us?"

Harriet took a deep breath, and then she said yes to the offer she couldn't refuse.

"I'm meeting them at the art gallery first – she likes art apparently – and I'll call you when we get to the restaurant. Okay, darling?"

"Which restaurant?"

"We haven't decided. We'll decide tomorrow, and I'll call you when we get there. Are you excited?"

"I'm thrilled."

"I knew you'd be thrilled. Bye, darling."

Harriet returned to her research on the Capitol Theatre, the old movie palace (originally known as Loew's Ottawa, then B.F. Keith's) built in 1920 at the corner of Bank and Queen for vaudeville acts and silent movies; wired for sound in the spring of 1929 (just as Fiona Chester was finishing her schooling on the Isle of Lewis); and demolished in July 1970. It had been Ottawa's biggest and most luxurious theater, replete with marble staircase, sweeping balustrade, chandeliered domes, and a spacious stage that for years was home not just to movies but to the Tremblay concert series, which brought to town the likes of Lily Pons, the Sadler's Wells Ballet Company, the Peking Opera, Ezio Pinza, Paul Robeson, Marian Anderson, Artur Rubinstein, Jascha Heifetz, Lois Marshall, Joan Sutherland, Teresa Stratas, Leontyne Price. In reading about this lost past, Harriet's own ideas began to take shape. She would have another series – an ongoing neighborhood series that would be lively, informative, and sexy: Leading Men from Grant to Gere; Leading Women from Garbo to Binoche; The History of the Movie Kiss; The Cowboy as Lover; The Rise and Fall of Joel McCrea; The Best Bedroom Scenes in the Movies. Why not have a month of Preston Sturges? A month of Cary Grant? A month of Buster Keaton? Why not have Screwball Heroines from the Dirty Thirties; Cross-Dressers in Screen History; Jane Austen Unbuttoned; Kurosawa Till You Drop. If book clubs could be all the rage, then why not movie clubs? Why not cater to the appetite for movie talk with book-and-movie groups, guest speakers, debates? Why not start a non-profit cultural institute that would bring back the winter matinée, the double feature, the documentary?

She would be the new Grierson.

In time there would be a plaque on the side of the Strand (renamed, though what that name would be she hadn't yet decided) lauding her indefatigable energy and keen business sense. Harriet Browning: Purveyor of cheap movies. Rescuer of talent. Cultural adventurer.

Though *venture* not *adventure* was what she stressed to puzzled lenders, since ads were to be banned, along with *Dr. Zhivago* and *The Sound of Music.*

"Tell me," Dinah had asked her recently. "What have you got against *Dr. Zhivago* anyway?"

"It's romantic in the worst sense of the word. Wait! Maybe that could be another series. Romantic in the Worst Sense of the Word. Rock Hudson and Lana Turner Revisited. People would come to that."

Buttonholing Kenny, Dinah said, "Do I understand that you and your sister have never seen *The Sound of Music?*"

"*She* won't let it in the house."

"They've seen the anti–*Sound of Music*," said Harriet.

"Don't tell me."

"*The Commitments.* And they loved it."

Since her deep sleep she felt capable of anything. Unlike Samson, shorn as he slept, she had acquired confidence. It sprang from her head like a big wig.

One morning she dropped in on the song detective, who was looking dejected, until she described her ideas for the movie institute, though *institute* wasn't the word and nor was *cultural center*.

He replied thoughtfully, "There used to be something called the 'Radio Theatre from Hollywood' introduced by Cecil B. DeMille. Movies were adapted for radio, and movie stars came on as guests. Maybe we could do a sort of 'Saturday Afternoon from the Strand' like the Saturday-afternoon opera broadcasts from the Met in New York, complete with a quiz. We could play clips from old movies and interviews from the archives."

"You could be the quizmaster," she said. "You could be Milton Cross."

"A lowbrow Milton Cross," he said. "Not which sharp was Joan Sutherland able to reach, but what cup size did Jayne Mansfield wear?"

"'Movies Without Pictures,'" said Harriet. "'For Movie-Lovers Everywhere.'"

It was Friday, the day she was to meet Pauline Kael, and she opened her notebook and wrote, *Dear Pauline, Leah claims to know you, but then she claims to know everyone. I hardly expect to see you today, but I can't help think-ing about what I'll ask, if by some miracle you're actually here. Cary Grant, first and foremost. We'll talk about him. Then why you're impervious to the charms of* Casablanca *but susceptible to the dubious appeal of* Tequila Sunrise. *Then how you maintained a friendship with Jean Renoir after his work went downhill, and you said so. And whether you've ever met Sean Connery. And how you ran your repertory house in Berkeley, and what advice you would give me for running the Strand.*

One o'clock came and no call from Leah. Two o'clock, and still no call. At two-forty-five the phone rang and Harriet picked it up.

"Darling, we're at the Château Laurier, in the restaurant with the piano. We're about to have coffee and dessert. Would you like to join us?"

Harriet took a moment to control her temper, and succeeded. And then she called a cab.

By the time she got to the hotel, and to the restaurant inside the hotel, it was nearly three-thirty. Her aunt was at a table near the grand piano, alone except for a potted plant trembling at her side. "Darling," she said.

"Leah." Harriet looked from her aunt to the used coffee cups and saucers, the used cloth napkins.

Leah signalled to the waiter. "Would you bring coffee? My niece is here."

Harriet, with help from the waiter, removed the coat draped over her shoulders, and sat down.

"You didn't miss much, darling. She's on her last legs and her nephew is an idiot."

"I've always liked it here," said Harriet, looking around and pretending not to be bothered, or taken in, or affected in any way at all by having walked straight into the trap she'd known was here. It was an old railway hotel, the main lobby not so different from the day when her mother brought her here for tea on her thirteenth birthday, though much else was gone: the old registration counter of black marble and brass, the barbershop frequented by Mackenzie King, the Canadian Grill, where so much politicking got done. Gone too was the Jasper Lounge, formerly the Jasper Tea Room, that her mother had described as having a double row of totem poles. Also the famous Peacock Alley, furnished with writing tables and easy chairs, which Gladys called the prettiest place in Ottawa. Even the moose and caribou heads in the main lobby had been spirited away to England by a previous general manager, who wanted them for the walls of his own inn, or so said Dinah, who got her information from a reliable bellman.

After Harriet's coffee arrived, Leah said, "That's the same waiter we had the night we came for dinner."

"Is he? I wasn't here."

"That's right. You didn't come. Lew took a turn that night. Did he tell you?"

"Dinah told me."

"Yes. Dinah looked after him. I think she looked after him very well."

Leah's insinuation was so grim of purpose that Harriet reached in her mind for something sane, something peaceful – and remembered the time when Lew came home from a fractious meeting of a local heritage committee that was bent on saving a building on Laurier Avenue, but divided about its methods. He had stood in the bedroom doorway – it was late – and told her that at the start of the meeting everyone was suspicious and hostile, darting looks around the table, all set to lock horns, until an older man reminded them of what had brought them there in the first place – their common desire to save a gracious old house – and once they were reminded of that, Lew said, all of their ill will fell away. She had lain in bed listening to him, a book in her hands, and as he talked she too had felt released from her own and everyone else's ill will.

"Leah," she said. "Why this charade about Pauline Kael? Let's stop needling each other. Let's stop." She reached across and put her hand on Leah's. "You're my aunt," she said.

But Leah didn't need to be reminded of that. "Then you should treat me better." Leah picked up her coffee spoon, dislodging Harriet's hand, and said, "I worshiped the ground my aunt walked on, and she worshiped me. She took me into her home. She opened up her arms to me."

So this was at the bottom of it all: Leah had been waiting for them to offer her a home.

But Harriet wasn't about to take her aunt in.

Cornered by her own ungenerosity, she fell silent. She took off her glasses, she rubbed her eyes. "What did you and Pauline Kael talk about?" she asked finally, and not without a trace of sarcasm.

"I didn't say much. She and Jack did most of the talking."

"Jack was here?" Harriet put her glasses back on.

"They talked about Lionel."

Harriet stared at her aunt.

Leah said, "You hate it when I'm right."

"What else are you right about?"

"You."

Her coffee was getting cold. She took a sip, and wished she hadn't.

"You can't resist smooth talkers," Leah went on. "Your face lights up when Jack comes in the room. You don't even look at Lew."

"You don't know what you're talking about."

"Let me tell you a story. For two years, when my Sarah had her daily TV show in Toronto, she'd fly home to Montreal on the weekend, and every Sunday she'd fly back to Toronto, and Jack would ask, Why Sunday? Why not leave early Monday morning so we can have the weekend together? But no, she had to be there the day before to get ready. Of course, she was having an affair with the producer. This went on for two years."

"You said that." Harriet's voice was scalding, but it had no effect on her aunt.

Leah said, "She broke it off when Jack found out, but he left her anyway. He couldn't trust her. And she's been scrambling ever since, trying to get him back. He'll never go back to her. You should pay more attention to Lew, or you're going to lose him."

"What a moralizer you are," Harriet said. "You're like a kindergarten teacher." Her arm was throbbing and so was her head.

Leah sucked air through her teeth. "You're not the first person to be disappointed in her husband. Anne, I mean my Anne in Chicago, she thought she married the wrong man too."

"I married the right man," said Harriet. "He married the wrong woman."

Leah smiled. Insecure women were her specialty. "How's your coffee? Shall I tell him to bring you a fresh cup?"

Harriet shook her head.

Leah signalled the waiter and asked for the bill. But Harriet said, "I haven't had dessert." And the waiter stopped in his tracks.

"You invited me for coffee and dessert," she said stubbornly, determined to get something for her pains. "I haven't had dessert."

Harriet took her time over the menu, and she took her time over dessert. *Had I seen you, I would have paid close attention to how you dealt with Leah. I would have told you that Kenny is reading your reviews now. And I would have explained why I like your writing so much. It's because I see you reacting to things on the spot. Being overcritical and overgenerous, but thinking, feeling, reacting.*

Leah eyed the slowly disappearing hazelnut torte.

"Is it good?"

"It is."

"Let me taste." She reached across with her greedy spoon, and Harriet drove her fork into the back of her hand. She wasn't one of six children for nothing.

She didn't draw blood, not that she would have minded drawing blood, but she certainly got a response – a yelp, a retreat, a widening of those remarkable eyes whose beauty she once commented upon. "Leah, you have the most beautiful eyes," she'd said to her years ago. And Leah had said, "I've never noticed. People tell me that, but I've never noticed."

But she noticed the fork in her hand. Her eyes were as surprised as Sean Connery's in *The Next Man* when Cornelia Sharpe raised a gun to his head and pulled the trigger, thereby putting an end to an Arab with a Scottish accent. Also, to a very bad movie that Harriet sat through twice after getting her wisdom teeth pulled.

"*Excuse* me!" said Leah.

Harriet went on with her cake. "That's all right, darling."

"You're cruel."

"Not cruel," Harriet said. "Heartless."

"Unfeeling."

"Yes."

"That's what I told Kenny."

Harriet put down her fork. "What did you tell Kenny?" she asked softly.

They were alone in the dining room except for an elderly couple drinking tea in silence. Show tunes were on the sound system. Doris Day. Frankie.

Leah said, "I want to talk to you about my will. I want you to know what you can expect."

"Leah, I don't expect anything."

"I don't mean you," she said. "I mean Kenny."

34

The Seduction

Spring came earlier that year than ever before. The warmth began in February, causing a long and thorough melt that followed Dinah's surgery. Doctors opened her chest and removed the tumor, after which her recovery was slow and painful. On the first weekend of that remarkable month, Harriet and Lew paid a visit to Dinah in the hospital, then drove to Gatineau Park and followed a trail so littered with fallen ice that walking on it was like treading on broken chandeliers. Around them were all the battered trees. Rather than dark branches reaching up and out, snapped white arms were hanging low. Everywhere. Torn tree flesh like long pieces of white chicken meat.

During that month, when they went to see Dinah, first at the hospital and later at the rehab center, they crossed paths every so often with Jim Creak. But it was Jack Frame who was invariably there. He couldn't have been more attentive, standing for long hours by Dinah's bedside without ever tiring. "I was made for this," he said. "I have the stamina of an ox." During one of these visits, Harriet asked him what it was like to talk to Pauline Kael, and he said, "I haven't the faintest idea." That was how she learned that she'd been right all along, though wrong to think she'd been wrong.

On the last Saturday in February, Harriet walked to the Arboretum and found, piled high, bundles of prunings from the damaged trees. To stand in the tall spruce grove was to imagine herself in a barbershop on a floor covered with dark curls of hair. A week later, at 5:40 a.m., she heard a robin and looked up from her book. It was March 7. She'd been reading about the history of early movies, and it occurred to her that what they'd been through in the ice storm was something like the rough passage of silent movies to talkies, and, just as happened then, there were many casualties. Leah had flown back to Italy on Valentine's Day, after a sour farewell. She spoke to Harriet on the phone as if she were the last person she wanted to see. It was Jack who took her to the airport.

March was unnaturally warm, more like May two months early. Dinah was home again, and Ida had returned to look after her. The prognosis was good, and they thought the worst was over. In the middle of March Lew went away for two weeks, to Mexico and Chile, and while he was gone Jack phoned Harriet several times.

"I don't have your e-mail address," he said to her the first time.

"I don't have e-mail."

"Ah, but you should. E-mails are much less invasive than telephones. It's like whispering. You can say, 'I love you, darling,' at two in the morning."

"I miss letters," she said doggedly.

"Oh, they're *gone*."

He called her for the name of a restaurant. Someone's phone number. The distance from one town to another. Was she his secretary? His voice flat, cool; and a phone call every other day, until she thought, He's calling because he wants to hear my voice. And deliberately she made her tone brisk and clipped, as you might turn your face to show its most unattractive side to someone whose interest in you is certain to vanish at the first minor test.

Outside, the early warmth brought buds to the point of bursting. She could hear them popping in the night like tiny fish leaping out of water. Pale sources of minuscule light.

Soon color washed over them. A hat of color descended over the bald head of winter.

Harriet knocked on Dinah's door. "Put on the kettle," she said. "I have something to ask you."

Bristly old Buddy made the hallway nearly impenetrable. It was like going through a carwash, without the car.

"Why won't you give Jim Creak the time of day?" Harriet said, once she achieved the kitchen and discovered that she and Dinah were alone.

"This is what you wanted to ask me?"

"I'll get to that."

Dinah spread her hands wide, but before she could speak Harriet said, "I've come to like him so much. It's true he can be stubborn, and he's not the fastest knitter in the world with those surprisingly small hands of his, but he'd have no trouble washing out the insides of jars. Besides, he's kind and interesting. And I think he's really devoted to you."

"That's the trouble."

"What is?"

"He's much too serious about me."

Harriet studied her. "What are you afraid of?" she asked.

Dinah could have answered, since she knew the answer. If she was going to be involved with the wrong man, then let him not be too earnestly in love. She said, "They've scheduled my chemo. It's going to start the week after next."

"That's what I was getting to."

Harriet had been leaning against the counter. Now she sat beside Dinah at the kitchen table, and asked what day they were starting. "April 8? But we won't be here. We'll be in Havana."

"Don't worry. My mother's here," she said. "And Jack will take me back and forth to the hospital."

There were so many birds now that when Harriet stood up and went to the window, she expected to see a flash of color. All she saw was a big ugly starling on the porch roof. But there were crocuses at the foot of the garden, like a line of purple feathers: near the fence, a semi-circle of purple feathers like an Indian headdress. She said, "I don't trust Jack, but I guess that's obvious."

"It isn't obvious. Sometimes you seem to like him very much."

"He unsettles me."

"Jack's good at that."

"So he unsettles you too?" Turning away from the window.

"No. He doesn't."

"But Lew does."

A sound came from Dinah's throat – the almost-laugh you make when you recognize, out of the blue, an old tune from childhood that you haven't heard in years. Then she said, "Not everybody can have Lew."

And with those gentle words a thorn was removed from Harriet's heart.

But Lew didn't call while he was away. More than a week went by, and not a word. Harriet removed old leaves from the tender tips of tulips coming up. Examined the beautiful red of the rhubarb, pushing up like the red tip of a dog's aroused penis, surrounded by cauliflower-ear leaves, wrinkly and almost black-green in color.

Inside, she looked at two old pictures of Lew. One picture included her, the other did not. She put the pictures side by side. She compared his face in the photo that included her with his face in the photo taken ten months earlier, before they had met, and discovered that when she wasn't in the picture he was entirely attractive to her, but when she was in the picture his attractiveness vanished. Is this why she liked movies so much? Because she wasn't in the picture?

She could love someone who wasn't looking at her, didn't know her, hadn't been shaped by her, but not someone whose face had been blurred and compromised by dealing with her.

Jim Creak was outside with his shovel, in shirt-sleeves, spreading the last vestiges of snow far and wide to melt even faster. She went over to tease him about his anti-snow avidity, then went on to the fruit-and-vegetable store, where her mind drifted to Jack Frame and his continued, inexplicable attentions. They had their foundation, she was sure, in some sort of ill will generated by her resistance to his writing, a resistance crudely worded and guilt-ridden, but firm. *No*, she said, she wouldn't read his first chapters about Lionel: find yourself a real editor. Dinah, she knew, had also told him to seek out a professional. But Dinah was Dinah. She could get away with anything, being straightforward and free of doubt. Being brave. For a moment, standing in the fruit store, everything Harriet disliked about Jack and everything she disliked about herself took hold of her with such force that she bent double over the green beans and apples in her grocery cart. Then she straightened up, and there he was, her date with fate, pushing his way through the turnstile.

He misread her blush. And why not? She was as revealed in her embarrassment as a shade plant suddenly exposed to the sun.

"Hello, beautiful," he said, looking her up and down, until her blush deepened.

He bought bananas and a pineapple, and offered to drive her home.

"I always buy too much," she said. "My eyes are bigger than my arms." And her bags were indeed heavy.

In Jack's car, feeling at a disadvantage, Harriet said almost nothing and then too much. She said yes, when he asked if Lew was still away. Then she said, "I dreamt about him last night. I don't recall the particulars except that in a general way he was very nasty to me." Her voice was rueful and only slightly amused.

"Where did you say he was?" Jack asked her.

"Mexico, then Chile. Or maybe Chile, then Mexico. I can't remember. He hasn't called."

"He's been away for a week and he hasn't called?"

"Not once."

And then she was telling him about the two times she'd called home collect from New York, when Lew answered the operator by saying, "I guess so." The first time it was "I guess so." The second time, "Well, I guess so." She laughed, shaking her head about it all. Dream, husband, life.

In truth, she had wandered blind afterwards, sick at heart. And having stirred up the old memory, she felt heartsick all over again.

"I don't mean to whip things up," said Jack, "but that's mean."

And so we make our confessions to the wrong person, and bonds that we have no intention of forming get formed.

By this time they were in front of her house – he had pulled up to the curb and she was about to get out, her hand was on the door handle, when he reached over and slowly and deliberately ran his hand up her long leg, from ankle to knee. She was wearing black tights. Then he sat back and looked at her. She stared at him.

"I love your face when it gets worked up," he said.

"Worked up?"

"When you blush."

"That's menopause," she said dryly.

"I don't think so."

Again, she moved to get out and this time he grabbed her hand, and held it. Then he turned her hand over and his eyes fastened onto the scar tissue visible on her lower wrist. He pushed up the sleeve to see more of the shiny, corrugated flesh. Then he bent his head and kissed her wrist.

"What are you doing?"

"You could invite me in, you know," he said, raising his head and looking at her.

Her other hand was still on the door handle, and some movie memory – the image of a woman's hand hovering around the handle of a pickup door – pressed in as she turned away. But he tugged her back, and she remembered a party years ago when she sat on a sofa between two drunk Russian violinists. Every time she tried to stand up, they pulled her down again. They were wild, even if they did play classical music. Vodka. But once she stopped trying to get up, once she stopped saying she had to go, and waited for a few minutes, then it was easy to get up and leave. She took her hand off the door handle and sat back.

When Kenny came around the corner, he saw a blue car in front of his house. He came up from behind, and recognized Jack Frame through the rear window. His mom was sitting beside him and they were talking. And then – hey! They pulled away as if he wasn't there.

He stood in the street and watched the car zoom to the end of the block, turn right and disappear.

So she forgot. She forgot it was a half-day at school. The front door better be unlocked, because he didn't have his key.

It was locked.

He couldn't believe it. What was the matter with her anyway? *I've been waiting for an hour! Where were you? I told you this morning! What's the matter with you?* And what a sorry look she would have on her face.

After an eternity of five minutes he walked down the street to Dinah's, and lucky for him she was home. He was mad, but all he told Dinah was that his mom wasn't there and the door was locked. Ida and Dinah made a big fuss over him. They fed him lunch, and kept him busy talking and eating. It was hard work being liked so much. After lunch Dinah needed to rest, so he watched TV with Ida, and every so often he phoned home, but there wasn't any answer. Later, when Dinah woke up, she phoned too, but there was still no answer, so the three of them played poker for high stakes. Dinah asked him what news there was from his dad, and he didn't have any news because his dad hadn't called. Where is he this time? asked Ida. Chile then Mexico, he told her. That man sure gets around, said Ida. You know where I'd like to go? she said. Greece. She turned to Dinah. After your treatment's over let's go to Greece – the sun will put you back on your feet in no time.

"What treatment?" asked Kenny. Nobody told him anything!

"You'll be in Havana," Dinah said. "You lucky dog. You'll be drinking *dulce de leches* laced with rum."

"Bacardi," said Kenny. And mimicking Jean Simmons, "'This would be a wonderful way to get children to drink milk!'"

Dinah laughed her rollicking, appreciative laugh, and he said, "Who was better in that movie? Marlon Brando or Frank Sinatra?"

"What kind of question is that? You know the answer."

This time Harriet picked up the phone. Dinah said to her, "Kenny's here and we've been playing poker. He whipped my ass, but only because I let him."

She handed him the phone and he said, "Where have you been?" He was blazing mad all over again. "I told you it was a half-day. Where did you *go*?"

"I'm sorry. I really am. I forgot all about it. I got a movie for us," she said.

"Which one?"

"*My Fair Lady*."

"I don't want to see *that*." He was disgusted.

"You'll love Rex Harrison. He was a great actor and a terrible man," she said. "I know a reporter who kept hoping he'd hit one of his fans so he could print the headline, SHIT HITS FAN. Come home," she said. "I've made cocoa."

When he came through the door, she called out to him from the kitchen. Her face was sorry and the cocoa looked good. Jane had a marshmallow in hers. He looked around. "Where's Jack?"

His mom gave him a strange look. "Jack isn't here."

"So where did you go?"

"How do you mean?"

"When you drove away and left me here."

Jane intoned from *Charade*, "'They left me there, Mrs. Lampert. They left me there. Six bullets in my legs and they left me there. They deserve to die!'"

His mom sat down. "Go easy on me, Kenny. I've had a bad afternoon."

After she'd sat back in the car, Jack said, "I want to show you something. It won't take long."

"Where are we going?"

But he didn't answer. After they turned the corner, he reached for her hand again. His hand was bigger than Lew's, and she didn't bat it away.

"Don't look so worried," he said with a smile.

He drove to his place on First Avenue, the first floor of a side-by-side in a block near Bank Street. His living room had an armchair and a large table covered with piles of paper. In pride of place was what he wanted to show her.

"*Where did it come from?*" Having opened the old album and discovered, one after another, the most beautiful pressed ferns, mounted carefully and identified with a flowing script: *Asplenium flaccidum, Polypodium rugulosum, Asplenium lucidum, Cynthia dealbata.*

Someone who knew Lionel, he said, another screenwriter. Her great-aunt had put it together as a young woman in New Zealand.

Pasted between and beside the pressed ferns – this was what took her breath away – were pictures of old movie stars cut out of magazines.

"I thought you'd be interested," he said.

She was more than interested. He pulled up two chairs, and she sat down and he sat beside her.

Here was Garbo. Sharing a page with *Diplazium proliferum*.

She said with wonder, "Do you recognize it?" It seemed to her it was the same one – the same fern that Lew brought back from Cuba, the same spear-tip fern that he'd put in her lap.

"Which?"

"I showed you this fern."

"I remember you showed me a fern –"

"It was this one."

She dipped down to the purse at her feet, pulled out her notebook, and wrote down the name. Then she went back to the beginning of the album – it was bound in green leather and quite thick – and found an inscription: *Mounted and Botanically named by Miss Hattie Partridge, Dunedin, New Zealand, August 6, 1884.*

A bluish white light of recognition flashed in her mind.

"Look." She pointed with her finger at *Hattie*.

"You were her in a previous life," he said.

No, she thought, that's not it. It's not that simple. You can't pin down these floating coincidences that way. And yet she liked him for saying it.

Below that inscription was another: *Diana Mills from H.L. Partridge, September 15, 1925.* She wrote both inscriptions in her notebook, pausing before she wrote down *September 15, 1925.* Then she went through the album, discovering Lillian Gish, Gloria Swanson, Mary Pickford, Ina Claire, John Gilbert, and thinking, as she turned the pages, about the almost physical nudge that sets a story in motion, or makes you aware that you're part of a story that's already in motion, and has been for a long time. Garbo arrived in Hollywood on September 15, 1925.

Jack sat close to her. When she turned to him to express her amazed delight, he reached up and took off her glasses. His mouth, when he kissed her, tasted of peanuts.

She felt her heart quicken and go heavy. Such a mixture of arousal and dismay. And now she remembered whose hand it was that hovered around the inside handle of the pickup door. *You'll like it*, he'd said. *She reminds me of you.* Was he setting her up again? Was all this part of a long payback by the man who hated Meryl Streep?

She pulled away. Then, putting her glasses back on, resuming her study of the album, she pitched into an embarrassed fever of talk about ancient ferns, the likely age of Garbo, what period this was, which movie; she turned again to the picture of Gloria Swanson and bending to look at it more closely, as if she were a little scientist, said that when Grierson visited her movie set she ordered him off. *There's a man here whose eyes are hurting me. Throw him out.* He had the fiercest eyes.

"What happened to her?" she asked suddenly of the screenwriter who inherited the album and pasted in the pictures of the movie stars. She checked the name at the front. "Diana Mills. Is she still alive?"

"Her son is."

"What happened to him?"

He was watching her intently, and then he smiled, and she realized that he was the son. Jack. And Diana Mills, "a screenwriter who knew Lionel," was his mother. Why hadn't she known this before?

"What became of her?" she asked him.

"She committed suicide."

Harriet stared at him. His eyes didn't leave her face. It was as if he were dangling the information in front of her. And then he let it drop.

"She swallowed arsenic," he said.

"*No.*"

"Like Emma Bovary."

If there was a correct response to this, Harriet couldn't think what it was. She sat stunned. No wonder his novels are full of suicide, she thought. Jack took on another dimension in her eyes as she sat there staring at him. But when she looked down at the album, ran her hand across a page, she wondered why Leah had never mentioned Diana Mills, why no one had. And her old wariness returned, not just about what he'd told her, but about the creepy, manipulative way he'd told it. Jack and his mother, she thought. *Jack and his women.*

She stood up. No, she didn't want a ride home, she had a few errands to do downtown, she would do the errands and take the bus home. She got herself to the door – Jack looked less surprised than amused, privately amused – and then she fled. She fled on foot and was halfway home before she stopped in her tracks. Her groceries!

Now what were they going to have for supper?

Pasta. They had pasta for supper.

Lew called that night, just before ten. Kenny and Jane came down the stairs as if it were Christmas. Thumping feet and pure excitement.

Afterwards, after he said he had found the perfect place for them on the southern coast of Chile, and she'd said, marvellous, we'll live like Neruda; after they'd laughed together and she'd pictured the ocean waves and smooth, black, volcanic rock and felt a great and welcome surge of love so that she was able to say with genuine warmth, I was worried, I know it's hard to get to a phone, but I was worried; after the kids were back in bed, then she walked up to Bank Street to return the movie, and the air smelled wonderful. It smelled like fragrant dust. Young and old were out walking or sitting on porches. There was a light wash of green on the trees, and crocuses were ankle-high. Ottawa wasn't so bad, after all, she thought, and really Lew was a peach. He had a beautiful voice. Always she noticed it on the telephone, a voice as flexible as a dancer's spine, as flexible and relaxed as he was himself, despite the failings he had that he wouldn't admit to.

She passed the old school, newly renovated on the corner, then crossed the street and went down to the video store to drop off *My Fair Lady*, one of Audrey's lesser efforts (even Audrey failed from time to time), although Jane had loved it until the end, when Eliza told Henry goodbye. "I hate it when she talks like that," Jane said. "I wish she'd speak normally." But Audrey, turning her neck into a concrete giraffe's and pursing her mouth, said, "'Goodbye, Professor Higgins, you will never see me again,'" and then she walked off in that ridiculous pink soup of a dress, as if rigor mortis had her in its grip.

On the way back it was light enough under the streetlights to see the dead squirrel, and to stop and study it. It was dead as a doornail. A dead black squirrel on its side, like a tiny black horse, really very elegant – one dark slit in its side, and one dark slit of an eye, lying on a takeout carton with spaces for four coffees. She straightened up and walked on, thinking of elegant horses painted on the walls of caves, or worked decoratively onto the shields of warlike cultures, as if death itself had a sense of design.

At home in the kitchen the tulips she had bought five days ago were in a state of utter openness, leaning as gracefully as Audrey's Eliza-neck refused to do, and reminding her of the long curve of the canal, which she considered Ottawa's loveliest attribute, along with the two rivers and the green cliff beside the locks. The tulip stems made eight long curving canals above the surface of her white kitchen table. The phone call had been a happy one, beginning with the operator's heavily accented Santiago voice, which she answered with a quick yes. Then on he came, his words making an odd echo that disappeared after a minute or two, so that she heard, unechoing, the curving, graceful lines of his voice.

One less squirrel to eat her tulips. Alerted the first time it happened by the movement of a single blossom, in a row of ten, bowing down, and then the little hands reaching higher and pulling lower as if for a kiss. Munch went the squirrel and stuffed the tulip into its mouth.

One less squirrel. And one more image from a day that encompassed beautiful ferns and another tricky kiss; Audrey Hepburn's neck and Cecil Beaton's flowers; a long-awaited phone call from a country far away; then a walk up Sunnyside and a walk back, during which a plop of rain fell on her forehead and she thought that's why the smell is so strong, so dusty, it's about to rain – past the dead squirrel lying on its coffee-carton bier, and inside, to her sleeping children and her wide-open tulips.

35

Love

The morning after he got home, Lew looked closely at Harriet's long, pale, earnest face: all bones, all structure, and thinner than ever. Since the ice storm she had peeled forward, capable and tough, while Dinah recovered from the sickness that advanced in the fall. And yet it was Harriet who was losing weight.

At her behest he had begun to make drawings for possible renovations of the Strand when, and if, they were able to purchase it. They had taken a good look inside its cavernous interior, empty of seats but with stage and hardwood floor intact. It made sense to divide it in half, and he was trying to bring her around to his view – the screens would still be ample, and she could run more than one series at a time, bringing in film students from Carleton University, conducting her movie clubs, her dinner-and-movie nights, her Oscar Night in Ottawa, her Old Cannes on the Rideau Week, her series of silent movies accompanied by local musicians, her historical nights to mark the anniversaries of old classics in what she now described, in her business plan, as a genre-breaking non-profit cinema that would be part movie house, part museum, part film school, part coffee shop. Yes, she would make the pastries; indeed, she had plans to market Harriet's Movietime Biscotti around the city. He was going along with her, since he had never seen her more intent, and perhaps it would work. But how like his father she was, how like his melancholy, obsessive, unravelling dad, who kept for years the pottery made by his teenage sons, and even mended it. But mended it in hostile fashion: thick rivers of glue ran down the sides of every reassembled bowl. Well, his dad had hated the pottery teacher in the end. Hated him for dismantling his sons' ambitions and encouraging them to follow his own offbeat, unillustrious path. How like his erratic dad.

"What are you looking at?" she asked him, as he studied her face that morning.

"A beautiful woman," he said.

And that was all it took.

"I love to watch you come," he said afterwards. "Your nipples go hard, your tits jump, you shake, and you get so warm."

Then, moving in his mind from one sensuous pleasure to another, he described the meal he'd had the day before in Mexico City. He started with a cold beer, and then he had broad-bean soup with *chipotles* floating on the top, then *nopal* salad, then mushrooms in a hot sauce, then *romeritos* – fresh rosemary sprigs cooked in a sauce – then *guana-bana* ice cream and *café de olla*. How delicious it was, he said, lying on his back, his gaze on the ceiling. Then, putting his arm around her, he returned to the mild and rainy present of this early spring.

Over the next few days Harriet would remember their brief exchange the first night he got home, and her irritation: the thing he said, and her reaction. Her love expanded after that. But was that the reason? That sad little thing he'd said that made her feel so annoyed and contemptuous at the time, but not later? Perhaps many things have been happening for a while before you realize they're happening at all. In our minds. In illness. Out of sight. Then there they are, already formed.

Her love came with a wide, almost soft feeling of loss and rolled over their usual routine. Every night he called from his office to say he was on his way and to ask if he should pick up anything for supper. Usually she said no. Sometimes a baguette. Then she would wait for him, glad that he was coming, and thinking in the back of her mind (not painfully, unless there was some unaccountable delay) of how one night he might not arrive. She thought of pioneer women whose men went out into the woods with an axe, and it was a daily miracle when they came back in one piece. Jane was reading all the books in the *Little House on the Prairie* series for the third time. Jane, who was large enough to wear her mother's black cashmere sweater but was still dreaming her pioneer dreams.

The sad little thing he'd said was, I can lose interest too. He said it after she hunched away from him in bed, too tired, too indifferent to even talk; and his words irked her.

He'd turned out the light. A few hours later she woke bathed in sweat and he spoke to her the way he usually did, calmly, unresentfully, to help her fall back to sleep. He was a little achy, and wakeful too, but he soothed her, and slept again. He was the baking soda that cancelled out the sour soup, the ointment on chapped hands, the good coat she counted on, the quiet man who never snored. *I can lose interest too.* And lying awake, she'd felt touched by his sad honesty. Early the next morning she'd brought coffee upstairs and found him standing in the doorway to her study. He turned and looked at her thoughtfully. When she asked him what he was looking at, he told her. And she'd taken his hand and led him back to bed.

It was what Rhett Butler waited for in vain. A wife who fell in love with her husband.

Now she let her glance linger on his dark-gray corduroy jacket and striped shirt, on his tired, intent, scholarly face as he went over receipts, numbers, tax forms – and she thought, No wonder women fall in love with capable men; what could be more reassuring and restful than watching a man pay the bills and figure out the taxes? His long wrists came out of his jacket sleeves, his long fingers sorted papers, his wrist-watch was neither too tight nor too loose.

She found herself doing things for him, and stopped. That way lay doom. No, he must continue to do things for himself, and she things for herself, and things for each other as they had always done, no more, no less, in order to avoid the sloppiness, the loss of shape, the artificial smoothness of early love. She stopped in mid-gesture and put the carrot into her own mouth.

Then one day Lew came home early and said, "I don't have great news."

"What's wrong?"

"Come into the kitchen and I'll tell you over tea."

"Let me go turn off my computer." And while she was upstairs, she thought, Either he's been fired or some colleague has been fired: there's been a shake-up at the university; or he's ill; or his friend Duncan has died. And as she walked through the dining room to join him in the kitchen, she called out, "So what is it? Tell me."

"Kenny's new teacher called me. She tried calling you first, but nobody answered."

"I must have been out buying food."

"She wanted to know if we had any idea that Kenny is being bullied by three boys in his class."

Harriet stood rooted to the spot.

"She said she's suspected for a while. This morning she called him in to ask him about it, and he was visibly upset."

"What are they doing?" She was afraid to hear the answer.

"Teasing him about his hair, his clothes, the way he talks, the books he reads. She said she asked him if he'd talked to us about it and he said, *oh no*, as if he didn't want us to know."

They stood looking at each other, dismayed and unprepared.

"Doesn't he have any friends?" she asked. "Doesn't anybody stick up for him?"

"I didn't ask."

"Did she say what we should do?"

"She said the school would handle it. There's a strict procedure they follow – the three boys will be sent to the vice-principal and given an ultimatum. She advised us not to talk to him about it, since he doesn't want us to know."

"Can that be right?" asked Harriet. "Surely we have to talk to him." They stood there thinking, worrying. She said, "Wouldn't it be unnatural to pretend we don't know? It's always better to bring things into the open."

"I guess she doesn't want us to make it worse. To make it bigger than it is."

An hour later, Kenny came home. All he seemed to have on his mind was their imminent trip to Havana. He could hardly wait. "Let's go to the Hotel Nacional," he said. "That's where Frank and Ava stayed. And the Hotel Riviera built by Meyer Lansky. Let's go there."

"How was school?" asked Harriet.

"Fine. Do you think we'll be able to see the room Frank and Ava stayed in?"

"Do you think they stayed there together?" she asked. "Or at different times?"

"It had to be together. Frank would never stay there after they split up if Ava stayed before. I know Frank. When Peter Lawford went out with Ava he didn't talk to him for five years."

"He held grudges."

"You follow my logic?"

"I do."

After supper, when they were alone in the kitchen, Lew broached the subject. He was washing the dishes, Kenny was doing his homework at the kitchen table. Lew said simply, "I hear there are some kids who are giving you a hard time."

"Only two," Kenny answered immediately, quite ready to talk, and eager to minimize the problem. "Ms. Neff says they're doing it because they were the new boys last year and I'm the new boy this year."

Lew asked what sorts of things they did, and Kenny told him. They took his things. They took his books and hid them. They flicked water at him. They left mean notes on his desk.

"Well, you can't give them the pleasure of seeing you squirm."

"One of them," said Kenny, "is really big."

The next day, at her desk, Harriet heard a dragon breathing fire and looked up from her notebook. Then she went to the window and watched a hot-air balloon rising off the open field at Carleton University. *They loom up like something out of Stephen Spielberg's imagination, if his imagination were peaceful, since the balloons are bright, beautiful, and without incident.*

You had a spectacular enemy in what's-her-name, the one who also wrote for The New Yorker *and said everything you'd ever written, every last word, was without merit. Renata Adler. In a way, that's the best kind of enemy to have. The mouthy, self-immolating kind. But how did you defend yourself?*

She had dropped in on Fiona Chester earlier in the afternoon, and because nothing else was on her mind she found herself talking at length about Kenny's troubles. To her surprise Fiona said, "You need to be aggressive if you're going to have a satisfying life." The tiny Scot said there was an art to not being bullied, and an art to bullying back. Kenny would have to learn how to stand up for himself. And then she talked about her years as a union organizer. After she left the Sun Life Assurance Company, she spent six years unionizing garment workers in Montreal. She said it was the best job she ever had.

Kenny is aggressive, but not in the way she means. He is aggressive in his questions and frustrations, and in his enthusiasms. I'm thinking of the utter pleasure he derives from hearing something praised.

Last night I was reading your essay about trash, art, and the movies, in which you say the romance of movies isn't just in the stories and the people on the screen, but in "the adolescent dream of meeting others who feel as you do about what you've seen." And I thought of my son, and wondered what it's like to be a boy who's filled to the brim with old movies that none of his schoolmates has ever seen. There was the day last year when Jane brought a friend home and said to her, "Let's watch Rear Window, *it's by Hitchcock." And her friend replied, "Who's Hitchcock?"*

Harriet had called Kenny's teacher that morning to find out more, and learned that it was two girls in his class who had come to her a few days ago and said, You should know what's happening to Ken. Boys were taking his pencil case and throwing it, so that he had to run to get it. Or his hat – they were throwing it around until *they* decided to give it back to him. He would have to run – this was at Brewer Park – to get his hat.

"I saw that once. Last fall. And I wondered –"

This had been going on for months, in other words. No wonder he never brought anybody home. No wonder he was quieter than he used to be. Dinah was right about that, if wrong about the reasons.

In the afternoon, when Kenny got home from school, she asked him if things were any better. He said they were, and he seemed greatly relieved. They weren't bothering him now, not since his teacher spoke to them.

But the teacher had warned her that while the bullying might ease off for a while, there was no guarantee it wouldn't resume. And so she pressed him for more information. "Who are they, these boys who are giving you a hard time?"

And he told her their names.

"Are there any kids you like?"

She wanted to know if he had any friends at all, any allies, and he answered defensively, "I don't dislike everybody in my class." Then he listed half a dozen names to prove it. But the list – several girls, a couple of boys – only confirmed her suspicion that he was quite alone.

She began to ask another question, uncomfortably aware that this sort of intrusive persistence was exactly what the teacher had warned them against, but he interrupted her. "It's over," he said. "I don't want to talk about it any more."

"But I need to know. I need to be able to ask you."

"I'll tell you."

"Will you?"

"I'll tell you if it starts again."

"Or I'll ask," she said. "But just from time to time."

She knew it was always possible that it wasn't as bad for him as she thought it was. The other day she had been saying to Dinah that she always felt so sad for Buster Keaton – there was nothing sadder than wasted talent. But Dinah got impatient. It's sadder for us than for him, she'd said. It's not sad for the person with the talent, it's sad for the observer of the person with the talent. Maybe it's the same when you die, she'd said. Awful for the people who care about you, but not so awful for you. "Maybe," she had said, "it's not so awful for the people who care about you either."

"Dinah, what's the matter?"

"Tests," she answered. "Where would doctors be without their tests? They'd have to use their brains."

And then they were in Havana, and it was nothing like *Guys and Dolls*. They rented two rooms in an apartment occupied by a large extended family (one of whom, an affectionate deaf-mute, uttered the most astonishing array of bird-like trills and ejaculations whenever she encountered Kenny and Jane in the wide hallway). A huge apartment full of ceiling fans, on the top floor of an old mansion. They arrived late at night, not realizing until morning that it had as many artificial plants and flowers as any little house on the barren rock of Newfoundland.

In their rooms there was a whole world in the fittings of each window, the workings that allowed air without sun, light without wind or rain, and this by means of a double ladder of wooden slats that opened at any number of angles, the slats covered by long glass inserts that also opened and closed, as did the entire window. It opened outwards, like French doors, onto a beautiful city riddled with decay, swept by hurricanes, and inhabited by roosters that didn't know the meaning of dawn.

They found Frankie the very first morning, in the Hotel Nacional's Club of Fame, an airy glassed-in terrace overlooking an unused swimming pool. He was with Ava in the mural representing the fifties, and so was John Wayne, Nat King Cole, Mickey Mantle, Lola Flores, Yma Sumac, Spencer Tracy, Marlon Brando. But no Jean Simmons. A mural for each decade, with Buster Keaton, Gary Cooper, Jack Dempsey, and Meyer Lansky consigned to the thirties; Fred Astaire, Betty Grable, Rita Hayworth, and Churchill in the mural for the forties; García Márquez, Josephine Baker, Yuri Gagarin in the post-revolution sixties, Francis Ford Coppola in the seventies, Muhammed Ali in the eighties, and so on. They spent quite a while looking at these well-known faces, Harriet remembering something Lionel had said about the universal language of the movies. He was referring to silent pictures and the short, golden time when they made language unnecessary, when it was possible to believe that flickering images on a screen might bring everyone together, no matter what country they came from. And then, he said, that hope was lost, like every other.

They took an elevator to the upper swimming pool and paid the daily rate to lie in luxury, in swimsuits and sunglasses, on four cushioned lounge chairs. "So are you going to have a daiquiri, Alfredo?" Kenny asked his mom, and when the wind picked up and blew around the pool, he called out, "'Fred? Where are you, Fred? It's cold. The snow is blowing in.'"

Lew looked up from his book. "What's that?" he asked.

Jane answered, "Audrey Hepburn's worst line in *Breakfast at Tiffany's*."

And Harriet said, "She was talking in her sleep."

Later, resting on their bed before going out into the warm, dark, crumbling city in search of supper, Harriet and Lew heard the movie talk continue in the adjoining room.

"Everybody in *The Godfather* was good," said Kenny. "And they were all unknowns. Except for Marlon Brando. Even Diane Keaton was an unknown."

"Everybody *was* good," agreed Jane.

"Except for Diane Keaton. I didn't think she was so good."

"I don't know," said Jane. "Maybe the role?"

"What are your top three endings?" he asked her. "I'd say *Godfather, Part II*; *Some Like it Hot*; *Local Hero*."

Lew spoke from his pillow into Harriet's ear, "Movies and comparing. And comparing movies. When will this stage be over?"

Perhaps never, she thought.

"I wonder what they're looking for," he said, "what they find in those old movies."

"What's your guess?" she asked.

"I really don't know. In Jane's case, I suppose it's the dream of doing that herself. Of being an entertainer. And in Kenny's case, I just can't say. Maybe it's knowing everything about something. Knowing who's who and having an opinion."

But she remembered herself at that age and what she'd been looking for: glamor, sexiness, excitement. And they find it, she would think later. *They know Frankie. They know Ava. They feel electrified by the things they do and say and wear, and how they carry it all off. It's more real to them than life.*

There's a price to pay, of course. Watch Guys and Dolls *in the afternoon, and the price you pay is evening gloom.*

I caught up with Rio Grande *a few weeks ago, and watched John Wayne and Maureen O'Hara being very effective together. What a beautiful face she has, very strong; and at times the camera made her almost plain – pale, and almost plain in her expressiveness. Kenny sat beside me and couldn't help remarking on how racist it was, and sexist and silly, but he liked it too, and wanted to know if I did. That itch he has to talk and compare that baffles Lew – it's how he keeps himself entertained. But it's not just that. It's how he makes the movies a part of his life, and his life a part of the movies.*

Now she heard the two of them talking about their top three beginnings, the opening scenes of *Nashville, Get Shorty, Breakfast at Tiffany's*, and she couldn't help herself. "*The Godfather, Part II* also has one of the best beginnings," she called through the open doorway. "The funeral in Sicily, remember? It paves the way for the final scene when Michael is all alone with his ghosts." She laughed at herself and turned back to Lew.

And the conversation turned to love.

"What about you?" she asked. "What search are you on?"

"You think I'm searching for something?"

"I think you might be. I think you might be looking for love."

"Oh, I've found that," he said.

"Where?"

"Right here." And he pulled her towards him.

For a while they lay like that, in each other's arms. She said, "To-morrow Dinah starts her chemo."

"Yes," he said, holding her tighter. But he didn't say anything else and she was left to wonder what he was thinking. She could have asked, but she didn't ask.

That week they would hear the slap of sandals on marble floors, the tremendous bang of a door slamming repeatedly in the wind, the crash of old molding falling from a great height, and the long, tuneful siren of an ambulance, as if a parade were going by. Since it often took so long to be served, they developed the habit of going to restaurants before they were hungry, and taking their books along to read while they waited. "Recommend some books to me," Jane said to her mother.

"There's Alice Munro. There's all of Steinbeck."

"Olive Steinbeck," Jane said, and wrote it down.

"Mommy?" said Kenny. "What ever happened to Jean Simmons?"

"Lord knows. Don't ask."

But he was relentless, a master especially of the unanswerable question. "Which would you rather be right now, as cold as an icicle or as hot as a burning log?"

"Why don't you ask me something I can answer?"

"All right. Who would you rather have dinner with, Kevin Costner or Tim Robbins?"

She thought for a second. "How about Kevin Kline or Sean Connery?"

"Okay. Who would you rather have dinner with, Kevin Kline or Sean Connery?"

She thought again. "Sean Connery."

"All right! Now! What about Sean Connery or Cary Grant?"

"Cary Grant."

"All right! Who do you think was better-looking? Peter O'Toole or Cary Grant?"

"Which period? Which film?"

"Peter O'Toole in *How to Steal a Million* and Cary Grant in *My Girl Friday*."

"That's hard."

"Come on. You have one minute to answer."

"Peter O'Toole's face was better-looking, but Cary Grant's body wins by a landslide."

"Was Peter O'Toole his real name?" asked Jane.

"Yes."

"Cary Grant wasn't his real name," Jane said. "His real name was Archibald Leach. Yuck."

"There's nothing wrong with that," said Harriet.

"Leach! Yuck!"

"Archibald Peach," said Harriet.

"Now," trumpeted Kenny. "Who was the better actor, Peter O'Toole in *My Favorite Year* or Cary Grant in *Notorious*?"

And Harriet reached forward and wrapped her hands around her son's neck.

That week she felt a new exhaustion, and blamed it on the heat. Lew noticed, and urged her to lie down more often, and she did. One night, while she was resting after they'd changed out of their beach clothes, and before they went in search of supper, they wrote a postcard to Dinah. The kids told her about seeing Frankie in the Club of Fame, and drinking daiquiris beside the pool. Harriet wrote, *The Bacardi is swell, but the flies are driving Kenny nuts*, recalling how they'd eaten one day in a tiny restaurant on a slummy street, and when the ceiling fans stopped working the flies descended and Kenny fled. He stood in the street, shaking himself and stamping, and only recovered when they went back for another afternoon at the Hotel Nacional. She passed the card to Lew. His pen hovered in the air, and Harriet looked away. She heard the pen make contact, and before they mailed the postcard at the airport, she read what he'd written. *We love you. Hang on tight. Lew.*

(When Dinah got the card two weeks later, she would be struck by their different styles of handwriting: Harriet's minuscule script, Kenny's scrawl, Jane's round printing, Lew's tall, evenly spaced lettering. She tucked the card between the mirror and the frame of her bureau, thinking as she did so of Lew's desk – his neat but expansive ways, his tidy but imperialistic papers spreading from study to dining room to basement, where his office was almost finished. Thinking he was a man divided between his radical inclinations and his enormous patience, representing to those who loved him a mixture of idealism and security. For children, and women over fifty, there was nothing more attractive.)

It was after they finished writing the postcard that the argument began, and for once it wasn't about the movies.

Kenny said, "It would be interesting to watch a revolution, but I wouldn't want to be in one. You'd be too worried."

He'd been thinking about this for several days as they stepped over broken sidewalks and around mangy dogs and away from people who bothered them with requests to buy things or hire their taxis or give them money. People who were after your stuff. He knew about that. People who wouldn't leave you alone.

"They want things to be both fair and equal, but that's impossible," he said. He'd been listening to Harriet and Lew. He'd been reading. "People want to use their abilities, that's fair. But Castro wants everybody to be equal. So they *can't* use their abilities, and that's not fair." Already he was worked up. "They can't have both. If people are better at things they should make more money."

Jane said, "Do you think it's fair that the extremely rich use their talents on the stock market and make loads of money? Is that fair?"

"It's fair, but it's not equal."

"I think it's disgusting greed. You're a disgusting capitalist," she said to her brother, and Harriet, listening with keen amusement, thought, They'll be all right, these two. No matter what happens. They'll defend themselves.

"Hey! This is a statement!" Kenny was standing up, waving his arms now. "Everyone's different. Some people are smarter. If someone's good, if someone's better than somebody else, it isn't fair to hold them back."

"Who is *good*? Are you saying the prime minister of Canada is good? *He* made it. Is he good? There is such a thing as doing something you love not for the money. Everybody can go to university in Cuba, right? University is free. Say you're a doctor. You can do all sorts of things, work in a hospital or do research. You just don't get paid a lot."

"But that's the point," shouted Kenny. "You can't do research because there's no money to do it. That's the paradox. You're doing what you love but you can't do it, because there's no money to pay for it. My final statement." He pointed into the air. "Eat or be eaten!"

Harriet stood up. "Let's eat," she said. "I'm weak from hunger." And then, "Where did you learn the word 'paradox'?"

She meant it when she said she was weak. It had been a long day spent in markets and museums, and in old Havana, where Kenny leant against a pillar in the cathedral and said *bugger, bugger, bugger,* just like Hugh Grant in *Four Weddings and a Funeral.* Then a taxi ride to the nearest beach, where Lew said to her, knowing she would be interested, "What you're seeing is Cuban women with Canadian and Italian men. Or Cuban men with Canadian women." A long day but not a bad day, until they set out at eight in the evening to find something to eat.

The next morning Harriet opened her eyes in the darkness and whimpered with embarrassment and shame. For in her mind they were still following the tall Cuban who trod the ground like an Indian guide, erect and never varying his pace, down the middle of unilluminated streets away from his family-run *paladar,* which was closed, to another that he swore was open. Block after block after block, as she muttered and fumed, while the others bore up with better grace. At one point he crossed a street just as the traffic light changed, and now in her mind she returned to this sorry point: Kenny was directly in front of her and she gave his back an impatient push, meaning for him to head across rapidly, then plunged across herself. But when she reached the far sidewalk, where the Cuban stood waiting impassively, and looked back – there was her family, standing on the other shore. And she was flooded with shame.

Lew opened his eyes and took in her face. "You didn't sleep," he said. And she shook her head and turned, so that she was lying on her side, away from him. He wrapped his arm around her and her shoulders began to shake. Look at you, she said to herself with contempt, look at you trying to get sympathy. The tears kept coming, however. Ah, said Lew, and held her tighter. He asked what was the matter, and after some little time and a lot of effort she managed to say how ashamed she was of having plunged across the road, leaving him and the kids "on the other side."

"Yeah," he said in quiet agreement a few inches from her ear, and her heart contracted. Then, after a moment, he added, "Well, that's not so bad. I've done the same thing."

And her heart eased.

"Especially at night," he said, "I get flooded with embarrassment about things I did a long time ago. Especially at night." And then he told her a story from his childhood that he had never told her before.

The window above their heads was open. The sound of traffic, of singing caged birds, of a single, punctual rooster came in with the early-morning light as they lay on the blue sheet, resting their heads on flow-ered pillows in this semi-elegant, kitsch-filled room, while Kenny and Jane slept on in the adjoining bedroom. He was five or six years old, he said, and he had made a flower basket at school for May Day. You were to give it to someone as a surprise, and he decided to give it to his mother, even though he had to ask her to cut the flowers for him. She did, cutting him some daffodils and other spring flowers which he put in the cone-shaped basket before hiding it in the living room, under a book of all places. But in the morning, when he pulled it out, the handle tore off, and then he didn't know what to do. You were supposed to hang it from someone's doorknob, but without the handle the basket was useless. He couldn't give it to his mother, and so he took it with him on his way to school with Stevie Brooks, thinking he would leave it at a neighbor's house. But standing on the road next to the neighbor's he thought, How can I leave it if it doesn't have a handle? Stevie lost patience with him. I'll show you what to do, he said, and grabbed the flowers and broke them in half and threw them on the ground.

He was laughing as he told the story into her ear, and she was laugh-ing too, but still crying. "Do you want me to stop?" he asked, and she said no, keep going. Something echoed in her mind as he spoke, something to do with flowers, and it was Marlon, she realized, Marlon Brando in the early-morning hours bending down to pick up a broken flower, which he put in an old tin can and gave to Jean Simmons in a tender, humorous gesture that itself had echoes of silent movies and of childhood. She knew the scene so well, its effect on her not unlike what she was feeling now. When he got home, said Lew, the first thing he did was to attack his mom, lash out at her, say it was all her fault. There was no place in the house to hide anything. If he'd had a place to hide the basket none of this would have happened. So she got him a cardboard box to put in his room and promised she would never look inside it. Anything he wanted to hide, he could hide in there. "And that box was in my room for years," he said, "and I never hid anything in it. But it was there for years."

She had to get up – her nose was so blocked she had to snort to breathe – and she was crying afresh, though less now, at the story: the kindness of the mother to the boy, the boy's long dilemma and longer shame. She had known Lew for many years and never heard this story, though he was fond of telling stories from his childhood, and so, for that matter, was his mother.

Under the chandelier that caught light and shed light and hung lightly suspended in the morning air – assembled in Cuba, she had been told, before the revolution, from cut glass made in Bohemia – she lay down beside Lew again as the day gathered strength and the warmth began to pour in.

They would go later that day to the famous ice cream garden known as Coppelia. It wasn't their first visit, but it was the first time they approached from this direction, and on foot. A block away, and across the street from the ice cream garden, they came upon Don Quixote in a tiny park. He was riding Rocinante, who was rearing up, all skin and bones, and they made a wild and skeletal pair, bronze horse and man, very endearing and sad. The sharp ribs of the noble horse were so like blades that Harriet, back in Ottawa and putting away her skates for another year, would dub them Rocinante. At Coppelia they ate their ice cream at a small table, surrounded by tall royal palms whose gray trunks, long and tapered, were like the Plasticine worms she used to roll out on her desk in kindergarten. From somewhere nearby came the sound of sweeping, and from near and far came the sound of cars.

"You liked *Don Quixote*, didn't you?" she asked Kenny. He had read a children's version that was very good.

"I loved it," he said. "But it had such a sad ending."

"But funny too," she said gently. "Right?"

"The book was funny, it was a great story," he said, "but he died at the end! And before he died, he got defeated by trickery!"

"What did Sancho Panza say at the end? Something about love."

"'He was a man in love. No one knows why.' He said that at the funeral."

"Yes."

She had read the book in high school. Her father used to give her a ride to school early in the morning, on his way to his office, and she would sit in the library reading until the bell rang. What a surprise to discover how rollicking and readable the old classic was. Well, to be accurate, she read parts of it. It was a very long book.

"The adult version has a different ending," she said. "He realizes that all his dreams were figments of his imagination, and he turns his face to the wall and dies from the truth. Like Emma Bovary. That's a wonderful book too. But her death was terrible."

"Where do you suppose we'll die?" asked Lew thoughtfully. "Will we die in Ottawa, do you think?"

Kenny said, "Let's talk about something else."

Jane said, "It's not thinking about what happens after death that's interesting. It's realizing that one day you'll know."

Harriet said, "I think I'll die in Sean Connery's arms."

36

The Wedding

"Why Jack?" asked Harriet.

"You think I'm making a mistake." Dinah was at home, resting between bouts of chemotherapy that were intended to stop anything further in its tracks. Just to be sure, her doctors said.

"I'm just asking why."

"He's been wonderful, dealing with doctors and nurses. I need someone like that. Someone aggressive. Besides, he's terrific at cross-word puzzles."

"I'm not saying he's not aggressive." Harriet wasn't about to be drawn out of her pensiveness. "Has he told you about his mother?"

"That's the saddest story I've ever heard."

"I can't believe that I never knew about it." She had hoped Dinah might have some doubts about the story too.

"Well, it's not something you'd want to talk about, is it?"

Harriet went to the window and looked down at Jim Creak's house. He happened to be outside in his sweatshirt and black pajama bottoms and black Chinese shoes, spreading a brightly patterned cloth over his picnic table. A warm March had stretched into a warmer April.

Dinah said, "I know what you're thinking, but Bill thought he had a screw loose, and I've wondered myself."

"You haven't watched *Vanya on 42ⁿᵈ Street*, have you? Even though I told you to. Have you read the play? You should read the play." Harriet turned her lightly tanned face away from the window and looked at Dinah. "They were too much alike, Jim and Bill; they were bound to clash. You don't like Fred Astaire either. You're hopeless."

"How were they alike?"

"Devoted. Honest. What you see is what you get. Eccentric, of course, and very independent, but not up to no good."

"Jack's up to no good? I'll tell him that." She let out a long, amused chortle.

It was childish to want Dinah to agree with her, and pitiful to feel displaced. She sank into the chair beside Dinah's bed, stretched out her legs, and let her hands fall into her lap.

They looked at each other.

Dinah said, "The Duke of Windsor was a big knitter too, and his penis was tiny."

"His penis isn't tiny. At the sleep clinic I saw him in his briefs."

Dinah's lips twitched with amusement. "Sometimes I forget how lucky I am to know you."

"Buster Keaton knew how to knit too. In *The Railrodder* he's knitting when he goes through the Rockies on the handcar." She was remembering him in the Club of Fame, how old he looked, his whole face like the pouch under a sleepless eye. Not a face that ever would have made it into that strange, beautiful album that Jack had shown to her.

"Hattie?"

"I'm here."

"We've decided the middle of June. We want Jane to be our best girl, and Kenny to be the ring bearer."

Harriet's face relaxed into a smile, and in this light Dinah saw the tan for what it was, and asked if she was sleeping. Harriet shrugged the question away.

From her study she had a view of Bill Bender's flattened garage, whose tattered shingles used to slide all summer long into the raspberry patch. Also, the flattened raspberry patch. Ottawa was a low city, and wide. Movement was horizontal – roads, rivers, the canal – cars, cyclists, joggers, people with dogs – except for the falling snow which made everything rapidly so much taller than before, a triumph of adolescence: the very thing that Kenny and Jane knew firsthand.

Not that you could count on deep snow any more, she thought. And what had happened to all the beautiful wallpaper of her childhood? The leaves, silvery and filigreed, the satiny surfaces, the reassuring repetitions of lines and stripes and dots that coalesced into flowers? Where would Cézanne have been without wallpaper? Or Matisse? And what had happened to the minds that made those designs? Deep-sixed, that's what, along with the stars of the silent screen.

I watched College *last night. You call it a beautiful comedy, and I agree. All the athletic feats Keaton can't master he suddenly does in one gliding tour de force when he has to rescue the girl at the end. It has the shape of comedy, as you say, the first half being one long humiliation, and the second half vindication – with the streamline zip of romance.*

Buster was so short. I didn't realize. And so obviously athletic and strong. A strange sort of handsomeness when he darts a look at the girl, or whenever he registers feeling by withdrawing into himself, hurt. Then you see how well chiselled his features are, how striking the dark hair and dark eyes, the bare, beautifully shaped legs. But the handsomeness vanishes as soon as he heads back into the world, dressed in a baggy suit and walking his stiff-legged walk, wearing his too-small boater: shorter than everybody else, and stricken, made monotone, by embarrassment. Always out of place, no matter where he was. Yet in place, no matter how precarious the setting.

Then I put on Bells Are Ringing. *By this time it was very late, but I began to watch, then kept going to see more of Dean Martin, who is paced through the movie as sparingly and irresistibly as Rhett Butler. His loose, casual, unbuttoned ease – funny and at sea, until Judy rescues him.*

A Saturday morning. She heard Kenny get up and, knowing she'd be interrupted soon, flipped to another page and began to jot down rapidly: Repertory, Revival, Classic Cinema, Film Society, Movie Museum, Movie Guild – turning over in her mind the various possibilities.

On the way downstairs, she poked her head into Kenny's room. He said, "I've decided to live it up and die in bed. Will you bring me something to eat?"

"You'll choke."

"I'll sit up," he said.

That day two goldfinches came whizzing across Bill Bender's lawn, then *thump*. Both lay in the grass, having crashed into the side of his house. The dumb blondes of the bird world, thought Harriet sadly. When did you ever see a starling barrel into the side of a house? After an hour she climbed over Bill Bender's fence and picked up the two birds, still warm but lifeless. She blew on their feathers and studied the infinite shades of yellow, olive, russet. Perhaps the Museum of Nature would want them. So she put them into a plastic bag, and put the bag in the freezer next to another plastic bag that contained the ice-swollen twig-cigar, a souvenir from the ice storm.

On the last day of April the For Sale sign in front of Bill Bender's house came down.

A few days after that, when she was in the garden, Harriet heard a dry clacking, as of an old typewriter, and looked up to see a swallow on the clothesline. The song detective was in his backyard. She went over to tell him that the swallow had arrived – in his tuxedo – only to waltz away. "How can we entice him back?"

"With music," he said. "I have a tape of a musician called Steve Swallow, and it's called 'Hello Hotel.'"

He went inside, and came back out with a tape deck that was playing jazzy strains that she'd never heard before. But Fred Astaire didn't return.

It was the time of year, early May, when she could never find slippers or shoes, since she went in the front door and out the back, into the street or into the garden, changing her footgear accordingly: a season of shoe confusion and basketball-thumped tulips and winter-old dogshit so weathered it was white.

Then one day a big metal dumpster, painted blue and wider than a grand piano and taller than an upright, appeared in Bill Bender's drive-way. Before the end of the day it was filled, removed, and replaced with another dumpster. His sons were throwing out the contents of their father's house.

Neighbors gathered. The front door of the house was wide open, and from inside they could hear the sons directing a crew of teenage boys in baseball caps who came and went, their arms filled with one overflowing box after another. Dinah, alerted by Harriet, headed up the front steps and intercepted the first sweaty son she came upon, a thin-haired man of fifty, built large like his father.

Papers? There was nothing in his will about papers. Manuscripts? There was nothing in his will about them either, he said. They were selling the house, that's right, and first they had to clear it out.

"Will you let me have a look?" she asked, telling them who she was. "I know what he was working on. He showed it to me several times."

The other son appeared, beaded with perspiration, circles under his eyes. He said to Dinah, "We don't want his things spread around among strangers."

"But I'm not a stranger. I'm an old friend of your father's." And again she said who she was.

"He never mentioned your name to me."

"Just let me see the filing cabinet that's got his book in it. I want to make sure it doesn't get thrown out. It's valuable."

The son looked at her with complete distrust. "We're taking whatever has value," he said.

Then Dinah erupted. "Does Fiona know about all this? Does Fiona Chester know what you're up to? Have you been in touch with her?"

The sons looked at each other. The heavily perspiring son, older, two inches taller, said, "The lawyer's taking care of Fiona."

And so Dinah and Harriet, and for a while loud Ray, stood on the sidewalk and watched filing cabinets, crates of books, crockery, kitchen implements, old tables, framed paintings, framed maps, gardening tools, and jars of every shape and size get dumped topsy-turvy into the great steel bin. After a while, Ray went home, started up his lawn mower, and blasted any remaining quiet to kingdom come.

Harriet told Dinah not to worry: We'll come back after they've left and go through it all. But the sons oversaw the dumpster's removal, and the setting-down of dumpster number two. Dinah, in fury, walked away and left them to it. It was madness, possessive madness, she raged, not to let others have what they had no use for themselves. The second dumpster was only half full at the end of the day, when the sons drove off with a sofa and a television set stuffed into the back of their van. That evening first one neighbor and then another scaled its steel sides and rescued Bill Bender's walking stick, some of his photo albums, part of his shell collection, a couple of paintings, numerous books. But Dinah, convinced that his filing cabinet of writing was gone, stayed in her garden, tearing a leaf into tiny bits, until Lew came over. He still walked Buddy almost every evening, and Buster too, since Jack had no fondness for dogs. He and Dinah sat on the back step, and she dropped her head on his shoulder. Lew, a battle-weary heritage architect, didn't offer false comfort, for which she was grateful.

That night the windows were open and Harriet's winter ears, still unaccustomed to the sounds outside, were overstimulated, as if by a Cuban fan a foot away. She couldn't sleep. The moon was full. It was warm.

Kenny woke up in the middle of the night, rolled over, and was falling back to sleep when he heard a crash, and then the sound of somebody moaning outside.

Another moan, another feeble cry, and he got up and looked out the window. The moon was bright enough for Jean Simmons to read by and Marlon Brando to tell her so. The sound came from Bill Bender's driveway next door. He got his dad.

When Lew hoisted himself over the side of the dumpster and found Harriet spread-eagled on the detritus of Bill Bender's life, apparently having slipped and toppled and cracked her head against the hard edge of a video box (*The Treasure of the Sierra Madre*), what moved him most was finding in her pocket, not the tissue he was hoping for, in order to wipe the blood off her head, but the fern he had given her months ago, laminated, like a library card.

She opened her eyes and said, "Revival House."

"Film Society," he said. "The Fern Film Society."

She closed her eyes. "You're right. That's it."

Two weeks more, and prim, conservative Ottawa took off its glasses and revealed its breathtaking summer face. Suddenly, it was lush, wild, profuse. Big bosoms of lilac barged forward, overmastering any sidewalk that stood in their way. Banks of honeysuckle spring up on all sides, lilies of the valley perfumed the ground, Virginia creeper clambered up telephone poles and across the wires. Surrounded by such greenery, Harriet felt the iron come back into her blood and the blood into her cheeks. There would be free movies on Saturday mornings at the Fern Film Society, with post-film discussions by Kenny Gold; a glassed-in crying room for mothers with babies; Saturday afternoons designed for old parents with young kids: "*The Crimson Pirate* Meets *The Court Jester*: See What Your Folks Saw When They Were Young"; weekdays planned around the schools: "Mario Puzo Meets Francis Ford Coppola: Contrast and Compare Movie and Book."

One Saturday night in late May, Kenny undertook to make Fat Clemenza's spaghetti sauce with meatballs and sausage. He said, "Once a week I'll make Clemenza's spaghetti." He stirred vigorously. "No," he told his mom, "the wine is last." Spatters of sauce covered the stove. "Who's the most famous actor living today?" he asked her.

"Marlon Brando."

"Marlon Brando? Marlon Brando?"

"Who do *you* think?"

"Al Pacino."

"Well, that shows there are limits to what you know."

"But Al Pacino won an Oscar for *Scent of a Woman*."

"So what?"

"He must have been good."

"Not that good."

"Oh." Pause. "Now I know who your favorite actor is of all time. Are you going to deny it? Are you going to deny that Marlon Brando is your favorite actor of all time? For years I've been trying to find out who your favorite actor is and you've always said you don't know. Now you've admitted it. You're disappointed now. You've finally given in. You've given in. You do not have the will, you do not have the power to restrain your answer."

"Kenny," said his mom. "Drop dead."

Kenny would remember her fierce attachments and antipathies: that she couldn't abide Jack Nicholson (he looks, she said, as if he's about to pick his nose and show you the results) or Katharine Hepburn (that faker) or Steve Buscemi (I'll call him when I need a rat catcher) or Nicolas Cage (stay out of his bed, whatever you do), but she had infinite patience for Cary Grant and Sean Connery, for Audrey Hepburn, Ingrid Bergman, and Greta Garbo, congratulating herself on the latitude of her tastes and on her subtle generosity. Not a word would she hear against Peter O'Toole or Jeff Bridges, mounting the barricades on their behalf, engaging in hand-to-hand combat with anyone who besmirched O'Toole's acting abilities, and writing furious letters to the editor when Jeff Bridges was dismissed as the forgettable star of another forgettable movie, "the overrated scion of a hack in a wet suit."

Your reviewer, she wrote, should be made to watch *The Fabulous Baker Boys* over and over again until he admits he's wrong.

Dear Richard Gere, she wrote. You should be forced to watch Cary Grant, over and over again, until you get it right.

These letters lay in piles next to the business plan on her desk, and one day Kenny would read them and be transported back to a boyhood when he never went anywhere without his bible, when he had a dad who knew all about the world and nothing about the movies, a sister who scolded him for wasting water and being a filthy capitalist, and a mother whose friend got cancer and urged her to get herself checked, and the friend survived – but his mom did not.

The wedding happened on a cloudy morning in June, and Harriet realized exactly how much weight she had lost when she put on a dress. She and Lew were the first to arrive (best girl and ring bearer having gone to the wedding breakfast at a secret location). They went around to Dinah's back garden and sat on folding chairs on the grass, and waited. A petal pathway ran like a pink-and-red carpet between the two rows of chairs and came to a halt under a trellised arbor threaded with roses.

Lew said to her, "We could do this too. We could have a proper wedding."

"I'd rather chew glass," said Harriet.

"But you're happy for them."

"Ecstatic."

"Hattie."

"Jack is awful," she said.

"He's not good enough for her, but he's not awful."

"Lew, just say he's awful. I want to hear you say someone is awful."

"He's not so awful."

And then they laughed, since it was obvious that his mild stubbornness was a perfect match for her miserable disgust.

Others gathered, but slowly, and while they waited Lew told her that he'd heard Garbo mentioned on the radio the other day. Someone who knew her had died. Some actor she admired. She had gone backstage to see him once, after one of his performances, but when he heard who was waiting outside his dressing room, he refused to let her in until he had made himself up all over again. No, he couldn't remember the actor's name.

A sprinkle of rain fell and moistened the guests and the petal pathway. Fiona Chester opened her umbrella, and Harriet saw Jim Creak arrive in shirt and tie. She glanced at the back door of Dinah's house, from which the wedding party would emerge, but no sign of activity yet, and she lost herself in the murky pleasure of uncharitable thoughts. It seemed to her that the bride, though hardbitten, was pudgy in her thinking: her weakness for Sinatra, for the royal family, and now for weddings. What was she thinking of, marrying Jack Frame?

Lew was talking again. Recently, he said, he'd learned about a new idea called "the complexity theory." He began to explain what it was and she barely listened, until he made a wide gesture with his hands and said something about a flock of birds. As soon as he uttered those words, *a flock of birds*, her mind cleared. How oddly disjointed so much of life is, she thought, and how little it takes – a few words, arranged a certain way – for it to make sense again. Her eyes cleared, her heart cleared, her mind cleared. Here was Lew, dressed in his dad's old linen jacket, explaining that a team of theorists decided to study a flock of birds to see how they managed to fly great distances towards a common goal, something every organization would like to emulate, and they discovered, he said, that the formation keeps to a route set by one or two head birds (who have read the wind and figured out what path to take), and holds its shape by virtue of each bird staying an equal distance from two other birds. They exercise self-control, in other words, after accepting an overall direction.

But without the phrase *a flock of birds*, she would have missed everything he said. To her, complexity lay in the absence of anything she could visualize, and simplicity, disarming and life-restoring, in being able to see by means of images.

Her relief upon hearing *a flock of birds* wasn't unlike Lew's relief at accepting the general direction in which they were all headed: Dinah and Jack would be married, he and Harriet would stay together. With Dinah he had an understanding, vividly tender, that they could openly worry about each other, favor each other, seek each other out – appreciate each other – as a reward for not having an affair.

Jack came around the side of the house with the minister, and they stationed themselves under the arbor. Harriet thought more uncharitable thoughts: about sentimental weddings in general and unreliable Jack in particular. I give them two years, she said to herself. In that moment a burst of music filled the air and the back door of the house was thrown open. Then out came Jane in her polka-dot sundress and brand-new patent-leather shoes, and Harriet's eyes welled up and over. Jane, all smiles, came slowly down the steps, but Harriet was rooting blindly in Lew's pocket for his handkerchief. Kenny, in his gangster jacket, a rose in his lapel, followed Jane, and then Dinah, looking lovely, really lovely in pale blue with a wide hat, came out behind him. Tears gushed down Harriet's face. Then stepping onto the petal pathway, Jane's feet shot out from under her and she landed on her bottom with a thud. Her mother nearly keeled over with laughter.

Lew jabbed her with his elbow – *Stop it, you're embarrassing her* – but try as she might she couldn't stop. Her intrepid daughter scrambled to her feet and carried on, and so did Harriet. She was helpless. In hysterics. Ignominiously, she had to abandon the garden for the front of the house, where she leaned against the porch and sobbed and wheezed with laughter.

It was the music, she would say later, congratulating the couple, and trying to explain what got her started. They were drinking champagne in Dinah's living room. A friend of Dinah's put on a CD and tears filled her eyes once again. "What a great song," she said. "'Moon River.'"

"Actually, it's 'As Time Goes By,'" said Lew.

He recognized her fit of tears and laughter for what it was too. Were she not so susceptible to emotion, he thought, she wouldn't deride it so fiercely. Soldiers, he had heard, were the most sentimental of men, and Harriet was a sentimental woman who masqueraded as a soldier. Then, when she least expected it, she was ambushed by herself.

The wedding kiss was much commented upon. It lasted so long, and was so passionate, that even Jane had to look away.

37

The Third Visitor

The wind changed in the early morning. From her study Harriet saw hot air balloons receding rather than advancing, and when she stepped onto the porch to get the paper, she smelled Thurso, the pulp-and-paper plant downriver. An east wind.

And then, at nine, a little rain.

Again, she had trouble finding a place to park. Again, she took the elevator up to the fifth floor, and this time she was alone in the waiting room, except for one other woman who was tanned and talkative. Her family had sent her to Paris for her fiftieth birthday, and she loved it. Italy next!

A woman in slacks and a striped shirt took her to the room that had the magic table. But they were looking in the wrong place. The trouble lay elsewhere. It was lurking in the lower left-hand corner of the screen.

That summer Harriet had wooden blinds installed in her study, and awnings on every window. In her shaded room on hot afternoons she liked to think she was living in a rich part of old Havana. I could be Hemingway, she thought. In truth, she was more like Lionel, putting her papers in order by throwing them out, and steadying her life by clinging to a wobbly idea. *I was reading about Grierson's efforts to get documentaries into movie houses and came upon your picture, the two of you seated together with Claude Jutra, the other judge at the 1962 Vancouver Film Festival. You're wearing glasses, and your hair seems to be in a bun. You look like a librarian, but I happen to like librarians. I watched a documentary about Grierson too, and at that stage, a few years before his death, he looked like a cross between Gregory Peck and Blind Pugh. What a face. Like you, he was* small, *as was Claude Jutra, and now you're the only one left, Jutra having jumped off a bridge into the St. Lawrence River, and Grierson dead of cancer at the age of seventy-three.*

Not long ago she had driven past the spot where the National Film Board got started in 1939 in an old sawmill next to the Rideau Falls. The sawmill – gone now, of course – housed not just Grierson and Norman McLaren, but for a time a man called J.P.R. Golightly, a name not coined, as she'd thought, by Truman Capote, after all. She parked at the French embassy and walked over to the falls, feeling the stir of temperaments in the cold and empty air, those odd couplings in history that make you stop in surprise. And she thought of the winter past, the ice-storm winter, as a stage set crudely rigged for sound, which meant it was a transition, and also the end of something. The next morning she stepped out into Miami: the softest air. A sudden change that made her wonder about conversions in novels: "After that, nothing was the same." *For a time, I want to say. For a time, and then familiarity and indifference settle around us once again. Life washes over most of us. It just keeps coming and washing over us; and, in time, we stop trying to stand up and sit down.*

After the wedding, Dinah and Jack went to Nova Scotia for their honeymoon, and to find a house to buy, since for years Dinah had been longing to live by the sea. No doubt they would move there for good, thought Harriet, and the neighborhood would break up even more. Old Buddy they left in the care of the song detective (to lose the girl and inherit the dog!) and after a week of pining the old protector wandered off and didn't return.

"I was looking forward to him biting Jack," said Harriet, who was also sorry that they hadn't been able to look after Buddy themselves, but her allergies were worse than ever.

She and Jack had shared fewer than a dozen words since he'd taken such elaborate measures to steal her groceries, but that strange afternoon often floated into her mind. What had he really been up to? she wondered. Another notch in his premarital belt, or did he actually care for her in some peculiar fashion? The fern album haunted her too, bringing her one day to a pitch of sadness. Everything was sad, the way, in November, every remaining leaf is yellow. She could barely stand up. Barely lift a finger. She felt like Jean Harlow before she died, so tired she couldn't lift her hand to take off her makeup.

She left her desk, took off her glasses, and lay down, and Kenny strolled in with a couple of movie books under his arm. "Is Paul Newman among your top five actors?" he asked her.

"You exhaust me," she said.

"Come on. 'Do it for me, Tony. For Riff.'"

"Why is it always too early in the morning when I talk to you, no matter how late in the day?"

"Just tell me."

"The trouble is, I know what your next question is going to be. All right. He's one of the top five."

"Is Dustin Hoffman one of your top five?"

"No."

"Did you say *no*?"

"I know it breaks your heart, but no. Who are *your* top five?"

"Marlon Brando, Al Pacino, Paul Newman, Humphrey Bogart, Charlie Chaplin."

She sat up, put on her glasses and stared at him. "What happened to Frankie?"

Kenny looked sheepish. "They're better actors," he said.

And your top five movies?" she asked, her voice quite sharp.

"*The Godfather, West Side Story, Some Like it Hot, The Wizard of Oz, Gone with the Wind.*"

"Kenny," she said broken-heartedly, "you've been reading too many top–one hundred lists. You've been corrupted. Be *truthful*."

But he gave her an incorrigible smile and said, "I have to pester you about one more thing. In this list *Sunset Boulevard* beat out *All About Eve* by four places. What do you think about that?"

"I don't. I don't think. Not about that."

"You're a cinematic idiot," he said good-humoredly, and tucked his books back under his arm and turned to leave.

"Wait," she said, hit by an idea. "What would you ask Peter O'Toole, if you could?"

He didn't hesitate. "Why did you get a nose job? You have three seconds to answer, you bum, you unruly alcoholic."

"You're hired," she said. They would include a column called "My Favorite Questions" in the *Fern Spectator*, to be published every other week and in a bilingual edition once it really got going.

This was the summer, the long, endlessly warm summer of 1998, when she showed her kids the spot where she first saw Sean Connery. They made the trip in the dog days of July, driving across Ontario to the small town on the Bruce Peninsula where she grew up. What they found when they got there was an empty lot.

"I was twelve," she told them, standing on the sidewalk and staring at what used to be the Berford Theatre. "Twelve when all the foolishness began."

They lived in an old house on the hill, she said. The "ghost house," people called it. It was set back in the woods, a big stucco house with a wraparound verandah on which her brother with the flat feet ran laps on tiptoe. The rest of them would be eating cherries on the steps, elevenses after some sort of hard labor, and her father would order Owen to do fifty laps.

After she saw Sean Connery in *From Russia With Love*, she said, she walked home in the dark, up that steep hill over there – and she pointed to it – to Gould Street. Then she turned right on Gould, and went past the Gilberts' on the left, one of whom was madly in love with her, and the Hyatts' on the right, who had a brainless red setter that ran back and forth on the flat roof of their house. She passed the Hahns' on the left, who had greenhouses, and the Germans' on the right, who had the blue baby. She passed their own ramshackle barn on the left and turned up the flagstone walk that wended its way under the elm tree (which would die and break her mother's heart) and through patches of thick-growing myrtle up to the three-sided verandah, and she went inside and upstairs, and put her head on her pillow and closed her eyes, and watched every second of the movie all over again.

"I consider it a form of progress," she told Lew and the kids as they drove up the hill in search of the old stucco house, "that young Sean turned into old Sean, and that I went from enjoying the sight of young Sean forcing himself on women – two years later it was Pussy Galore, gloriously, in *Goldfinger* – to Cary Grant being seduced by Eva Marie Saint."

They were on the hill by now, and then they were even higher, on the little hill upon which sat the old house, and it was utterly transformed. It was a white mansion in a landscaped garden. "Believe me," Harriet said, "it was nothing like this when I was a kid." They parked on the road and got out and looked, and the thought Harriet had been having – that the most powerful influence in her life after childhood movies was probably repeated movies: the same scene over and over again until she moved past monotony into fine-honed harmony, a great and soothing familiarity that was both restful and exciting – that thought went out of her head. A woman came down the driveway to where they were standing and asked if she could be of any help. No, said Harriet. We're just taking a look at the house where I grew up. Well, come in, the woman urged. Come inside. They went inside, but it was so different – walls had been taken down and all the wallpaper removed – that Harriet felt just like that crazy red setter down the street.

That night in their motel she dreamt about Sean Connery. It went on for a long time. She called him Mr. Garbo, fully believing that that was his name. Mr. Garbo, she called to him, as he entered the room. He was about sixty-five in the dream, and he was writing books. On the last page of one of his books he wrote a line towards the bottom that said he wasn't going to make love, he was going to save himself for his books. *We went for a drive together after dark. I don't think I was driving. I don't think he was driving either. He had a wife. He seemed to want to stay with his wife. There were children. In the dream I thought it prudent to pretend I like children a whole lot more than I do, since he seemed to expect that of women. These children – there were several – were small, blond, smiling. I guess they were his. I was certainly in the running for him and he knew it and responded in a charming, gruff, noncommittal way. Towards the end of the dream, when he was deciding to save himself for his books, I put my hands on his bare back, and he was old – it was a sixty-five-year-old back, though not as old as Sean is in reality, a fact I was aware of even in the dream.*

The next day they drove home, across country scoured by glaciers – pressed under ice a mile deep, and pressed repeatedly, until the ice melted for good and the land made a scarred rebound into the marvellous light. Like my childhood, she thought. It too had been a kind of ice age from which the parental glacier had finally retreated, and then what a lot of work it had been to get anything to grow on the boulder-filled, back-breaking personality that remained.

Looking out the window as the land went by, she began to think about all the things she would never know. She would never know, to remember, the names of more than a few trees and flowers. She would never know how to play chess. She would never read the Bible from cover to cover. She would never know the true story of Cary Grant's sex life. She would never know what she really thought about Jack Frame. She would never know, to meet, Pauline Kael.

I wonder if you watch movies at all any more, or if, like Don Quixote and his books, you've thrown them over. I watched Camille *the other day and got tired of Garbo's neck. The way she arched it back – her signature gesture – to show sexual surrender, and her half-laughing way of speaking when attracted to a man – that became a little tiresome too. You say she did her best acting in* Camille. *And yes, she's good, and Robert Taylor not quite as bad as I thought he would be – the man who broke Barbara Stanwyck's heart – but that's because Garbo helps him along, amused to discover that she finds him attractive.*

She's very good at near collapse. Her body in sickness is very expressive, her face moving between hope and despair.

At a roadside picnic table, Kenny glanced over his mother's shoulder as she jotted things down in her notebook. "You're writing about me," he said.

She didn't bother to dispute it.

"If you're going to write about me, at least call me something else. I'm Jean-Claude," he said. And he beat his chest with his hand. "Jean-Claude de Frontenac."

Jane looked up from her tomato-and-cheese sandwich, hold the bread. "Are you writing about me too?"

"What should I call you? Carlotta?"

Kenny said, "No wonder your book didn't sell. Who wants to read about people called Kenny and Jane? I mean, where's your imagination? Kenny and Jane. That's so bad it's pathetic."

"I like simple names," said Harriet. "Maybe I'll call you Mutt."

"Natalie?" pondered Jane. "Melissa? Nicole?"

Kenny said, "I like Nicole."

"Okay," said their mom. "Nicole and Jean-Claude. Pardon me. Jean-Claude de Frontenac."

"De Front-nac," he said. "Not Fron-te-nac. Front-nac." He was pretending to be Kevin Kline in *French Kiss*. "Not Luke. *Luc.*"

While they were at the picnic table, the wind picked up. It brought windy heat, which would follow them home and last for twenty-four hours, then turn into deep humidity, then rain. The air after the rain would be soft and smoky. But when they pulled into their driveway all was well. They were glad to be home again among the clotheslines and lilac bushes. In the distance they heard the pipes of the Ceremonial Guard practicing on the fields at Carleton University, and Harriet remembered quite vividly seeing the preview to *Brigadoon* at the Berford Theatre – Gene Kelly and Van Johnson lost in the mist, Cyd Charisse in her apron and dancing shoes.

That night a house burned down at the end of the block. Three days later, a raven flew down into Harriet's garden and walked among the marigolds. A few hours after that, what sounded like a cuckoo called loudly, oddly, and she looked up to see on the curving trunk of a neighbor's tree a pileated woodpecker. It took off with great sweeping wing-beats, landed on a telephone pole on Sunnyside Avenue, and called again. Visitors come in threes, she thought. Where was the third visitor? It must be the terrible stranger.

That year was a bountiful fruit year, 1998. Trees were laden with apples, pears, plums. Bushes were heavy with berries. The gooseberries in Harriet's garden had never been so fine. The blueberries at her parents' cottage were larger and more numerous than ever.

One day in August, when they were at the cottage, and had picked until they were tired and thirsty, they stopped, and old Martin said to his daughter, "We had no psychology in those days, thank God."

He was speaking of his youth. They had left their berry buckets on the porch and come down to the water, and from there they looked back up the slope at the ice-damaged woods over which he and Leah had quarrelled nearly thirty years ago, Leah wanting to sell her share to him, but for a price he refused to pay.

"I know as much about my past as I want to know," he said. "I know more than my sister, who thinks she knows everything."

"I don't think Leah's speaking to me any more," said Harriet.

"You'll be able to live with that," he said.

Then something happened to his eyes. Those eyes like Harriet's – like José Ferrer's. He took his hand and whacked the side of his head to keep the tears in place. A family ambushed by its eyes. Harriet had told him her news.

They went to sit on the bench beside the water, and looked out at the lake without speaking. They sat comfortably in their discomfort, without speaking.

Then her mother came down the path and joined them. Gladys, whose idea of entertainment was watching *Nails*.

"She's thirteen now," Harriet said to her mother of Jane, who was on the raft. "That's a relief."

"She's growing up," said Gladys, entirely missing Harriet's point.

"I mean your second sight didn't pan out. She's thirteen, and Lew is alive and well. Remember?"

"Oh, I know what that was," her mother said, and her voice was as self-dismissive as when she'd once talked about her girlish infatuation with Jean Harlow, as if indulging herself in such pap should have been beneath her. "It was my own reflection in the glass doors at the end of the hallway. I wonder how many so-called ghosts can be explained in the same way?"

"Maybe it was me you saw."

"You?"

"My glasses. My skinniness. Had you thought of that?"

Her poor mother had to put her hand on the bench and sit down.

In September Harriet stopped coming downstairs for breakfast. She changed in less physical ways too. She turned against videos, and became obsessed with the damage they were doing. *Movies, like letters, used to require geography. You went out to them and returned from them. You wrote a letter and went out to mail it; it travelled a distance and you could visualize the distance; it was delivered to a mailbox and you could visualize the mailbox. Your correspondent took out something made of paper and ink, something handled by you and all the people in between, and now by him or by her. But videos, like e-mails, have killed geography and time – the time it takes to mail the letter and for the letter to arrive, the time it takes to go to the movie and watch it and return home in a musing frame of mind. There is, of course, the time it takes to go to a video store and mill around in perplexity. But that turns movie watching into another form of shopping, which I hate.*

The truth is, I've lost my taste for movies. I haven't the slightest desire to see a movie any more.

It was so sad, thought Kenny. It was like what happened to Robin Williams. He didn't want to be funny any more. His mom didn't want to watch movies any more. "I'm sick to death of them," she said. "I'd advise you to read the classics. You can start with *Jane Eyre*." And often now, when he looked in on her in the morning, her reading light was on and she had fallen asleep over a pile of books. She had never really given Dostoevsky a chance, she said. To say nothing of *Moby-Dick*.

Kenny read alone at the kitchen table, elbows spread wide, hands wrapped around his ears: one fantasy book after another. To hell with *Jane Eyre*.

His mother lay outside in the hammock. This had become the new bedside. Every few days Dinah came over, though sometimes she brought the wrong thing. *People*, which his mother said made her feel more dead than alive. He and Jane spirited the magazines away to their rooms. Dinah also came with new snapshots of her place in Nova Scotia: she and Jack would be moving there in early December, she said, but she would keep her house in Ottawa, renting it to some people she knew, "since you should never put all your eggs in one basket," she told Kenny. Fiona dropped by too, and of those conversations he heard every word, since everything had to be repeated at least twice. Fiona was in the habit of bringing cashews, and again, he and Jane were the beneficiaries. Jim Creak came by, not just to check on Harriet but to take Lew out for a beer. And even Jack's weighty footstep came through the house from time to time. Kenny overheard his mother ask how the book about Lionel was progressing, and Jack replied that it was done; he even had a publisher. After he left, his mom said, "Kenny, if there's anything worse than an envious writer, I can't think what it is." You mean Jack? "I mean me," she said.

In October the house was quiet. Jane stopped picking on him. Lew stopped playing piano. He himself used the soft pedal whenever he practiced. His mom nursed her sore belly. She couldn't even read, she said; she had time on her hands, but no brain power.

Then one day in late October, when it was raining outside, Kenny said to her, "Just look at this." He made her come into the living room, made her lie on the sofa, put a pillow behind her head and a blanket over her knees. "Just watch for twenty minutes."

He slipped a movie into the VCR and on it came: the strains of "Moon River"; Fifth Avenue at dawn; the yellow cab pulling up to the curb and Audrey getting out and the cab pulling away. His mom sat up and he sat beside her. Jane joined them, and they watched the whole thing, from beginning to end.

They saw their mother's face soften and her shoulders relax.

"It's still wonderful," she breathed when it came to an end. "And so is Audrey. She's so beautiful."

"You liked it?" asked Kenny, eager to hear her say it again and at length.

"I feel one hundred percent better," she said. "I feel like I've had a blood transfusion."

The next day he said to her, "Just watch the beginning of *The Russia House*."

And on it came: the clouds in the end-of-the-Soviet sky, the gilded domes, the painted spires, the black umbrella, Michelle Pfeiffer's lovely face and Sean Connery's bewitching voice, and once again Harriet sighed with satisfaction. "You know, I knew him when he didn't have that accent."

"Shhh," said Kenny.

"In *Goldfinger*. He doesn't have that accent, except when he says 'Pussy.'"

Nothing so relaxing for her as watching these old movies, and watching them with Kenny and Jane, her two comrades-in-arms from the very beginning. Old movies had been mother's milk to them, and an escape from motherhood for her.

Kenny would say to her, "Just watch for half an hour." And on would come *North by Northwest*, *The Grass Is Greener*, *Notorious*.

One day it was *Ninotchka*. She said, "I *like* that scene," when Melvyn Douglas kept telling one joke after another to get Garbo to laugh. *Here goes*. A man comes into a restaurant. He sits down at a table and he says, Waiter, bring me a cup of coffee without cream! Five minutes later the waiter comes back and says, I'm sorry, sir, we have no cream. Can it be without milk? *Oh, you have no sense of humor!* And he told her there wasn't a laugh in her. Not a grain of humor. None whatsoever. Everybody else laughed. *But not you!*

"That's a good scene," said Harriet.

"He's good," said Kenny.

"He *is* good," she said. "And that's a good situation: getting some-body serious to laugh. You should work that into one of your stories."

That was the fall when Kenny began to ask everyone what kind of lawyer he should be. Criminal? Corporate? Environmental?

"Divorce," Dinah told him. "And this is what you do."

Dinah's hair had grown back, thick, bristly, multidirectional, and her laugh was as wild and crumpled-sounding as ever. She said, "You accept only the richest clients – the richest! And on your desk you've got a special red telephone – that's a direct line to me – and every day at four o'clock you call me with the hottest gossip."

"I'll have my office in New York," he said with satisfaction.

They were on the back porch. Lew had moved an old sofa out there, and another table, where he worked while Harriet lay resting in the hammock. Now he looked up. "I thought you were going to be a sportswriter."

"No," Kenny said. "Newspapers will soon be a thing of the past and I don't want to do Internet journalism."

"It's still writing," said Lew.

"No. I don't want to do it."

Then it was November again, but this time there wasn't any snow. A warm November followed upon a warm October, a warm September, a warm summer, a warm spring. The warmth had become endless. It was 1998, the warmest year in Ottawa's history. On the back porch the hanging plants were still hanging, the folding chairs were unfolded, the hammock was still up. On this particular day, so memorable it was pho-tographed, his mom lay in the hammock, wrapped in a quilt. Dinah had finished packing up her house. Jack had gone to Chicago to ship his belongings east. And at Kenny's instigation they decided to have a final meeting of the Fern foursome, and at Dinah's suggestion they dressed up. But first they had to decide which movie it was going to be.

Harriet said she had a hankering to see *Summer Stock* again. "That was a wonderful sequence of scenes: Gene and Judy on stage in the empty barn singing – what were they singing?"

"'You Wonderful You,'" said Jane.

"And then the kiss that takes them by surprise. Then later, on the verandah, when she sings – what was she singing?"

"'My Friendly Star,'" said Jane.

"And she doesn't know he's there listening, but the camera catches his face at the end of the song, and you know that suddenly *he* knows how in love with her he is. A lovely flow to it." She made a curving gesture with her hand, her face wistful and relaxed. "Charles Walters was the director."

Jane said, "I loved the 'Get Happy' song at the end. That's my favorite."

"She lost weight for that. She went to a fat farm, and they shot the scene three months after the rest of the movie was done. Poor Judy. Well, she was having one of her breakdowns. But there was something between her and Gene. Some attraction."

Harriet's glance moved from Lew, who was bent over the report he'd spread on the table, to Dinah. She'd been thinking a lot about what would happen to Lew and the kids after the doctors had finished with her. "What are we going to do without you?" she said to Dinah, who answered gently that Nova Scotia wasn't so far away. She wasn't going to the end of the world.

"It's far away."

Harriet turned her head and looked out over the garden. A small, purple clematis flower still bloomed, unbelievably. What was it Bill Bender had said? Something about the yellowy, balmy atmosphere that stretched through Christmas in 1918 as thousands died of the Spanish flu. Unusual weather coupled with unusual illness. One reversal leading to another.

In the end, they settled on *Guys and Dolls*. "Kenny," said his mom, "you can wear your gangster outfit."

Dinah said, "It's always so easy for men. Put on your tux. Put on your gangster outfit."

"I'm Ava," said Jane.

"Okay," said Dinah, "then I'll be Adelaide. And you can be Sarah Brown," she said to Harriet. "It's time you sang a few hymns."

"No, I'll be Frankie. I'll be Frankie on top and Ava underneath."

Dinah looked at Jane and Kenny. "Your mother," she said, "is out of control again."

They dressed their mom. From the basement chest they pulled out a gold sequin gown with narrow straps, a pair of kid gloves, a metallic

silver coiled belt. Jane took her long black Morticia Addams wig off her
doorknob and put it on her mother's head, and Harriet was Ava. Then
Kenny found his grampa's pre-tied bow ties and chose the red-and-blue
polka-dot one. He also contributed his dad's black fedora and old tweed
jacket, and now Harriet was Frankie.

They made her go to the mirror and she said, "All I need is a cigarette."

As it happened, Kenny had some. Not the Airmail cigarettes that
Harriet's brothers used to buy in the little candy store next to the
Berford Theatre and smoke in the woods, but a pack of candy cigarettes,
one of which she hung off her lower lip as she practiced standing with
her back to her kids, then turning around to give them the look Frank
Sinatra gave Doris Day in *Young at Heart*.

"I missed my calling," she said to them, her voice a mixture of
wonder and conviction. "This is what I was made for." And she meant it,
heart and soul. "I should have gone on stage."

She felt like Margot Fonteyn after she took up with Nureyev. Like
Cyd Charisse after she discovered silk stockings. Like Garbo after she
got the joke.

Lew snapped a picture of the Sinatra gang: Jean-Claude Sinatra in his
typical outfit of gangster jacket, blue shirt, pink floral tie; Nicole Sinatra
in capri pants, Cuban top (the first and only time she ever wore it), fur
stole, and dangling earrings; Harriet Sinatra as Ava/Frankie; and Dinah
Sinatra in mink jacket, pink pants, high heels, and glass of champagne
provided by Jim Creak, who saw the goings-on and came over.

Jim Creak had a parting gift for Dinah: the sweater he'd been knitting
for her when he and Harriet were at the sleep clinic together. "The sea air
is damp," he said, as she pulled it over her head. "Does it fit?" It fit. But
convincing him of the fact required full-scale reassurance. Then he asked
for her address. She told him she couldn't remember the postal code, but
would write the whole thing down for him later, and he said, "Promise?"

Dinah promised, "if it's the last thing I do before I leave."

38

Afterwards

Dinah Bloom moved away in early December, on a day so unseasonably warm that Kenny, coming home from his piano lesson, saw a man run into the street in stocking feet. It was Jim Creak, waving a pair of gloves and shielding his eyes from the bright sunlight. "Where are you?" he called, looking around him. And to Kenny, "She's gone."

He stood in his socks staring after Dinah's car, which had turned the corner and disappeared from sight. It was December 4, 1998.

The following day, when he opened the paper, he read about the discovery of the world's earliest flower, a 142-million-year-old spindly twig with peapod-shaped fruit and a woody stem. The flowering plant fossil, he read, was found 250 miles northeast of Beijing in a rock formation of limestone and volcanic ash, from which fossilized insects, birds, and plants had previously been unearthed, but never a flowering plant, until now. He clipped the article and kept it, since the longevity of flowers was something he wanted to believe in.

The article got lost among other papers on his desk, the letters that kept coming with their oddly touching requests: a woman who wanted to hear Edward Johnson's voice because the great tenor stayed with them one night when she was a child, sleeping in the same room where the seamstress stayed twice a year when she came to sew all of their clothes; a man who wanted to hear "Don't Sit Under the Apple Tree with Anyone Else but Me," because his mother sang it when he was a boy picking potatoes in eastern Scotland, where the wind came directly off the Russian steppes, "a lazy wind," they called it, because it didn't blow around you, it blew right through you. His own letter to Dinah, the one he mailed with her gloves, didn't get a reply. It wasn't until a full year went by and he was cleaning off his desk that his eye fell upon *world's earliest flower*, the partial headline of an article folded in half, and since only the day before he had gone to Harriet's funeral, he sat down to write to Dinah.

I don't know whether you've heard, he wrote. *Perhaps not. Perhaps this will come as a shock, though it won't be a surprise.*

Dinah read the letter in her house by the sea. She knew about Harriet's death. She had heard from Lew, but not until after the funeral: she'd been away, an impulsive trip to Paris to sort out her thoughts about Jack. Lew's call came a few weeks after her own last phone call to Harriet, itself the briefest of conversations, during which she'd confessed that there were worse things than being alone. And Harriet had said, "I never understood that man."

In another month Jack would move back to Chicago, leaving Dinah not sadder, but wiser, since, except for his roving eye, he had turned out to be a lazy man. Several months after that, in June, she would turn her car left on Sunnyside Avenue and enter the old, familiar network of tree-lined streets.

Which door would she knock upon first? Fiona Chester's, she decided, knocking very loudly in order to be heard. But a nurse answered the door, then led her into the living room, where the matriarch of the neighborhood, dressed in a skirt and blouse, was seated on the sofa eating half a boiled egg, just half; she would save the rest for later when she had more appetite. A tiny figure, bowed down, bent low over her egg. But, "I'd recognize you anywhere," Fiona said, although there was little recognition in her face. There was pain. She was living under a low roof of pain, which is what shingles are – ripples of fire that travelled down her back, under her arms, and across her chest. Ceaseless, except when she managed to sleep.

Dinah sat beside her and took her hand.

"You've come to see Lew."

"Partly."

"It's hard to lose a wife." Fiona couldn't lift her head, and so she was speaking to Dinah's hand, as if into a microphone. "They'll be glad to see you. Kenny takes out my garbage, Lew walks Buster, and Jim Creak comes over and reads to me." She gestured to a book on the table. "Not every man loves Jane Austen."

Dinah leaned over to see what it was. *Persuasion*. The book where nearly everything to be learned isn't spoken so much as overheard.

"How is Lew?" she asked.

"Lonely. It's a lonely business, losing your wife. I've seen it before. But," she said with an effort, still speaking into Dinah's hand, "you haven't told me about you."

Half an hour later, Dinah was walking up the lane where, according to Bill Bender, kids used to hunt bees among the hollyhocks, and coming towards her was the boy who loved Frank Sinatra. Easily a foot taller, and alone, as he was the first time she saw him. In T-shirt and shorts; long arms, winter-pale knees. Knapsack on his back, book in his hand, eyes on the ground.

"Frankie," she said.

He looked up – tall and skinny, a triumph of height and light – and he brightened and flushed, advanced and retreated, in the way of thirteen-year-old boys.

She hugged him, and it was like holding wooden scaffolding that hugs back. Then he didn't know quite where to look or what to say, and his shoulders slumped.

"What's your book?" she asked.

He showed her what it was. *5001 Nights at the Movies*, held together with an elastic band.

Dinah took the heavy book out of his hands and the past flowed into her eyes. She stood there, blinking hard. Then she said, "You really should write to her. She'd like to know that a young writer carries her under his arm."

In fact, the old typewriter was back in the basement, and for long stretches of time Kenny barely said a word. But that wasn't the case now. "So," he said, coming to life, "what did you think of *Pulp Fiction*?"

"I'm glad to see you haven't changed."

She walked him home, and he wanted to know if she was going to watch a movie with them later, since it was Friday, movie night. "As if you need to ask," she said, but she would check on her house first, letting her tenants know that she was here. Then she inquired after his father and sister, and asked about their plans for the summer. Kenny said he was going to Italy for the summer. "Well, not the whole summer. The month of July."

His voice had deepened so much she had to smile. "Jane must be excited."

Jane wasn't excited, she was jealous. She was staying here. He was going to Italy by himself. He was staying with Leah.

"Leah," she said, and became aware of the world again.

Car horns were blaring in the distance – either a wedding or an accident, or both. Kenny, as if reading her thoughts, said, "Can you believe that Pauline Kael didn't like *Chinatown*?" And the image in her mind sharpened and cut deeper, of John Huston's kindly, horrifying leer as he reached into the blaring car to claim his granddaughter for himself. The transition to motherless. Motherless, and taken under the wrong wing.

An hour later Jim Creak looked out his upstairs window and saw what no one ever sees: a garden in the moment of blooming. Dinah Bloom, moving about in the openness of her old shade garden. The oak tree had been hauled away and loud Ray's loud pool hummed next door, but Dinah was back. He stood transfixed, waiting for her to look up, or come over. But she went up her back steps and inside. He wouldn't see her again until later that night, when he looked out the window before going to bed.

What Dinah did next was drive to Metcalfe Street and buy an extra-large pizza from her favorite pizzeria. She drove back with it and carried it up the steps to the Golds. Kenny and Jane were home, but not Lew. It was just after six o'clock.

Another half-hour went by. Dinah was at the kitchen table, talking with the kids about Nova Scotia, when she heard the front door open. Then she heard voices. Lew and someone else. A colleague, who perhaps was more than a colleague. Valerie was bearing pizza too.

Jane would say later of this moment that it was like watching a movie. The girl who at the age of four sat on the grass in Riverside Park unable to take her eyes off the couple locked in a steamy embrace farther down the slope; the girl who shook off her mother's hand when she offered her a sandwich with a "No, I'm watching a movie"; this girl was now fifteen and no less keen-eyed about the workings of romance. She saw her father's sad face transformed by the pleasure of seeing Dinah, and she saw Dinah's face respond. Dinah stood up, and her father wrapped her in a hug.

"You came back," he said.

But then awkwardness took hold. They had supper together and there was too much pizza and too little talk. Valerie asked questions that Dinah didn't feel like answering, and after a while the table fell silent.

Jane and Kenny insisted that Dinah stay and watch a movie with them. They wouldn't let her leave, and so she stayed, while Lew drove Valerie (who didn't care for movies) home.

Jane put on *Crossing Delancey* (despite Kenny's plea for *This Is Spinal Tap*) and Dinah remembered her disagreement with Harriet about how long they would last: Izzy and the pickle man. She remembered saying that Izzy would be ashamed of him. Every time they went to some literary party and she introduced him as her husband the pickle man, she would be ashamed. It'll be over in two years, she'd said. "I don't know," replied Harriet. "He knows what *ambivalent* means, and he's crazy about her. It's a good dilemma too: falling for the wrong man, while underestimating the right one."

Lew came back before long and watched the last half of the movie with them. "Finally," he said, when Izzy dumped the writer-jerk for the pickle man. "It took her long enough."

It was after that, after the movie was over, after the kids were in bed, that he and Dinah found themselves alone in the kitchen.

"Are you thirsty?" he asked. He got a glass from the cupboard and filled it with water from the faucet. She wasn't, but he was. "Where are you staying?"

"In my house. One of the tenants is away."

She had told him this earlier, but he'd forgotten, either out of nervousness or fatigue, or both. She could see how tired he was.

"You've had a terrible year," she said, as he drank down the water.

He ran the back of his hand across his mouth. "It's still terrible. But people have been good. They've been wonderful."

She thought his smile, while tender, meant to imply that the people who had been wonderful were the ones who had been on the scene – not far away.

"Hattie missed you," he said. "We all missed you." And he reached for her hand and gave it a squeeze, then turned and set his glass down beside the sink. "*Muchacha*," he said. "I've got to get to bed. You'll be around for a few days? I'm so tired I can't stand up any more."

Dinah remembered then that she didn't know where Harriet was buried, and she asked him. There wasn't a gravesite, he told her. He and the kids had sprinkled her ashes in the garden, after the snow was gone.

"I like that," she said. "I like that you did that." And she touched his arm.

Her purse was hanging on the back of a kitchen chair. She picked it up, then opened the screen door onto the porch, and stepped outside. The door clicked shut behind her. And then she heard the rustle of leaves and felt a warm breeze.

She walked across the porch and down the steps onto the grass, taking the back way to her house. A dog began to bark and she half expected Jim Creak to come outside and call for Stella. She looked up at his house. There was a light on upstairs, and she saw movement in the window, and then the light went out.

Halfway down the garden slope she paused again, feeling the soft air on her face, feeling her own fatigue. All around her lay the dark garden, but it was city darkness. She knelt down and put her hand on the grass. By morning there might be dew, she thought. Even now it felt cool, a little damp. She pulled out a blade of grass, and it stuck to her fingertip. When she examined it, in this light, it looked to her like a long eyelash.

Acknowledgments

For invaluable guidance and support, my thanks to Ellen Seligman, Dawn Seferian, Jennifer Lambert, Peter Buck, Anita Chong, Mark Fried, and Bella Pomer.

For their generous help with the world of this book, I would like to thank Sheila McCook, the late Rhoda Barrett, Isabel Huggan, Casey and Bess Swedlove, Bruce White, Alain Miguelez, Earl Crowe, Alex Fried, Stuart Hay, Bill Cody, Jack Holliday, Wayne Grimm, Pat Gorman, Adrian Shuman, Peter Harcourt, Gary Draper, Stuart Kinmond, and my two cinematic comrades-in-arms, Ben and Sochi Fried.

My thanks to CBC Radio and The National Library in Ottawa.

The idea for an album of pressed ferns that also includes pictures of early movie stars comes from *Basil Street Blues* by Michael Holroyd.

The song detective's call-to-love on page 216 is taken from one of Dennis Lee's "Night Songs" (*Nightwatch*, McClelland & Stewart, 1996). It is used with the author's generous permission, and the permission of the publisher.

The lines of poetry by Anna Akhmatova are from *Poems of Akhmatova*, © 1973 by Stanley Kunitz and Max Hayward, published by Houghton Mifflin. Permission has been granted by Darhansoff, Verrill, Feldman Literary Agents.

The Pauline Kael quotations from her reviews of *Nashville* © 1975 and *Last American Hero* © 1973, reprinted in *Reeling* (Little, Brown and Company, 1976), are used with the permission of Curtis Brown Ltd. The line from her essay "Trash, Art and the Movies," reprinted in *Going Steady* (Marion Boyars Publishers, 1994), is used with the permission of the publisher.

Quotations from his stories, "The Sinatra Sisters" and "Brackett Brackenwood," are used with the permission of the author, Ben Fried.

Quotations from "Our Footloose Correspondents: A Spanish Shawl for Miss Garbo" by E. W. Selsey, published in *The New Yorker*, April 23, 1938, © 1938, 1966 The New Yorker Magazine, Inc., excerpted by permission of the publisher.